A RELIC OF
MAGIC & MYRRH

Ebook ISBN: 978-0-6454516-3-4

Print ISBN: 978-0-6454516-4-1

Edited by Sarah Proulx Calfee, Three Little Words Editing https://threelittlewordsediting.com

Proofread by Jo Speirs, Nurturing Words

https://www.nurturingwords.com.au

Front cover design by Amanda Pillar from Smoking Hot Covers

https://www.smokinghotcovers.com

 Created with Vellum

For Henry - a man of many talents who we love and who without his input, this story would not have been nearly as much fun to write.

PROLOGUE

Isadora Smith had seen death many times, but never her own. Until today.

Inside the remodeled barn, Isa kicked off her shoes, flicked on her favorite playlist, and with the warm, earthy smell of turpentine tingling in her nose, loaded a scoop of paint on her pallet knife and approached her canvas. Isa just had to find the light ... She adjusted the easel. And there it was. Her mind cleared. Her world brightened.

Not that she wasn't happy outside of painting, and she enjoyed her life here in Maleny, mostly. It *was* gorgeous. But it was also in the middle of frigging nowhere, and as someone who didn't drive—much—near to impossible to have a social life. The perfect hiding spot.

She'd been hiding for how many months now? Probably the same length of time since she'd banged someone. At least she had her steamy fantasies and daydreams with her sexy mystery man from her visions.

With heavy beats filling her studio, Isa applied the pallet knife to the canvas in deliberate strokes, building up the color layer by layer. She reached out to pick up more paint, but stars gathering at the edge of her vision had her stop midway.

Damn. Not now. This commission was due—

The stars intensified until they filled her sight, and she crumpled forward. Cried out as her knees smacked into the hard floor.

-((●))-

Her mystery man, this time wearing a black suit and holding a gun, stands in the middle of a luxe bedroom. Beyond him, sliding glass doors frame a stunning harbor at night, lights shimmering over the water.

At his feet lies a woman in a massive puddle of blood. She's wearing a ruby dress, and the silk material is turning black soaking up the liquid, and red spatter covers the bare skin of her neck, arm and chest. Her figure is so familiar, though her face is covered by dark wavy hair.

Her mystery man drops to his knee and, with shaking hands, brushes the strands aside. Isa sees her own face, pallid, still, dead.

((●))

Isa slowly woke up—gagging and stiff. She curled up into a ball, forcing in shuddering gulps of air. How long had she been out?

Then she recalled the vision—that face, her own frigging face. Shit, shit, *shit*. She was going to die, sooner rather than later, and what had she done lately but cower in fear?

1

One Month Later

Isa stared at Raph's apartment door and rubbed her palms on her denim skirt as she waited for him to answer. Her big brother was going to lose his shit. But that didn't matter—learning how to control her visions did. The problem—there was next to nothing on the internet about divination for people with Isa's heritage.

Isa knew she had to paint some invitation for Eve, but what she really wanted was intel on what Eve knew about divination.

That, and to see *him*. Her mystery man. Would he be here yet?

After the death vision, she'd been caught in a revolving door of emotions, from devastation to disbelief to convincing herself she could outrun fate—but in her heart, she'd known the truth from the moment she woke up.

Her visions always came true.

And for way too long, she'd let that asshole Liam turn

her into a fearful mouse, just because he'd stalked her and tried to kidnap her. Well, no more.

She was going to learn how to control her gift—and use it for good in whatever time she had left—and, given *he'd* also been in this morning's vision, meet her mystery man after all these years.

Finally, Raph opened the door and let Isa in, scowling. Isa gave him a giant hug, then turned to Eve—a powerful witch who knew a lot about the magical world. Isa threw her arms around her, but Eve clearly didn't hug much because she gave Isa an awkward pat on the back.

"All right," Raph said. "So what's so important that you drove all the way here—especially when ...?"

"When what?" Eve asked.

"When Isa's had issues with past clients, making her prefer to stay away from crowded places." Raph's voice held a note of caution. "And she's not meant to drive."

Isa rolled her eyes before she answered—and made sure Raph saw it. Enough with overprotective big brothers wanting to wrap her in cotton wool. As frightening as that death vision was, she'd discovered the power in knowing *when* her end came: until a ruby-red dress and luxe bedroom, Isa might as well be a frigging superhero.

"I had a vision this morning." Isa reached into her handbag and pulled out a lead pencil drawing of the invitation she'd seen herself hand painting. "I sketched this as soon as I woke up. This is what I'm going to do for you. So, I'm going to be here for a while." *With access to Eve* and *her mystery man.*

What would he be like in person? Tall, authoritarian—

"Isa, did you hear me?" Raph gave her a funny look.

"Oops. Sorry, just ... thinking." Isa answered all the questions Eve and her brother asked her about the invite, but one part of her mind stayed with the mystery man. She started telling Raph about him, but had to swallow the lump stuck in her throat.

"You okay, Issi?" Raph asked. "Damn it, you shouldn't have driven so soon after a vision."

"No, no. I'm okay. It was something else. Anyway, there's this man in the vision too; he was accessing a computer system and adding your details to a registration list to match the invitation I make for you."

The buzzer rang over and over, and Raph hit the intercom button. "Yeah?"

"And hello to you too, sunshine," a voice rumbled on the other end of the line. "So, I'm all set at the hotel but wanted to work on our ... job. Let me up."

That voice ... Her belly tightened. She knew that voice. Raph hit the door release and turned his frown on her; his lips pursed as if to shape the word no. Ha. She wasn't going anywhere. "Okay, so where can I set up my workspace?"

"Isa, we need to talk." Raph glanced at Eve. "Could you let Grayson in—he'll be up in a moment." Overprotective big bro dragged Isa into his bedroom. Raph lowered his voice. "I'm not joking, Isa. There's a serious sicko out there threatening to kidnap you. Kidnap! And you've come right here to where ..."

Blah, blah, blah, stay safe, blah, blah. Fuck staying safe, fuck Liam, fuck hiding. Need didn't even come close to explaining the ... drive so deep inside her; it might as well be part of her DNA to *do* something useful with her gift ... *before*. What truly mattered was gaining control, and that meant getting one-on-one time with Eve.

There was a loud rap at the door.

"Raph? You in there?" The same voice that had rumbled over the intercom echoed into the room.

The hairs on the back of Isa's neck prickled. That voice ...

"Yeah, yeah. Be there in one minute," Raph called out.

Isa forced her attention on her big brother and glared. She wasn't leaving. She didn't care what he said.

"Okay," Raph muttered. "Fine, but you stay right here in the apartment. You don't go out at all. Deal?"

"Deal."

Isa yanked open the bedroom door. What was she going to ask Eve first? There were so many—

A giant stood at the doorway, his fist raised and about to knock again. Her breath punched from her chest. Her mystery man! The same who'd been starring in so many of her visions for the past decade. Midthirties, close-cut hair and beard, brilliant cobalt-blue eyes. Huge shoulders and a muscled build.

He held himself like a coiled spring, ready to lunge in a heartbeat. The hard, firm line of his lips tightened the longer he stared at her. He stared so hard—so forcefully, Isa almost took a step back.

Her own personal harbinger of doom.

Isa wheezed in a breath, and with it, the most tantalizing scents of sandalwood and bergamot filled her lungs. A delicious heat bloomed low in her belly. Holy. Shit. This man ... *this* man! Isa shoved down her fear and focused on temptation. Her future might be limited, but fate be damned, she had one more thing to add to her to-do list: bang her mystery man in real life—not just in her dreams.

Then her heart took flight, and she had to squeeze another breath past the tightness in her chest. Finally, after all these years, he had a name.

He had a name.

"You're ... Grayson?" Isa said.

"Just Gray."

‹‹●››

"Last chance," Isa ground out as Gray drove her out of the city. Ugh. Why did her dream-man have to be such an a-hole? "Listen, you can stay here and do whatever you Templars do when you're in a foreign country, and I'll drive myself home. It's a three-hour return trip you don't have to make. You've been working nonstop the past week on this job with Raph, so you could even take some time to enjoy Brisbane."

"And like I said every other time. No. I promised your brother I'd get you home safely. Raph would kill me if he found out I let you drive. And if he's busy killing me, he's not working on my job, so it's a double hell no, you're not driving."

"Is everything about work to you?"

"Yes."

"Then stay here since it's that important. I'll get a bus—"

"Nope. I also know about the crazy stalker guy. You don't want your brother worrying about you when he's in the middle of an investigation, right?"

"More like *you* don't want my brother worrying about anything other than your job."

"That too. So don't huff. You already told Raph you'd go with me."

"I'm not huffing." Ugh. Being treated like a child by her big brother's friend topped her all-time most-hated moments. Especially since she couldn't look at him without remembering—

"We need to fill-up on the way," Gray said. "I haven't

driven in your country before, so have zero idea about gas stations."

"We call them petrol stations to start with." Isa sniffed and checked out the dashboard gage. Half a tank left. "We should make it back. I drove down here on half a tank, and I can refuel when I'm back home."

"Petrol stations. Got it." Gray's deeply tanned hands competently turned the steering wheel. "But I'll refuel while I'm there."

"No, I can do it. I don't want to take up any more of your time."

"Five minutes for gas—petrol—won't hurt."

Argh. She could scream with all this protectiveness. She'd had it from Raph her entire life—she didn't need it from Gray, too. And it was even more excruciating with him because while she was hyperaware of Gray, he had eyes only for the road—not for his friend's little sister.

Pfft. She was only ten years younger than Raph. No big deal. Raph was in his midthirties, and Gray had to be about the same age.

"Are you wearing anything scented?"

"What?" She glanced down at her outfit—she had on her favourite wide-leg cotton pants and a black tank.

"You know, like a perfume or soap wash."

"No. I mean, I washed my hair and I use soap. But no perfume." She shot him a look. What was he on about?

"Something smells like cinnamon rolls. Like—"

"Like what?"

"Nothing." He shook his head.

Isa took a strand of her jaw-length hair and sniffed. "My shampoo has a kind of cinnamon smell. It's also sandalwood and—"

"Never mind."

"Seriously? 'Do you wear perfume and cinnamon rolls,' and then *never mind*?"

"Yes." He clenched his jaw and went back to focusing on the road.

Righto. She mentally rolled her eyes, then spent the next eighty-five minutes in a tug-of-war between wanting to watch him and not wanting to make her fascination obvious, given his absolute disinterest in her.

And why would he be interested? Even now in his casual jeans and tee—the opposite of the stiff business shirt and pants he'd worn in most of her visions—it was clear that whoever Grayson No-Last-Name was, the sexy ice prick played an important role in the Templars.

Memory of a not-so-businessy vision played through her mind. A man with a bear of a chest, standing alone in an icy field, mist in the air and frost coating the grass, as he moved through some kind of martial art flowing movements. Strength in his body.

She squirmed in her seat.

"Anything wrong?"

"Nope. We made a great team," she blurted out.

"Huh?" Gray glanced at her. "What?"

"You know—my artwork and your computer hacking. Together, we got Raph what he needed to complete the job. That was impressive, right?"

"And we broke a million laws."

"Aren't Templars above all that?"

"We still work with local law enforcement agencies when there's a crossover, so we try not to make it harder on them than it has to be. Too much red tape."

Isa snorted. "Sure, you do. Well, I thought it was remarkable."

"Yeah, yeah, it was ... impressive."

Something warm unfurled in her chest, and she switched her gaze back outside as they turned onto the main road through town. Even though she and her dad had moved up three years ago, this was the village where she shopped, went to the hairdresser, saw the doctor. It had become home.

So why did her stomach pang like she hadn't eaten for a day?

Damn it. Because after working on the forgery for Raph and Eve, being part of a team and using her gift for a purpose, returning to this life left her hollow.

"I'd like to do that more often." The words were out before she realized she'd spoken.

"What, make forgeries?"

"Yes."

"You going to the dark side?"

"No, I'm not planning on using my mad forgery skills for evil." Yet. But she kept that to herself. Evil and good were just two sides of the one coin, after all. But Gray saw only black and white, and she didn't think he'd appreciate her more ... gray approach. She snorted. Why did this man have to be named for a shade she liked so much?

"What are you laughing about?"

"Nothing. It wasn't a laugh. It was a snort—for a private thought. And what I'm saying is that Raph needed my forgery to complete whatever secret task you've got him working on." She glanced at him. "And I still don't see why you won't trust me if you trust my brother."

"It's not about trust. It's about the job."

"Pfft. You're the boss, aren't you? And whatever it is, it's clearly important since you've come all the way from ..." She cut herself off before she said too much.

"From?" he said after a beat.

"America. Your accent *is* a giveaway, you know—just in case you don't want anyone to know where you're from." She stared outside the car window as they drove through the small community of Maleny.

"So why the sudden interest in making forgeries?"

"It's not the forgeries." She turned back to face him. "It's just that I haven't felt ... useful ... for a long time. I liked it." She crossed her arms. Why had she gone and told him that?

"But you've got your artwork. You should concentrate on that."

Of course she should concentrate on her art. Grayson, the mighty Templar, had gone and said so. Ugh. Why did the men in her life always tell her what she should frigging do?

"You're obviously talented and your pieces make people happy," Gray continued, oblivious to her mental teeth gnashing. "That's good."

"*Good*? Good is when you drink a warm cup of tea instead of piping hot. Good is when all you have is milk chocolate, but you love it bitter and dark. Good is ... not something that makes you feel alive, sends your heart racing and your blood zinging."

"Nothing wrong with good." He cut her a look, but his inscrutable poker face didn't change.

"Oh really, Mr. Tell The Little Artist What She Should Do?" She shifted toward him in her seat. "So what's so *good* about being a Templar? And I'm serious; I have no clue what you do other than order my brother about."

Gray snorted. "No one orders your brother to do anything. Except maybe Eve. But I can't actually tell you—"

"I know, I know, you work for the supersecretive Templars—who are common knowledge—but I can't ever mention the T word."

"And yet ..."

"We're alone in my car. Don't think anyone's going to hear what we say."

"I'll fill her up," Gray said as he pulled into a petrol station. He shot her another of those cool looks as if to say don't even think about arguing. Well, bad luck, buddy.

"No. You drove me home. I'll fill her up. I *can* do some things for myself."

"Never said you couldn't." Gray held his hands up. "Just trying to help."

She snorted. There it was—*only trying to help*. Knocking back his offer made her feel like a dick. But if she kept letting others help, she'd never do anything for herself. And that was not on.

Walking across the small lot to the garage, she pulled her wallet out of her handbag. A screeching noise shattered the quiet—she whirled and saw a black sedan careening off the road and rushing toward her.

"Move!" Gray shouted, and he appeared out of nowhere, his body ramming into her.

She hit the hot pavement, shoulder and hip bouncing off the concrete. Her head would've hit too, but something warm cushioned her cheek and temple.

She blinked and stared into the silhouette of Gray's face —the bright summer sun shining behind him, casting a halo around his head.

"Gray," she whispered. She wanted to say his name over a thousand times. A name to the face after all these years.

"Stay here." Gray sprang to his feet. She twisted around as he ran for the car that had come to a screeching halt where she'd been standing moments earlier.

The driver's window rolled down, revealing a man with sandy hair swept back from a bland face. Blue eyes stared down at Isa. "Liam." His name fell from her suddenly numb lips.

Gray yanked the driver's door open. "Get the hell out of the car!" Gray yelled.

How had Liam found her? Ignoring the pain radiating up her shoulder and hip, Isa scrambled to her feet. She had to get out of there—they both had to—Liam was too unpredictable.

"Isadora!" her ex shouted.

Gray shifted to block her view, but not before she caught the glint of a gun in Gray's hands. Where had that come from?

"Stop looking at her and look at me instead," Gray ordered Liam. "I said get out. Now. Turn around and put your hands on the car. Make one single move and I'll put you down."

Ice trickled down Isa's spine. Gray had never sounded so lethal. But something in his words made the instinct to run pause inside her. She was so sick of being the casualty. Of always running. Of others protecting her because they believed she couldn't do it for herself.

And now, with her death vision looming on the horizon ... would she be dealing with this shit to the end?

No. No frigging way. She'd had enough.

"Liam." She hid her surprise at her calm voice when inside her belly was rioting and her heart was racing. "What are you doing here?"

"Isa, stay back," Gray ordered her over his shoulder.

"No, I will not *stay back*. I'm not letting this ... creep have one more minute's sway over me and my life." She limped to Gray and put her hand on his arm. He tensed but didn't move. "I need to talk to Liam. Alone."

"He just tried to kill you. As if I'm leaving you on your own with him. We need to call the police."

"Yes, the police can be called. But I need to talk to Liam. And fine, you can stay. But stand back." She stared at Gray, willing him to see how much she needed to do this. The heat of Gray's body made her want to lean into him, but she didn't. No leaning on anyone, ever again. Finally, he shifted a slight step back.

She turned to Liam. "You won't hurt me now, will you?"

His eyes widened, and he looked from her to Gray as if seeking permission from the hulking Templar.

"Hey, dickhead. Look at me. Not him." Why did Gray make Liam shit scared, but not her? How could she get the men in her world to treat her on the same level? "I'm going to tell you this once, and once only. Are you listening?" She waited for his nod. "Then know this. I will never, ever read for you again. Not if you kidnap me. Not if you hurt me. Not. Ever. And if I see your face—even one more time—I'll use every vision needed to destroy your frigging precious business. Do you hear me?"

Liam's eyes narrowed, and something ugly crowded in his gaze before he glanced back at Gray.

"Hey! I said don't look at him. He's got nothing to do with you and me. I meant it. Never, ever, again. Now get out of here. You might make it back to Victoria before the police catch up with you."

She kept her gaze on Liam and forced a calm expression even as her insides jangled.

Finally, he nodded and slid back into the car. He gave her one last look before he slammed the car door and ripped out of the parking lot.

As if all the strings holding her up snapped at once, energy fled her body and her knees wobbled.

"Here, I've got you." Gray's warm hand supported her elbow. Isa leaned into him before she recalled her new promise to herself and forced her jelly legs to straighten.

"I'm good." She glanced around. The few other people nearby looked at Gray and her warily, unsure whether to intervene. Ew. She hated attention like this. She moistened her suddenly dry mouth. "Think I need to sit down, but need a water first."

"Why don't you sit in the car? I'll take care of the gas and get you water. If that's okay?"

She blew a slow breath and eyed the distance to the petrol station shop. "I can make it." She ignored the doubt in Gray's expression and shuffled inside.

The girl behind the counter stared at her wide-eyed. "Are you okay?"

"Yep." Thankfully the girl said nothing more, and Isa paid for the petrol and two bottles of water and then limped back out to the car.

She sank into her seat, grateful to sit and not fall.

"You good?" Gray murmured as he slid in beside her and started the engine.

"Yeah." She took a long sip, almost sighed in relief as icy water soothed her raw throat. "I've needed to do that for a long time."

"You took a risk there. And as much as you laid the law down, Liam gives me zero confidence he'll take your warning on board. And he knows where you live now."

"I know." She stared through the windscreen as they drove through her quirky little village. It was a sweet town where the locals knew each other by name, and the tourists came on the weekend and left them alone throughout the week. She recalled the look in Liam's eyes. That hadn't been acceptance. That had been *I'll wait for another time.*

A shiver shook through her. Damn it, damn it, *damn it.* She banged her fist on the dashboard.

"Who—what now?" Gray glanced around.

"Nothing out there. It's all in here." Isa scrubbed a fist over her chest. "I just wanted to stand up for myself. To ..." She snapped her mouth shut.

"What?"

Not be the victim. But she didn't say the words. She wasn't even going to *think* the V word anymore, let alone say it.

"I want to work with you," she blurted out. "You said it— we worked well together. And fine, I don't know what you actually do other than the Templars are police in the world of witches and daemons and anyone basically nonhuman. Mind you, I still don't know who gave you that right, but that's not the point. My visions can be useful." She ignored the whisper in her mind ... *If you could control them.*

Well, so what if she didn't have control? She'd damn well learn it. Because this was a chance—maybe her last—to use her gift for something worthwhile.

"Come on, Grayson. I can help, I know it."

2

GRAY GLANCED over at Isa's beautiful green eyes as she scowled at him. She wanted to work with him? His gut tightened. Fuck, no. No way under any circumstance was a civvy like Isadora Smith getting closer to his world than she already was.

"No." He turned his attention back to the road.

"*No*? That's it? You saw what I did for Raph—how my vision helped him. I can help you too. I know it."

"Yes, you helped Raph. But don't you have another painting to do for someone? Raph said your art is constantly in demand."

"No. I just wrapped up my last commission and haven't taken any more."

"What? Why?"

"Just because. But it means there's nothing stopping me from working with you."

"Except for the fact my work's freaking dangerous. It's a place for professionals, not civilians. Okay?"

"No, not okay. I'm serious. I can be useful, you know. And not just with artwork."

"Isa, what I said about your painting being good—"

"This has nothing to do with that. I told you, I want, *need,* to do more now. To be helpful. I've spent my entire life being 'looked after,' but you saw with Liam just then—I could literally destroy his business, but he didn't even listen to me. Well, no more. I'm taking charge of my life now. I'm *making* this gift work for a purpose."

"Fine. Help your local community. Help your neighbors. But no way in hell are you helping me."

"Why?" Isa crossed her arms, and that little chin rose high. He held in a groan—she was every bit as stubborn as her brother. Which was admirable—but didn't change a thing. "Because I'm a woman?"

"Hell, no." He snorted. "Some of my best operatives are women. It's a no because my work involves people who will kill you just as soon as they look at you. And there are things far more deadly than humans. Not to mention, Templars are professionals who have trained for years."

"And I've had years training with my visions."

"Isa, it's a solid, absolute no. Now I need to get you home. I'll let Raph know about the fuckhead Liam. But then I've got to get back to work. The case I'm working with your brother is almost done, and as capable as Raph is, I want to be there as backup."

"So Raph can help, but ..." As her voice tapered off, the color in Isa's cheeks paled.

A chill flew through him. "Isa?"

Her arms unfolded, and with her eyes open, she slumped forward, the seatbelt arresting her momentum.

"Shit! Isa, are you okay?" No response. No movement. He pulled the car over to a screeching stop in the gravel. "Isa, can you hear me? I'm going to rest you back against the seat. There you go. Isa? Did you hit your head earlier?"

But she still didn't respond, and her vacant gaze stared through him.

Was this a vision? Goosebumps flew over him. Isa was totally defenseless right now. What if he hadn't been there? What if she'd been walking along the street and fallen over and hit her head?

And hell, what was he meant to do now? Raph would know. As much as Gray hated to call while the other man was in the middle of retrieving a Templar relic, he had no choice.

"Dial Raph Smith," he directed his voice-activated intercom system, not taking his hands off Isa in case she fell forward again. "Loudspeaker."

The ringing of a phone filled the car for several seconds, but Raph didn't pick up.

"Hell." He maneuvered one arm around Isa and cradled her slight frame against his chest—ignored the sudden sensation of rightness at having her there—while he fumbled in the back seat for something to use as a pillow. Finally snagged one of Isa's jackets and stuffed that between her and the door.

"Isa? Isa, you there yet?"

But she just stared out the windscreen. Fuck it.

"Hold on. I'm taking you home." Only the gods knew why he was talking to her, but he did anyway—maybe she could hear him somehow, and she'd come out of this quickly?

He phoned his second in command, Marcella, for directions to Isa's property, then turned the car back onto the road. As he did, the hairs on the back of his neck prickled.

He checked the rearview mirror. Nothing suspicious popped. But those little hairs continued to crawl the entire drive.

Ten minutes later, he reached the turnoff to Isa's farm. Please let her dad be home.

"We're almost there, Isa."

"Gray. What's—?"

"You're awake. Finally. Are you okay?"

She blinked and shook her head, her cheeks ghostly, and her eyes widened.

"What is it? What's wrong?"

"Cobwebby. Hold on," she muttered. "Where are we?"

"Your place—almost. Driving you up to the house now. This is your driveway, right?"

"How?"

"How did we get here?" He glanced at her. Clearly still out of it. His stomach tightened, but he kept his voice even. "You blanked out back there."

Her face went paler still.

"Hey, don't pass out. Lean forward and put your head between your legs, deep breaths."

"No—I'm okay. Just tired. Need to sleep. And the vision …" Her eyes drooped.

"Hold on a little longer. Is anyone else home?"

"No." Her eyes shut. "Just me. Dad and Leilu are out."

"Eyes open, Isa. Good girl. Who's Leilu?"

"Dog."

"Got it. Okay, there's the house. Where do I park?"

"Not house. Barn. My studio. Indigo door. Red couch. Keys in …" Her eyes closed again. "Handbag."

"Isa?" But this time, her eyes stayed shut. Fuck. The barn? Why not her house?

But he followed her instructions and drove to an outbuilding with a blueish-purple door.

"We're here," he said as he turned the engine off. "Come on, Isa. Time to wake up."

Nothing, except the even whisper of her breathing.

Double fuck.

With a sigh, Gray hopped out and opened the passenger door. Isa's dark curls fanned over her cheeks, hiding her face from him.

"Isa, you there yet?" He shook her arm. Nothing. What kind of sleep was this?

And hell, not another person in sight. Blue door it was.

Gray grabbed the key from Isa's purse and left her sleeping in the car. He knocked hard first, then unlocked the door. "Hello? Anyone here?"

Of course not. Just his freaking day.

A short entry corridor led to a bright open space with soaring beamed ceilings flooded with light from an entire back wall of glass doors and windows.

This wasn't a barn. Where were the hay bales and pitch forks?

A kitchenette, a small dining table and the couch Isa had mentioned took up one end; dark pops of jewel shades filled the room, from the red cushions to the peacock rug on the floor. Three easels held canvases in varying stages of work, positioned near the back glass wall. More canvases stood up against the only wall, not in the direct light. Gray climbed the stairs to the mezzanine level where Isa had a bed, but she'd easily fit on the couch downstairs.

He jogged back to the car and tried one more time to wake sleeping beauty. No go. But she was tiny, and he lifted her into his arms with zero issue.

As he did, Isa nestled into his chest. Dark eyelashes feathered over the tops of her cheeks, with perfectly defined black brows arching above them.

And hell if she wasn't perfect all over. Sleeping anyway. The rest of the time, she was like a terrier with a bone. She did not give up. Which he'd admire if her goal wasn't to join his freaking world.

She mumbled something, and Gray tightened his hold around her. She even fucking fit his arms perfectly. *Like I was made for her.* Something pinged in his chest. Something warm and right.

Hell no. His breath whooshed out. Isa was his closest friend's little sister. She was everything bright and light. He was cranky and fucked up. And he didn't do relationships. Period.

He stomped inside—maybe if he walked heavily enough, she'd wake up—and laid her down. Forced himself not to stare at her again while he grabbed a cushion and stuffed it under her head. Didn't want her waking up with a sore neck.

And now what was he meant to do?

He tried Raph again ... still nothing. The job to retrieve R-104A better be going to plan.

Gray turned back to Isa. If she was a Templar, she'd be a useful team member.

But she wasn't. And he already had one member of the Smith family on contract, which he'd had to work his ass off to convince the Templar Council to agree to.

Although he privately disagreed with the council's reluctance to deal with the Smiths. So what if they had an interesting family tree? It was what they did—not who their parents were—that counted. Just look at him.

And it was time for Gray to get back to his job. He wasn't leaving Isa like this, though. Not until she was awake and okay. But he could use the time efficiently.

He sat at the table near the kitchenette and called Marcella. She picked up immediately.

"Any updates?" Gray asked.

"Yes. The council are becoming nervous about R-104A's status."

"Release an interim update that our contract man on the ground appears to be on track for recovery. And while we're on the one hundred and four relics, has Cyn checked in re her project?"

"Only that she's following up the latest lead. I swear she mentioned a love whisperer or something."

"Okay, at least she's got a lead. That's been a long time coming. Any other updates?"

"One. The Daemon Congress petitioned for a meeting with one of their representatives. The council wants you to take that meeting on priority."

"Now? I'm in the middle of tracking down a missing relic in another country." Gray shoved a hand through his hair. "All right, send me the rep's details. Also, have the jet on standby in Brisbane; hopefully, we'll wrap up R-104A tonight, and I can get back to the US. One more thing—I need you to get the local law enforcement here onto a person of interest. I'll shoot the info through shortly."

He'd just sent the fuckhead Liam's details through to Marcella when Isa mumbled something from the couch, although her eyes were still closed.

"Isa? What was that?" He knelt beside the couch and shook her shoulder. "Can you hear me, Isa?"

"Gray?" His name was a whisper on her breath, and he leaned closer.

"That's right, I'm here. Can you wake up?"

Those beautiful lips pursed, and she mumbled something more, but he couldn't make out the words.

"It's Grayson. Gray. Can you hear me?"

She cupped his jaw. Her thumb rubbed his skin, and

goosebumps rolled over him. Then the pad of her thumb brushed his lower lip.

He sucked in a breath, and the instinct surged through him to turn and nip that firm flesh—but, gods, she was *sleeping*. He had to stop this.

"Isa," he whispered, pulling back.

But she followed him, and before he could say anything, lush, silky lips pressed into his. Heat flashed through him.

Intoxicating, mysterious. Beguiling. The urge to sink into that kiss clawed through Gray. She was fucking perfect. Just like he'd imagined from the second he'd met her less than a week ago.

A growl rumbled through him.

The sound cut through his haze. Shit. Fuck. He was kissing Isa—his best friend's little sister—while she was *asleep*.

He backpedaled to the other end of the room.

3

"GRAY," Isa breathed.

He was in Isa's vision again. Like he inhabited a hidden nook inside her mind and no matter what she did, he was there. But he had a name now. Finally.

His warm, clipped voice echoed in her ear—clearer than ever before—like he was right there in the room with her.

So close she could do what she'd dreamed of from the moment she'd run into him at her brother's apartment. Touch him. Kiss him. Experience him.

But when Isa tried to draw him closer, he backed away. No. No, this was her vision. Surely, she could control what she saw, just for once?

So, she went after what she wanted and leaned up. Captured those firm, sensual lips with hers. A moan whispered through her—was it hers?

Yes, this was exactly what she wanted. Gray's heat and fire and spice infusing her world.

But then he disappeared.

Damn it.

Except ... she blinked, opened her eyes. Wow, that hadn't

been a vision. It had been a dream. And, of course, Grayson had been the main act. Over the years, she'd had plenty that went way further—he'd featured in those, too.

Gray! Where was he? She sat up but stopped midway as her head swam.

"Isa." Gray walked over and stopped in front of her. And the rest of the room came into focus. She couldn't stop her mouth from dropping open.

"What—how—we're in my studio."

He jammed his hands into his pockets and rocked on his heels. "Are you okay? You've been out of it for half an hour."

Okay? *Was* she okay? How did she even get here? Oh shit. "You carried me in?"

"Yeah, you weren't moving. How do you feel? Need a drink?"

"Water would be good." She licked her dry lips as she swiveled her legs around and planted her feet on the ground. "Give me a sec."

"I'll grab it."

"Thanks, but I need to move. Need to get rid of the—" She waved a hand at her head. "Cobwebs."

"Sure?"

"Yes. I'm not going to fall." At least Gray stepped back. Although he stayed tense. No doubt ready to spring into action if she stumbled. Damn it, would there ever be a day when the men in her world didn't feel like they had to catch her every single second?

"Just trying to help," he said. "Are you always this independent?"

"I wish." She snorted. "You see how I get with visions— they make me way too dependent on others as it is. Getting myself a water is a big deal some days."

Conscious of his gaze on her, Isa did her best not to

stumble to the fridge, and took a bottle of cold water for herself. Held up another for him. "Want one?"

"No, I'm good." He folded his arms—his biceps tightened—and leaned against the kitchenette. Damn, but he looked delicious. "So, do your visions usually wipe you out that much? And it came on so fast—what if you'd been outside and fallen over and hit your head?"

She took a sip of the water and did her best to pretend she wasn't enjoying the view before she responded. "No. That was ... unusual."

"Huh." His lips tightened.

"What's wrong?"

"I don't like things being ... unusual." He rubbed the back of his neck. "I like normal. Explainable. Events and actions that fit into the compartment they're supposed to."

"So you can be ready to handle anything, right? Like an attack or something?"

"Exactly." Gray stared hard at her. She shifted, uncomfortably warm under that regard. Damn. She had to be careful, or she'd give away too much. "What was so out of the norm?"

He sounded casual, but his interest remained locked on her. At least they were talking about the vision, though, and not him.

"I usually get enough of a warning to sit down," Isa said, "but this one slammed into me. And then it wiped me out longer than normal, too."

"Any clue why?"

"No. I got a vague sense of unease—my belly knotted up —so it might be something bad. Although, I've had worse reactions to other visions ..." She shut that thought down. "And now I have a damned sore head. Like the vision shoves itself inside me and everything gets screwy after."

"Bad?" Gray visibly tensed. "Why? Was someone hurt? Killed?"

"What? No. That's awful."

"Sorry. Occupational hazard."

"I know." She searched his gaze. How many times had she seen him standing over terrible scenes? She turned away and wandered over to the nearest easel. She'd hated seeing Gray in those scenes. Not because of what they were, but that he always seemed so alone.

"What did you see this time?" he asked, following her over.

"It was two visions. It started with Raph and Eve ..."

"Yes?"

Isa chewed on her lip. Just how much did Gray really know about her and Raph's true heritage? Until she knew for sure, she had to be careful.

"Raph and Eve were holding hands." She refused to give in to the urge to shiver at the rest of what she'd seen. "But then the vision morphed into someone wearing latex gloves, using fancy tweezers to open an old brass incense burner. They were going super slow like it was glass, not metal."

"An incense burner?" Gray froze. "Who was the person? What else did you see? Tell me everything in precise detail, exactly as you saw it."

"Okay, okay, calm the farm." She blew out a slow breath and replayed the vision through her mind. "I didn't see a face. Just the hands in the gloves. The incense burner is on a stainless steel surface. I didn't see if they opened it."

"Did you see any marks on the censer?"

"You mean the incense burner? Let me think ... a small flared cross—near the bottom."

"Fuck." Gray grabbed his mobile phone, punched in

something. "I want a priority check-in for R-104B. In person," he barked. "Then get a helicopter—I don't care who—for priority pickup at this location, and move the jet to the nearest viable airfield." He fired off Isa's address and ended the call.

"Gray, what's going on? What's R ... whatever you said?" A shiver trickled down her spine.

"Forget you ever heard R-104B. And I hope to hell it's nothing."

"The way you're pacing doesn't *look* like you think it's nothing." He cut her a look, and she shrugged. "It's true."

"Let's just say it's pushing coincidence too far. What else can you tell me about your visions? Are the events you see happening in real time? In the past, the future?"

"The future, always. But the timeframe has been anywhere from seconds to days to even months." She suppressed another shiver. "Why?"

"Because maybe we can stop it from coming true."

"You can try," Isa whispered.

"Has that ever happened?"

She shook her head.

Gray's phone pinged with an incoming message. His mouth tightened, and then he rapidly typed something before he held the phone up to his ear. "I need to make a call—can I go out that way?" He gestured toward the back of the studio.

Isa quickly slid the door open. Gray passed her without a look, and while he didn't ask, she closed it after him to give him privacy.

Through the glass, Gray snarled something—she didn't have to hear him to know his voice was terse—his jaw tightened, and fury glittered in his navy eyes.

She headed to her easel, stared into the painting that

would be her last commission, searched for the peace and calm and sense of right she had in her happy zone.

A chill flew up her arms instead.

Damn. What was so important about an incense burner?

The scrape of the sliding door pulled her out of her thoughts.

"I have to go," Gray bit out. "Now. A helicopter is picking me up here ASAP. Local law enforcement will station a unit at your house until Liam's picked up." His phone pinged with more messages, and he turned his attention back to it.

Isa's mouth went dry. Gray was leaving—and she might never get another chance to prove what she could do.

"You need me there too," she blurted.

Gray flicked her a look. "No can do."

"What if I have another vision of your ... thing? If I'm with you when it happens, I can fill you in right then."

"Still no."

"Grayson, look at me. I know this is serious. But I am too. I can help you."

"Why are you hell-bent on doing this?"

"Because I want—"

"What? What do you want so much that you're talking about stepping into a world where plenty of people end up dead?"

"Because you need me." And she needed him. To give her a chance to prove her mother's legacy was a gift—and not a curse. "I can use my visions to search for ... whatever you need."

"You can make a vision happen?" His gaze sharpened.

"Yes." She battled back the urge to bite her lip and fold her arms, forced herself to meet his stare. "I can do this." *She hoped.*

Stuff that. No more hoping. She would *do this.*

"You can't just call me after a vision?"

"I can—once I wake up. But more than that, if I'm at the scene of whatever is going on, it might help me channel the visions to get you more relevant information, and fast."

"Near real time?"

Isa, Isa, Isa, what are you doing? She shut down the urge to say no; she had no chance at doing this, and instead, held Gray's gaze and nodded.

"Shit. Doesn't matter. The answer's still no. I can't let you get involved—"

The rumble of a vehicle engine had them both go still.

"You said your dad was out for the day?"

"Maybe he's back early."

Gray shot her a look. "And it could also be your ex. Stay here. I'll check it out."

As if. Always trying to protect her.

"I said stay." Gray's lips flattened.

Lips she'd swear she knew way better than she did. She dragged her gaze up to his eyes. The storm brewing in their deep blue depths did little to ease the roiling in her belly.

"I'm not one of your minions you can order around. And I'm also not a piece of fancy-ass delicate glass that's going to smash into smithereens if you look at me the wrong way. Come on, someone is at *my* house. I'm going with you."

"Fancy ass?"

"Well, fine. My ass *is* fancy. But I'm not delicate. Oh wow —is that ... a smile? Oops, guess not."

"Fine." Gray held up one hand. "But be quiet. I'm the professional here. If I say you run, you run like hell."

She held in a sigh. They lived in a rural town, and even then, the farm was a ten-minute drive farther into the countryside, up a long winding driveway in the middle of cow paddocks. Danger didn't live on her doorstep.

"Whatever you say." She plastered an appeasing smile on her face.

"Don't give me that BS. I know you think I'm overreacting, but until we open this door, you—and I—don't know what's on the other side. And this is another reason I'm not bringing you with me. My operatives always do as I order."

Damn. "In that case, you say run—I run."

He cut her a look and then held his fingers to his lips as the car engine stopped.

Multiple doors clicked open; feet crunched on gravel. A husky, feminine voice called, "Spread out and search all the buildings. She's got to be here somewhere. Remember, I need her alive."

Isa couldn't stop her mouth from dropping wide as she met Gray's glittering gaze—all traces of humor vanishing from his expression. Oh shit. Now what?

4

FUCKING HELL. What was going on now? Gray had zero time for this—he had to get to R-104B.

He also needed a weapon ... and his were in the car. Fuck, fuck, *fuck*. He'd dropped one of the basic rules of ops. Never go unarmed. He needed his ass kicked.

"Do you have any knives here?" he whispered as he locked the door. Not that the little latch would hold anyone off who really wanted in.

"A butter knife," she whispered back. "And a palette knife."

"Grab them and let me see. I'll pull the drapes and lock up."

Isa ran toward her art supplies, and he raced to the back sliding door.

"Here." Isa joined him holding two knives and a screwdriver. "I had this, too."

The butter and pallet knife were close to useless. But the screwdriver was sturdy enough to do decent damage. He took that.

"Where can you hide?"

"Upstairs—the mezzanine has a closet."

"Go now. I'll sneak around the front from the back. Don't come out for anyone else but me, got it?"

Isa swallowed hard, but she nodded and took off. At least she didn't panic under stress. Thank the gods for small mercies.

Gray took one moment to check his watch. Fifteen minutes till the chopper pickup. He just had to deal with whatever this next bullshit was first.

He eased the curtain back at the corner of the glass sliding doors. Still only rolling green paddocks. No sign of anyone else. He checked the mezzanine once—no sign of Isa—and headed outside.

As he reached the front of the studio, a male voice called out, "Farmhouse is clear."

"Door's locked on the barn," another male voice responded.

"Smash it," the female voice said. "If the woman's there, don't touch her, but kill anyone else inside."

A crash echoed from the front.

Shit. Time to go.

He rounded the corner. A black SUV had parked in behind his car. Unoccupied. So, two males and one female going by the voices so far.

Bangs and crashes rang out from inside the studio. Fuck. Fear cut through him. Isa better be hidden—no. No thoughts of Isa. Fear, any emotion right now, would be zero use. One obstacle at a time.

At the front door to the studio, a bulky man wearing jeans and a navy tee held a handgun—looked like a Taurus G3—pointing at the ground, and watched whatever was going on inside. If this was the guard, he was doing a piss-poor job.

But the dude still had a weapon. Gray had a screwdriver, for fuck's sake.

Then a scream echoed from inside the studio.

Oh fuck. *Isa*.

Gray grabbed the guard around his meaty neck and drove the screwdriver through the jugular vein.

The guard stiffened. A gurgling, choking gasp sounded from his chest, and Gray stole the gun from the guard as he crashed to the floor.

A second figure deeper inside the studio whirled around and whipped a gun from his jacket. Gray aimed for the center of mass, pulled the Taurus G3's trigger twice, and the guard dropped to the ground.

Isa's scream pierced the air again, reverberating through the studio like an alarm. Gray spun and trained the gun up the stairs, ready to fire.

Isa and a blue-haired woman appeared at the top step. The woman had one hand with wickedly sharp claws wrapped around Isa's arm and held a knife to her ribs.

"Let go of me!" Isa pulled at Blue Hair's grip. "Gray! Run!"

Like fuck. He steadied his aim.

"Who the fuck are you?" Blue Hair snarled.

Isa's cheeks were pale, but then she looked at her artwork. A red tinge hit her cheeks. "The painting! That was an important commission."

Gray stopped for a moment—as did Blue Hair. Man, Isa had spunk. Reluctant admiration tugged at him, warred with the need to keep her safe.

"Isa, stay calm," he said in a careful voice and turned his attention to Blue Hair. "What do you want?"

"Down. Now." Blue Hair jerked Isa's arm and forced her down the steps.

Gray maneuvered so that he blocked the front door.

"Well, this is interesting." Blue Hair glanced at the bodies. "You took out both of them?"

"They shouldn't have tried to kill me," Gray said.

"At least you saved me the job there. But don't get in my way; otherwise, this one will have to go too."

"Really? I thought you needed her alive?"

"Alive, yes, unharmed? No." Blue Hair swiped her clawed hand over Isa's arm.

"Hey!" Isa hissed. She grabbed her bicep as blood welled between her fingers.

"Get the fuck away from her, or I'll take you down, too."

"Uh-uh, no shooty-shooties now. These are poison tipped." Blue Hair waggled her clawed fingers as her lips curled. "If Her Highness here doesn't want to go the way of the angels, then she should come with me. Now."

"Highness?" Isa's face went chalky.

Highness?

"Oh yes," the female purred. "I know exactly who you are. And you're going to bring me one helluva payday. No pun intended."

Fuck no.

Gray carefully set his aim. "I have zero idea who you are, and I give zero fucks. I'll pull the trigger right now and put you down, and you better believe I can make the shot with ease. Now drop the fucking knife."

"Shoot me, and you lose your chance at the antidote."

"I'd prefer to shoot you and take my chances with my medical team. Either way, you're dead. Last time I'm going to say it. Drop. The. Knife."

Blue Hair's gaze locked on his gun, and her lips thinned. Then she dropped the knife and slowly raised her hands.

"Isa, get over here." Gray kept the Taurus G3 trained on Blue Hair. "Isa!"

Isa clambered down the stairs, holding on to her bleeding arm, and stood by Gray. She glared at Blue Hair and asked, "Who are you?"

"Just the bounty hunter who's going to bring you in."

"Over my dead body," Gray growled.

Blue Hair's eyes narrowed as she looked from him to Isa, and her lips tilted in a knowing smile. He bit back a hiss—why had he said that?

Fuck. Fuck, fuck. He should kill Blue Hair right now—but if what she said about the antidote was true ... Hell. He couldn't risk killing her until he had more information about the poison.

"Whoever the fuck you are, if you come near Isadora again, I *will* put you down." Gray nodded to the door. "You're going to walk out of this building, get in your car and drive far, far away. And I mean it. You take one single step toward us, and you're dead, poison or not. Got it?"

"Never mind. You'll come to me. I'm getting my card from my pocket. You'll need it when you're calling me to save Her Highness here."

Keeping the gun trained on Blue Hair, Gray stepped in front of Isa and yanked a white rectangular calling card from the bounty hunter's clawed fingers.

((◆))

Heart pounding, arm on fire, Isa stood in the middle of her studio surrounded by blood splatters and globs of ... oh shit, was that a body? And another there—her gut roiled.

She darted to the kitchenette and vomited into the sink.

A scraping behind her made her stiffen and whirl around.

"She's gone," Gray bit out as he stalked back into the studio. "But we need to go. I don't want to be here when she comes back."

"What about those men? Should we call an ambulance?"

"They're dead. No, don't look at them—look at me. Isa, they were here to kill me and hurt you—at the very least. Don't even think about them."

Isa's stomach threatened to come up again, but she swallowed the bile.

Look at Gray. Look at Gray.

Something she'd been wanting to do in person her entire adult life. And now, finally, that wish had come true.

And in Gray's implacable, icy gaze, she found enough calm to draw a deep breath, and the violent urge to be ill eased back to a roiling gut.

"I'm okay." She went to wipe the hair back from her face, but pain ricocheted through her arm.

"What's wrong?" Gray took her hand.

"Stop!" She yanked back.

"Hell, how bad is it? Here, sit down." He dragged over one of the dining chairs.

"Just scratches." She breathed through the pain. "But they hurt like a bitch. Don't touch them again."

"Okay, okay. Let me look. I won't touch. Shit, these are nasty. Listen, we don't know what this poison is, what it will do to you, or how fast it's going to act."

"That doesn't matter right now. I have to get word to Dad. No one from Mum's world is ever meant to come near us." The memory of her vision from earlier about Raph and Eve swept through her. "And I need to call Raph for something important."

"Are you loco? Hell yes, your poisoning matters. Call your father and Raph later. Right now, I've got something in the car for the poison. Stay there." Then he spun and ran out of the studio.

Isa opened her mouth to yell no, this poison wasn't going to kill her—but shit, he'd ask why. And no way could she tell Gray the truth about her death vision. He'd tell Raph, and then they'd both try to lock her away somewhere *safe*, and any hope of using her gift for good would go up in smoke.

5

"FUCK, FUCK, FUCK." Every second counted. Gray ran for his car and grabbed his bag.

Back in the studio, Isa still sat on the chair, but she was talking on her cell, and she held up one hand when he reached her. Damn stubborn woman. This was her life! He set the duffel bag on the table and laid out his medical equipment.

"Thanks, Dad. You, too." She hung up and looked at Gray. "I let him know what happened and to stay away until I can figure out what's going on."

"I told you that could wait." He flipped open the poisons kit. "Arm out. I need to inject you intravenously to counteract the poison." He filled a syringe with the masking agent. He didn't tell her the medication was a temp fix only. He'd face that problem once Isa was out of immediate danger.

"I was just sitting here, so calling made total sense. And no, it can't wait. What if that bitch goes after Dad?" Isa gasped, and her cheeks went a ghostly hue.

"What? Don't like needles." He grasped her uninjured

arm. "Isa, you need this—"

"No. Not that. The scratches hurt." She gasped again. "A lot. They're hurting so much frigging more." She hissed, and tears welled in her eyes as she turned her arm over.

Fuck. Her *arm*. Red and blue streaks spread out like the roots of a weed, trailing up and down from the wounds.

"Is that bad?" She let out a whimper.

Yes. Very fucking bad. But all he said was, "You need this now." He slid the needle into her vein, then he took out a blue marker, drew a line around the angry red streaks, and checked the time. If those streaks kept going ...

Come on, come on, come on.

"The masking agent will kick in fast." He glanced at her face. "How's the pain?"

"Still hurts like a bitch. And the nausea is ..." She made a see-sawing motion with her good hand.

"Okay. Listen. I need to identify the poison."

"I need to call Raph."

"No. Identifying—"

"Gray. This is important. I have to get a message to him."

Frick. The job Raph was working was far too vital to risk being jeopardized.

"Poison first so we can work the fuck out what antidote you need. Then Raph. But you can't mention what happened here. I don't want him distracted."

"Fine by me. He'd go all protective big bro mode all over again."

"He cares about you, that's all. Hell, *you* need to care more about your life, Isa. And you're coming with me, by the way. No, don't get all excited. We'll talk on the chopper since I can't leave you like this."

He took the poison identification satchel and a sterile

scalpel. "This is going to hurt. I have to remove some skin from around the wounds."

"What?"

"I'll give you a painkiller after, but I need you to stay still and steady for me now. Can you do that?"

"Do I have to?"

"If you want a cure that doesn't involve a blue-haired bounty hunter, yes."

"Fine." She clenched her jaw.

"Good girl. Okay, here goes."

He shaved a sliver of skin away from the largest wound on Isa's arm. She tensed and hissed, but she didn't scream or jerk away. His gut clenched. But he kept going and took one more sliver.

"All done." His breath whooshed out. Shit, had he been holding it that entire time?

He glanced up at Isa, and his chest tightened.

Tears ran over her cheeks, and sweat gathered around her forehead.

"Sorry," Gray whispered. "I'm—"

"No. I know. I'm okay."

"Identification is next." He dropped her skin samples into the poisons test vial and snapped the bottom to mix the serum in.

Please don't turn green. Please don't turn ... Fuck. Ice washed through his veins, and his gut curdled.

Amoricinae Venenum. Shit!

"So what is it?"

If he told her the truth, would she panic? At the very least, it would be distressing. No, better to keep her comfortable and calm for as long as possible. He put the poisons kit away and took out a dose of morphine before turning back. "How's the pain? Sorry. Loco question. Here, take this." He held out a tablet. "It's strong, so it might make you lightheaded."

"Then I'll wait. I need to call Raph."

"Frick, Isa. Really?"

"Yes. Really." She lifted her chin in that way of hers that screamed she wouldn't back down. "I told you it's important."

"Fine. Call him now. But make it quick." He checked the time. "Chopper is inbound." Sure enough, the *whomp, whomp, whomp* of rotors spinning echoed through the studio.

"Now?"

"Yes. Now. You've got one minute. And I need to let him know he's on his own tonight, as well, so I'll call first."

He'd barely wrapped up his terse conversation with Raph when Isa grabbed the cell from him. She filled Raph in on a vision she'd had of her brother and Eve—although why the hell that was so important, he had zero clue.

While they spoke, he checked her arm. The red streaks hadn't progressed past the blue marker.

Thank the gods. Because if the masking agent hadn't worked ... well, not even a human hospital could help Isa then. Only the true antidote would do.

"Time to go." He took his cell and ended the call for Isa.

"Hey—"

"Chopper's here. Painkiller now." He waited until she'd swallowed the tablet before grabbing her good arm and helping her to her feet.

"Oh crap." She wobbled. "Don't feel so good."

"Are you going to—"

She vomited all over his feet and slumped against him. "Sorry."

"Ah hell." And there went the pain medication. "Come

on. I'll give you an injection for the pain when we're on the chopper."

"My stuff—"

"I'll grab your purse. We'll work the rest out later." He wrapped an arm around Isa and walked her out of the studio as the helicopter landed in the grass. He covered Isa's face as the rotor blade downwash sent debris toward them.

As soon as Isa was strapped into the rear passenger seat, Gray administered another painkiller via injection, then took the co-pilot seat for the twenty-minute flight to the closest airfield where the Templar jet could meet them. But after they'd landed and he helped Isa out, she let out a giggle.

"Isa—you okay? Come on, we need to board the jet."

"Holy shit, Grayson. Gray... son. Have I told you I really like your name?" She waved one hand through the air. "You're my favorite color—actually, gray's not a color. You're a shade. My favorite shade."

"No."

"And your eyes. They're this brilliant blue that makes me want to paint them. And your lips. They make me want to—"

"Okay, okay. I get it." He checked her pupils. Damn. The painkiller he'd given her hadn't been *that* strong.

"Well, I do. And I like that plane, too. Is it a plane? Or a jet ..."

He took her still-waving hand and guided her up the stairs. "Careful. You're high as a kite."

"Think it's the inect ... inject ... that thing you put in my arm."

Shit. Just what he needed. "Think you're right. And it's a jet. Bombardier Challenger. Templars have a fleet. Here you go, ease into the chair now." He helped her strap into one of the reclining chairs for safety during takeoff and tightened the seatbelt right up. Frick, how did such a big personality fit into such a tiny package?

"A fleet. Of course you do." Her nose puckered, but her eyes drifted shut. Finally, thank fuck. The quicker she slept off the effects of the pain meds, the better.

As the jet took off, Gray sat beside Isa so he could monitor her vitals and check his watch. Thirty-five minutes since a bounty hunter had poisoned his best friend's little sister while he stood right fucking there.

For one heartbeat, he stared at her lips.

Then he shook his head, dispelled the urge to lean over and kiss her, and instead grabbed his laptop, brought up the case file on his relics, and put a call in to Marcella.

"We're on our way to LA now. I need you and Tank to meet us there. Set the apartment up for the three of us and one extra. Then I want a file on all known daemon poisons and another file on everything we know about a blue-haired daemon bounty hunter, name unknown at this stage. And get the Daemon Congress rep to meet us as soon as we land. I want to speak to them first up." Regardless of what the daemons wanted, Gray was going to find out what they knew about amorice and its cures. "Marcella, wait, one last thing. Get Tank to organize a change of clothing for our guest."

Confident his team would follow through on his orders, Gray sat back beside Isa and checked her over.

Heart rate, blood pressure, temp, all normal. About time something went right. Even if the masking agent was a temp fix only.

Hell—what to do now? At least by taking Isa to the US, the Templar lab was an option for an antidote—he'd call them shortly. And the daemon rep might have information about the poison that could help too.

But if not ...

A chill flew through him. No. Not thinking like that. Keep going. One obstacle at a time.

And hell, he should let Raph know about the poison ... except distracting Raph midjob on retrieving R-104A? Not happening.

Gray's gut knotted. Raph would kill him for keeping this secret—let alone for bringing Isa into this world.

But facts were facts. R-104A was stolen a week ago. R-104B was missing now. And R-104C had been missing for decades.

All three relics missing at the same time.

A shiver trickled down his spine. Coincidence? Zero chance.

And now Isa, with her unique ability, was coming with him to the US. It would be irresponsible *not* to use her to trace R-104B. He just had to keep Isa safe along the way and rein in the loco-ass urge to get close to the stunning diviner.

Which meant he needed to get to work.

He called the Templar's chief financial officer.

"Atticus, I need a favor," Gray said.

"And hello to you, too. What do you need?"

"You keep a quiet, close eye on our strategic partners, right?"

"I do indeed."

"Perfect. Can you make some extremely quiet, let's say *invisible*, inquiries into the St. James Corporation?"

"Interesting you should bring them up. Chatter is that the SJC have been making some ... out of the norm business decisions lately."

"I hate out of the norm. How so?"

"Taking on projects at the upper end of the risk profile. And in volumes unusual for SJC. Since Kai has been in charge, he's always had a taste for the higher risks, but never in the volume we're hearing about now."

Alarm bells rang in Gray's mind. Another coincidence.

After Gray hung up the call, he stared at Isa.

Fucking hell, if someone was out to unite the three gifts, the entire world was in immense danger. Because whoever held all three gifts together could control the hearts, minds and bodies of humankind.

He set his jaw. That wasn't happening today. He'd throw everything he had, pull every lever needed, to make sure the three gifts were safely contained, including using his best friend's little sister.

6

Isa woke to a throbbing ache in her arm, pounding in time to a dull thud at the back of her head.

Was it another vision? She tensed—then a scent she only associated with one person reached her, and she turned her head.

Gray sat across the aisle, standard scowl in place, his head bent over his laptop. Surprise, surprise. He practically lived in front of that thing, issuing orders. Making calls.

Except for killing those two men and handling that woman back in her studio.

Then, as if seeing Gray had been her grounding, her surroundings swam into focus.

A plane. Creamy leather armchairs facing each other on both sides of the cabin, with a matching leather couch farther down. A screen on the wall displaying an image of her favorite Waterhouse painting, *Hylas and the Nymphs*.

"Hi," she croaked. "Any chance they have toilets on this flight?"

"Isa." Gray shut his laptop. "How are you feeling?"

"Like I had a huge night out and drank too much."

"Sorry, party girl, you had something, but it wasn't alcohol."

"Not a party girl." She unclipped her seatbelt and shuffled to her feet. "Where are the loos on this thing?"

"Bathroom's at the back. Careful on your feet."

She shot him a look, but at least he didn't walk her to the loo. She followed his direction on unsteady feet, only to stumble to a stop after passing the last partition.

An enormous bed took up this entire section of the plane. And at the far end, another door led to an actual bathroom. Holy shit. Who traveled like this?

After she'd used the loo and washed her face, the cobwebs in her head fully dissipated.

And her heart picked up pace. She'd done it! She gave her reflection a high five, only for the scratches on her arm to protest.

Damn. Poisoning aside, she'd still taken a step toward action.

"Do you remember what happened in your studio?" Gray asked when she returned to the front cabin.

"Yep." She held her arm out as she slid into the seat opposite him. "The poison. The masking agent. The chopper ... things get woozy from there."

"Turns out you're among the small percentage of the population who can't handle both painkillers and the masking agent. That's why you vomited, and why the injection affected you so strongly."

"Huh. That makes sense. So, no more masking agent or no more painkillers?"

"Definitely the latter. The masking agent is critical until I can get you the antidote."

"But why do we need a cure at all if the masking agent is

... how did you put it, counteracting the poison? Gray? Why are you looking at me like that?"

"I'm not looking like anything." He ran a hand through his hair.

"Yes, you are. I see the same look on Raph's face all the time. You're hiding something."

"Not hiding. Protecting." He opened his laptop. "Right now, we need to discuss your visions—"

"No." She leaned across and closed his laptop. "You said you want me to take this seriously. So I am. And do I need to remind you I'm the poisoned one here?"

"Not like I can forget," he muttered. "Okay, but don't freak out. I will fix this—"

"You're worried I'll panic after everything that happened today? Gray, cut the BS and just tell me already."

"Fine. The masking agent requires a top-up every six hours. But ..." His lips flattened. "The agent stops working altogether after ninety-six hours. And based on your body weight, I'd use that as the maximum duration."

"So I do need the antidote. No worries, I'll look that up next."

"Isa, it's not that simple. You need to take this—"

"Seriously. I get it." But Gray didn't—and wouldn't—know this poison wasn't going to kill her, so she shut her mouth. "Back at my studio, you did the test, right? So what's this poison?"

"*Amoricinae Venenum.* Street name amorice. It's a poison from a daemon-realm species of plant. The toxin is like ricin here in the human world because it interrupts the molecular function of your cells. Basically, the cells die off. And when enough cells ..." His expression tightened.

"And the antidote?"

"The cure has to be made from the same plant as the

poison. I checked with our lab in the US, and we don't have it."

"When did you ask them?"

"While you were passed out from the painkillers."

"Ugh, I hate that." A shiver crawled down her neck.

"You were in pain—"

"No, not the injection. The unconscious bit. *That's* what I hate." She crossed her arms. "That's a big part of why I don't go out often, even locally. Imagine not knowing when—where—you might suddenly lose consciousness. Who's there? What will they do?"

Gray eyed Isa for a long moment before he said, "I never thought of it like that. I can see why you'd be uncomfortable in public places."

She almost said, "except around you," but bit back the words. It sounded batshit—she'd only known him for a week. Except that wasn't true. Years of seeing him flew through her mind.

"Is your arm hurting? Shit, I can see it is."

"What—no. No, just thinking. So this poison is deadly?"

He nodded. "You can take the masking agent for ninety-six hours—four days—but if we don't have the cure by then …"

"I die."

If possible, his jaw clenched even tighter.

But Isa's death was coming in a luxe bedroom with Gray at her side, the two of them dressed to kill. So this poison couldn't be her undoing, which meant Isa would get the cure.

She stared at Waterhouse's *Hylas and the Nymphs.*

Dead … dead meant never painting. Never experiencing one of her dreams of Gray for real. Never seeing Raph again. Her father. Her mother.

Isa's stomach clenched. *Her mother.*

Although there *might* be one other option to save her from the poison. Except, by taking that option, Isa wasn't really saving her life. She'd be ... losing it, for whatever time she had left.

"Well, that's not going to happen," she muttered. Both dying from the poison and the other option.

"Exactly. Because there are four days to find a way out of this. That's a long time in our world. Our US lab might come up with an option, and the daemon rep I'm meeting in LA might have some intel as well."

"I can't tell if you're being optimistic or realistic here."

"I'm not a naturally optimistic person."

"Okay. Realistic. Good news, I can be an optimist for the two of us." And Gray's calm helped *her* pulse even out. "How long was I unconscious?"

"An hour. You need your next shot in five hours. I've set a timer on my cell and watch."

"I need to set a timer on my phone, too."

"It's in your purse. I grabbed it before we left. But I've set my alarm—"

"Thanks, but I need to set my own. I can't hassle you every six hours. And you need to show me how to inject myself, too."

"You're not a hassle, Isa. It's the opposite. I need you alive. Right now, you're my only link to the item you saw in your vision."

"Good to know I have a use." Gray the Templar—first and always. But she'd signed up for the chance to be useful, so she didn't argue that point. "Nonetheless, I need to do this for myself."

"Isa, back at your studio, you said no one from your mother's world is meant to come near you. And the bounty hunter called you Highness. What the hell is going on?"

Isa swallowed the lump in her throat. Shit. Where did she even start? "How much do you know about who I really am?"

"You mean the fact that your mother's father is the Lord of Hell?"

"Yeah. That. How did you know?"

"It came up one night several years ago when Raph and I were working on a case together."

"It doesn't bother you?"

"Isa, believe me, no one should be judged based on their parents. I trust Raph—count him as a friend. But he never went into the details about your mother, and after what just happened with the bounty hunter, I need to know more."

"I think the Highness thing is referring to my grandfat— I can't even say it? But no one's ever called me that before today."

"Okay. What else?"

"The way it was told to me, Raph and I each were born with a gift—yes, Raph calls his a curse—from our mother. He sees the past; I see the future. Because our powers were so strong, our grandfather wanted Raph and me on his side of Hell. I was just a baby, and Raph would've been ten. Still a kid. But Mum made a deal with our grandfather—she'd return home and let him lock her behind the thirteenth gate, keep *her* powers on his side of Hell, on the proviso that Raph and I could live human, normal lives. Well, as normal as possible, given our gifts. And no one from Hell would interfere with us."

"So this bounty hunter is going against an order from the Lord of Hell?" Gray asked.

"Which doesn't make any sense." Isa rubbed her arms.

"Are you okay?"

"Yep. Just ... getting my head around it all." She straightened her back. "But I'm fine. In fact, I want to do something. I need to do something. So come on. Put me to work. Let me find this thing you're after." She held her breath. Come on, Gray. If her death vision came true in four days or forty, it didn't matter. She needed to use her gift for something worthwhile while she had the time.

"Hold up, you've moving too fast. I said we'd talk about it."

"Well, clearly, I'm coming to LA. So why waste the chance to find your missing item?"

"It's not that easy." His grim expression made her instinctively lift her chin. She might be a full foot shorter than him, but she refused to back down. Not when she could finally prove her gift's worth *and* spend more time with this man, right here. Right now.

"Isa ..." His jaw clenched. "I'll pull every lever needed to keep the items under my protection safe. But there are three things you need to know if you do this. One, you'll have to sign a nondisclosure agreement with the Templars. Two, you do everything I say when I say. That includes that if I think something is too dangerous, I'll bench your ass, and wherever we are in the world, you'll stay there until we can get you some place safe. And three, the beings who might be involved with this are not human." He regarded her, his expression grave, his eyes narrowed on hers. "Are you ready for that?"

Daemons. A chill flew up Isa's back, and she couldn't help a shiver. But she still held Gray's gaze. "I know what you're saying, Gray. That just makes me the perfect person to help you."

"Fuck. Can't believe I'm thinking of doing this." Gray shook his head.

Isa held her breath. Was he—?

"You can work with me. At least it'll get you away from Blue Hair while we find the cure."

"She's a daemon, so not sure how I get away from her for long," Isa said.

"You know what she is?"

"Of course." Isa suppressed a shiver. "Not like I could miss that, given everything."

"Then yes, getting you away from the daemon bounty hunter is also a benefit of you coming with us."

"Whatever you say." Her heart leaped. She was doing this! She was using her gift for something good.

"Fine. You're coming with me." Gray clenched his jaw even harder. Too much more and he might break his teeth.

"And I hate to push you after today, but this is critical." Gray linked his fingers and sat forward. "Are you up to looking for the incense burner now?"

Her stomach lurched. Maybe because of the poison—or the medication. More likely, the lie she'd told.

"I'm ready. Can you show me an image, or do I go off what I saw in my vision? Is there anything else you can tell me about it?"

"You need to sign the nondisclosure agreement first. What you're dealing with here goes beyond anything you've ever heard about. But there's one other thing. Once you sign the NDA, it'll be on record that you're helping the Templars. We also have an arrangement with most governments for our operatives to travel across borders. Most of them, anyway. I'll fill out the paperwork."

"Paperwork?"

"Even Templars can't escape bureaucracy. Well, we can, but there'll be hell to pay afterward."

"And is that what I am? An operative?"

"No." Gray scowled. "I haven't figured that out yet. For now, we'll call you an advisor."

"Ad-*vis*-or." Isa teased the word out. "Advisor Smith. Isadora comma advisor. Okay, what next?"

Gray's eye twitched as he stared at her, then shook his head. "We have standard fees that pay for routine work, like spells and tracking services, but your gift is unusual. Diviners name their price. And the top diviners—the ones —name big figures."

"As in level one? Of course, you categorize them. It's all about the business, right?"

"Don't look at me like that. What we do is important, so yes, we have processes to ensure we achieve the expected outcomes."

Isa couldn't stop a laugh—only a little hysterical— escaping her.

"What?" Gray muttered.

"You sounded so ... so ... businessy." She forced her lips into a straight line. No more inappropriate laughing.

"And what does an art major know of business?"

"I know corporate speak from when I used my visions to help Liam with his business. How do you know I majored in art?"

"I have a full file on you. I ordered it when you arrived at Raph's. From school, university. Boyfriends—"

"Not much to report there," she muttered.

"—who your commissions have been for. And we have nothing about you working for any corporations or busi- nesses while you were studying."

"This is batshit. Why do you need to know all that?"

"Because what we do is vital for the safety of this world —and others—and knowing who we're dealing with is critical to our success."

"Well, your fancy file doesn't know everything. I worked for Liam, but we were seeing each other, so maybe he kept me off the books. Not that it matters. I hated all the corporate jargon and focus on deals and money. Give me my studio and genuine, one-on-one interactions any day."

"And yet, here you are."

"For a purpose, remember? But good to know the Templars are yet another corporation. All right. Back to the levels of diviners."

"To assess payment, we grade power levels one through three. One is for a ninety percent or higher success rate. Two is fifty-to-ninety, and three is anything below fifty."

"Okay, easy. Level one—that's me."

"That high?"

"I've never been wrong that I know of. So, I could charge anything I wanted?"

"Now who's all about business?"

"I never said doing business wasn't okay. People need to make a living, after all. Wait up." She held up a hand. "If my name is on the paperwork, will you list me as a diviner?"

Gray drummed his fingers on the arm of the chair. "Yes."

"See, that's the thing. I'm not using a spell here. My visions are part of me, like breathing. And who in your organization would have access to that information?"

"My immediate ops team on the ground working with us will need to know."

"I guess." Isa nibbled her lip. "But who else in your organization could look me up and find out what I do? Look at what happened with the last person I told about the visions."

"Not everyone's like Liam," Gray said softly.

"Really?" She stared at him. "Because what if they are? I'm here to help. But I'm not ready to have my name and gift shared with the world."

"Then we'll keep you listed as an advisor, but you won't get the same rates as a diviner."

"I'm good with that." She'd work for free if it meant using her gift and keeping her name out of the spotlight.

As soon as she'd signed the paperwork, Gray sat back at the table, this time in the chair opposite her.

Damn, she'd enjoyed having him so close, and the temptation had been high to rest her head on his shoulder. *Uh-uh, Isa. Don't go there.* Banging Gray if the opportunity came up was one thing. Getting attached to him—leaning on him—was a hard no. Isa was standing on her own two feet from now on. Which meant no to borrowing a hot, hulking, hard-muscled body for the job.

"Okay, I'm ready," Isa said.

"Then let's get this done. Look there." He nodded at the image of the Waterhouse painting and pressed a button on his laptop.

The Waterhouse image disappeared, replaced by a photo of the incense burner from her vision.

Gray tapped the laptop again, and a close-up picture of the incense burner, taken from the top, came up. Something brownish filled the receptacle.

"What's that in the bottom?"

"Myrrh."

Isa looked from the monitor to Gray. "Like the incense?"

"Correct. This myrrh came from a special *commiphora abyssinica* grove over two thousand years ago. The grove has long since disappeared, and this is the last known resin from those trees."

"What makes it special?"

"Those eight myrrh trees had the power to help humankind speak to their gods."

"Wow. The only myrrh I ever heard of was the … myrrh from legends."

"Not legend. And yes, that's this myrrh."

"But how?" she breathed. "And why do the Templars have it?"

"There's more I can't tell you here, Isa, even with the NDA, but I can say that two thousand years ago, three gifts were given—and after that, they were separated, taken to three different locations all over the world. As an organization, the Templars are here to protect those gifts, and other dangerous supernatural objects, to keep them from falling into the hands of those who would do terrible things with their powers."

Isa's chest tightened. She looked at the screen again. At the cross on the incense burner. *Oh frig*. Right there—an ancient gift, a relic …

"Isa, if you need some time—"

"No, no. Just … taking it all in. Um, so someone stole it? How? Where was it even kept?"

"Inside one of the most secure facilities in the country. The vault has around-the-clock surveillance, with access restricted by keypad and biometric locks. R-104B sat in a polycarbonate case two hundred times stronger than glass, spelled with an alarm ward."

"That's a shitload of security."

"Which should've been impenetrable."

"So, what do you want me to look for?"

"I've got my team looking into when—and how—R-104B was taken, and we'll follow that line of inquiry as well, but I want you to find where the myrrh is now. Can you do that?"

"Give me a moment of quiet and I'll try."

"I can be silent. What else do you need?"

Damn, she hated to say this. So much for standing on her own two feet. But the last time she'd seen the myrrh, she'd crashed.

"Just be on hand in case I topple. I should be okay, though—I always have been until this morning, anyway." Isa took a deep breath and stared at the picture of the incense burner.

Please let this work.

7

GRAY FORCED himself to breathe evenly when all he wanted was to scream *no*—*don't take one more fucking step into my world*. But that ship had sailed. And Isa was right. She might be the best person in this world to find R-104B.

And while she tracked the relic, he'd focus on the antidote and keep any more daemon bounty hunters off her tail.

Fucking bounty hunters. What the hell was that about? Another question he'd follow up with daemon rep.

Isa closed her eyes, and then an electric hum buzzed across him, leaving the hairs to stand up on the back of his neck. Like when Isa's vision had hit in the car, although this buzz wasn't as strong.

Isa's eyes snapped open.

"Did you see the myrrh?" He leaned forward.

"No." Isa rubbed at her temple, exactly like last time, too. "Damn it, it was weird—and only a flash. But I swear it looked like a restroom in a club. A nightclub." She ground her teeth, frustration pouring off her.

"It's okay." Except, it wasn't. And she looked at him like she knew that, too. "Fine, it's not, but you're trying. Maybe it's the poison—or even the medication? Could they get in the way?"

"Maybe." Isa drummed her fingers on the tabletop. "I want to try again, but this time I'll lie down. The bedroom back there. Can you keep the cabin crew out?"

"Yes, but they're Templars. Even if they went in, they wouldn't bother you."

"It's not about that." She rubbed her arms. "I don't know them. Just thinking a stranger might be watching me while I'm out of it makes me antsy. And as you've seen, it's not like I'm in a light sleep and can easily wake up."

"Tell me about it." Gray relayed the message to the crew and then turned back to Isa. "What about me?"

She shot him an odd look. "You're not a stranger." Then she stood up, only to sway on her feet.

"Hold on—" He darted to her side.

"I'm fine." She pushed his hands away and walked—wobbled—up the aisle.

"So freaking independent," he muttered under his breath.

"I heard that."

"Good. Since you're on my payroll, don't go falling over and braining yourself. At least let me walk close to you. Just in case."

"Trust me, I know you need me in working order to find the relic." She snorted as she rounded the last partition. "You know, this is beyond-level fancy, right?"

"It's a bed and bathroom." He shrugged. "Trust *me*, when you're traveling nonstop and need to be on top of your game, good rest is important."

"Sure. Nothing to do with how uncomfortable a normal airplane seat is."

"Well, there's that." Gray looked at the bed and then at

Isa. His body tightened and a lick of warmth curled through him. He bit back a groan. *Not the time. Not the time.* He cleared his throat. "So, do you need any help …?"

"Actually, don't think I'm batshit, but I'm grimy and still bloody, and maybe if I have a shower and get clean, I can start fresh."

"Go for it. I didn't get you any clothes before we left, so can you stay in those?"

"I'll make do. But thanks, I'll be quick."

"Right. Well, I'll wait out there. I'll get you a water-proof bandage to protect your arm. You don't need a hand, right?"

"No! I can handle a shower. But … just to be safe, maybe don't go too far. If you hear any odd thumps, call out. And if I don't respond, *then* check on me."

She disappeared into the bathroom. And now she was hopping into the shower. Isa naked, wet, only a few feet from him.

Gray bit back a groan and dropped onto the bed to wait for her. A bed perfectly made for Isa and him, especially since she was already naked. And hell if *he* didn't want to be her towel. To lick every drop of moisture—fuck. He sprang to his feet as if the bed was on fire.

The job. *Head. In. The. Game.*

A million—ten—minutes later, Isa emerged from the bathroom. Rosy cheeked. Hair damp around her breath-taking face.

"So I've been thinking." Her cute nose wrinkled. "How about this? I'm going to lie down and shut my eyes. You sit on the end of the bed, and if I see anything, I'll let you know before I pass out."

·《●》·

As Isa settled on top of the luxurious bedspread and closed her eyes, a fantasy of Gray on the bed with her flew into her mind. She chased it away. This wasn't about her. Or about Gray. Only about the relic. Messing up this chance to prove herself—to do something truly purposeful—because of a hot bod wasn't on the cards. Even if it had been forever since her last sexual interaction with an actual person.

Enough. No more sex thoughts.

Closing her eyes as the mattress dipped beneath Gray's weight, Isa took a deep breath, only for his warm scent to ease through her. An answering heat gathered in her belly.

Holy shit. Even his smell made her horny.

Well, it didn't look like she had any hope of stopping her physical reaction to him, so she didn't bother fighting it, and instead focused on the image of the relic.

Pinpricks of slivery stars gathered at the edge of her vision, and she relaxed her mind ... let everything else drop away ...

A red neon light strobed once, twice, three times, and then the red neon filled her vision.

Black mirror tiles lined a wall above a dark velvet couch. Opposite the couch was a row of hand basins and faucets.

A door opened. Thumping music crashed into the room as three young women—barely out of their teens, if that—laughing and yelling at each other above the music danced through the door. One wore a gold-sequined halter top, the second a red silk dress, and the last a black strapless top.

The first woman, Gold Sequins, walked to the mirrored wall, and black stenciled letters with fancy scrollwork became visible, etched into the glass.

Behind her, Black Strapless opened her clutch bag. "Look what I got!" she said.

"What the crow, girl?" Red Dress gasped. "How'd you get that?"

"It's not what you know, it's who you know ..."

"Gimme!" Gold Sequins lunged for the bag.

Strapless jumped back. "Uh, uh, uh. We have to share."

All three piled into one of the toilet stalls. The door slammed shut behind them.

And then it was just the empty restroom, the mirror ... with those letters. But Isa wasn't close enough to make them out. Damn it. She needed to be closer! Why bring her to this place—show her these letters—if she couldn't make them out?

If she could just walk over—

The restroom spun like a globe on a stand, and by the time Isa blinked, the fancy black scrollwork had shifted right up close. Prickles crawled over the back of her neck. Holy shit. She'd done it. She'd moved closer to the mirror.

But how? And why now?

What made this vision so important—a scene from what looked like a nightclub bathroom—that she could control her movement? Whatever it was, she'd focus on that later. Right now, she had to capture as much of this room as possible.

She peered harder at the letters.

A curdling scream shattered the silence. The cubicle door where the three women had gone slammed open. Strapless and Red Dress fell backward onto the floor, and Gold Sequins was nowhere to be seen.

The first stayed still, but Red Dress flopped to her front and pulled herself over the other woman.

"Help ..." She looked up. Blood filled her eyes, dripped from her nose. "Me."

Isa screamed. The vision disappeared.

8

GRAY DREW IN A DEEP BREATH; a delicious combination of earthy and woodsy air, with a hint of cinnamon made his mouth water. Hazy, distant memories of cinnamon rolls on frosty mornings teased at the edge of his dream. His hands tightened around a lush, warm weight. A tight, velvety nub pressed into the center of his palm. He shifted his grip, ran his thumb over that point.

Heat curled through him, and his balls tightened. He fitted himself against the warm body at his chest, and a succulently curved butt rubbed against his rock-hard dick.

Gray smoothed a kiss along the nape of the neck in front of him.

A moan echoed into the dream—

His eyes flew open, and he shot to full wakefulness. What the hell? Where—fuck. Not a dream. He was in the bed. With Isa's breast in his palm.

And then she rolled toward him. A smile touched her lips.

He yanked his hand away—his fist clenched, already missing that firm, silky flesh—and he jumped off the bed.

Isa's eyes opened just as he landed on the floor, and they widened as she looked at him—at herself—and her lips curved even more.

Had she realized? He'd been asleep, even so. What the hell did he say?

"Now that's a way to wake up," she murmured. "And was I imagining it, or was your hand up my top while we were spooning there?"

Shit. "Totally reflex. I fell asleep, and I'm sorry—"

"Stop right there. Don't you dare say sorry for spooning me and copping a feel. I'm a single, healthy, consenting being. And you're a single ... wait, you're single, right?"

"As if I'd spoon someone if I wasn't."

"So, what's the problem?"

"Because it's unprofessional." And distracting as all hell. And she was his best friend's *little sister.*

"What, there's some rule that diviners and Templars can't hook up? You really are a stuffy bunch."

"Of course, there's no rule. And we're not stuffy. We're *professional.*"

"Then I don't see the problem. And damn, but it's cold now. You were a good blanket." Isa shrugged and pulled the comforter up over her chest. Which was just as well. He needed to focus, and not on her body.

And did she really not care that he'd had his hand on her breast? His palm itched at the memory.

"To be clear, I don't normally sleep beside my team."

"Oh? So I'm special." She grinned, and he ground his teeth.

"No. I mean, yes, of course," Gray said. "But you'd been in the vision for a long time. And just when you seemed to come around, you passed out within seconds. Then you got really restless, so I sat on the bed to monitor you."

He didn't say that she'd calmed down as soon as he'd sat beside her. Or that each time he'd tried to leave, she became fidgety, until, finally, he'd brought in his cell and laptop and stayed.

"And fell asleep." Isa's grin grew wider.

"I didn't want to leave you in case the poison caused any issues."

"You were worried about me?"

"You've been poisoned, and you're working on a case. Of course, I was worried."

"Well, thanks for looking out for me." A softness entered her eyes that made him want to fidget.

"No need to thank me," Gray said. "You're my—"

"Let me guess. Asset? Business?" She shook her head like he'd disappointed her, the silky ends of her hair flicking over her shoulders.

"Yes." The urge to say something softer, *nicer*, sat on the tip of his tongue, but he bit back the words. He wasn't either of those things, and he wouldn't lie or defend the fact that he had a job to do. "So the vision? Did you see R-104B?"

"Oh damn. The vision!"

"Yeah, that's what we're talking—"

"No. Gray, the vision was ... odd."

"What this time?"

"I controlled it—from inside! I've never been able to control a vision like that before. And no, sorry, no sight of the myrrh. But—"

His watch beeped, and his cell alarm pinged. "Hold on. Time for your next shot."

He grabbed the medical kit, and by the time he returned to the sleeping cabin, Isa's cheeks were flushed and her eyes bright.

"You need this now. Sit down." He jabbed a finger toward the bed. "This is cutting it too close."

"Hey, calm down. I'm fine. And the medicine right's there."

"This is your life, Isa." He searched her beautiful eyes. "You're not taking this seriously enough."

"And *you're* wrong, Gray. I know exactly what's at stake." Her mouth tightened. "Here, I'm ready. I won't let you down."

Let him down? He shook his head, but wasted no more time and slid the syringe into her vein.

"I'll check your dressing next. You're looking a bit ... off. Are you okay?"

"Yeah, just low. Could be because we haven't eaten in ..."

"Hours. Right, your arm's looking good, so I'll organize a meal, then you can tell me about the rest of the abnormal vision."

Fifteen minutes later, Gray sat opposite Isa in the forward cabin where the flight crew had served a hot meal.

"I could get used to traveling like this," Isa said as she took a sip from a porcelain teacup. "They even have chamomile tea."

He just nodded. No need to tell her he'd sent word ahead to make sure they'd stocked the herbal tea.

"Okay, back to business." She put her cup on the table.

"We can wait till after you've eaten—"

"No, this is important. I get it." Isa rubbed her arms.

"Do you need a sweater or are you that rattled?"

"Well, it is cool. But the vision was ... freaky, to be honest."

"Here, take my jacket."

As Isa settled beneath the fabric that swamped her like a blanket, a sensation bordering on ... satisfaction ... tugged in his chest. Isa wearing his jacket. Warmed by his clothes. Surrounded by his scent.

It soothed the stupidest, freaking need in him to be the one to make her feel that way.

Fuck. Wherever the hell these cave dweller instincts sprouted from, they needed to dry the fuck up.

"So what happened?" he growled.

"Are you okay?" Isa wrinkled her nose in that way she did. "I can give it back if you're cold—"

"Keep the freaking coat. I'm not cold."

"Okay. No need to get pissy."

"I'm not pissy."

"Sure." She shot him a look that screamed she absolutely thought he was pissy.

And he was, fuck it. "Just get to the vision."

"Okay, okay. This is what I saw."

He let her talk it out the first time and then asked her to repeat what she'd said to double-check her recollection.

"And you think R-104B and this restroom are linked?" he asked.

"Well, I can't be sure of that." Isa chewed on her lip, and he did his best not to stare at the plump surface. "But that's what happened when I focused on the myrrh as you showed it to me."

"How many visions do you normally have?"

"Completely out of the blue, you mean? Every few weeks —but it's not like a clockwork thing that I can set my watch by. I might have two visions in a row, then none for a few weeks."

"What about the sleeping thing? What's normal?"

"Anywhere from a few minutes to half an hour, depending on the length of the vision."

Isa took a bite of steak, her lips parting before she closed them over the meat. His pants grew tight, and he forced his gaze to his own meal. Isa finished chewing and then waved her fork in the air. "Why all the questions?"

"If I'm going to use you—work with you, I mean—understanding how your visions work is imperative."

"Using me is fine to say, you know. I asked to be here, don't forget."

As if he could.

She chewed another mouthful, then licked those lush lips with the bottom fuller curve that made him want to bite it. Lick it. Suck it into his mouth. Freaking hell. If he got any more wood around her, she'd think he had a problem.

"You okay there?"

He shot her a look. Okay? No. He was hot and frustrated because he wanted to get his hands back on her flesh—*and she hadn't minded*? That just made his dick even harder. And then frustrated at his lack of gods damned focus on the job.

"Don't worry about me," was all he said, though, and stood up.

"What about your meal—?"

"I need to check in with my team," he muttered. "You just ... sit, eat. Stay warm. I'll be back."

Raph's little sister. Raph's little sister. *Raph's little sister.*

In the middle cabin, Gray sat at the desk and contacted his team for an update.

"I've reviewed the surveillance feed from inside the vault," Marcella said. "It looks like the R-104B is still there."

"So someone hacked the SJC system. That's meant to be near impossible." Fuck. "How long since our last visual inspection?"

"We're on a monthly schedule there, and it was twenty-five days ago."

"Then R-104B could've been gone for at least that long.

All right, make sure everything's ready at the apartment. And I want a meeting with Kai St. James today."

"We haven't been able to locate him yet—we're trying."

"Try harder. And then I want the rest of the SJC facility's internal surveillance feeds."

"All of them?"

"Every floor, door, parking lot. Every single inch. And put in a formal request for all other feeds from local law enforcement, government buildings, private citizens—anything and everything that will show who's been in and out of that building in the last twenty-five days."

At least his body was under control when he hung up from Marcella and rejoined Isa.

"Why do you look like you're ready to murder something?" Isa asked as he slid back into the chair opposite her.

He scowled. "Because we still don't have R-104B."

"Okay ... so, where are we heading now?"

"LA. We're flying into a private airfield. I have a meeting as soon as we land, and from there, I'll head to the vault facility."

"What about the nightclub my visions took me to? I think the letters stenciled into the mirror are the name, or the logo, of the nightclub. Can you look into it?"

"I'm already working my team overtime on this recovery."

"I went looking for your relic, Gray, and the visions took me there. Twice. And if those women are in trouble, we need to go there too. We might help them."

His gut knotted again.

"Fine. But I'm not searching for the women. They took whatever was in that purse; they can handle themselves. I'm worried about the relic. Nothing else."

"Handle themselves?" Isa's mouth dropped. "Those

women were dying. Maybe one already did. Three women went into the stall, and only two came out. And they were bleeding from their eyes and noses. That's not *handling themselves.*"

"That's awful, no question. But one—or even three— people who choose to do that to themselves can't compare with what I'm working on."

Isa recoiled from the table. "You can't mean that. Where's your empathy? Your compassion?"

"Yes, I can." Gray refused to let his brother's image come to mind. And refused to let the twinge of weak emotion creep into his chest. "I've got empathy for people who don't deserve the shit that's coming their way if I don't locate R-104B." He ignored the churning in his gut. "Now, could you draw the letters you saw?"

"Why are you so cold?"

"There's no room for anything else, that's why. You said you wanted to help me, well now's your chance. Again, can you do the drawing?"

"I'm an artist." She snorted. "Of course I can. But I can also help those other women. Because they do need it. Whether it's in one month or one minute, or damn, maybe it's already happened, and they're lying there needing help *right now.*"

"Fine, draw the letters. Maybe you can help those women that way."

"You really have ice in your heart, don't you?"

"It's not about ice. It's about—"

"R-104B." She threw her hands in the air. "Of course. Get me some paper. I'll draw the logo or whatever it was."

Gray clenched his jaw and bit out an order for the cabin steward to bring over paper and pens. Isa stared out through the window until the paper was there, and then she bent her head to that task, not meeting Gray's gaze at all.

She didn't get it. Hadn't seen the devastation that addiction left behind. And not just the users, but everyone else too.

Gut churning, Gray forced himself to stand up smoothly.

Because hell, what could he say right now? Any words that came out would just make Isa hate him even more. She was too softhearted for this shit. No freaking question.

He ordered coffee for himself, a chamomile tea for Isa, then opened his laptop and called up records of all the security procedures and risk mitigations they had in place for R-104B.

The relic had been in the safekeeping of the St. James family for close to a thousand years, passing down through the hands of consecutive generations. As one of America's wealthiest families, and with their facilities considered among the strongest anywhere in this world, the myrrh should've been safe.

Absolutely.

So why wasn't it?

9

KEEP IT PROFESSIONAL. *Purely professional.* Isa repeated the mantra once more in her head as she sketched the logo. She peeked up at Grayson again. Don't yell at him and tell him he's an asshole with an ice heart. Huh. An icehole.

But after all these years of him invading her visions, she'd never imagined he'd be such an utter dick. And damn it, why did he have to be a walking, talking wet dream? No wonder he'd featured in her steamy dreams for years ... even before she'd known his name. Which made things a whole lot of bizarre sitting opposite him.

He'd changed into a fresh white business shirt and black pants shortly after they'd boarded—the casual rough-edged jeans-and-tee-wearing man replaced with the urban professional. Except he couldn't quite blunt the edges of his personality, even with the business clothes.

Did he have any more ink? The last time she'd seen Gray's tattoos, he'd been in a chair, having words added beneath a cross on his chest. But that vision had cut off fast, and she hadn't seen the final design.

He rolled back the sleeves of the shirt, revealing strong,

tanned forearms, and picked up his coffee cup, the porcelain too delicate for his large hands.

Those forearms and hands would make an amazing study for a sketch or an artwork. Muscular. Capable. Gentle. Beautiful. A contradiction in form and use—

"Everything okay?" Gray took a sip of the coffee, his lips parting on either side of the cup as he regarded her over the rim.

"Yep, absolutely." She ducked behind her sketch pad. Damn, she'd gone all hot and bothered watching him have a coffee! She was going to need some self-care soon or go insane.

Or … she could tell him about her wet dreams and invite him to join her in that amazing bedroom on board to spend the next twelve hours.

Shush, inner sexpot. He was an asshole. He'd probably give her freezer-burn with his ice blood.

But he'd leave behind a beard rash in all the right places with that delicious stubble.

"Are you finished?" Gray asked.

"Here it is." She turned the pad around with the sketch of the logo from the club from her vision and ignored the thrill his rough voice sent through her.

"You're good," he breathed.

A curl of unwelcome pleasure flittered through her at the praise, but she ignored it and inclined her head once. She'd be polite because it was the right thing to do. Something Gray seemed to have no clue about.

"I'll take a photo and send it to my team."

"Who's this team you keep talking about?"

"You'll meet Marcella—she's my 2IC and in charge of our tech—and Tank, our driver and second gun, when we land. They're my ops team for this job."

"There's more than one team?"

"Okay, fast version. The Templar Knights have three divisions: Ops—operations—R and D, and corporate. We split the ops teams into global regions."

"You sound like every other major corporation I've heard of."

"These days, we pretty much are. I head up the US ops division. We're in charge of the physical aspect relating to all items under our purview, from monitoring our jails to tracking down missing relics—thank the gods that doesn't happen often—and occasionally acting as a … control … for otherworlders living in our community."

"Hah. I knew it. The magic police."

"Sometimes."

"And all this paperwork—like the NDA and paying me a wage. You're just another company."

"No 'just' there. We're unique in our work and in our responsibilities. And, like I said, bureaucracy is everywhere. I answer to the Templar Council."

"Who are?"

"The governing body who ensures that everything the Knights do is for the greater good."

"So what, you're a real live knight while you do the job? What if you leave and do something else?"

"Once a Templar, always a Templar."

"Wow. That's … serious. And R-104B—the myrrh? What's its influence?"

"Alone, not so much. But if it falls into the wrong hands, and its sisters do too, then we're in a world of shit. I cannot —no, I will not—let that happen."

Gray's mobile phone lit up with an incoming message, and as he read it, his lips tightened.

"The team tracked down the logo. It belongs to Fathom

LA, a nightclub near Santa Monica Beach. Part of a chain of clubs, apparently."

"Can someone go now? What time is it there?"

"They're seventeen hours behind Brisbane, so ... we've been on board for eight hours. That makes it about 2:00 a.m."

"They'll be open then. Can you call? No, I'll call—"

"Don't get in a snit." He tapped something into the phone. "I've instructed one of my team on the ground to check it out."

"Snit? Gray, you really are an ass." She snapped her mouth shut. Damn it, she'd gone and said it. She folded her arms and looked out the window into the night sky.

(((●)))

The sun had risen a good two hours earlier, and Isa was back drawing the last of the three women from her vision when Gray's rough voice interrupted her.

"We're landing soon."

She stared at the drawing. Strapless's eyes weren't quite right ...

"Are you still pissed at me?" he asked.

"Yes." She didn't look up. Not that she needed to see him to know where he was. Trapped in the cabin, every time he'd spoken, moved—or damn it—just breathed, she'd been aware of him.

It was batshit.

In her visions and dreams, Gray had been a dominant, fearsome force. She'd never have imagined he'd be even more so in person.

"Good to know you're honest about that kind of shit," he said.

Isa used her lead pencil to shade in a little more of the woman's cheeks, then shifted back in her seat and considered the drawing. But instead of the person on the paper, Gray's face filled her mind.

She slammed the paper down on the table.

"Whoa. You're really steamed, aren't you?"

"Steamed? I'm appalled that you think me caring about the lives of three women makes me in *a snit*."

"I knew you didn't like that," he muttered.

"You think? And yes, I'm not hiding my feelings—no matter how much you don't like it."

"What? I never said I didn't like that. I admire it—good on you for not hiding yourself."

"Well, thanks." Isa tapped the pencil on the table. "Although, I guess in some ways, if I'm honest, I am still hiding a part of me. It's not like I'm telling everyone about my visions."

"That's called being smart. So, that's all three women?"

"Yep. I've almost finished. Once we land, I can color the images." She held up the three drawings.

"Wow." Gray took the first. "You're really skilled. I mean, I've seen your paintings, so I know you're good. But these ... I can't believe you drew them from memory. If I saw this woman walking down the street, I'd recognize her."

Warmth curled through Isa, but she squashed it. Going all soft and gooey because Gray the Icehole appreciated her skill with a pencil wasn't part of the plan. "Good. That means we might find these women, let them know what's coming. And since there was no incident at the club last night, it could be tonight instead."

"We still don't know the R-104B connection. Listen, the

plan is to meet the daemon rep when we land, then head to the vault facility."

"What about the club? I'm serious, Gray. That's where vision led. We should go there first. I was searching for the myrrh after all—"

"Fine. We'll stop there on the way to the facility. But that's it."

"Wait—it's what, eight in the morning? Will the club be open?"

"By the time we land and drive into the city, it'll be nine, but I'll put a call into the club management."

"They'll open up just because you ask?"

"Of course."

Isa didn't hold back a snort. Gray, the mighty Templar, had spoken, and the world dropped at his feet.

Oblivious to her thoughts, Gray stood up and strapped a tan leather gun holster over his white business shirt. Then he removed a compact black case from the overhead compartment.

"What are you doing now?"

He unlocked the case and flicked the lid open. "Weapons. Standard Templar issue." From the case, he removed two black handguns, did some kind of fast check with each weapon, then slid them into the holster.

Holy shit but he was hot! Isa clenched her thighs.

"What?" He stared at her as if she'd spoken.

Get your thoughts together, Issi! "Just thinking I'll need some clothes."

"I've arranged for a change when we land. We don't have time for shopping, but give me a list of what else you need, and I'll take care of it."

"Just like that?" She clicked her fingers. "You're like a fairy godmother. And I bet you even know my size, right?"

His hooded eyes skimmed her body—and then met hers. A buzz sizzled through the air. Her belly tightened. Oh stars, that look ... now she wanted to reach over, grab his tie, haul him in for a hot, carnal kiss ...

She looked away.

Uh-uh. No fantasizing about exciting, steamy kisses. Look at what had happened when Gray had copped a feel on the bed. He couldn't get away from her fast enough.

Thirty minutes later, they'd landed at a Los Angeles private airstrip—apparently the Templars owned multiple hangars at the airfield—and when the steps to the plane lowered on the tarmac, a gleaming midnight SUV, and a man and woman, both outfitted in matching tailored black suits, waited for them.

"That's Marcella and Tank." Gray nodded at the two people.

Tank stayed with the SUV, but Marcella met them at the bottom of the steps.

She looked dangerous, shadowy, and expensive. She had an earpiece peeking out from behind one ear, mirrored sunglasses, gorgeous dark skin, and close-cropped, red-tipped black hair.

"Are snazzy black suits a Templar uniform?" Isa asked.

His snort echoed in her ears.

"Hi." Isa smiled at Marcella and held out her hand. "I'm—"

"Where's the Daemon Congress rep?" Gray bit out from behind her. "They're meant to meet us here."

"No word," Marcella said.

"—Isa." She dropped her hand.

"Shit," Gray said. "If the rep still wants to talk, they need to meet me at the club; otherwise, I can't confirm my next location."

Isa hid a laugh at Gray's scowl. He really didn't like having plans changed, did he? Well, life wasn't always about structure, a concept that might be good for the icy Templar.

"Hi," Isa said, held her hand out again.

"Make the niceties fast." Gray strode off for the SUV.

"Sorry about him," Isa said in her sweetest voice. "He's grumpy because he didn't get enough sleep."

Marcella grinned. "Looks like you're giving Grumpy a run for his money, chica. Call me Marcie."

"Don't encourage her," Gray growled over his shoulder. "And I didn't sleep because I was taking calls for the last six hours trying to find R-104B. And other things." His gaze pierced Isa so swiftly she was left with no mistake that he was talking about the antidote.

"Of course, Boss. No encouraging here. There's a garment bag in the back seat as per your instructions."

Isa made straight for Tank when they reached the SUV. "Hi, I'm Isa."

The driver smiled, a huge grin that Isa returned. "Welcome to LA."

"Thanks."

"Seriously, no time." Gray opened the passenger door. "Isa, change now if you want privacy. We'll turn around. Marcella, you stay here in case the daemon rep makes an appearance. We'll meet back at the apartment."

Yikes. No wonder Marcie called him boss. "Do you ever say please?"

Tank's eyes widened. Marcella choked on a cough. Gray turned around, his expression hardening from icy lake to frozen tundra.

"Guess not." She bit her lip and scampered into the back seat, yanked the door closed. Note to self. Do *not* piss off the mighty Templar who held her dream of using her gift for a purpose in his frosty hands. And was helping find an anti-dote for her poisoning problem.

Isa unzipped the garment bag. Well, he might be a prick, but he'd organized a bra, panties, shirt and pants. Correctly sized. Huh. Did her file even have her cup size? Or ... had Gray figured it out from when they'd spooned?

He'd certainly gotten a healthy feel. And damn, but his grip had felt fine. How would those hot, calloused hands feel in other places?

Warmth pooled low in her belly.

"Ready?" A knock hammered at the window.

Shit. No time for fantasizing over the grumpy, delectable Templar. She scrambled to strip and yank on the new clothing—didn't even stop to admire the pretty rust-hued top with a drop shoulder.

"Done!" She stuffed her dirty clothing in the garment bag.

"About time," Gray muttered as he yanked the passenger door open and slid into the seat. "And remember, your next shot is due in—"

"Three and a half hours. Got it. I've set two alarms on my phone. I'll be fine. Now I want to see LA. Apparently, Mum brought me here when I was a baby."

Gray glanced over his shoulder at her. "Really? Why?"

"This was where Mum left ..." Isa eyed Tank. Where her mother had left Isa and her existence in the human world behind and crossed into hell. "Anyway, I'm interested in seeing the place."

Gray stared at her for a beat, then turned back around without pushing for anything more.

Isa forced herself to look outside the window, at the buildings and people and sun-drenched city that rushed by.

Isa's mother had sacrificed everything for Isa and Raph.

And right now, Isa could finally use her gift for good, to help those three young women.

So what if Isa had kept a few tiny details from Gray? He'd said it himself—the greater good outweighed everything else. And Isa was playing her part.

-‹‹‹◈›››-

As the SUV pulled up in front of Fathom LA, Gray closed the file with the club schematics and the dossier on the human they were meeting—one Rochelle La Seine, witch, successful businesswoman, and part owner of the entire Fathom family of businesses spread across the country.

He checked his watch as Tank double-parked but left the engine running. Ten minutes past nine. Shit. Traffic had been a bitch, so they were late. Two hours and fifty minutes until Isa's next shot. If the daemon rep didn't meet them here, there was always the option of putting Isa back on the plane and sending her to the Templar's Boston research and development lab.

The lab team there would be Isa's next best chance at a cure if Gray couldn't turn up anything today. And if the lab *didn't* find anything ...

He swallowed the lump that jammed in his throat and shut that thought down. He *would* get an option for Isa that didn't include going anywhere with the blue-haired bounty hunter.

Before he could leave the SUV, his cell pinged with an incoming message from Marcella.

"Thank fuck," he muttered.

"What's that?" Isa asked, breaking her silence since her

comment about her mother. Whatever she'd been about to say earlier, clearly Tank had put her off.

"The daemon rep is meeting us here," he replied. "Tank, find a place to park, but stay close."

As soon as Gray and Isa approached the black-mirrored glass entry doors, stenciled with the same logo Isa had drawn, a hulking security guard in a black shirt and pants met them, and after requesting their names, led them through an entry foyer and into the club.

A man and woman sat at a high table toward the back. Gray didn't recognize the man, but even from across the room, the woman with her silvery-blonde hair resembled the image of the club owner Marcella had sent through.

"One moment, please," the security guard said. "I'll let the owner know you're here."

Gray was pretty sure Rochelle La Seine could see this for herself, given she was right there, but he just nodded and checked the place out. Schematics were good, but nothing beat eyes on the ground.

Stairs to the right led to a second-floor balcony. A bar ran the length of the wall at the bottom of the stairs, and a stage ran along the opposite wall. They were all empty. Not another person in sight.

"Creepy," Isa muttered under her breath. "Too much open space without purpose. Too much light showing up the hard edges and tacky floors."

"Hopefully, it's better at night. Listen, I've got an idea for the reason why we're here. Play along." Then he forced a smile as Rochelle approached them.

Her red leather pencil skirt and fitted jacket showcased a toned, tall figure, and her smile revealed blindingly white, perfect teeth.

"Well, hello." Rochelle looked Gray up and down first,

interest lighting in her gaze before she shifted to peruse Isa. Her interest there dimmed, and she turned back to Gray. "Grayson, I take it?"

"Good morning." Gray smiled and held his hand out.

"Now I'm very glad I said yes to the meeting," Rochelle said.

"So are we. This is Dora. I guess this is early for you, right?"

"Indeed." Rochelle nodded to the table where the man sat in the only shadowed area on the entire ground floor. "But when two tall, hot drinks of deliciousness walk into my club, I don't mind an early start."

"Two?" Isa asked before Gray could speak.

"Well, yes. He said he was your associate. Is that right?"

"Absolutely," Gray lied. "Thanks for making him welcome, too."

As if the man knew they were talking about him, he stood up. Easily as tall as Gray's six feet three frame. Shoulder-length hair more red than brown. Muscled, but holding himself with the ease of someone who understood their body and capability.

Gray tensed, but he maintained a calm expression.

"So how can I help?" Rochelle smiled at him.

"Actually, could we trouble you for a coffee? We'll see ourselves over to my associate."

"Of course." The club owner's cut-glass smile belied her words. Interesting.

Once Rochelle had left, Gray leaned into Isa and whispered, "Stay behind me. This is likely the daemon rep, and I want a word before Rochelle comes back. But given the bounty issue, safety first."

"Hello," the man said as they approached. "Grayson?"

"You are?"

"Rohan, here on behalf of my world's congress. I missed you at the airfield."

"Prove it."

"What?"

"You heard me. Prove you're who you say you are." Gray eased his jacket back to his hip for fast access to his holster. "And make it fast."

"Your second in command sent me here. Marcella. Cool sounding chick." The daemon held one hand up. "I'm going to show my mark. Don't shoot me."

Gray raised one eyebrow.

"Shit. That was a joke. Okay, here you go." Rohan rolled up his sleeve to reveal a tattoo covering his inner forearm. The ink showed a gateway with an eye between the gates. The eye glowed green before returning to normal.

"Haven't seen the mark of the daemon's High Congress in a few years." Gray let his jacket fall back into place. "Okay, you're cleared."

"What's that tattoo?" Isa leaned around Gray. "And what's your congress?"

Rohan stared at Isa, his eyes narrowing. "And you are?"

"This is Dora. She's with me." Gray smiled but couldn't fight the urge to stand between Isa and anyone who might want to use her—or harm her.

"She's also right here," Isa said, too sweetly in his ear right before she stood on his foot. "Oops, how clumsy of me. Hi, I'm ... Dora. Nice to meet you both. Rohan, was it?"

Gray blew out a surreptitious breath. Thank the gods Isa hadn't challenged him on her name.

"Dora?" Rohan turned his entire attention to Isa, and everything in Gray went on high alert.

Gray pulled Isa to his side. He needed to deflect this male's attention, Congress rep or not. "Yep, Dora is keeping me company this trip, if you know what I mean." He squeezed his little diviner as if they were a couple. *C'mon, Isa, go along with this.*

"Didn't realize Templars took their plus ones on the road," Rohan said, his gaze dipping to Gray's hand for one moment. Then his face relaxed into a bland expression.

Gray aimed for the same look. "When you're the boss, you get to set the rules. Now, what can I do for you?"

"I have a proposition." Rohan looked round. "Interesting choice for a morning coffee."

"I take it you want privacy for this discussion?"

"You'd be right."

"As soon as I'm done here, we'll talk. Can you come with us?"

"Works for me." Rohan's expression morphed into an affable grin, and Gray didn't have to turn around to know Rochelle had rejoined them.

"So, what can I do for you?" the club owner asked, passing out the coffees.

"Dora and I are looking for a venue to host our engagement party."

"We'd be delighted!" she said.

"Excellent," Gray said. "Actually, Dora, sweety, didn't you want to visit the bathrooms earlier?"

She stood up, a smile plastered on her face that was too sweet for even her.

"Oh, you're such a doll to remember everything I say. How lucky am I?" Isa shot Rochelle a look. "How did you put it? A tall drink of deliciousness *and* he cares about me."

Gray turned a laugh into a cough and glanced away— and found Rohan staring at Isa. Hell. The daemon might be there on legit business, but his intense focus had Gray's internal radar pinging.

"So lucky." Rochelle looked at Isa like she was loco and gestured. "The closest restrooms are back through there."

Gray spent the next ten minutes asking everything he could think of about venue hire until Isa finally rejoined them. She gave a brief shake of her head.

Damn it, had this been a complete waste of time?

His gaze fell to her arm—she was due her next shot soon. Fuck. And he still needed to talk to Rohan about Isa's poison and find the fuck out what the daemon congress wanted. Time to move.

"Rochelle, thank you so much for meeting with us," Gray said as he stood up. "Your venue looks perfect for our event. Unfortunately, Dora and I have to get going now, but I'll have my assistant reach out and discuss dates."

Gray left Rochelle typing on her laptop at the bar and ushered Isa toward the exit, but as he did, the front doors to the club opened and a familiar man with pale slicked-back hair, wearing a precisely cut silvery-gray suit, walked into the bar. Fucking Kai St. James. Gray tensed, and adrenaline rushed through him.

"Grayson," St. James said. His customary million-watt smile blinked on, and he cut fast looks at both Isa and Rohan before turning back to Gray. "How lovely to see you! Didn't realize you were out here on the West Coast."

"St. James." Gray forced a fake smile. Especially as the billionaire's gaze once more went to Dora. Fuck it, he didn't want to play games here. But the stakes were too high for any mistakes to be made. "Good to see you, too." Not a lie.

St. James leaned in close. "I understand you've been trying to see me. Something about a sensitive matter."

"My team is handling that. I'm actually here for other business."

"Kai, do you know my guests here too?" Rochelle came over and placed a casual hand on St. James's arm. *Interesting.*

"Two of the oldest families from Boston?" St. James said. "Of course, we know each other. But I haven't had the pleasure of meeting your other guests."

"Oh, let me introduce you to everyone," Rochelle said. "Dora, Rohan, this is the illustrious Kai St. James of the St. James Corporation. You're fortunate to meet him—he's such an important figure in our world today with the medical research his foundation does. We're holding an event for him here tonight, in fact."

Oh, fuck no. Like watching a movie he'd seen a million times over, Gray knew what was coming next, but there was no fucking way to stop it.

"And Kai, Dora is Grayson's fiancé."

"Dora, is it?" St. James held out his hand. "Lovely to meet you. You should all join us here tonight. Rochelle, we can do that, right?"

"Well, the event is full."

"No, no. I insist."

10
———

Isa couldn't help but watch Gray as they left Fathom LA and stepped out in the bright morning sun. Hot tension poured off him like his vitality had gone up another notch, which was saying something because that man practically had his own personal energy force field.

"What's going—?"

"Wait." He held up a hand and grabbed his phone. "Marcella, change of plans. I need you to look at St. James's facility without me." Gray barked out a series of orders, then ended the call and gestured for Isa and Rohan to come close. "We need to talk. Away from the club."

"I know a place that's open air," Rohan said. "No need to worry about who's coming in—or out—of doorways."

"How far?" Gray frowned at Isa.

"Hey, I can walk, you know. Country girl, remember?"

"At the beach. One block over."

"Let's go, then. I want Isa off the street."

She rolled her eyes, but within a moment, found herself caught between the two massive men, Rohan leading the way, Gray at her back. Something told her that wasn't unplanned.

Isa glanced at the daemon as he led them to the beach-front. She couldn't put her finger on why, but she didn't feel uncomfortable around him. Kind of like how Gray made her feel calm, too.

And it couldn't be because of the daemon aspect—the moment the bounty hunter had found Isa back at the farm, Isa's internal alarms had shrieked. But there was none of that with Rohan.

Then he stopped, and she ran right into him.

He whirled and grabbed her arms when she stumbled. "Sorry. Got you."

She glanced up. Found him staring back, and his pale, icy-green eyes held such an intensity her breath caught.

"You okay?" Gray's brusque voice—the opposite of the low and smooth Rohan—cut through her daze.

"All good. Just ... thinking."

In no time, they'd reached the shoreline cafés and shops. Rohan stuck to his word and took them to a café over-looking the beach, even getting a table at least semi-separated from everyone else.

"All right, we need to talk," Gray said as soon as they'd placed their order. "And after Fathom, plans have changed."

"Why?" Isa crossed her arms—the bandage around her wound tightened.

"Not now." Gray's gaze darted to her bicep. "Rohan, what does the Daemon Congress want with the Templars?"

"I'm—we're—searching for a key. A very specific key. We'd like to propose a binding contract between the daemons and the Templars where we provide something for you in exchange for information on the location of the key we seek."

Wow. What kind of key would make a daemon willing to go into a magical contract?

"You need to be more specific than *a key*," Gray said.

"And I will be. After I know, are the Templars open to a mutually binding contract?"

"I'll check with the council. Why start with me?"

"Because we believe the key is in your country."

The two men were like a tennis match with their question volleys. Definitely two alphas here. Right now, their sparring was verbal, but with the tension pouring off them, it wouldn't take much and they'd be leaping at each other's throats.

"Then I have a proposal for you." Gray leaned forward. "I need an antidote for *Amoricinae Venenum*."

"What the fuck?" Rohan's eyes narrowed. "Why? Who? What's going on?"

"That's need to know." Gray returned Rohan's hard gaze with his own glacial look that had no doubt sent lesser daemons into a freeze. "Now, if you have information on the antidote, I'm open to a trade."

"Wait up," Isa blurted. She grabbed Gray's arm; his muscles tensed beneath her hand. "Gray," she whispered to him. "You don't need to do this."

"So?" Gray said to Rohan. Ignoring her.

"Hey!" Isa slammed both hands on the table. "I said wait. You can't do this without talking to me first. This is my life."

"And it's your life I'm trying to save here." Gray scowled and glanced at Rohan. "We're going to a freaking party tonight instead of getting you the treatment you need, so yes, since you're working for me, I'll do what I fucking need to keep you safe. You're my—"

"Asset." She scowled right back at him. "Just because you're trying to help doesn't mean you don't talk to me first."

"Excuse me, but I have a question," Rohan said.

"What?" Gray and Isa said in unison without breaking their mutual glowers.

"You two argue like an old married couple. Are you really together?"

Isa transferred her glare from Gray to Rohan. "You know perfectly well Gray and I aren't a couple."

"I hoped. But good to know for sure." Rohan shrugged.

Gray groaned and dropped his forehead onto the table. "Isa."

"What? And don't hit your head so hard. You'll give yourself a headache."

"Swear to the gods, Isadora—"

"What? What do you swear to the gods, Grayson I-Still-Don't-Know-Your-Last-Name?" She waited, but he just shook his head. "That's what I thought. So, Rohan, I have an option for you. I need information—and not just about an antidote—and I'm willing to help you find your key if you help with my questions."

"Isadora ..." Rohan sounded out her name, and something like anticipation sharpened in his gaze. He smiled, and suddenly she knew what a fish felt like right before it got gobbled up by a beautiful, wicked-toothed shark. "I'm willing to enter a binding contract if you are."

"Hold up." Gray held both hands up. "You two need to ... what's your expression? Calm the farm. Let's work our way through this one step at a time. Rohan, you're looking for a key. Isa and I also need information about *things* that are important to us. I'm sure we can work this out with no binding contracts."

"What, show me yours and I'll show you mine?" Rohan smirked.

"You came to us, not the other way around here. But fine

—I'll give you two questions we need answered. That's a big show of faith on my part."

"Hell." The daemon glanced between Gray and Isa. "Done."

"First, why would a blue-haired bounty hunter be here in the human world? Second, what are the antidotes to amorice?"

Rohan's eyes flattened. "Triulf's here?"

"Who?" Isa leaned closer.

"Blue hair, black claws, stunning six-foot female?" Rohan said.

"That's her." Isa restrained the urge to rub her arm.

"Her modus operandi is to tip her claws with a variety of poisons or acids—depending on what she's after. And she's not only a bounty hunter. She moonlights as an assassin."

"Just great." Isa sat back in her chair. She couldn't stop herself from running a hand over her sleeve.

"What the hell?" Rohan shot forward and searched Isa's eyes. "Why aren't you showing any signs? How are you even walking?"

"A masking agent. But it's a temp solution. In fact, I need my next shot in less than an hour."

"Fucking gods," Rohan breathed out.

"Those are our questions," Gray said quietly.

Shit, those were Gray's questions. Isa had more of her own—like exactly who was Rohan, but something told her now wasn't the time to go there.

"What are yours?" Gray continued.

Rohan checked over his shoulder as if he expected someone to be eavesdropping before he turned back to Isa and Gray.

"First, you're not telling me everything. Why are the Templars so invested in one person?"

Gray tensed, and Isa met his guarded gaze. But she didn't say a word—this was his issue to discuss or not.

"The Templars are looking for a missing object, too," he finally said. "A relic. And no—I can't tell you what it is."

"Shit." Rohan leaned closer. "The missing key I'm here for belongs to a hellgate. We believe it's here in the human world."

"Well fuck," Gray whispered.

"Who is 'we'?" Isa matched Gray's volume.

"Your grandsire."

Isa's stomach dropped, and a wave of dizziness swam through her, but she forced it aside and locked her gaze on Rohan. "You know who I am?"

"You know who she is?" Gray grabbed Rohan's wrist.

"Yes." Rohan stiffened, looked down at Gray's hand. "And I'd let go, now. Otherwise, we're both going to end up in a scene neither of us wants."

"That's not how this works," Gray said. "*You* need to stop messing with us because *I* don't give one little fuck about a scene if it means protecting Isa. So I'm going to ask this once only. *How* do you know who she is?"

"Okay, boys." Isa leaned forward over the table. Shit, but it was both incredibly sexy and scary at the same time between these two. "How about no one makes a scene and we just all lower the testosterone, huh?" She pried Gray's fingers one by one off Rohan's wrist.

But the alphaholes didn't break their staring challenge.

"Well, how about we go with not touching?" She shrugged and sat back. "I'll just leave you two to your pissing match while I sit here and wait for my next dose of the masking agent. How's that sound?"

Gray's nostrils flared, although his gaze stayed locked on Rohan. "How long?"

"Let's see ... an hour and a half. So, can we get this over with? Come on, on the count of three, you both look away. That way, you both win the pissing match. Come on. Three, two ..."

"Fine."

"Fine."

She barely held back an eye roll. "Finally. Now, Rohan, *I* want to know, how do you know who I am?"

"Every daemon knows *of* you. I just put your name, the fact you're with a Templar, and that Triulf"s sniffing around together. But that last part ... Man, there's going to be one pissed off Lord of Hell. There are strict orders in place for you—and your brother—not to be touched. Anyone who crosses that directive is a goner."

"So why would she be after me?"

"No fucking idea. But when I report this back, there's gonna be literal hell to pay."

Isa glanced at Gray. His face was stony, and his diamond-hard gaze was so dead it lacked any brilliance at all.

"So, we have three problems," Gray said in a tone that matched his eyes. "Each of them fucked up. Isa's problem could kill her. The thing I'm looking for can lead to the destruction of all humankind. And you, Rohan, have an issue that affects both our worlds. So, all three of us are going to work together."

"What do you want?" Rohan said.

"Kai St. James is expecting us all at his event tonight. That's the perfect cover for me to get a good look at what the fuck is going on in that club. I'll recommend the Templar council agree to a binding contract to help find your key on the provision your end of the contract is to work with the Templars to assist us when requested. *And* you'll provide information on an antidote for Isa."

"Done. But I'll tell you about the amorice right now. There are only two options. One is the antidote made from the poison itself."

"The other?"

"There might be a spell. But even if you can find it, you need one hell of a skilled practitioner to perform the rite. This isn't a spell for a minor witch. Maybe a Watcher? But not sure you'd get anyone from that coven right now— word is they're scattered around the world searching for one of their own—so maybe a high priestess? Rumor is there's one here on the West Coast that might be powerful enough."

"A high priestess?" Gray rose to his feet. "I need to make a call. Isa, stay here. Rohan—keep an eye on her. We don't know where this Triulf is or if anyone else has joined the hunt for Isa."

Isa spluttered over her coffee. Stay? Keep an eye on her?

"There's one bit of good news," Rohan said. "There won't be many bounty hunters willing to take on your grandaddy. Hell, I'm stunned even Triulf is. The payoff must be damned enticing."

"Doesn't matter," Gray said in his usual icy tone. "One bounty hunter is one too many. And don't give me any shit on this, Isa. I see that look. Remember, you're"—he glanced around and lowered his voice—"needing this option. And I need you to be fit to do your job."

As soon as Gray left the table, clouds chased the winter sun away, and Isa rubbed her arms as a shiver coursed through her.

"Isadora," Rohan murmured her name and looked at her with steady, serious eyes. "You know you could come with me. If you cross a hellgate, the poison won't kill you."

"Because if I cross over, then I'll become ..." She swallowed the lump that lodged in her throat. She couldn't even say it.

"Immortal. Fully daemon. Subject to the Hellcourt. Yes, that's the consequence."

Hellcourt? Isa shook her head at the new term, then ducked a glance at Gray. Far enough away that he couldn't hear her. "So who would have ... control over me? Just curious. I'm not thinking of actually crossing over."

"You're one of a kind, Isadora. The only female part human who's a direct blood relative of the Lord of Hell. For certain, your mother and your grandsire would have control over you. Possibly the other High Lords, Forneous, Kryakis, Demondus, Alastair and Lilith. You've heard of them?"

"Vaguely. They're like the devi—my grandfather's inner circle, right?"

Rohan's jaw tightened. "They're also your relatives. They're your grandfather's siblings and half siblings."

"What? I never knew that."

"Not many do."

She grabbed Rohan's arm. "Who are you, Rohan? Really?"

"I'm the representative of the Daemon Congress."

"Which is exactly what?"

"The congress runs Hell—it's made up of your grandsire, his inner circle and each of the gate lords."

"And you? Who are you really?"

"That's a story for another time." Rohan's eyes softened for a fraction before he took her hand off his arm.

"Done," Gray said from behind them. He slid back into his seat. "There'll be a high priestess at the club tonight."

"Whoa, you have one on speed dial?" When Gray just stared at her, Isa snorted. "*Of course* you do. Okay, since we're going to a party tonight, I need more clothes."

11

AFTER ROHAN LEFT THE CAFÉ, Isa couldn't shake the need to watch him leave.

"Finish up." Gray took out his mobile phone again. "Tank is heading back here now, twenty minutes out."

"What about shopping? I need something for tonight, remember?"

"Marcella can pick up some options."

"But why? There're shops here—look, across the road."

"I can think of three reasons. Bounty hunters. Visions. And your next shot is due in thirty minutes."

"We have the medication here. How would any bounty hunter know where I'm right this second? And I can have a vision anywhere. Plus, Tank isn't even here yet. Come on, the shop is right there. I can cross one street." She stared him down.

"Fine. But if I say run, you run, if I say drop—"

"I drop. Got it." *Again.*

"*And* if Tank arrives and you haven't found something to wear, we're leaving, and you'll wear whatever Marcella picks up. And if you keep rolling your eyes, your face is going to freeze like that."

"Then stop with the bossiness."

"This isn't bossy. This is making decisions in line with our overarching goal so that outcomes meet expectations, every single time."

"*In line with our overarching goal*?" The corners of his lips tilted up a fraction. "Ugh. Did you do that on purpose? You know I hate corporate speak."

"Zero idea what you're talking about."

"That makes two of us, dude."

Seriously. You'd think she was going to get run over the way he guided her. But at least there was a clothing shop close with some stunning, vivid creations in the window.

"You know"—Isa opened the shop door a fraction—"you don't have to come in if you don't want to, and going by that look, you're coming in. And good eye roll—you're learning fast. Wait a second, does that mean ... are you ... loosening up?" She gasped in mock horror.

Gray grabbed the door above her head with one long, muscled arm. He held it still, forcing her to pause or rub up against the expanse of his hot, hard-muscled chest.

"Isa." A dangerous light entered his gaze.

Her mouth dried up, and she licked her lips.

His eyes narrowed, and a tinge of red hit high on his cheeks. Oh shit. That look. Warmth pooled at her core.

"I'm not in the mood for playing," he growled.

And there went her nipples, tightening as if his hand were back on her breast. She almost whimpered. Why did Gray the Icehole have to be so frigging sexy that one growl and she was wet for him?

And damn but *she* wanted to play now. Wanted to run her hands over that chest. Down his hips. Find out if his dick was as big as the rest of him. She eyed his hand where he held the door.

"Why are you looking at my hand?"

"Oh, you know." She grinned up at him. "The saying about a man's"—she glanced at his crotch—"size compared to his pinky. Because one day, Grayson I-Still-Have-No-Idea-What-Your-Last-Name-Is, we *are* going to play."

Gray stared at her for one beat. "Minx, *if* we ever play, you won't be laughing. I'm not some kid who's all sugar and sweet."

The warmth in her core deepened. And she couldn't contain a hum as she brushed past him, her nipples grazing his chest.

"I like my chocolate dark and bitter, remember?" she said over her shoulder. "Now take a seat, Grayson. I'm getting my dress on."

((●))

Fifteen minutes later, Gray's cell pinged with yet another message from Tank. Still in traffic.

Gray leaned against the wall right beside Isa's changing room and made sure the shop assistant was at the other end of the store. He'd paid her enough money to close the shop to anyone else while he and Isa were inside and insisted she stay at the front. Random requests for privacy mustn't have been that out of the ordinary because she'd taken the money and not batted an eyelid.

Another ten minutes of hell standing guard outside a changing room, for fuck's sake. And it wasn't just the fact he was on guard duty—it was who he guarded. Because the line between keeping watch over her and keeping watch while they had mind-blowing sex grew thinner and thinner.

He wanted Isa. No fucking question. He'd have to be dead not to. And even then, he had the sinking sensation his body would rise from the grave for Isadora Smith.

"Everything okay?" Isa called out from where she was trying on yet another outfit.

"Tank's still caught in traffic." He held in a sigh. Traffic was a bitch. Fact of life.

"Well, think I've found the one. Although there's one last dress to try on. Want to see?" The drape pulled back.

"No, I don't need—" Hell. The air punched from his gut. "You know I can see the underside of your breasts, right?"

Isa pivoted, checking herself out in the mirror as she gathered her hair up and piled it on top of her head, revealing the sweep of her neck. The tiny black dress pulled tight across the curve of her butt.

He bit back a groan as his cock stiffened to full attention.

"Yeah, I kinda like it. What about you?"

Like it? She looked like a fucking wet dream walking.

"But the color of the last dress is amazing. Although this works as a backup." She winked at him and pulled the drape shut, closing off that freaking magnificent view.

And hell if he didn't want to yank the swath of heavy material open, sink his teeth into the skin at the base of Isa's neck, grab that ass and dig his fingers in deep.

Fuck, fuck, fuck. *Isadora.* His best friend's little sister. Trouble. What the hell was he doing?

"Hey, Isa?" No, no, no, Gray, do not flirt with your asset.

"Yeah?"

"Thought the deal with men's cock length was their shoe size?" He thunked his head against the wall. He was an idiot. A fucking death-wish idiot.

There was a moment's silence before Isa replied in her usual sunshine tone, "Urban myth, sorry, your lordship. But your little finger ... I read that if it's close in length to your ring finger, then your dick has some extra *length*, too. So ..."

"Yeah?"

"How long is your pinky?"

"That would be for me to know."

"Ooh. And me to find out?"

He couldn't stop himself from groaning this time. A zipper rasped. Fabric swished. He stared at the drape so hard his eyes burned. Just like his body.

"Hey, Gray?"

Do. Not. Open. That. Drape.

"Yes?" he ground out. Fuck. If she opened it, he'd see her again—maybe more of those breasts. Or that lush butt. Maybe she needed help with the clasp? Maybe he could just get a little closer—

"Why did you send Marcella to see the ... thing we *were* going to see, instead of going yourself?"

"Marce—" he stopped. Shook his head. Isa wanted to talk about R-104B? At least one of them had their head in the game. He shifted to relieve the tension in his pants and cleared his throat.

"The ... matter we're talking about?" He checked the shop assistant was still well away and lowered his voice. "St. James owns that vault. My team has already pulled the internal vault surveillance feeds, so no question St. James knows something is up, and yet he played dumb when we met him this morning. As of now, he's my number one suspect. So, I'm going to play dumb, too. We've got an invitation to the party tonight, and I'm going to use that to get close to him."

"What if he's trying to keep close to you?"

"I have zero doubt he is. Which means I need to convince him I'm merely the boss at the top who never gets his hands dirty and lets his team do most of the legwork."

"Most?"

"He doesn't know me—even though he makes out like he does. But he knows my rep, so I can't be a totally useless figurehead either. I need to play the part of a doting fiancé, too focused on paperwork to get into the field much. Which means you, Isadora, need to play a part, too."

Playing a part. That was all this was. But Isa as his fake fiancé ... He bit back another groan. Why did that sound like both heaven and hell?

·(((◆)))·

At 8:00 p.m., Gray worked alone at the dining table in the Templar's LA penthouse and eyed Isa for the millionth time, where she sat near Marcella and Rohan on the plush lounge. The city lights glittered outside the floor-to-ceiling reinforced windows, but something—someone—sparkled even brighter right here in the apartment.

And it wasn't the long-sleeved, backless, ridiculously short sequined dress that matched her eyes. It was Isa. She shone from within. Bright. Powerful. Priceless.

And how did she look so effortless here? Gray had lived in the most lavish accommodations for over twenty years but still didn't fit the urban, suave mold. Yet Isa came from a farm in Australia, had arrived in the US with nothing more than her pants and tank top, and now here she was with her dark hair falling in silk waves around her shoulders, like a lover's hands had been running through it, with her eyes glittering like they held the secrets of all the worlds—hell, maybe they did—and talking with Rohan and Marcella as if she was a queen.

A chill swept through Gray.

The granddaughter of the devil had a pedigree unlike any other. And way better than his.

A cold weight sank to the bottom of his gut, but he refused to acknowledge it any further and instead reviewed his preparations one more time. Three doses of masking agents and backup syringes, earpiece and mic combos—

"What are you doing? Didn't you go over all this earlier?" Isa stood up and wound her way between the furniture to stand beside Gray. Her scent reached him first. That delicious combo of cinnamon and earthiness that made his mouth water and his dick go stiff.

At least the table hid his reaction.

"This is about the five Ps," he muttered. And he didn't need to look at her to know she was staring at him like he was loco. Hell, maybe he was. But ensuring the successful completion of every operation was his life—and if he fucked up and things went bad, then it was a hell of a lot of lives hanging in the wind. Which made his motto even more important. "Perfect preparation prevents piss-poor performance." He did a fast mic test.

"Yes, but we're going to a club. Not a ... a ..."

"Isa, we're going to the nightclub where your vision showed some disturbing shit going down, and that may be linked to R-104B. I'm leaving zero to chance on this. So you'll wear an earpiece, as will Rohan and I. These are so tiny no one will even see them."

"And what are those?" She pointed at the other items lined up on the table.

"Carbon fiber pen. Also doubles as a shiv. And two

knives made from a nylon composite strong enough to drive through wood."

He placed the pen into his pocket, then lifted his pant leg and strapped one knife to his calf, then rolled his shirt sleeve up and strapped the other along the inside of his forearm.

"That's a lot of weapons for a club." Isa nibbled at her lip. "Do you really need all that?"

"After what's happened to you in the last two days, I'm not going anywhere unarmed ever again. Now, let me help with your earpiece." He motioned her closer. And hell, he must love playing with fire suddenly because he should keep Isa far away, but instead, he leaped at the chance to touch her.

"Can I push your hair back?" he murmured.

She nodded and turned, and he brushed the silky strands back from her cheek.

His body surged into overdrive. Blood pounding. Heart racing. Freaking cock so stiff he'd have a zipper imprint for a month.

Fuuuucking hell. He was in trouble.

"Does it go all the way inside?"

Oh, he wanted it *all the way,* all right—but fuck. Fuck, fuck, *fuck*. He bit back a growl and restrained the cutting, clawing need that surged through him to crush her to him. He forced himself to only touch the lobe of her ear—and insert the earpiece.

An image of inserting his cock between Isa's thighs flashed through his mind. Gray swallowed hard. Fuck, mind off Isa's thighs.

"Is that it?" She licked her lips. Her gaze dropped to his mouth. Color hit her cheeks. Then her gaze lifted to his—

and everyone and everything else disappeared as something hot, intimate, passed between them.

"Gray, are you done with Isa? I need her over here," Marcella called out.

The pulse at the base of Isa's neck visibly throbbed. Ah hell, it would be so easy to lean in, clamp his lips over that point and suck her skin into his mouth.

"Gray?" Isa whispered. "Am I done?"

Shit. He whirled back to the table.

"Yep, you're good." Could his voice get any gruffer?

"I'm all yours, Marcie. What do you need?" Isa said a moment later.

Gray kept her in his peripheral vision as she spoke with Marcella.

"I'm taking your biometrics—height, shape, weight—so I can feed them into our tech," Marcella was saying. "Your earpiece also lets us monitor your location within the club, and then once the tech recognizes your body, I can pinpoint where you are within the space itself."

"Wow. You love your tech, huh?"

"Yep. That's my specialty."

"Well, you can add looking stunning in a suit to the mix. I've never seen anyone pull off a black suit and white shirt with such style. You're going to look amazing in the club."

"I'm not inside tonight. I'll be managing the tech from the car." She shot Gray a dry look. "Not that I'd mind checking out the view. I bet there are some stunning women —present company included—there tonight."

"In that case, you have to come!" Isa whirled to him. "Gray, can't Marcie be inside tonight? She's single, and who knows—the love of her life just might be there."

"No." He didn't even bother to ask how Isa knew all

about his field tech's love life. Isa had this way about her that opened people up like flowers for a bee.

"Why?"

"Because we're working, and Marcella's job is in the SUV."

"What about the end of the night—?"

"No. No, no and still no. The job isn't over until you're back in this apartment, locked up tight for the night. Now enough, I need to go over the club specs one last time."

Gray snapped his laptop open, forced himself to ignore Isa's laughter as she joked about his prickly, icy ass with Marcella and Rohan, and instead focused on schematic plans.

Isa laughed again, and resisting the urge to look at her took everything he had.

Shit. Enough was enough. "All right, we're out of here. Testing mics now. Can you all hear me?"

Isa nodded, followed by Rohan.

"I just have to grab my coat." Isa stood and the hem of her dress slid up one thigh. How could someone so short have such long legs? She was back in a flash, smiling up at him with that irreverent grin that made his heart thump.

"Okay, handsome." Isa looped one arm through his. "Let's go pretend to be a couple for the night."

His gut tightened.

Fuck. Was that anticipation? Dread? Both?

12

Isa couldn't stop herself from scanning the city and crowds as Tank drove the SUV past a queue of glamorous people lining the sidewalk and pulled up in front of Fathom LA.

A doorman opened the passenger door and Isa slid out, did her best to avoid flashing her panties at anyone close by in her seriously short skirt—and waited as Gray and then Rohan followed her out of the car. She didn't need to glance at them both to know their impeccably cut dark suits hugged their broad shoulders and lean hips. The glance of most women there—how they looked at Rohan, and then Gray, and did a double take as if to say *holy fuck* said it all.

Can't blame you, girls.

Then Gray put his hand on her lower back—and even through her dress, through her jacket, something hot gathered where he touched her.

It's for show. All for show. But no matter how much she told herself that Gray's possessive touch wasn't real, she was so damned into him, *her* reaction wasn't for show. How was she meant to hide that?

Gray said something to the doorman, and then a security guard ushered Isa, Gray, and Rohan through the smoky-glass double doors.

Lights pulsing above the dance floor, the pumping of loud music, and the odor of mingled perfumes, sweat, and alcohol met them. Dark and alluring corners where velvet and leather booths lined the walls and the gallery level.

And people filled every available space.

Isa had just handed her jacket over when Gray touched her elbow, and she turned to find Rochelle, stunning in a shimmery black halter-top pantsuit, standing in front of them.

"The VIP areas are upstairs," the club owner said over the music. "Kai has the entire upper floor for his event tonight, and your name is on the list, so head on up any time."

"Thanks. We might have a look around first, though." Gray squeezed Isa's hand. "Dora still wants to check out the place for our little event."

"Of course, of course—look around. I've also set you up a bar tab, so grab a drink whenever you want."

As soon as Rochelle disappeared back through the heaving mass of bodies, Gray motioned for Rohan and Isa to come in closer.

"Stick to the plan." He placed an arm around Isa's shoulders, his fingertips grazing her collar bone. She tried—failed—to hide a shiver at his touch, although if he noticed, he didn't let on. "Meet back in thirty."

Rohan nodded and set off, his long, laconic gait taking him effortlessly into the crowd.

"Just you and me now," Gray murmured into her ear. Another shiver trickled through her, and her nipples pebbled—thank frig he couldn't see them right now; otherwise, he'd know exactly how hot he made her. "I'll keep the boyfriend stuff to the bare minimum."

She nodded and pressed into his side. "No issues here, Ace."

"Ace?"

She glanced up at him. "You're definitely the top dog here." She shrugged. "Let's stop by the restrooms on the way to the bar—I want to check them out again."

Witches, humans, and who knew who else, filled the restroom, all showing miles of gleaming skin and beautiful faces. And Isa had to be the shortest one there, of course. But none of the beings present were the three women from her vision.

Isa made her way to the makeup mirror and pretended to fuss with her hair while she listened in on the nearby conversations.

Snippets of talk about the VIP section and some billion-aire in town, a reference to two built guys, one with long reddish hair and the other with black hair, and then some chatter about an illicit drug that made a few of the crowd ooh and ah.

But after five minutes, Isa couldn't stay much longer without looking conspicuous, so she headed back to Gray.

He stood against a pillar surrounded by four women. They circled him so tightly their arms were packed together.

Something possessive flared inside Isa, but the absolute disinterest on Gray's face made the sensation relax. What-ever turned Gray on, it wasn't them.

Though they didn't seem to see that because they all crowded closer.

Isa couldn't hold back a smile. Gray was so damned hot that his aloof expression was probably having the opposite effect to what he wanted, the poor darling. Hmm ... to rescue or not to rescue?

Then he caught her eye. He jerked his head once toward the women.

She pretended to think for a moment while checking them out—they really were great looking from the back.

Gray's eyes narrowed.

Oh well, fun time was over, apparently.

"Baby cakes, there you are," she cooed. She made her way around behind Gray and wriggled under his arm. "Thanks for keeping him company, girls. I've got it from here." She rose on her tiptoes and pressed a fast kiss to Gray's jaw.

Gray stiffened. Pulled back. Yikes. Too much? She needed to check how far this pretense was meant to go.

But instead of moving farther away, he stared at her eyes, and then his gaze traveled down to her mouth. And damned if she didn't feel that look on her lips.

"Isa." His whisper drifted over her. He moved closer. Those firm, delectable lips she'd dreamed of kissing hovered above hers—

"All right, you two." Rohan's voice broke through the haze that consumed her. "Enough. You've convinced everyone down here you're a couple."

"Fuck," Gray whispered. "You're dangerous, woman." Then he pulled back and turned to Rohan. "Thought we were meeting at the stairs."

"We were." Rohan rolled his eyes. "Except you two were nowhere to be seen, so I came back this way to make sure you hadn't ditched me."

Isa resisted the urge to touch her tingling lips. She was dangerous? Uh-uh, Gray was the dangerous one here.

She glanced sideways at him.

Found his expression impassive. What the hell? Who was this man—a cyborg or something? If it wasn't for the ridge of his dick pressed against her for that fleeting moment, she'd have thought he wasn't into her at all.

Okay, so maybe he wasn't a robot. And the heat that stirred low in her belly shifted to a simmer.

"We're not ditching anyone," Gray muttered. "Let's go."

·(((●)))·

"Anything stand out?" Gray asked Rohan as he walked, with the daemon on his right and Isa tucked against his left, up the stairs to the VIP section.

"Nothing about any missing relic," Rohan said. "The most noise was excitement over some new street drug."

"I heard about that, too," Isa said. "It was all the talk in the ladies' restroom. Apparently it's like riding out an hour-long orgasm that will get you so high, you'll be talking with the angels."

Shit. *Talk to the angels.* Surely not? The hairs on the back of Gray's neck rose.

"Listen," Gray said, "we're not the local cops, and it sounds like they need to be all over this new drug, but I think we need to get a sample, too."

"What? Why?" Isa asked.

"Can't say."

"Of course not."

He ignored the way she rolled her eyes. "But for now let's focus on what we're really here for—"

"Saving those three women," Isa said.

"Finding the relic." Gray cut her a look.

"We can do both!"

"But one comes first—"

"Okay, okay, you two," Rohan said. "You're arguing like an old couple already. Are you sure you're not married?"

"Married? What's this?" St. James said, standing at the top of the stairs holding two glasses of champagne.

Shit.

"I just popped a bottle of Louis Roederer," the billionaire said. "Sounds like perfect timing."

"Always good timing for champagne," Gray forced a relaxed tone. "But no, Rohan's joking. Still only engaged."

"And on that, please let me offer my—and my family's—congratulations." St. James and Gray shook hands; then, the billionaire pressed a kiss to Isa's cheek.

Gray wrapped an arm around Isa, and when she leaned into him, he had the insane urge to preen. But he shut that shit down. If only it didn't feel so fucking right.

But St. James's cheek kiss had been a lot longer than what Gray would give a relative stranger. What was the other man's game here?

The billionaire led them over to another area, separated from the rest of the VIP floor by a red velvet rope. Gray held back an eye roll. Really? A velvet rope? Nothing but a statement of who's who in the zoo. St. James's entourage and other quasi-famous people looking for the best place to be seen in LA that night crowded the space. As introductions were made, Gray took careful mental note of them all.

And then a server handed around glasses of sparkling champagne, and St. James once again toasted them and then gestured for Isa to take a seat with him on the velvet lounge. Gray pretended to take a sip and sat beside her.

"So, Dora, do you have much family here?" St. James leaned in close to Isa. A smile crossed the handsome fucker's face that probably looked charming but put Gray's radar on an even higher alert. "Grayson's based in Boston, so I assume that's why you're having your engagement party here?"

"Some," Dora replied smoothly. Shit. St. James had asked casually enough, but why the interest in Isa? Could be the marrying Gray story—that alone would put Isa into the high-value category, given the link to the Knights' organization. And St. James was very good at maintaining the ties needed for his business. But was that the real—or only —reason?

Isa glanced over to Gray, her eyes sparkling as she gushed about something inane—she was doing a damn good job of giving nothing critical away, the clever minx. But as she did, St. James's gaze raced down Isa's dress.

The fucker. He wanted Isa. No question.

Not happening. Not ever—even if Gray and Isa weren't really a couple.

"So, St. James, it's good to see you again." Gray put an arm around Isa. At least he could play the jealous role easily enough. He never let his feelings show, though, which the billionaire would know, so Gray had to play this with caution and restraint instead of what he really wanted—get Isa the fuck out of there. And follow that up with another kind of fucking. "What are you doing over the festive season?"

"Heading to New York tomorrow, then down to St. Barths in the Caribbean for New Year on my superyacht, *Enchantress.*"

"Sounds like a blast."

"It always is. What about you?"

"Not straying too far from the office. You know how it is, always something going on."

"Yes, my team told me about the issue we have with ..."

St. James pulled up short and glanced at Rohan and Isa, then back to Gray. "Actually, can we have a word in private? Business, you know."

"Sure." Gray stood up. "Be right back," he murmured into Isa's ear.

"No worries, go do your thing. Actually, I'd love to have a look around. Rohan, fancy a walk?"

Gray bit back the urge to order her to stay the fuck up on the VIP floor. She was going back to the ladies' restroom. No question. But there was shit all he could do about that right now.

Maintaining the easygoing smile, he followed St. James past the balcony that overlooked the rest of the club and into another room altogether.

Sconce lighting illuminated three walls, with the last wall covered in a dark-glass mirror. A floor-to-ceiling pole took pride of place in the center of the room, and a leather sofa sat at the far end.

"We can chat better in here," St. James said, no longer yelling over the music.

"Much better. So, what's up?"

"While I don't know the nature of the item in the vault that the Templars are concerned about, I'd still like to help. I understand an item is missing, and I hope you can appreciate how much of a predicament that puts me in. If there's been a security failing—something wrong with my team or my systems—I need to know. And I'd like to help regardless of the issue we're dealing with."

"I haven't received the latest report, but my team is working on the matter now. Once I get their update, I'll be in touch—as much as I can, anyway," Gray said.

"I thought you'd be directly working the case? I heard Templars visited the vault today."

"My crew. These days I'm much more deskbound," he lied. Well, sort of. Bloody desk work. "The higher you climb, the less field work you do."

St. James laughed. "Tell me about it. Well, the offer's there ... but can you tell me what it is? Or is that not allowed?"

"Unfortunately, that's not something I can discuss—you know how it is. But thanks for the offer. And I understand your team is working with mine on security footage from around the facility, so I'm sure it'll be fine. But there's one thing—you have a lab here, is that right?"

"Yes, one of my medical research facilities. How can I help?"

"I need to run a sample of a local substance. Any chance I could run it past one of your lab techs tomorrow? I know it's a Sunday, but I'm not sure how long I'll be in town."

"Well, if it's for the Templars, my lab is your lab. I'll let the team know you'll be stopping by. We operate seven days a week, although not the full contingent on a Sunday."

"Thanks, I'll have my team reach out to your lab—manager? Director?" Gray said.

"My director can take care of whatever you need. Now, I should get going—party to host and all that. But this little room is part of my event, so if you and Isa want ... privacy, it's all yours. I'll let Rochelle know."

"Wow, good of you. Thanks." Gray barely kept an even expression as St. James slapped him on the back and left the room. And he'd bet every relic the Templars oversaw that the smoky mirrors were two-way. So that would be a giant fucking no.

Gray rejoined the group behind the velvet rope and checked the time. One hour until Isa's next dose. But where the hell was she?

"What do you think of Fathom?" Rochelle appeared at his side and tapped him on the sleeve. "I see Dora's dancing with Kai, so perhaps I can take you on a private tour?"

Hell, had St. James run for Isa the moment he'd left? And had the other man set up the private chat for that reason in the first place?

At least he knew where to find his diviner.

"Thanks, a tour would be great," he said.

Fifteen minutes later, Gray extricated himself from Rochelle's grasp on his arm and went to the balcony. Rochelle's expensive perfume clung to him, but it wasn't the scent he wanted to inhale. And even though the dance floor heaved with bodies under the deep red lights that shone over the dark club, only one person stood out.

Her dark hair swung as she moved, her dress swished over her curves and revealed tantalizing skin.

Then a tall man crowded so close to Isa that he blocked Gray's view.

St. James. *Again.* Fuck.

Before he could second-guess himself, Gray squeezed through the crush of bodies to Isa. She had her back to him, but then she spun as she danced, and her eyes lit up. Her smile made his chest hurt.

"I wondered where you'd gotten to," Isa shouted over the music. "Kai said you were with Rochelle—this entire time!"

Over her head, St. James met Gray's gaze and smiled, then he picked up Isa's hand and pressed a kiss to it. "I'll leave you to it, Dora. Lovely dancing with you. I'm heading upstairs. See you later."

Isa smiled like a queen giving a fucking favor and then grabbed Gray and pulled him into her. She rose on her toes and pressed against him.

His body tightened. Whoa, what—

"Dance with me," she yelled into his ear.

What the? "I don't dance!"

"You have to." She shook her head, the silky strands brushing over his jaw. "If you don't, it'll look odd. Plus, this is the perfect angle to watch the restroom door."

He groaned. Of course. Isa was hell-bent on saving those three women. But he had something more important than three lives—he had countless humans at stake if what he feared happening was actually in play.

He glanced up. St. James and Rochelle stood at the VIP balcony watching him and Isa. Hell. Isa had one thing right, he needed to play the game here because something was definitely not on the up with St. James. But was that something related to the myrrh or another matter entirely? Like the woman currently swishing her body to the music and rubbing right up against him.

"Five minutes," Gray ground out. "Your next dose is due soon."

"I know."

She said nothing else, just turned him around until she faced the restroom, and then wrapped his arm around her neck, pulled him close and danced.

And Gray's body went into hyperdrive—hyperaware of her every move as she danced and spun. The sweep of her breasts against his chest, her butt against his groin. The way her fingers sifted through his hair. And her scent. That intoxicating mix that was all Isa replaced the harsh perfume from earlier.

Holy hell, she was perfect.

She smiled up at him again and moved closer still, so that with every move she made—they made—their bodies brushed and rubbed. Blood flew to his dick and no question she'd feel him when she danced that close. But she didn't retreat. Instead, she rubbed even harder against him, and he couldn't hold back a groan.

"Isa," he muttered in her hair when she did that spinning thing again and pressed her back into his chest. He ran his hands down her shoulders, skimmed her figure from the sides of her breasts to her hips. He held her there as she moved, and then she tipped her head back and danced.

"Isa," he murmured her name again, and this time when she spun around, he left his hands on her hips. She stared up into his face, and there was no other option but to lean down and capture her mouth.

Lush. Divine. Decadent. He wanted to dive into her, but some remnant of sanity remained, and instead, he traced her lower lip. Against his mouth, she smiled and then tasted him back. Stroked. Played. Whispered. Nipped.

An inferno licked through his veins, and any lingering game play submerged beneath a wave of desperate, craving, clawing hunger.

Gray gathered Isa to him. All thoughts of dancing and the club, of people watching, disappeared as she kissed the ever-fucking life out of him.

Long, drugging kisses that obliterated the rest of the world and had only one thing taking over his mind. Tongues tangling and tasting, retreating, and surging.

"Grayson." Fucking St. James calling his name broke into the moment.

He slowly pulled back. As he did, Isa stared at his lips. A puzzled frown crossed her face before she quirked one eyebrow.

"What?" he asked.

"Never mind. We can finish this later, Ace." She winked.

Later?

Then St. James whacked him on the back before he

could respond—and hell, Gray had zero idea whether he would fling Isa over his shoulder and cart her off like a cave dweller to find out exactly what *later* meant, or if he'd be able to find that last strand of sanity and sit in an ice shower all night long.

And another zero clue was if this was in character or for real. But he was on the ride now, and neither he nor Isa were getting off the rollercoaster until they were back at the Templar apartment. Gray pressed his forehead to Isa's for one second, then turned around and wrapped an arm around her shoulders.

And he *would* ignore the perfect fit of her body against his.

"St. James." He nodded to the billionaire.

"I have to leave now, but I told you about the superyacht, right? Why don't you and Dora join me? I'll have my team send through the details. Rochelle's coming, and even if you can't make it, Grayson, Dora, you're most welcome."

Everything in Gray froze, but he scrambled to keep his game face on.

"Thanks, I'll see what we can do." Gray shook St. James's hand and then grabbed Isa and pulled her off the dance floor.

"What's going on?" Isa gasped when Gray stopped at a table in the far corner of the ground floor. "Hey, move aside —I can't see the restroom through you."

"Don't worry about the women. We've got bigger issues. But first, your dose. Are you sure you don't want me to administer it?"

"No, you showed me how, and I've got this."

"Isa—you don't have to do everything on your own."

"Actually, I do." Her stubborn chin rose. "I'm going to the restroom now. See you soon."

Shit. How much more independent could she get? "Fine. But check in via the earpiece if you need anything at all. I'll be right here."

"I know." Her expression softened, and she patted his arm.

As soon as Isa disappeared into the restroom, he monitored every second on his watch, tuned out the music and people, and concentrated on the earpiece in case anything came through from Isa.

Four minutes. She should be doing the injection now.

If the worst happened, he'd get Marcella to call an ambulance. They'd take Isa to the nearest human hospital, and if needed, he'd medivac her to the Templar lab in Boston. And then he'd call Triulf.

Seven minutes. Isa should be done by now.

He opened his wallet and flicked a thumb over the bounty hunter's calling card. That was the last resort—and one he'd take if he had to save his diviner's life—

Isa appeared in the doorway to the restroom. Cheeks normal. Hands steady. She gave him a nod and wove her way back to him.

His breath let out. And by the time she reached him, he had his wallet away and made sure zero sign of his concern remained on his expression.

"All done," she murmured.

"Good job. Listen, I did a recon of the club, and there's nothing screaming R-104B is here, except St. James. And right now, his focus on you is next level. I mean, hell, he invited you onto his yacht."

"So, can we trust him?"

"No. And if he wants us on his yacht, there's a reason. I just have to work out what."

"But we're going, right?"

"I'm going. Not sure about you."

"Gray! You've got to get over this protective BS. You know I can handle this. And how will it look if you and I don't turn up together?"

Gray grimaced. "St. James might know what you can do."

"What?" Isa went pale. "Why?"

"He invited us—you—onto his yacht. The first time he's ever invited the Templars on board."

"You think he wants me because of my gift?"

"Isa, you're so fucking hot I've got singe marks. So I have zero doubt his interest is only in your gift. But it makes you a desirable package."

"You think I'm hot?" She searched his gaze.

Gray couldn't stop his scowl. Was this girl serious? How could she not see how fucking stunning he found her? He opened his mouth to say something when Rohan appeared at their table.

"You two—seriously, why are you always disappearing? Whatever, your other guest is here."

"Well, that's one bit of good news." Gray glanced at Isa. Her eyes widened. Guess she'd realized who Rohan was referring to.

"She's here? Now?" Isa rose onto her tiptoes. "Where is she? I can't see her."

"Front door." Rohan nodded to the entry of the club. "Surrounded by the three hulking males. Private security, by the look of them. I only got a glimpse as she came in but recognized the tattoo."

"You know an awful lot for a daemon." Gray regarded Rohan mildly. Rohan met his gaze with the same expression.

"What tattoo?" Isa still searched the front of the club.

"Crescent moon," Gray murmured. "The mark of a high priestess."

"This one wears hers loud and proud," Rohan said. "Right between her eyes."

Gray said nothing, but since he'd been with Cyn when she'd gotten that tattoo, he knew it all too well. He'd gotten his own—not his first, and not a moon—that night, too.

He took out his cell and sent a fast message alerting Cyn to where he, Isa, and Rohan were.

The next moment the phalanx of guards—seriously, what was that shit?—shifted direction and walked over, forcing dancers to move or get pushed out of their way. Gray held in a sigh. Someone had really gone all out this time.

"Wow, they're all for your high priestess?" Isa said.

The guards stopped at their table, and then a long, black-painted nail tapped on the closest guard's shoulder. He shifted to the side and the high priestess lifted her chin.

Rohan made a low hum—Cyn glanced at the daemon. Her eyes widened for one second—so fast, probably only Gray had even noticed, given he knew her so well—before she regarded Isa, and then rested her gaze on Gray.

"Hello, lover." She stepped over—almost as tall as him—and pressed her lips to his.

Oh shit. What was she doing?

13

Isa couldn't stop her jaw from dropping when the three guards shifted, revealing possibly the most stunning woman she'd ever seen. *This* was Gray's high priestess? Shining blonde hair, heavily lined violet-blue blue eyes, a crescent moon tattoo on her forehead, more designs winding up her arms and legs, deep red lipstick. Stunning. Bold. A gaze that glittered with a take-no- prisoners attitude.

And then she kissed Gray.

Isa's breath whooshed out. And before she realized it, her fingers had curled into fists. Only Rohan's hand on her arm had her stop from doing something totally stupid, like flying around the table and ripping that breathtaking crea ture off Gray.

At least Gray stepped back. His eyes flashed a warning at the high priestess, and whatever passed between them, the woman didn't go near him again. Lucky for him, because he'd just been kissing Isa—except no, these kisses today had been pretend.

Their kiss had been hot. And sure, he'd been into her—

his dick made that clear—but neither gave Isa any right to feel jealous.

She'd had two visions of Gray being intimate with women over the years—thank frig no more—and this stunner hadn't been either of them. But there was nothing to say Gray and the high priestess still hadn't been together.

An oil slick washed through Isa's belly.

"What a greeting." Gray laughed, and it was good—it was almost perfect—but a note of strain made Isa peer closer at him. "But I'd like to introduce you to my *fiancée*, Dora."

"Oh, what a spoiler," the high priestess pouted those gorgeous lips. "The fiancée part, I mean. But hello to you both." Her husky voice made her even more appealing. Damn it.

"Hi, great to meet you. You're spectacular," Isa blurted out.

"Why, thank you. Now that's a greeting. So, you're looking for a high priestess?"

"Yes, she is," Gray said.

"Yes, I am." Isa glared at Gray. "I can talk for myself, you know."

"Never said you can't. But—"

"Ignore those two," Rohan murmured. "They've been spatting like an old married couple all day."

"And you are?" The woman turned to Rohan, but her expression had lost all the warmth from when she'd been talking to Gray and Isa.

"Rohan. Daemon Congress rep here on official business."

"Which gate?"

"None of your business." Rohan smiled—but there was

more shark than dolphin in that grin. The high priestess gave him a grin to match.

"Do you two know each other already?" Isa glanced between the two of them.

"Nope," Rohan replied, gaze still locked on the high priestess. "But I'm happy to get to know her more."

"Ew," the priestess said. "Please. I'm just making sure I remember the ass who I hope never to see again."

"Cut it," Gray muttered, then his voice lowered. "We need to talk. But not here. Can you come to the apartment?"

"I've got an appointment in my rooms in an hour, which is where I'm heading now. But I can come to you after that."

"Done."

"Can you give me anything to go on?" she asked.

"We need an antidote. Amorice."

The high priestess gave a long, low whistle. "That's not easy. I'll see what I can do. Ciao, babe. See you later."

Isa nodded back when the woman dipped her head at her.

She couldn't hold in a laugh when the high priestess gave Rohan a long head-to-toe once-over, then spun around in her killer stiletto heels and strode away with a sway to her hips. The three hulks surrounded her, and then they all disappeared out through the front entry.

"Thank fuck," Gray muttered. "Hopefully, we're on the way to getting one problem solved."

Isa absently rubbed her arm. "I hope so too. So does your high priestess have a name, or do we just call her HP?"

"She's not mine. And I'll let her introduce herself to you."

"So mysterious." Isa rolled her eyes. "Now, back to the—"

A single silvery star shot across her vision. Another star

shot past. Then more and more until a universe of them gathered at the edges of her vision.

"Gray!" She grasped the edge of the table and held on tight. Shit. Shit, shit, shit. This was why she didn't go out.

"Isa? What's—?" Gray was suddenly at her side. She glanced up at him, unable to make a sound.

"What's going on?" Rohan's voice came at an echo as if she was being torn from this world and he was shouting down a long, narrow tunnel.

"Fuck. Now?" Gray's voice followed Rohan's. The Templar's shoulder brushed hers. Warm. Steady. He was there. She'd be okay.

She struggled to nod before the stars closed in and everything went blank, but Gray was there, so it would be okay. It had to be.

««●»»

Not here. Not now. Fucking hell. Gray wrapped an arm around Isa and leaned her head into his shoulder.

"Grayson?" Rohan asked. "What's going on? Come on, man, fill me in. Why is Isa … vacant?"

"Stand on her other side now. We have to keep her standing and make it look like everything's normal."

"Fucking hell," Rohan muttered.

At least they were at the back of the room, but still. Gray snatched up his drink and pretended to take a sip.

"Isa's having a vision," Gray said as loudly as he dared over the music. He checked the room. Several people stared at their table, but every one of them glanced away when he met their eyes.

"Here?" Rohan shot a wary look at Isa.

"Yes. Here. Right now. And she can't move when it happens."

"How long does it last?"

"No fucking clue. Some go fast, some long. And she's wiped out afterward. We'll need to leave, but I don't want to move her until she comes out of it."

"You just want to stay here?"

"Right now, we also have zero idea what she's seeing. If this is about ..." Adrenaline surged through him. If the vision had anything to do with R-104B, then he needed that information from Isa immediately. He buried the urge to pick Isa up and get her out of there.

"Who can say what it's about? She needs to be out of the public eye."

"No. We stay. When she comes to, then we move."

"I thought you and Isa were for real. Or at least you had a genuine feeling for her," Rohan hissed. "All the kissing and shit—but you don't care for her at all, do you?"

"It's not about caring, it's about my job. Hell—you're here on a mission too. The hellgate key you need? Would you put anyone above that?"

"You don't know what I would or wouldn't do," Rohan said.

"You're right. But you know who I am. So no, we're not moving. And fuck, we can't argue. People are looking our way too much as it—"

"Gray?" Isa's whisper had him stop, and then she raised her head from his shoulder.

"What did you see, Isa?"

"They're here."

"Who?" He brushed the hair back from her forehead.

"The women." She blinked and dragged in a visible

breath. "There. I saw them from the other angle—they went in. They're in there. Now."

"Shit. Rohan, I need to get into the bathroom. Stay with Isa."

"Call ... an ambulance," she whispered.

"On it," Gray said.

As he ran into the restroom, he activated his earpiece. "Marcella, call emergency services now." He shouldered past two women trying to enter and ignored their outraged protests. "Stay out," he barked over his shoulder.

And then he pushed through the inner door. The restroom looked exactly as Isa had described—smoked-glass mirror wall, colored lights, one woman crawling over the floor bleeding from the eyes and nose. A second on the floor, legs hidden behind the toilet stall door, but her upper body was visible, motionless, staring up at the ceiling, blood tracking down the sides of her face.

The first woman raised her head. "Help ... me."

Adrenaline surged, and he ran to her. "Help's coming. I have to check on you all." He raced into the stall. A third woman slumped in the corner, eyes open and staring at him, red rivulets streaking over her cheeks.

Fuck. His blood iced over. No pulse on the woman in the stall. He checked the woman on the ground. Nothing either.

Fuck, fuck, *fuck*.

He updated Marcella on the scene, got her to contact the club security team—surely they had first aid training? And then started chest compressions on the nearest woman.

‹‹●››

Two hours after the vision had started, Isa sat at the same table huddled beside Gray under the too-bright lights of the club and finished her statement for the police. Rohan had disappeared when law enforcement arrived, but before then, the daemon had stayed glued to her side.

Paramedics had taken all three women out on stretchers, plus five other beings who'd also taken the drug in other parts of the club. Paramedics had even tried to check Isa out, no doubt because she'd looked so tired, but Gray had said something to someone, and they'd left her alone.

The policewoman who'd taken her statement said they'd follow up if needed and then left Gray and Isa alone at the back of the club before moving to the next table.

Isa pulled her coat tight.

"You okay?" Gray asked, his gravelly voice rumbling beside her. "Still cold?"

She shook her head. "No. It's just ... reaction, I guess. How much longer before we can leave?"

"Let me check. I need to get a sample of the drug for our lab before we go. I'll be right back."

"Sure." She frowned as Gray strode to the entry. Sample? Had she heard right?

He was back in a few minutes. "All done. And we can go now. But there's a ton of media out front, so we're going out through the back. I don't want your face on the television at all."

"Because of Triulf?" Not that she minded. She was happy to keep her anonymity.

Gray nodded. "Rochelle's cleared us to use her loading dock. Tank's bringing the car around now. You good to walk?"

She nodded again and stood up.

The brightly lit empty back-of-house area had a sterile,

spooky vibe, and Isa couldn't wait to get to the car, even if her legs were dragging by the time they reached the vehicle.

Isa sank into the warmed, ultra-cushioned back seat with a sigh.

"Fuck." Gray looked over his shoulder as they took off.

"What?" Isa twisted around, but nothing stood out through the tinted back window.

"Media. Coming around the corner as we left. I hope they didn't see us."

"Well, at least we're in the car now. And thanks for helping me lie to the police about why you ran into the restroom. I couldn't tell them about the visions. If word got out about what I can do, it'd be all over the news." And anyone who wanted to know the future would be all over Isa like oil paint on canvas.

"Yeah, and our cover with St. James would be blown."

"Of course." From where Gray sat in the front passenger seat, it was impossible to see his expression; but Isa didn't need to. The tension in his body screamed his displeasure, and he kept looking around them. "That too."

14

Isa only breathed easy when they reached the apartment, not helped by Gray glancing in the side mirror the entire drive.

"You can sleep soon." Gray scanned the lobby as he strode through.

"I'm okay." Of course he'd noticed how tired she was, even though she'd tried to hide it from him. "Are we safe here tonight?"

"Yes. Why?"

"You're looking around like someone's going to attack us any moment."

"Habit. And caution right now is sensible. But once we're inside, you can relax. Security is a combination of the best Templar tech, plus we have a ward spell from the Watchers in case anyone tries to circumvent our tech."

Gray's mobile phone pinged as they waited for the lift. His jaw clenched. "Fuck."

"What?" Her stomach tightened. What else was coming at them that night? Isa stared at Gray as the doors opened. "Gray, what is it?"

"Nothing. After you." He gestured at the doors.

"Don't manage me, Gray. Yes, I'm tired, yes, it's been an awful night, but don't lie to me."

"I wasn't going to lie. Now go. It's late. We're all tired. Can you please get into the elevator?"

She folded her arms.

"Okay. Yes, I was thinking about lying—but only so you can get some sleep. I would've told you in the morning."

"Then tell me now."

"Really? No, don't raise your chin at me. Fine. I'll tell you. But inside the damn elevator."

Isa relented. "So?" she said as the doors closed after them.

Gray sighed and looked away. "One of the women died."

Isa froze. "What? When?"

"About ten minutes ago. I asked to be notified if there were any ... developments."

The lift chimed at the top floor, and she stepped into the luxury apartment. But none of it mattered. That woman— dead. Isa swallowed the lump that lodged in her throat and forced her words out. "And the other two?"

"The one I gave CPR is still alive but in a critical condition. The other is seriously unwell but awake and talking. She'd had the least amount of the drug." Gray's nostrils flared, and he whirled to face the view of LA spread out in the last stretch of night. Tension poured off him. "Fuck, fuck, *fuck*!"

Damn, Gray was steamed. No—whatever this was, it was more than anger. There was a level of sadness and desperation there that made her chest tighten.

Isa joined him at the window and placed a hand on his shoulder. He was so tense his muscles were like iron. "Hey, now it's my time to ask ... are you okay?"

"I freaking hate it," Gray whispered.

"I heard the paramedics at the club, Gray." She walked around to look up at him. When he met her gaze, the pain in his made her heart stutter. "They said you saved one of them—"

"No, Isa, you saved them. But that's not it. I hate the waste. Watching someone die because of fucking addiction. That's what I hate. How it destroys lives. People. Old, young, those women. My brother."

Isa stopped breathing. His brother? Her chest tightened. "Gray, I'm so sorry. I didn't know."

"It is what it is." Gray's eyes closed and when they reopened, they were flat. Emotionless. "And it's not important now."

"Don't you dare say that! No wonder you've been on edge about this."

Suddenly his eyes glittered with another emotion, and then he reached for her. Maybe she reached for him, too. But as soon as his lips were on hers, she pressed into him. Tension still ran through his body, but heat replaced the ice pouring off him.

An answering fire simmered low in her belly.

"Wait." Isa pulled back. "One question."

"Now?"

Her nipples tightened. Damn, but he was hot and hard and so very fine. But she had to know one thing.

"Why are you kissing me now? We're alone."

His lips tightened, and the look in his eyes made her want to dive back into him. "Because I want to," he finally growled. "Not because I have to put on a show."

"In that case ..." She nipped a fast kiss on his lips and then kissed him fully. Heat and male and musk made her moan and kiss him harder.

"I swear we've done this before," she whispered between kisses. "Before tonight, I mean."

"Ah ..." Gray eased back.

"Ah what?"

"We—you—kissed before. Technically, this is our third."

"No, I'd remember that."

"Back in your studio—you were asleep. Passed out, whatever you call it."

"You kissed me while I was unconscious?" Grayson, the always serious, perfect Templar Knight, kissing someone while they were out of it? No frigging way.

"No! Gods, no." Gray raced through an explanation of what had happened. "Isa, seriously, I'd never take advantage of you like that."

"You know, that's so unfair."

"Huh?"

"You get to remember our first kiss and I don't."

"It was fast. And barely memorable."

"Ew." *Barely memorable* was his description of their first kiss? She couldn't contain a blanch.

"Not like that. Like I was so focused on making sure you were okay that I didn't get to think about it. Trust me, that kiss—the one you and I just had—was far better."

"Well, I still think we should try to make up for it. Kiss one was a wet blanket. Kiss two was for show. Let's make this one a firecracker."

She pulled Gray to her and fitted her lips to his. Licked inside his mouth and stroked his tongue.

A growl rumbled through him, and then his mouth slanted on hers. Tasted her. Owned her. But she wasn't about to be submissive. She tangled with him in the kiss, then nipped his lip. Stopped and sucked at the firm flesh she'd bitten.

Then Gray grabbed her thighs, lifted her, and fitted her to him. Isa wrapped her legs around his waist, and his cock pressed against her core. Yes. Exactly where she wanted it.

She squirmed closer, tried to feel more of his chest against her breasts, and ground against the hard ridge in his pants.

The chime of the lift doors opening echoed through the apartment, followed by a dry voice, "Well, well, the fastidious Grayson, Templar Knight, boss, and pain in the ass playing on the job? Wonders will never cease."

Isa tore her mouth from Gray's and peered over his shoulder.

Gray's high priestess stood inside the doorway. This time she wore skintight leather pants with icepick heels and a black sequin bustier. Over that, a sleeveless opaque black vest that looked like a modern-day cape, floated around her impressive curves. She was the hottest, most dangerous-looking woman Isa had ever seen.

Gray groaned and turned around. "You have the worst timing ever."

"I know. It's a skill."

"Wait. How did you get in?" Isa stepped back from Gray.

"I'm coded to enter any time. All Templars are."

Isa couldn't contain a scowl as she stared at *her* Templar. "And this isn't something you thought I should know earlier? HP is one of you too?"

⸨●⸩

Gray stared at Isa's frown. The rare emotion made him pause.

"HP?" Cyn quirked one eyebrow.

"High priestess," Isa said, the frown still on her face. "Gray refused to tell us your name."

"Call me Cyn."

"Sin?" Isa's frown deepened.

"With a C. But either works." Cyn gave one of her dry laughs. "You know, that scowl reminds me of someone else …" She tapped one black fingernail on her lip and shot Gray a mocking glance. "I wonder who?"

"Shut it." Gray nodded to the lounge. "Come over and sit down. This is important. We need your help, and there's no one else I trust on this one."

"Wow, I'm honored." Cyn's grin dropped, replaced by the focus she was renowned for, and she strode over to them, the long drape of material swishing behind her in an elegant sweep. "There's good news and bad news about the amorice antidote."

"The good?"

"While the toxin is the most lethal in the range, there's a spell to cure the poisoning."

"The bad?"

"I don't have that spell. Rumors are the Watchers have it, though."

"Fuck." Gray stared at Isa. There had to be a way here.

"Calm down. I might still have an option—I've put feelers out through the black market to see if there's anything I can access from here. But that type of inquiry needs time. Maybe twenty-four hours."

"The black market now? Great. This is getting better and better." Freaking hell. He raked a hand through his hair.

"Hey, like Cyn said, calm down. I'm sure it'll be okay."

"Calm down? As of right now, I don't have a cure for you. This is as far from okay as possible."

"And getting upset won't help either. Cyn also said she's

still looking into it. And if she can't find this spell, then I'll go to these Watchers. So no, it's not over yet."

"Looking into is far from having a fucking cure."

"It's one more day—hell, a few hours. Come on, Gray." Cyn crossed her arms. "It's almost dawn now. Let's tackle this one step at a time. How much longer can Isa take the masking agent?"

"Two-and-a-half days. Max," he ground out.

"Okay, so we know what we're working with."

"I need to contact the Watchers," Gray said. "Confirm if they have this spell or not."

"At least it's an option." Isa shrugged, and the material of her dress dipped off her shoulder, revealing that warm, delicious skin that he'd trailed his lips over—

He turned away. Not. The. Fucking. Time.

"I need to make this call in private. I'll be out soon. Cyn, watch our Divine One. She has a habit of getting into trouble." And of obliterating his thoughts every time she got near.

Then he made a fast exit to the study and slammed the door behind him. Bloody hell, why did Isa get to him so badly?

(((◆)))

Isa caught herself staring at the corridor Gray had disappeared down and forced her attention back to Cyn.

"Well, he's in a snit." She turned back to the high priestess. "Is he always like that?"

"Pretty much. But he hasn't had an ... easy road to get to where he is today. So we forgive him. Mostly."

"I guess not, especially after what happened to his brother."

"Oh shit," Cyn breathed out. "He told you about his brother?"

"Yes."

"Hmm." Cyn's eyes narrowed.

"What?"

"Gray doesn't open up to most people. He keeps shit to himself. But you can get why he's got such a hard-ass view about drugs. I'm more ... open to people's choices. But Gray, well, he is who he is. Now, tell me more about you. How come Grayson is so invested in you? And I'm not talking about the kisses."

"I'll tell you about me if you tell me why Gray doesn't use a last name?"

"That's next level getting to know our Gray."

"Our?"

"I've known him since he was a pimply faced teenager. We've gone through assessments, joined the Templar ranks, been through firefights and magic fights, and even banged a few times—no, no, don't get pissy on me."

"Ah, yes, yes. The man who I'm thinking about having sex with has been with a glamazon like you? Of course, I'm allowed to get pissy."

"Well, when you put it like that, okay. You can be pissy for one second. But that's it. Because trust me, Gray never looked at me like he looks at you. Ever."

A kernel of warmth eased through Isa's chest, but she refused to examine it. At all. She was a grown woman, and how a sexy hard-headed ass like Grayson No-Last-Name looked at her made no difference to the situation.

"So, you're a high priestess; any chance I can ask you about something ... not exactly magic related, but similar?

Especially since Sir Shithead over there doesn't want us to go anywhere until he returns?"

"Shithead?"

"Would Sir Asshole work better? Wait, my favorite is Sir Icehole. I'll go with that."

"Either or." Cyn laughed. "We call him Ice, so Icehole's not too bad. Okay, we might as well talk. Especially since I want to know how you got poisoned with amorice."

"That's a long story. Can we start with you? As in, what's the difference between you and a witch?"

"That's easy, and no state secret or anything. Witches work with spells and their will, whereas I work with spells and sacrifice. Sometimes mine, sometimes others, but always with a sacrifice."

"So, what spells do you do?"

"I mix spells into tattoos—either Henna for temporary or inked for permanent like my crescent moon. I'm also damn handy with potions and poisons. Basically, if it's got liquid and I can draw it, paint, slop or shake it, I can spell it."

"Do you practice divination?"

"It's doable through spell work, but it's my worst skill. Very unreliable." She winked. "Now, what about you— what's the deal with the Divine One thing?"

"One more question? Please? How do you become a high priestess?"

"Bloodlines. My heritage is human-witch and daemon. The daemon connection lets me turn a sacrifice into more magic than I could produce as a witch."

"Can anyone with ... daemon heritage do that?"

"Not sure. Daemon genes express differently in anyone of mixed blood. It's also got to do with the gate the daemon's belongs to. You know how that works, right?"

"Yes." Isa hid a frown. Was that why her visions were so

strong? There was no higher gate than where her mother came from.

"So ... we're playing turnsies or some shit, aren't we?" Cyn asked. "You're up, Divine One."

"Turnsies?" Isa laughed at the scorn in the high priestess's expression. "Haven't heard it called that before, but I guess so. And it's Isa, just Isa."

Isa quickly detailed her story, from Liam to the vision of the myrrh, the poison to what had happened at the club. "So that's me. And the hard part is that when the visions hit, I can't see or move or hear anything happening around me."

"Have you tried to learn control from inside the vision?"

"I began working with a coven several years ago, but after what happened with Liam ... I moved north and kind of retreated from the world. But that was the old me. The new me is going to figure it out."

"What about using crystals?"

"As in for control? I never have. The witches I worked with were trying spells to help me, but nothing made much of a difference."

"Well, given your visions come from your daemon side, and that daemons have an exceptionally strong affinity to crystalline elements in this world, I'd start there. Why don't you take this?" Cyn twisted a small silver ring with an oval-shaped stone set in the middle of her pinky finger. "The stone is citrine. Try focusing on the crystal next time you want to have a vision and see if it helps bring one on."

"Whoa, are you sure? I can pay you—"

"No way. You're part of the team. Now, I'd better scram. Places to go—spells to make and all that. Let Ice know I'll be in touch."

Places to go ... After the high priestess left, Cyn's words tumbled over in Isa's mind as she sat on the lounge, staring out into the last light of the night. Cyn had her shit together. Look how she'd blended who she was—her witch and daemon heritage—with what she did as a Templar.

So if Cyn could find that balance, then Isa would find it, too, for as long as she had left in the world.

She should go to bed, but everything inside her was too … wound, like a coil ready to let fly.

"Cyn's gone?" Gray's voice had her turn around. And her mouth dropped open. He'd changed into charcoal sweatpants and a tight black tee that did everything for his body, and sent heat curling through her.

"Yeah, she'll call you or message or something. And look —I even stayed out of trouble all by myself after she left."

"You didn't like that, huh?"

"No. Because I'm not a child and don't deserve to be treated like one."

"Ah, hell." He raked a hand through his hair in that way of his. The movement made the hem of his tee lift to show the ridges of his abs. Her mouth went dry. "Sorry. Protectiveness is a force of habit—"

"More like distrusting me to handle myself." She inwardly fanned herself. How hot could one guy be?

"Fine. That too."

"Well, at least you acknowledge it."

His lips twisted before he sighed. "Listen, you must be exhausted. Why don't you crash?"

"Actually, it's the opposite now. Can't seem to slow my mind enough to even think about sleeping." And thank the stars she hadn't. This sight was too fine to miss.

"Well, I need to sit. I want to review the police report while everything's still fresh in my mind."

"Now? Don't you ever sleep?"

"Of course. When I need to." He joined her in the lounge

area but moved to the long sofa opposite. As he sat, his junk pressed against his sweats.

"Why don't you have a shower? That might help."

Heat flooded her cheeks, and she yanked her gaze to his face, but he was still staring at his laptop screen.

Phew. He hadn't busted her perving.

"Sure. Good idea."

But the shower didn't cool her down either. And as much as she could've gone straight to bed and tried to sleep or even used the shower to take the edge off her sexual frustration, neither option was what she wanted.

So she changed into a tank and leggings, also provided by the wonderfully efficient Marcella, and padded barefoot to the living room.

Gray had turned all the lights out, bar a floor lamp in the corner, but instead of illuminating him, the pools of shadows seemed to encase him. Set him apart from everything else. Not light. Not dark. Just alone, somewhere in the middle. Solitary.

He looked up before she spoke, and something in that fierce, steady, implacable gaze called to her.

"Can I sit with you?" she murmured.

"Of course." He broke eye contact and nodded beside him. "There's enough room here if you want to lie down."

Did he know she didn't want to be on her own? And more than that, that she wanted to be with *him*? But she said nothing as she took a seat, drew her knees beneath her, and snagged a throw cushion to wrap her arms around.

With the city lights filling her view, and the security of Gray at her side, finally, the tension in her body eased. The whirl of her thoughts ceased.

What an amazing scene this would be to paint. To capture the sense of the city on the break of day. Lights still on, but the sky streaked with the deepest indigo, signaling the night had come to a close. And Gray, part of the night, and yet not. Working to daybreak because he lived and breathed his dedication to the cause.

"Gray, can I ask you a question?"

His sigh whispered through the room.

"Just one, I promise. Then you can go back to your work."

"Okay. Hit me."

"Tonight, at the club, you said you don't dance. Ever. And it got me thinking. What do you do to relax? I mean, I've only known you for a ... week." Not true, but this didn't seem the time to bring that up either. "And all I've seen you do is work on your laptop. Or protect someone, or investigate someone. Or order people about. You do that a lot. But I haven't seen you just ... relax."

"There's zero time for that."

"Okay, I get that for right now. But when you're not on a case, how do you relax, then?"

"I do jiujitsu."

"Ju—what?"

"Jitsu. It's a martial art, weaponless. Good for relaxing the mind."

"But that's still for work, right? What about reading? Watching a movie?"

Gray looked at her as if she'd sprouted paintbrushes for ears.

He shook his head. "I read reports."

"Reports?" He was joking, right?

"Yes, they have to be read."

"Oh. You're serious." She mentally shook her head. No wonder he was so uptight. The man never relaxed, let alone had any fun. He hadn't in person over the last week and never during the multitude of visions he'd featured in throughout her life.

"Don't look like that. I'm perfectly happy with my life as is. I don't need any ... silly things to waste time on."

Ah. And there it was. No wonder Gray was so dark. Well, Isa might only be in this world for a short time, but she'd make damn well sure she showed him some ... lightness ... while she was there.

She shifted to curl up on her side, her feet brushing his warm thigh, and rested her head on the cushion.

And finally, her eyes closed from natural fatigue. But before sleep claimed her fully, she swore a hand curved around her ankles. Solid. Firm. Comforting.

15

Five and a half hours after Isa had fallen asleep on the couch, Gray pulled into the restricted underground parking section of St. James's medical research laboratory.

Isa sat beside him, her beautiful face still pale—no surprise—and her chin raised in that way of hers that screamed of defiance and the steel rod she had for a backbone. She might be small, but she was tough. And hell if Gray didn't admire that about her.

The sense of falling deeper down a rabbit hole clawed at him.

"It'll be okay." The lie was out of his mouth before he could stop it.

"You don't need to say shit like that."

"I'm trying to comfort you."

"No need." Isa rolled her eyes at him, and that little sass almost made him smile. "I can see how worried you are. Ever since they showed my face on the news this morning, you've been ..."

"Not worried. Concerned." Understatement.

"Concerned. Got it. So exactly what are we doing here?"

"I'm meeting the director of the lab to hand over a blood sample."

"But you've got your own lab—why aren't you sending the sample there?"

"I did that too. This specimen is a dummy. The real reason we're here is to check out what research the St. James corporation is into. And give you a chance to see if your visions pick up anything."

"Damn, but you're sneaky. I like it." A flicker of pride shimmied through him at her praise. He held in a groan. Giving a fuck about Isa liking him played zero part in his plan. "Okay, I'll see what I can do with my visions," she continued, oblivious to where his thoughts had gone.

"Before we go in, two things. I know your cure is a priority, and that we're cutting this fine, but Cyn's working on it, and if her option doesn't work—"

"I can always call Triulf—"

"That's not what I was going to say."

"Well, she's plan C, right?"

"Hell yes, plan C. Although I'd prefer plan fucking never." Shit. He never wanted Isa within screaming distance of the bounty hunter bitch ever again.

"Listen, I appreciate the support."

"Why does that sound like a 'but' is coming?"

"Because it is." Isa's beautiful eyes darkened. "If I have to … take steps to save my life, like dealing with Triulf—or anyone else—then *I'll* consider those steps if it's the last option. That's all."

"Okay." Gray searched her unusually closed expression. Why was she hiding something? But she'd been subdued all morning, no surprise, so maybe she was just worn out? "Triulf is the last option. No arguments there. I was going to say, the next step is for you to go to the Watchers."

"That works, as long as whatever the step, if it's about my life, then it's my call."

Shit. Now he got it. "You're worried I'll force your hand and go to the daemon for help."

"You do have this habit of expecting everyone to do as you say."

"What do you want me to say? If it comes to saving your life, I'll do whatever's necessary."

"You'll do? No. *I'll* do."

"What if you're unconscious? Or if we're in a life-or-death situation and I need to make a call in a split second—what, then?"

"Fine. Apart from those two circumstances, *I* make all life-altering decisions."

"But remember, R-104B is still—"

"The priority. I get it. The relic comes first. Not being captured by a daemon bounty hunter will be a bonus."

"Is that a joke?" Gray groaned when her face lifted in a smile. "Not funny."

"Kind of is. I'm not about to sit here whining. Now come on. We're at the lab. I know the drill: stick with you unless you say otherwise. Do what you say when you say it. Or you'll send me to Boston and lock me up—"

"Keep you safe—"

"And handle the visions some other way."

"Fine. At least you listened. Let me check the lot before we get out." Three other vehicles parked in the VIP section. No people visible. Cameras at all entry points and every bay.

"That's new." He nodded at the ring on her right hand.

Isa twisted it, maybe in response to his query. "Cyn gave it to me last night. You're observant."

He didn't say anything. But considering how attuned he'd become to Isa, there was nothing he *wouldn't* notice.

"Last thing," he said. "The lab director's going to be curious about why you're here, but given the media coverage of the club last night, I'll play on the fact that you're still shaken up and don't want to be alone. Can you play a clingy, scared, helpless woman?"

"What? No way would anyone in their right mind would fall for that."

"I've got nothing else. Come on. Just lower your chin. And get rid of the promise to do battle in your eyes—I swear, I'm just asking you to put on an act here—I know this isn't the real you. Believe me, I know you're not helpless."

"Really?" Something in her tone had him stop and look back at her. Uncertainty clouded her expression.

"Isa, I've only known you for a week, but in that time, I've seen you command the people around you like a tiny general. You've almost been run over, have been drugged, had your life threatened, and yet somehow, you're here actively helping me on a case, even when it puts your life in even more danger. So no, I don't think you're helpless."

"Thank you." Her eyes brightened. "That means a lot."

He hadn't realized she felt that way. But his words seemed to have made a difference. And hell if he didn't want to do that more often.

"Okay," Isa said, "I can pretend to be weak and helpless. I should hang off your arm a lot. I'm needy, right? So just a warning, I'll be plastered to you."

And Gray was way too okay with that last part.

He cracked the car door open, but his cell pinged with an incoming message marked priority by the Templar Council and he paused midway out of the car.

"About fucking time," he breathed when he'd finished the first part of the message.

"What? Gray—what is it?"

"Raph completed the job he was working on for me. He and Eve actually finished the job together."

"Back in Brisbane?"

"No. In Rome. As in Italy." He read the rest of the message. "Shit."

"Shit what? Gray, I swear by all the stars if you don't start telling me—"

"There was a fight with a fucking daemon in the piazza of the Vatican ... Raph says it's Forneous. Eve was injured."

"Frig. How bad? Is she in hospital? What about Raph?"

"Both are walking. Raph is with Eve right now—she's about to redo the ward spell, then they'll head to Eve's. Shit, what's the time difference from Rome? It's what—seven o'clock there. I need to arrange provisions."

He made a quick call to his equivalent in the European Templar division and arranged for essentials—including coffee, knowing Raph and Eve—to be delivered.

"All right, time to go," he said to Isa after he ended the call. "What? Why are you looking at me like that?"

"Nothing. Just that you're not always the iceman. Thanks for looking after Raph and Eve, especially the coffee."

"Don't get squishy on me, Divine One. Raph's on contract—and I'd like Eve to be as well—so I'm looking after my crew."

"Sure."

"Seriously. But I will say one thing. That news has me looking up. Maybe we're finally getting on top of this shit. Let's go find R-104B. Ready?"

(((●)))

"Ready," Isa affirmed as she grasped Gray's arm. He glanced down at her but didn't speak as they approached the internal entry. The door opened, and a man in a white lab coat held up a hand as if to wave them over.

"That's not who we're meeting," Gray said into her ear. "Stay alert."

"Got it."

"Hi," Gray said. "I was expecting Director Levenson?"

"Unfortunately, the director is out of town with a family matter. But I'm her second in charge, Dr. Morris, so can help with everything you need. This way, please." The doctor led them through a heavy door into a completely white corridor with a lift at the end. "In the event of an emergency, follow all safety instructions. First aid compartments are on all levels behind the green cross."

Five floors up, they emerged into another long white-on-white corridor, although at least this one had sunlight at a far window. Dr. Morris led them into an office with a desk at one end and a round meeting table in the center.

The unrelenting, sterile, bleached environment had the hairs on the back of Isa's neck prickling, and she didn't hesitate when Gray took a seat facing the door and gestured for her to sit to his left.

Gray pulled a small case from inside his jacket and placed it on the table.

"Inside is a sample I'd like to have analyzed to determine its chemical composition. As this is Templar business, I'll ensure that fees match the rush on the order. But also, because this is Templar business, I'd like to see the security protocols for your lab."

"Of course," Dr. Morris typed something into the keyboard, and a knock tapped at the door.

Gray stiffened.

"Come in," Dr. Morris called out.

The door opened, and Kai St. James walked into the office. His smile shouted a warm welcome.

"Grayson, Dora, how lovely to see you. What perfect timing. And I heard about what happened at the club after I left last night."

"It was awful," Isa said honestly.

"I'm sure it was. So, Grayson, this is what you mentioned last night?" Kai nodded at the table. "What can we do for you?"

"I didn't expect you to see to it personally, but thank you. It's for a chemical analysis. I also wanted to review your security protocols. Only because the sample is sensitive. You know how it is."

"Of course, of course. I'll personally take you into the surveillance control room and have that information made available to you. Unfortunately, access requires security clearance—you've got that, Grayson, but Dora doesn't." Kai glanced with an apologetic smile at Isa. "Sorry. However, the control room is on this level, only a few doors down. We won't be far away."

"How do you feel about that, sweetie?" Gray picked up her hand. "I know you're still shook up after last night."

Sweetie? She resisted the urge to wrinkle her nose. "No worries." Although, being alone in this place featured last on her to-do list right now. It had creepy zombie apocalypse vibes.

Gray seemed to get her true feelings because he briefly squeezed her hand. "I'll be fast. I promise. And you can call me if you need anything. If you feel ... faint or anything like that."

Oh shit. He meant if she had a vision.

That would be bad. But then he squeezed her hand again.

Kai nodded. "If you're not feeling well, Dora, we can get—"

"No, just didn't eat much yesterday, and with hardly any sleep ..." At least that wasn't a lie.

"You'll be okay," Gray said again. "I know it."

Isa blew out a steadying breath. Easy for him to say—he wasn't the one who might end up inwardly comatose, completely unaware of his surroundings. But she nodded. He was here for the relic. That was the priority.

Plus, she was standing on her two feet. Sitting alone in the creepy lab was fine. Totally fine.

"I'll have the team bring you something to eat right now," Kai said. "We have full catering on site."

"Thank you, Kai. That would be ..." Impossible to even think about eating. "Lovely."

Gray gave her a tight smile, then he followed Kai and Dr. Morris out of the room, and the door closed behind them with a solid clunk.

Damn, but it was cold in here. Isa twisted the ring Cyn had given her last night. Then snatched her hand away. *Not the time for a vision. Not the time for a vision.*

One thing she could do was send a message to her father. What time was it back home, though?

She'd just sent her message and slid her phone back into her handbag when the door to the office reopened, and Kai strolled back into the office.

"Uh, hi." Isa glanced behind him, but the door closed before anyone else came through. "Where's Gray?"

"He's inspecting our security setup. I ducked out to order you something to eat—just need to know if there's anything you'd prefer or are allergic to?"

"How … considerate." Isa faked a smile. But if Kai was here, then Gray could hopefully get what he needed without the billionaire hanging over his shoulder. "Good news. I'm not allergic to anything, and the only thing I don't drink is coffee."

"Excellent." Kai took a seat two over from her. "It was a pleasure to meet you yesterday. And if I may say so, you really struck me."

What, like with a pole? She inwardly rolled her eyes, but kept her pleased expression.

"It was lovely to meet you, too. You were so generous to Grayson and me at your party."

"Well, Grayson and I go way back. But trust me, it's always a pleasure to spend time with someone so attractive, so … fascinating."

"What a compliment." If she wanted to puke. "But I'm not that interesting."

"Now, there I must disagree," he said, as smooth as liquid caramel.

Isa just stared at Kai. Where was this going? And how much longer did Gray need?

Kai leaned across the table. The Oxford blue sleeves of his shirt matched his eyes perfectly. "I've known Grayson for a long time, and that man would never marry someone of anything less than superior intellect or skill probably both. And *that* makes you interesting."

"Now you're flattering me." Without question. But why? And what would a needy, clingy, scared person do, that being the case?

"Ah, but not without reason, Dora." Kai shifted into the chair next to her.

"What—?" She eased back in her seat. "Kai, what's going on?"

"Dora, Dora, Dora ... not sure I can call you that for much longer, though."

"What—why not?"

"Because why be satisfied with the Templar? Rochelle saw him kiss another woman at the club—so whatever the two of you have, it's not his everything. And more than that, Gray's bound by rules and a system that will never let you reach your true potential. But I can give you the world, *Isadora*."

Isa couldn't stop her sharp breath at the recognition blazing in Kai's eyes. Her stomach clenched. Oh damn, damn, damn.

"What—how—?"

"It took some effort; however, my team have experience with challenging background reviews."

"You checked me out?"

"Of course. And my search paid off. Because you, Isadora Smith, are the epitome of *interesting*. My invitation to join me on *Enchantress* stands. Come with me—with or without Grayson—and see the life you could have by my side. More money than you can imagine. Luxury at your fingertips. Power. Respect. Your every wish and whim catered for and the world—all the worlds—at your feet. And I'll be at your side. I'll shower you with everything you can ever wish for. Can your Templar offer you that?"

"And what would I have to do in exchange for ... this privilege?"

"Work with me. Join me. I know what you are," Kai said. His eyes lit with a fervor that made her gut seesaw. "And I know what you can do."

Oh holy shit. Gray *had* been right.

A sharp rapping at the door cut through the room and Kai eased back, although his gaze stayed locked on her. Isa forced herself to stay still under the scrutiny.

"One minute," Kai called out. "Isadora, you're more precious than the rarest pearl, and I'll make the world your oyster. I'm heading down to St. Barths earlier than planned, but I'll have a jet on standby for you out of LA. Join me. Come and see what your future can—will—be. But right now, I have to go. Business calls." He picked up her hand and pressed a kiss just above her knuckles before placing it on the table as if she was made of delicate crystal. "I'll make sure Grayson takes good care of you until I see you again."

As the door closed behind him, Isa rubbed her palms on her jeans. Cotton filled her mouth, and she had to lick her lips to wet them. Had that really happened? Kai St. James had ... propositioned her?

And it hadn't been sexual. That proposal had been all about her gift. Gods, gift? Maybe her brother was right after all, and the sight of the future *was* a curse.

St. James wanted her to be his partner. *Sure.* He'd end up another Liam, but this time on steroids with his money and power and reach. Isa would never escape him.

Shit, shit, shit, *shit.*

And if she told Gray, he'd never let her go with Kai. No bloody question. But if she didn't tell Gray ... Damn it. She was already hiding the truth from him on so many levels. She didn't want to lie to Gray anymore—it was time she came clean, and then he could damn well treat her as an adult and an equal who could help in this hunt for the missing relic, even if it wasn't with the ease she'd said in the beginning.

The door handle turned with a soft snick.

This better be Gray—

Triulf sidled into the room. "Well, hello there." She shut the door behind her. "Fancy finding you all alone."

Isa's heart punched in her chest, and she scrambled to her feet. "What—how did you find me?" So much for security and the bounty hunter not being able to find her there.

"Trailed you from the Templar apartment. As soon as the media splashed your face all over the news, I knew where they'd stashed you. And I might not have been able to get into the apartment, but all I had to do was wait and then there you were."

"Why? You know who I am, yet you're willing to mess with *him*?" She eased around the table. Shit. How could she get out of this room?

Isa gripped the back of the nearest chair.

Please, please let Grayson—Kai—anyone at all come through that door.

"Oh, I know who wants you, and believe me, when he gets his hands on you, there's not much your grandaddy will be able to do in the human world."

What the frig did that mean? Not that it mattered. And it looked like she was on her own. Isa lifted her chin. "I'm not going anywhere with you. I wasn't in Australia, and I'm not now."

The daemon flexed her fingers. "Since you're still standing, your Templar Knight must've provided a masking agent for the poison." Triulf surveyed the tips of her claws. "But at my best guess, you've got two, maybe three, days at most before you either call it quits here in the human world or come with me willingly."

"Then why are you here now?"

"Because someone told your grandaddy about the bounty. The schedule's moved up, so we have to go. Now move it." She nodded at the door.

"And *I'm* saying for the last time—N frigging O. I'm not

going anywhere with you. Poison and all. It's not happening."

If only she had an edge ... Isa twisted the ring that Cyn had given her. The hairs on the back of her neck prickled. Maybe she did.

She twisted the ring again and stared hard at the daemon. *What's your next move ... what's your next move ... what's your next—?*

Stars gathered at the edges of Isa's vision. She grabbed the back of the chair ... and everything went dark.

"Bitch. You'll regret that." The bounty hunter wiped blood off the bridge of her nose.

Then Triulf lunged around the table, claws outstretched and reaching for Isa. A chair flew at Triulf, hitting her in the chest, and as she recoiled, the door to the office slammed open and into her, sending her headfirst into the wall. Triulf's eyes rolled back in her head, and she dropped like a sack to the ground.

The room swam back into view, but spun around. Isa shook her head to dispel the sensation. What had just happened? She glanced at Triulf. Her nose wasn't bleeding, and she still stood at the door.

Holy shit.

Adrenaline surged through Isa. Something had hit the daemon, enraging her. But what? The table held scissors, a stapler, a thick-based tape dispenser, paper and pens ... Isa stopped.

She racked her brain to replay the vision. One of those items hadn't been on the table.

Yes!

"Did you hear me?" Triulf ground out. "So help me. I'll make you bleed for putting me to all this trouble."

Isa lunged forward, grabbed the tape dispenser and

hurled it. The metal base connected with the daemon's nose in a solid thwack.

"Bitch," Triulf spat again, right on cue. "You'll regret that."

Oh shit, please let that vison be true … Isa grabbed the chair and held it like a lion tamer.

"That won't help you." Triulf shot forward.

Time slowed. Isa threw the chair right in time for the office door to … and yep, it hit Triulf, and an eye roll, and boom, down she went.

Holy shit. A hysterical laugh escaped Isa.

"Isa. Fuck!" Gray sprung into the room. His eyes were wild as he took in the daemon, then slammed back to her. "Are you okay? Did she hurt you? What happened?"

"I—" Isa shook her head—as much to get her mind around what had just happened as to stave off the lethargy rolling through her. Damn. That vison had been over fast, but the fatigue was like normal. "Sleepy. But okay. Had a vision."

"Hell." Gray pulled her around Triulf. "Tell me later. Let's get you out of here."

She let him pull her back all the way to the underground garage.

Crack! Crack! Thunder boomed. Something whacked into the wall beside them.

"Gun!" Gray shouted. "Get down." He pushed her back into the building.

"Not the girl," a voice yelled from deeper in the lot.

Gray yanked the door shut behind them. "Someone's fucking shooting at us."

"Not me," Isa squeaked. "You!"

16

FUCKING HELL. Daemon bounty hunter in the building. Armed assailants—at least two—in the garage.

Which way to go now? And how many assholes with guns was he up against? Gray eased to his feet and peered through the window in the door.

"Careful!" Isa whispered.

He silenced her with a hand motion. "Silver SUV, widows tinted too dark to see inside. The only car not there when we arrived. No one else visible."

"Gray." Isa grabbed his arm. "I can help."

"Not now. I need to—"

"No. Listen. I forced a vision before, with the bounty hunter. Just enough to see what was coming, and it got me out of that room. Let me try to do it again."

"How long?"

"A minute." Isa made a seesaw motion with her hand. But when her fingers trembled on the end of the motion, his gut tightened. These bastards were going down.

"Do it. I'll keep watch. But sit over there—out of the way of the door if it opens."

She nodded and dropped to the floor, then twisted the ring and closed her eyes.

In the harsh glare of the overhead lights, Isa's normally warm skin was pale, and for a long fucking minute, only their breathing—his even, hers harsh—echoed through the corridor. Where was everyone else? Just what the fuck was going on here?

Gray peered back through the window. Shit. Two doors had opened on the SUV. At the other end of the short corridor, the lights on the elevator lit up. It was traveling down from floor four to three.

Shit, shit, shit.

"Isa? Anything yet?" He glanced at her. But her eyes were still closed, although her breathing had evened out.

The elevator reached the third floor. Gray took the safety off his gun and palmed the pantographic knife from his forearm sheath. He flicked his wrist, and the hinges sprung, the blade snapped into lock.

And then Isa gasped. "She's—they're—coming."

"Who first?"

"Bounty hunter. From the lift with a gun in each hand."

He eyed the lift. Three to Two. The light on the display blinked on the down arrow.

"The people in the car park? How far away?"

"After we're back in the lift."

"The bounty hunter. Which way does she look first?"

"Ah—"

"Isa, did she look right or left when she comes out of the lift?

"Right. She—"

"Wait here. Do not move. I need to know where you are."

He didn't wait for Isa to agree, just sprinted for the elevator. Coming down from the ground floor. The down arrow blinked. Seconds, max.

The ping toned. The doors opened, and he dove for the wall as the bounty hunter ran out, a gun in each hand.

She swung to her right, just as Isa had said. Then she whirled left.

But Gray was ready. He stepped in close, made sure Triulf's weapons were pointing away from Isa. Then four cracks thundered in his ears. Gunpowder stung his nose, but as Triulf's body went slack against him, he shoved the knife between her ribs and twisted.

Her eyes widened, and her breath gurgled as he shoved the blade even higher and made sure she was done.

He pulled the blade free, and Triulf toppled to the ground. Her weapons clattered beside her, and he kicked them away even as he leaped over her body and ran back to Isa.

"Don't look at her, Isa. Focus on me. What next?"

"Wh—what?"

"Isa. Look at me. She's taken care of—for now. But we don't know how long she's down for, and there's still people in the car park. What did they do in your vision?" He knelt between her and Triulf. "Focus, Isa. What happened? How many people did you see? Male or female?"

"Two—two men. One on each side of the car—a third person in the backseat, but I never saw their face. Both men have guns, and they approach the door and come through. We weren't sitting here. That's it."

"Okay, get up." Gray grabbed Isa's arm and helped her to her feet. Hell. She was wobbly. Too wobbly to run far. And her eyes were closing. Reopening. Closing. She sagged against the green cross of the first aid kit on the wall.

"Isa, wake up, honey." He gave her a shake, and her eyes popped open.

Shit. They weren't getting out of there easily if he had to carry her out. What he needed was a way to keep her awake ...

Most medical kits carried epinephrine pens.

He slid Isa back to the floor and jammed a hand against the green cross. The compartment doors retracted and the kit opened up, including an anaphylaxis kit.

"Isa, I'm giving you a dose of epinephrine. Hope to the gods this works and wakes you up."

He hit her thigh with the pen, waited for the click to confirm the needle had engaged, and held it in place.

As he counted, he kept his gaze on the door to the garage.

One. Two. Three.

"Okay, Divine One, time to go." Fuck, this better work. He helped her to her feet. She was still wobbly, but her eyes were open. "You okay?"

"I'm here."

"That'll do. Right, we're going back to the lift. Lean on me as much as you need."

"Is Triulf ... dead?"

"That's an unknown." They reached the bounty hunter. "But she's not moving. And that way out is the best option right now."

He put a call in to Tank. "Priority pick up, under fire. St. James laboratories' main entry."

The elevator pinged. He silently pushed Isa inside and hit the button for the ground floor. As the doors slid closed, the parking garage door opened. Two armed men eased through, guns drawn. Eyes alert.

"Fuck," a man shouted.

Gray gave him the middle finger as the metal doors shut between them.

‹‹‹●›››

Holy shit, what was coming next? Isa's heart thundered in her ears as she forced her wobbly legs to run—shuffle—down yet another long white corridor.

Gray pressed his hand into the center of her back, urging her forward as much as keeping her steady. Good. Not the time to stumble.

Because if she fell, he'd stop. And while those men weren't gunning for her, they were for Gray.

He barked commands at the surrounding people; get out of the way, move to safety, as well as demanding exit directions from Marcella through his earpiece.

And it worked. At the next turn of the corridor, a sliver of daylight shone at the far end.

Please, please, please let that be the way out.

Rapid cracks boomed through the lab. Isa yelped.

Around them, people screamed.

"Go. Go. Go!" Gray shouted close to her head. His hand pressed harder.

Two security guards ran past them toward the gunshots.

"Look out! Don't go—" Isa waved them down, but they ignored her and kept running. She tried to turn around and yell at them to run the other way, save themselves and everyone else, but Gray pushed her forward.

"Leave them," he grunted. "They're doing their jobs. I'm doing mine and getting you out of here."

More gunshots cracked. More screams echoed throughout the floor. Closer.

An empty security desk loomed ahead, and the exit doors were closed with a swipe-card port next to them. The sliver of a window flashing the daylight beyond beckoned, but with no visible way through.

"Damn it," Gray snapped. "Fucking mantrap—double set of doors. You need to be buzzed or carded through one before the other can open. There must be a buzzer somewhere."

He ran around the desk and hit every button. Nothing.

Behind them, the screams were lessening now. The gunshots sporadic instead of constant.

And somehow, that was worse.

"Fuck it. Marcella!" Gray barked. "Open the exit doors remotely. Isa, get under the desk. Duck in nice and tight now, honey."

"Oh shit," Isa whispered as she crammed herself into the farthest corner. "You only use sappy words when you're worried."

Gray hunkered down, and she tried to squeeze in even farther to make room for him.

"Isa, take a breath and listen up. Tank is almost out front. As soon as Marcella gets the doors open, you run and don't stop until you're with Tank."

"Wh—? Oh no. You're going back there."

"Right now, we're sitting ducks."

More gunshots. Rapid again. Another scream. Isa jolted.

"Isa, last thing. What you don't want to do right now is have another vision. That will leave you zero control. So no visions. Can you concentrate on that?"

She nodded, then swallowed hard. *Do not have a vision. Do not have a vision.*

"Good girl. Okay, I'm going. I'll be back. Promise."

And with that, he rose to his feet and disappeared from view.

And in the sudden emptiness, only the roaring of her blood and the harsh breaths dragging into her lungs filled her ears.

The cramped space beneath the desk spun around her. Oh no. No, no, no. Not having a vision now—

Except, this wasn't a vision. There were no stars.

Panic attack.

Okay, she'd had these before. She knew what to do. She tapped her little finger and thumb together and counted, *one, two, three, four* ... Again. *One, two, three, four.*

The desk cavity stopped spinning.

Okay, she just had to inhale, exhale. Steady. Even. And stay still. Breathe and still.

And then the exit door lock clicked. Her breath whooshed out. Thank frig, they were getting out of there.

Gunshots fired. Close—the closest yet. Again. Again. Isa tensed.

Footsteps pounded toward her.

"Dead end!" an unfamiliar voice shouted.

"Back to Forneous," another voice shouted. "The myrrh's gone, anyway."

"Then let's get out of here. I want to be gone before that fucker finds us."

Holy shit. They were after the myrrh? She had to tell Gray. Had to *find* Gray—

"Too late, boys," Gray's voice rang out.

Relief made Isa sag, then four gunshots thundered. Split the air. She couldn't stop a scream, and then her ears rang. An awful smell filled her nose.

Thuds, followed by clatters and gasps and gurgles, echoed beside the desk.

"Isa, it's me. Out now," Gray growled.

She scrambled to her feet.

Oh holy shit.

Blood and body ... stuff ... splattered all over the desk. The floors. The wall. Heavy metallic and acrid stinks tainted the air. Two men lay motionless on the ground.

Her stomach revolted and flew up her throat. She turned away. Swallowed hard and breathed through her nose until the urge to gag stopped.

"Hey, step this way." Gray reached out.

And without pause, she took hold of his hand. The man who had killed three people in front of her in the last fifteen minutes.

A hysterical laugh escaped her. She must be batshit, because for all his violence, she trusted Gray, felt safer with her hand in his than she had with anyone ever before.

17

BLOOD HAMMERING, adrenaline streaming, Gray pushed Isa through the door. His world narrowed. Isa's safety. Coming threats. Next steps.

Lab workers ran from the building. Screams echoed.

"Marcella, exiting the building now," he snapped into his mic. "Make sure first responders have medics incoming; there's a high number of injured." *And worse.*

In the distance, sirens wailed, but he couldn't wait for them to get there. Stashing Isa was the priority.

The squeal of rubber on road screeched around the side of the building, and as he and Isa ran, Tank hurtled toward them.

Then Isa stumbled and fell to her knees.

"Shit." He grabbed her shirt and yanked her up, but she didn't budge. Her eyes told him everything. Hell no. Not now. *Not now.*

Then Isa blinked.

"Thank fuck," he breathed out. "I thought it was a vision—"

"It was. That's not Tank." Isa nodded at the SUV barreling for them.

Gray threw himself and Isa onto the concrete pavement, rolling so he took the hit of the fall, then covered her with his body. The vehicle jumped the curb and screeched to a halt where they'd been standing.

The driver's door slammed open, and a man with silver braids jumped out. His lips flattened, his eyes did a weird twitch, and he took a gun from his jacket.

Fuck no.

Gray rolled to his side. Took aim. Shot. Shot again.

Twin holes bloomed on the guy's forehead. Then he crumpled to the ground.

Gray surged to his feet but stayed crouched with one knee on Isa's back, shielding her as best he could.

"Let me up!" she snarled.

"Wait." He opened his mic up. "Tank, where the fuck are you?"

Another black SUV hurtled around the corner. Gray tensed, but this vehicle stayed on the road, screeched to a stop at the curb, and the passenger door swung open.

"About time," he muttered. He leaped to his feet, hauled Isa up, and dragged-walked her to the car. He threw Isa into the rear seat, then piled in after her.

"Go," he yelled. "We need to be gone before the police arrive; otherwise, they'll stall us to make statements on the scene. And I'm not risking Isa out in the open any longer. Take us to Cyn's."

As the car took off fast and smooth, he stared at his diviner. "Buckle up. And fucking hell. Is there anyone not trying to get you?"

-‹‹◆››-

Tears burned Isa's eyes when Tank stopped the SUV in a downtown LA alleyway. From the fatigue that clawed at her from head to toe. From the awfulness of the lab attacks. And from a heart-pounding combination, equal parts terror and fury, that Gray could've been injured. So. Many. Times.

"I'll help you down," Gray ordered after he'd hopped out.

"I can get out on my own—"

Except she couldn't. Every limb shook, and the tears were close to overwhelming her ability to contain them. A hot lump lodged in her throat, but Isa couldn't swallow the knot, because even that act might break the dam wall.

And damn it, Gray knew. He opened the door and helped her down. The fury that had tightened his expression for the last hour still tugged hard at his eyes and lips. She wasn't adding to his stress now, so she shut her mouth and focused on staying upright as he helped her down.

"Take care," Tank said from the driver's seat. Sympathy radiated in his expression.

"Thank you," Isa squeezed out, past the tightness in her throat.

"Liaise with the locals," Gray ordered Tank. "I'll provide a statement later, but I want an ID on all shooters. And remember, Cyn's undercover, so keep the fact you dropped us here off record. As far as anyone knows, we've headed back to the apartment."

"Yes, boss."

"Come on," Gray bit out. As he ushered her through the alleyway, he crowded her so close she couldn't see a damn thing. A red door opened before either of them could knock, and Gray pushed her inside, then slammed it behind them, encasing them in darkness.

Isa reached out a shaking hand to steady herself, found a wall. Once her eyes adjusted, she made out a neon red skull glowing at the end of a long, skinny corridor.

"Steady." Gray grasped her shoulders, and she sank into his hold.

"I'm okay." Isa shrugged his hands off when she had her balance. *Stand on your own two feet, Isa.* While she could, anyway. "Just tired."

"Well, that wasn't as pissy as before. So either you're even more tired than you look, or you're not angry anymore."

"Of course, I'm still pissed at you. But first—why is it so dark?"

"Zero idea," he replied in that icy, controlled voice that she hated more than his pissed-off tone. "Cyn let us in, but we can't proceed further until she disengages the next lock —it's a motion sensor combination tech-and-spell ward lock. Now, what's going on? Why are you angry?"

"Me?" Isa whirled around. "Oh, I'll tell you why I'm pissed off. Don't worry about that. But you go first. You're icier than your normal glacier self and don't deny it."

"In case you've forgotten, they almost killed you today. Multiple times. Reason enough, don't you think? Now your turn."

"Don't BS me, Gray. I've been *almost killed* plenty of times before, and you weren't this angry."

"People died at the lab who were just doing their jobs because those fuckers back there didn't give a shit and gunned them down. That pissed me off. I need to find fucking R-104B, and instead, I'm running around keeping you out of bounty hunters' hands. That also pisses me off.

And I just killed—I think—the one freaking person who has the antidote in case we can't cure your poisoning. And *that* is the piss-me-off trifecta. So yes, I'm angry. But I'm also fucking furious that you could've died today, Isa. So many fucking times. I'm beyond words speechless with how angry that makes me."

"Oh." Isa stopped and stared. He'd never been so ... open before.

"Hell." His sigh brushed over her. "Sorry. I shouldn't have—"

"No, no, you're allowed to get angry, Gray. Everyone is. Thanks for being honest with me."

"Shit. I yell and swear, and you say thank you?" He shook his head. "And for the record, no, I don't get angry. Anger does zero to help the situation. It makes people react in less than controlled conditions and is my absolute least desired position."

"Well, this is another point where you and I disagree. Because I'm all about the emotion. And to be clear—right now, I'm angry at the pricks, too. And at you."

"Me?"

"Yes, you. Grayson No-Bloody-Last-Name."

"Hold on. What've I done?"

"*You* almost died, too." She couldn't stop herself from jabbing a finger into his chest. "Those people who attacked us—they weren't trying to kill me. They were after *you*, and the relic—"

The words of the gunmen in the lab came back to her.

"What?" Gray asked. "Are you okay?"

"Yes, I mean, no. I'm shaky and angry, and I really don't want to fall flat on my face. But I just remembered what those men said—the ones you killed."

"Tell me."

"The first one said something about Forneous. He attacked Raph, too, right?"

"Fuck. What else did they say?"

"That they should just get out anyway because the myrrh wasn't there. Gray, they were there for the myrrh—not me, after all."

"So R-104B *was* there. Hell. How close were we? Okay, Marcella already hacked their network to open the door. I'll get her to do it again and search their records."

"Damn," Isa said. "So Kai really is involved."

"Somehow, yes. But the one piece of good news in this morning's fucked-up-ness is that Forneous doesn't have R-104B."

"Well, good to have one thing go right. Now about why *I'm* pissed—"

"Still?"

"Yes! You manhandled me back there, Gray. And then you put yourself between the bounty hunter and me when you know they're not out to kill me." Damn, maybe she should tell Gray about her death vision. What if he got hurt trying to protect her?

Her entire being shuddered at that thought.

"Isa, this is my job. There is no fucking universe that exists where I will not take action if you're being attacked. And I can't just stop and say, 'excuse me, would you mind if I put you out of harm's way?' No freaking way. And you're wasting your energy getting angry with me over that, because zero is going to change."

And that was why she couldn't tell him. If he knew about the death vision ... about the possibility of crossing over and becoming a daemon ... he'd decide for her in a heartbeat if he thought it would save her life. He'd said it right here.

The fatigue dragging at her mind sank its claws in deep, and Isa sagged against the wall.

"Shit. You're out on your feet."

"Because I wasn't leaving you and Marcie unprotected while you were protecting me. At least awake, I might have another vision if someone else was coming at us."

"Isa, that's our job. We're Templars—"

"Well, hello, you two. Still arguing, I see." Cyn's beautiful voice floated up the corridor. "I disengaged the locks. To what do I owe this visit?"

"Hey," Isa muttered.

"About time, Cyn," Gray bit out. "You heard what happened at the SJC lab? Triulf followed us there from the apartment. It's a compromised location for Isa as of now."

"Where's the rest of the team?"

"Marcella's wrapping up at the vault now. She'll stay at the apartment and run point between us and the police on the incident."

Incident. Isa shook her head. How could he be so ... cold about what had happened? The echo of the screams and gunshots and the smell of the air ... She shivered.

"Can you walk?" Gray said in a low voice as he reached for her arm.

"What's wrong?" Cyn asked. "Are you injured? Is it the poison?"

"Just tired." Isa pushed him away, but he re-secured his arm around her.

"Stop pushing me away. The adrenaline will wear off soon, so you'll be extra shaky. Let me, us, help. You did your job, now let me do mine. Cyn, do you really have to keep this place so dark?"

"It's called ambiance. I'm a high priestess. My customers need to feel the gravitas of the moment and all that." She went around to Isa's other side. "I'll help too. I'd love to know what your job is, Divine One."

"Just Isa."

"Hell, no. If I had a title like that, I'd be using it."

"Hell's right. And all I did was the visions. Gray did the ..." Her voice trailed off.

"I did the killing," Gray said.

"Standard stuff, then." Cyn nodded. "Sounds like you two make a good team."

As they shuffled down the corridor, Gray filled Cyn in on the attack at the lab, the myrrh.

"That's why we're here," Gray said. "With the apartment location compromised, I thought it best to come to you directly."

"Is that real?" Isa blinked at the skull.

"As real as it gets." Cyn touched something on the wall behind the grisly bones, and the wall slid open to reveal a windowless room that looked like a witchy ultra-luxe dominatrix boudoir. There was a red velvet chaise, shelves filled with crystals, jars with ... things in them, a wall with whips and chains, and a sideboard with candles and knives.

"Welcome to my place of business."

"Wow," Isa breathed out as they entered. "I like this."

"Where to?" Gray asked.

"Through the door at the end—that's my bedroom."

Isa was still cataloguing the fascinating room when Gray led the way into the next space. A giant bed filled the far end, with a reading chair and a square timber coffee table opposite it. There was also a small dining table with one chair and then an entire wall filled with tech equipment and computers.

"You've got a full apartment, right here," Isa said. Still no windows, though. She held back a shudder. "Do you live here?"

"Nope," Cyn replied. "This is my crash pad. Some spells take a long time to complete, and I like my full comforts while I'm working. Now, I have a meeting in ten minutes with a contact about your poison, so I'll reset the wards and locks as I leave. Just stay here and you'll be fine. Isa, use my bed. Gray, standard Templar tech, so you can use all the equipment as you need. There's a full bath through there as well."

"Got it," Gray said. "And thanks, Cyn."

"Coolio. See you soon."

Isa didn't wait around to be told twice. The firm mattress sank comfortably around her, and a yawn overtook her.

"Hell, you're almost out," Gray said. "Here, let me look at those scrapes."

"What about you? We hit the pavement together."

"I'm fine."

"Come on. You took the brunt of my fall. You're not sore at all? Is this some Templar magic thingy?"

"No, smartass. And fine. I'm a *bit* sore. But I'm two times as big as you."

"I'm not that small. I might be short, but I'm strong."

"Never said you weren't."

Isa snorted. "You don't have to say it. It's been obvious since I first met you."

"Fine. I'm bigger than you are. But I'm okay. I'll be uncomfortable and bruised, max."

She held his stare. "Then I'm the same."

"I hate it when you do that."

"What?"

"Tilt your chin like you're waving a flag at the world

shouting *'warning: mind made up and don't even attempt to change it.'*"

"I'm not that bad." Isa eased to her back. "See, I'm even lying down."

"Hate to keep you awake any longer." He nodded at her cheek and arm. "But those are deeper than I realized. They need to be looked at before you go to sleep. Want me to do it?"

She groaned and forced herself to sit up. "Maybe I could just have a little sleep now and do the whole plasters thing later ..."

"Sorry, Isa. This won't take long, though." Gray opened a cupboard in the kitchenette. "Standard operating procedure is to keep a basic first aid kit beneath the sink."

"Good to know." She couldn't stop another yawn from rolling through her as she swung her legs from the bed. "I'll do it. I should use the bathroom, anyway."

"You sure?"

No, she wasn't. But she was doing it, anyway.

As soon as the bathroom door closed, she leaned on the vanity to keep herself upright. Damn, but she was a mess. Screw it. She barely had the energy to do the plasters, let alone worry about her appearance.

Isa ripped open the first plaster, and as she did, the *crack crack crack* of gunshots replayed through her mind, followed by the screams echoing through the lab.

Her heart took off.

Shit. She sank onto the toilet and forced herself to step through her panic attack process. Eventually, the counting overtook the memory of those sounds.

Maybe she could just sit here and fall asleep?

"You okay in there?" Gray asked.

She hauled in a breath. "Uh-uh," she lied with as much energy as she could muster.

By the time she'd cleaned up the scrapes and taped plasters over the worst of them, she barely made it out of the bathroom. Thankfully Gray said nothing else, but he still hovered close by as she shuffled each step, as if he knew exactly how close she was to falling flat on her face.

"Thanks," she muttered when she was horizontal once again. As her eyes closed, she gave in to the one little urge she couldn't get rid of. "Can I ask one more thing?"

"You can ask."

"Always so guarded." She didn't even have the energy to roll her eyes. "Can you sit with me? Here on the bed? Those screams ... the gunshots ... they're replaying in my mind. But it stops when you're close. Just until I'm asleep?"

For a moment, he said nothing. Had she asked too much? Then the bed dipped beneath his weight. His warm scent settled around her.

"Sure thing, Issi."

18

ISA WOKE up under the bedspread and to the immediate sensation of being watched. Not in a hair-creeping-at-the-back-of-her-neck way, but an awareness that someone whose regard she enjoyed had their eyes on her at that very moment.

Gray.

A lone lamp lit the corner of the room where her Templar sat in the reading chair, his laptop open on the coffee table, but his gaze on her.

As Isa sat up, the bedspread fell to her waist. Goosebumps rippled over her bare stomach, chest, and shoulders. No wonder. She only wore her plain black sports bra. She lifted the cover. Well, she was wearing panties too, so that was something.

She left the blanket over her lap and legs and met the gaze boring into her from across the room. "What time is it?"

"Almost five. You've been asleep for three hours," Gray said in that low, raspy tone that made a different awareness ripple over her skin.

"What about you—did you get any rest, or have you been locked to the laptop?"

"I'm fine."

Of course he was. "So, was it Cyn or you who took my clothes off?"

"Both of us." Gray winced. "You were whimpering in your sleep, and when we checked you out, you had more skin scraped off along your side and over your shoulder that we didn't see earlier." He put his laptop aside. "There's food if you're hungry, and Cyn said to have a shower and use anything you need in there."

"Bathroom first." She hopped out of bed—aware the moment his gaze dropped away from her without looking at him.

"Your clothes were pretty messed up, so Cyn's getting you something new. She has a robe in there you can use until she gets back," he called through the door.

Sure enough, a full-length, deep-plum swathe of silky material hung off a hook on the wall. Isa took her time in the shower, and after the day from hell, passed on re-wearing her underwear. At least she had Cyn's robe. The silk was cool and light, and Isa couldn't help but smooth her hands over the beautiful material.

When she returned, Gray's attention was on the laptop. A mug with steam curling up into the dark sat on the dining table.

"You need hydration, so start with that." He nodded without looking up. "It's chamomile."

"Thank you." A kernel of warmth unfurled in her chest. She sat on the chair and took a sip.

Ah, she needed that. She rolled her neck and shoulders. Huh. The soreness was gone.

"Can't believe how deeply I slept after ..." She shook her head. "I can't even put into words how terrible today was."

Gray finally glanced at her. "You were exhausted, banged up, and witnessed some awful shit go down. And remember, I jacked you up with adrenaline. That alone would make you crash hard."

"I've never used adrenaline before."

"I did some research while you were out, and it's not a good idea to do it again. Plus, you still crashed. It only held it off for half an hour."

"At least I don't feel as bad as when we got here. Even the scrapes feel better."

"That's probably because Cyn did a healing spell."

"She did? Wait—doesn't she require a sacrifice for her magic?"

He held up his arm. A plaster covered the vein on the inside of his elbow.

"You bled for me?" Isa put her mug down and moved to sit on the coffee table beside his laptop. "How much?"

"Doesn't matter."

"Yes, it does." She searched his face—had no idea what she was looking for. But the mask of cool indifference wasn't it. "You made a sacrifice so I'd feel better when I woke up. That's not a small thing, Gray."

He sighed and met her gaze. Finally, something simmered in his eyes—a heat and depth that called to an answering fire inside her.

"Isa," he murmured. "I'm learning there's not a lot I wouldn't do for you."

He should look tired, but the ever-present strength in his jaw and eyes, the pure brutal force of his personality, rang strong still.

She took a deep breath—and as she did, Gray's gaze

dropped from her face to her breasts. Her nipples tightened. Color hit high on his cheeks, and he jerked his gaze back to his laptop.

After everything that happened—the death, the violence, the certainty of fate coming for her no matter what —one thing flowed through Isa with utter certainty.

She wanted Gray.

Right here and now, she had a chance—maybe her only chance ever—to be with the man from her dreams in real life.

"So ... how long did Cyn say we're here for?" She trailed a finger over his hand. Up his thumb, back down, and then across each of his fingers. His skin warmed under her touch.

"Three more hours." He shifted his hand. But his gaze prowled over her before returning to his laptop. The low heat simmering in her belly shot to a boil.

"Maybe there's a way to spend those three hours." She shifted closer. Stroked her bare foot up his calf.

"Isa." He snapped his laptop shut.

"What?" She let herself smirk. That little emotion ... ah, but she loved seeing him react. "I'm just here, a woman in a silk robe, rubbing a man's calf with her foot." She gave a little shrug. The robe dipped low over her shoulder. His eyes tracked the movement.

"You're distracting me."

"About time."

He leaned forward and grasped her hips. A dangerous tilt curled his lips. "Diviner, what are you after?"

Diviner.

"Well, Ace, I'm after this." Isa pushed him back and ran her foot right up his leg to his thigh. Kept going until she toed the hard, thick bulge in his pants.

Hot damn, Grayson No-Last-Name. Her body dampened. *At a frigging toe nudge.*

He inhaled sharply, then his normal cool expression slid into place. She was going to delight in stripping that away.

"I didn't think ... this ... was on your mind." He nodded between them.

"Grayson No-Last-Name, *this* has been on my mind since I first saw you." She almost added, *and that was years and years ago.* "And 'this' means sex. Full-on penetration, orgasm-inducing sex. Is this clear enough?"

"Clarity's important." His gaze locked on her shoulder—why? Ah, the silky robe had dipped lower.

"Is there any other reason we can't do this?" Isa asked.

"I'm working."

"What on?"

His gaze traveled from her shoulder to her neck and down the line of skin exposed by the parted robe.

"Well?" she nudged him with her knee.

"St. James. The team are working up a surveillance plan."

"Are they expecting an answer from you in the next ... fifteen minutes?"

"Fifteen?"

"I don't want to take you away from your work any longer than absolutely necessary."

"They'll report back in an hour."

"Wow. An entire hour." Things were looking positive then. Just a couple more hurdles to get over. "So, is there anything else you need to do right now?"

"Keep an eye on you," he rasped.

"Are we in any danger? This very second?"

His turbulent eyes deepened, giving her the answer.

Her pulse picked up, and in a fluid motion she stood and

straddled him. The confines of the chair meant she squished in nice and tight, and she hissed when his body brushed exactly the right place.

"One more question," she whispered.

"What's that?"

"How do I seduce you?"

"*Issi.* You already have." He cradled her cheeks, then drew her down and captured her lips with his.

There was no soft melding or easy tasting.

He owned her mouth. His tongue surged inside, and a pool of heat drenched her core.

She grasped his hands and met his tongue with hers. They tangled, stroked. She gasped for air and went back for more. His taste filled her mouth. His scent filled her lungs. Heat and spice and ... Grayson.

Isa pressed harder against him. His hands left her cheeks to skim down her neck, over her shoulders. Down and up her arms.

Goosebumps followed where he swept.

Then he drew in a shaking breath, and withdrew, pressed his forehead to hers.

"What?" she whispered.

"Nothing. Just need to ..." He skimmed the side of her torso, his fingers grazed the swell of her breasts. Her nipples tightened. The heat in her core grew. She shifted to give him more access.

A groan vibrated through him, and everything inside her quickened.

Then his lips followed the trail his hands had left. Feather touches along her jaw. Across the hollow of her neck. The sensitive point where her pulse beat.

Please, please suck there. Suck hard and long. Soothe the pres-

sure between her legs. But he ran his tongue so lightly over that flesh, every nerve flashed.

She turned her neck to the side, tried to bring him back to that point—

He blew over her skin; then his mouth trailed over her collarbone and down her chest.

Fine. Her breasts. He could suck her there—but he just pressed a kiss to the flesh exposed by the opening in her robe.

"Gray." His fingers traced a line to her navel. Her muscles contracted, and he did it again before he trailed back up her sternum, across to her breast, around her nipple ... please, please, this time—his trail continued back up her other side.

"Gray!" She grabbed his hand.

His eyes were heavy-lidded as he raised his gaze to hers. "Mm?"

"I'm not weak," she whispered. She lifted her chin and stared him down. "I. Am. Not. Weak."

"I never thought you were," he said, his voice hoarse.

"Then why are you treating me like a piece of glass that's going to shatter if you hold me too tightly? I *want* to shatter. Right now. With you inside me. On me. Around me. Fucking me so hard, you're all I feel. That's what I want. So, Grayson I-Still-Have-No-Idea-What-Your-Last-Name-Is, what do you want?"

Gray ran his hands up her side, and she shivered under his large, hot, calloused hands. But his eyes locked on hers, and flames rose to burn right in his gaze.

His lips pulled back tight, and his nostrils flared. "Want?" The word sounded guttural, torn from him. "Minx, I want you so fucking much. I want to imprint myself on you. I want you to wear my mark, so everyone knows you've been with me. I want to dive into you and not come up for air for a day. A month. Hell, a year. I want to eat you out and lick you up, and I want to be inside every single part of you. My cock is so hard I'm going to come just putting it in you. And I don't want easy, I don't want slow. I want full throttle. To pound into your body and make you scream. I want to touch the heavens with you. *That's* what I want."

Isa's body flooded, and it was all she could do not to dissolve into a puddle right there. She tried to speak—but his words had dried her mouth, so she did the only thing she could.

She grabbed her handbag and rummaged through it, and slammed down a pack of ten condoms on the table. Found her voice.

"Give it to me like that."

"*Isa*. I'm not a gentle lover. I like it hard and when it comes to sex, I'm in control." His lips pulled tight. "Do you really want that?"

Her core throbbed so hard she almost whimpered. Hard? Yes, please. But apparently, Gray needed convincing.

She stepped back and dropped the robe. Kept walking back until the bed hit her legs, then reclined on the cover. Parted her thighs.

"I'm so wet for you right now," Isa said. "I could come from your words alone. But that's not what I want. I want your dick inside me. I want your body around me. And yes, give it to me hard." She stared him down. "Now, you're still all the way over there. What more are you waiting for?"

19

WHAT WAS HE WAITING FOR? Just to get his damned body under control so he wouldn't leap at Isa and devour her in one bite.

Hell. This was bad. So fucking bad. He glanced at the surveillance feeds.

"Stop overthinking," Isa said.

"Are you serious? Overthinking is my job," he snapped. "It's impossible for me not to overthink things." The locks were set. Wards in place. The feeds were live and clear.

Could he do this? Not should he do this, because no fricking question there ... everything about Isa turned him on so fucking much, tempted him to the point she'd been all he could think of every goddamn day for the last week. The very first kiss back on her couch haunted his dreams. But in his dreams, the kiss wasn't the end of it—he was between her legs and surging into her, owning her—

"Gray." She laughed, and goosebumps skittered over him. "I'm lying here naked. I couldn't be any more serious."

And so fucking good.

Desire hammered through his blood. Exactly like he wanted to hammer into Isa.

She inhaled and her breasts rose. Holy mother of the gods. Talk about perfection. High breasts tipped with dusky nipples. Curves at her hips. And miles and miles of that skin that made his mouth water to lick and taste and bite and suck.

And if there was any blood left in his body, it flew to his dick because he was so hard he'd have a zipper imprint from his fly for the rest of his life.

Gray was at the edge of the bed before he even realized he'd moved. He undid his belt. Ripped through the buttons and yanked it off. Pulled his shirt up and over his head. Threw it somewhere.

Isa's gaze traveled over his abs. Locked on the ink covering his pecs.

He kicked off his pants and his trunks.

Her eyes dropped to his cock, flared. She hummed. And hell if that didn't make the blood surge through his veins even hotter.

Gray palmed himself, and his cock, already primed, jerked in his grasp.

"Isadora, I need to ..." He stared at her breasts. Those tips called for his lips.

"Yes?" She inhaled. And before she could exhale, he'd lunged forward and sucked her nipple into his mouth.

Her moan echoed around the room, and then she pressed her hands into his hair, held him. He rolled his tongue around the velvety nub. His balls tightened, and he ran his palm over the tip of her other breast. Groaned as it pebbled against his skin.

"Closer, Gray. I need to be closer." Her hand ran between them, and she grabbed his cock, slid her grip up his length, then rubbed the pad of her thumb over the head. Spread a bead of precum over him.

Shivers shot up the base of his cock, and he jerked in her grip.

"Fuck." How could one touch be both heaven and hell? He rolled his hips to dislodge her grasp.

"Wait, I want to do this."

"Yeah, and I want to last more than one freaking second."

Isa's lips curved in the hottest smile ever as she knelt at the edge of the bed and grabbed his hips. He had zero clue what gods he'd pleased to be right here, right now, with this woman, but he muttered a thanks to them all as she swept her hand over him again.

"But I've been wanting to get up close to your package for an age." She licked her lips. "Come on, Ace. Let me take you to the edge."

"Isa, *you* are one hell of a package," he ground out when she pumped his cock again.

"Well, thank you. That's another compliment I'll take."

"There's something else you're about to take." He lifted her, flipped her onto her back. "Game time's over. I'm so close to coming, baby, but I need to make this good for you. Need you to take me. Are you ready?"

Her eyes shone with that fucking mysterious gleam of hers, and then she lifted her chin, stared him down like a queen ordering her subject, and nodded.

"Make me come, Gray. That's an order."

And hell if he didn't love her sass. Like he was about to love her pussy. "Glad you like orders. You're about to get a few."

He shifted down her body, grasped her thighs and held her wide. Then he licked up her seam. Hot musk hit him hard. Had him go back for more, and this time, he tongued her deeply. Isa's back arched off the bed and her breath caught.

He swept his tongue back up and swirled it around her clit.

"Tell me—do you come from penetration, the clit, both?" He sucked hard on the nub of flesh. She gasped and bucked against him. "Tell me, my little Divine One. How do you come?" He blew against her. Isa hissed and her hands jammed in his hair. "Tell me." He sucked her clit again.

"Both. But definitely—there!"

"Good girl." He licked her again, ran his tongue over and over her flesh until she was grinding against his mouth. Then he eased one finger, two inside her. Her inner muscles contracted around him. "Fuck, your pussy is wet. You're going to feel so good around my cock. But right now, come for me, minx."

He thrust his fingers into her over and over as he sucked on her clit.

Her breath hitched. Her body tensed under his hands and mouth. Her back arched off the bed again.

"Holy—Gray, I'm coming!"

Her body clamped on his fingers. Heat and wet silk flowed over them. She let out a keening gasp and convulsed in his arms.

⸨⦿⸩

Isa caught her breath as the last tiny pinpricks of sensation careened through her body. Her heart raced. Heat blanketed her limbs. And her core still hummed from the explosion Gray had detonated inside her.

Somehow, she raised her head.

And her breath seized in her lungs.

His mouth pulled tight. His gaze locked on her core. Then Gray licked his lips, and his eyes darkened with a dangerous edge that shot an entirely new thrill through her.

"My turn now." He ripped a condom packet open and rolled the sheath over his dick.

Heat flooded her all over again.

Then he prowled up her body until he loomed above her. With the dim light throwing shadows across him, the fierce glow in his eyes, the savage need pouring off him, he could've been scary. But this moment embedded in her soul as another experience to be captured.

She'd paint him wild and on the edge of control with fire burning in his eyes. Ridges of charcoal for his brutal energy. Gunmetal slashes at the danger lurking beneath the façade he presented to the world. Obsidian streaks for the hard core of this man.

Her own personal shades of Gray.

"What do you see?" he rasped.

"You." Isa wrapped one hand around his neck and lifted herself to kiss him. Tasted herself before he growled and then dominated her mouth. His lips demanded she open up. His tongue surged inside. Stroking. Filling.

And even though she'd just come harder than ever before, hot tension coiled through her again.

Then he grabbed her hips, dragged her to the edge of the bed, and stood over her.

Oh holy gods, this man was perfection. Isa might be the daemon here, but he was the god of the shadows, with the hulking body, tattoos inked over his chest and shoulders. Dark hair tapering in a vee. Ropes of muscles upon muscles, carved and gleaming with sweat.

Her mouth watered and she reached out to trace that arrow of hair—

"No touching." He batted her hand away.

"But—"

"Minx, I'm already on the edge." His jaw clenched. "Don't move one fucking inch." He ducked down to the jumble of his clothes and pulled the belt out of his pants, then tossed it beside her.

"Gray?" A thrill raced through her.

"Do you trust me?"

"Yes." She didn't hesitate.

"Good. Give me your hands. No. Don't ask why. I'm the boss, remember?" He drew her arms back above her head. "Now, stay."

Isa twisted to watch as he picked up the belt and looped the ends through a bedpost at the head of the bed, then yanked it on hard.

"Perfect. Hold these." He placed the ends in her hands.

"Why?"

"Because." He lifted her hips to his, splayed her wide, and fitted himself to her core. "I'm going to last all of one minute with your hands on me. So pull on the belt every time you get the urge to touch me."

She wrapped her legs around him and moaned when he nudged at her entrance.

"Issi, is that a yes?"

"Yes!"

"Thank fuck." Gray's muscles bunched, and his teeth clenched as he pushed inside deeper. An unending progression that filled her. Stretched her. Set every nerve alight. "Take me, Issi," he growled. "Take every. Single. Part. Of me." His hips flexed, and he seated himself all the way inside her.

Gods," she gasped, and tugged on the belt. Her back arched off the bed.

"That's it, baby. Shh, I'm in. Now, you ready?"

She opened eyes she hadn't realized were closed. And every part of her lit up. His arms trembled. His massive chest and shoulders strained.

"Ready?" She licked her lips, wiggled to find some ... ease ... from the unceasing pressure inside her. Then moaned as more sensation erupted.

Gray hissed and grabbed her hips. "Stop that. You're mine for this hour, right? This is my show now."

He let go of her hips with one hand and ran it up to her breast. Ran around and around one nipple, then the other. Fire arced from her breast to her core, and Isa undulated against him.

"Shit," he groaned. Then he swatted her hip. "No moving."

"At all? I thought it was just my hands. You're batshit."

"I'm also in charge. You move—I stop. And we have ... forty-five minutes left."

Isa laughed. "Always the boss. All right, Ace, I'm all yours."

"Yes, yes, you are." That wicked light entered his eyes, and then his hands went back to holding her thighs high off the bed, and he withdrew in one long slow glide—and then thrust back into her.

Nerves screamed. Tension coiled.

Gray did it again. The pressure climbed.

Again. Her body wound tighter.

Then he growled. His teeth ground. And with a groan, he surged faster, harder. The coil of tension twisted.

"Isa," he growled. "Yes, yes, yes."

Oh, holy shit— "Don't stop!" she gasped. She arched, pulled on the belt with everything she had.

"Fucking gods," he roared.

And the tension exploded into a million shattered pieces, obliterated the rest of the world as sensation coursed through her nerves, every limb. Every single part of her.

Long minutes later, Isa hauled in a shuddering breath and opened her eyes. Gray withdrew—her body shivered at the internal caress—then her hips dropped to the bed. He got rid of the condom, then was back in a flash and crashed beside her.

His incredible body took up most of the space, but she didn't care.

With her blood still humming, and Gray for real beside her, this was perfection.

(((●)))

"You moved," Gray muttered before he pressed a kiss to her shoulder. Isa turned her head to face him. And his heart clenched in his chest. Gods, she was fine. Cheeks flushed, dark hair a shining, curly mess. Lips red. Eyes gleaming.

"And you didn't need forty-five minutes," she purred.

"Is that a complaint, oh Divine One?"

"Divine One?" She did the nose wrinkle thing. And the clenching in his chest spread.

"As in your level, diviner-one."

Divine as in holy fucking special, because she was that and more. But Gray held that back and instead pressed another kiss to her shoulder. The delicate skin inside her elbow. The freckle on the underside of her wrist. Inhaled the intoxicating scent of Isa and cinnamon that made his mouth water and sent his blood simmering again.

"Already?" Isa's eyes darkened, and she glanced down his body.

"What can I say? You gave me an hour. Apparently, my cock is prepared to make the most of every single second."

"In that case ..." She laughed, and the sound made him smile. "Come on, Ace." She jumped to her feet. "Frig, but it's cold."

"I can warm you up."

"You better."

She danced into the bathroom, and the bounce of her butt cheeks lit an entirely new fire in him, and he registered zero cold as he grabbed the pack of nine condoms—a man could dream, couldn't he?—and followed her in.

20

GRAY WOKE up to the sensation of something changed—as if the air had rearranged itself. As was his norm, the fog of sleep gave way to instant clarity, and he pressed a kiss into Isa's dark hair before he could stop himself. Isa's cheek lay on his chest, one arm stretched across his belly, and her breasts warmed his side.

Pure. Fucking. Heaven.

Except for the fact they were being spied on.

"How sweet," Cyn crooned softly from the doorway.

"Spying is rude, you know," he whispered.

"Hey, you're in my bed. How's that spying? And don't tell me you didn't know I was there."

"Of course I did. Not a Templar for nothing. Now, shh. Don't want to wake her up."

"Too late," Isa murmured. He tightened his arm around her.

"Sorry," he muttered.

"What for? Too many orgasms to count? Or the excellent pillow of your chest?" Isa's lips curved against his chest, and his body hardened all over again.

"Ew," Cyn groaned. "TMI, thank you very much. Now, if you'd both like to get dressed, I've got something to try for Isa's antidote." She sent him a bland look, but held his stare for an extra second.

"Be right there." Gray checked his alarm. "Eight p.m. Next dose in three and a half hours."

"And Isa, I got you a change of clothes, but just pull on the underwear for now. Also, this spell needs to be done on completely clean skin." Cyn raised one brow. "I suggest a shower first."

"I'm up for that," Isa said, grinning up at him.

His cock hardened. Apparently, he was also up for a shower.

"While I'd like to be in that shower with you"—major fucking understatement—"I need to talk to Cyn about our next move."

"Okay," Isa said. "Your loss."

Yes, it fucking was.

"What is it?" Gray said as he joined Cyn back in her shop. "Can you do the spell for Isa?"

"Yeah, I'm ready. But that's not all. An update just came through from the council."

"Thanks." He grabbed his laptop and opened it on the reading table. "Holy hell," he whispered after he'd read the report. "Isa got it right. The club *was* the right place to be."

Dread filled his gut, and he clenched his fists to stop from punching the table. This was bad. As bad as it got. And instead of working to fucking find R-104B, he'd been fucking Isa instead.

"What do you mean?" Cyn asked.

"Remember the drug sample I took from the club? It has a distinct chemical marker linking it to R-104B."

"As in—*our* myrrh?"

"Yes. Fucking hell. Not only is that dangerous as hell for anyone ingesting the synthesized chemical, but that means someone has accessed the seeds, not just the resin inside." And by the gods, what if they'd cultivated one of those seeds? "Fuck. Fuck, fuck, *fuck*."

"What's wrong?" Isa's question had him turn around. She'd pulled her shiny hair into a high pony and had Cyn's silky robe on again.

"Nothing." This was need to know only, and right now, Isa did not need to know this part. He ignored his fellow Templar's look. "Cyn's ready to do the spell, right?"

"Sure. Right. But heads up, this spell will take a long time. And because of how I make magic, it requires a blood sacrifice."

"I'll do it." Gray rolled up his sleeve.

"No way," Isa said. "You've already bled once for me. I'll do it this time."

Cyn gave him a tight smile. "Actually, for the best effect, it needs to be Isa. This is a big spell I'm attempting, and the strongest sacrifice comes from those who benefit most."

"What's the process?" Isa asked softly.

"I'm making an unguent—a sort of thick lotion—with your blood, and then you'll have to rub it on yourself. I can't touch it. The catch is that it might be a bit, ah, painful."

"Is it dangerous?" Isa asked.

Gray glanced at Isa. How was she taking all this? But her gaze was squarely on Cyn.

"Not to you. But it won't be fun."

"So where does it go?"

"The seven major energy points," Cyn replied. "Crown, forehead, heart, solar plexus, stomach and groin."

"So everywhere."

"Don't worry, I'll talk you through that part to make sure

you get it right. Then it's a matter of time, letting the magic engage the poison. That part might take hours."

"Good thing I used the loo, then."

"Not the time for levity," Gray growled. He shoved a hand through his hair. "This is serious."

"You think I don't know that?" Isa stood up. "I'm one hundred percent aware of how critical this spell is. So keeping myself calm—and so I don't freak out on Cyn—I chose to take a moment for some levity. No, stuff the stuffy speak. I'm calling it humor. I *choose* to find a little lightness in this crap. Now. I'll be back in a few minutes. I want to use the bathroom again. You can sit here and stay, Mr. Serious."

Gray stared at Isa as she disappeared into the bedroom.

"Down, boy," Cyn murmured.

He snorted. "I haven't been down around Isa since the moment I first saw her."

"That's obvious."

"I just don't get how she's so ... so ... easy about all this. She says she gets how important this is, but then she makes jokes."

"Grayson, Isa is way stronger than you—or I—realized. Don't underestimate her, and don't mistake her choosing to find the light side of shit a sign of not respecting, or understanding, the gravity."

Hell. "Fine. The sooner we get Isa done, the sooner I can focus on R-104B."

"Take a seat at the reading table. Or you can stay in the bedroom so you don't get in the way."

Gray restrained a snort. Isa was about to undertake a painful—dangerous, no matter what Cyn said—spell. Not even a high priestess with mad skills could make him leave this room.

His diviner returned in moments, but she refused to

look at him, so he pretended to focus on his laptop and forced himself to ignore the thought of her in any pain.

(((◆)))

Isa's heart thumped so hard she had to take a deep breath to stop it from flying from her chest as Cyn set up candles in a five-point star in the middle of the wooden floor and placed a crystal orb at its top and a small animal skull at its bottom.

"Where do you want me?" Isa asked.

"Take off the robe and sit in the middle of the candles. Eventually you'll be lying on the floor—and this will take roughly an hour, so you'll get uncomfortable pretty soon."

"If you can help me with this poison, I'd lie on hot coals right now."

"Well, it'll be hot. So, next step. I'm going to draw blood from a vein, and I'll use a needle and syringe to fill a vial."

"No worries." Isa shrugged off the robe, folded it up on the chaise.

Gray was studying his laptop, and his gaze never strayed to her once. Way to make a girl feel sexy. But then—he'd already seen it, so maybe he'd had his fun and didn't want to see it again?

Something soured in her belly, but she and Gray weren't a couple. And he was perfectly within his—icehole—rights if he didn't want to have sex with her again. Even if sex with him had been out of this world. And even if her body was already yearning for more of those orgasms. Of *him*.

That was the scary part. It wasn't just her physical being that connected to Gray's; the deep attraction that drew her to him like a moth to a flame had grown too strong and she felt every shift in his guarded gaze, every twitch of his tense muscles.

It was as if he'd branded a piece of her, and forevermore, a part of her would belong to him.

"Well, hopefully, this will be the last time," Cyn said, thankfully oblivious to where Isa's thoughts had gone. "Sit there. I'll kneel beside you and conduct the spell from here."

Isa eased to the floorboards, and a shiver trickled down her back.

"You okay?" Cyn asked.

"Sure. Just cool down here. And it's a fascinating view of your shop. How do you not have any dust here?"

"Magic." Cyn smiled. "Okay, for the spell, I'm going to pour salt in a circle around us—just to be safe in case anyone's tracking my magic, not that it's likely. Gray, once the salt circle is cast, you can't step over—not for any reason. No matter what you see or hear, you do not cross. Got it?"

Isa glanced up as Gray's gaze cut to her. Something turbulent washed through his eyes—but whatever it was, he shut it down and ducked back to his laptop.

"Why does that sound bad?" Isa lifted her head as Cyn poured the last of the salt and closed the circle.

"You'll be fine. Standard spell safety tip. Now, once I'm casting the spell, you might be in more discomfort. But I'm going to spell you to sleep while the cure spell does its thing, because you don't want to be awake for that. In fact, you might fight it, which in theory would be even worse."

"Shit, Cyn," Gray growled from the reading table. "In theory?"

"First-time spell for me, remember?" Cyn gave her a tight smile. "But I've got this, Isa. And so do you. New spell and all."

"Thanks for reminding me." Lead-winged butterflies

fluttered in her belly. She twisted the ring Cyn had given her. "Okay, I'm ready."

"Then it's blood taking time. Here goes."

Isa didn't flinch at the tiny prick in her arm. What a fascinating process. Cyn injected Isa's blood into a stone bowl, then poured in the poison, and last, dripped wax from a candle into the mix.

Then she took a pestle and mixed them all together as she whispered, *"Blood and poison, here combine. Add the wax, count in time. Mix the rub, re-entwine. Negate the toxin, blood refine."*

"Isa, dip your forefinger and middle finger into the mix. You want to spread two lines, thickness doesn't matter, starting at your forehead."

Please let this be okay. Isa inhaled deeply and exhaled it in one long, even breath. She had this. She could do this.

21

GRAY'S GUT churned as he sat at the small dining table while Isa lay in Cyn's bed. "How much longer?" he ground out. "It's already been four hours."

"Like I told you last time, no fucking clue." Cyn sat on the bed, her fingers wrapped around Isa's wrist. "I'm monitoring her body for signs of any issues, and so far, all's good. We just have to wait until Isa comes around."

"And we can't rush her?"

"What do you want, an awake Isa with poison in her veins or a sleeping Isa fighting off the taint? You don't get both."

Hell. He held in a sigh. "I hate it when you're right. So, tell me the truth, what's the chance of this working? With Triulf dead, Isa needs a backup plan."

"The Watchers?"

"They haven't said yes yet. This is coming down to the wire—Isa's got a little more than a day and a half. I need to know how much pressure to apply."

"Pressure?"

"So far, I've asked nicely. But if this spell here is a lowball chance, then I need to light a fire under that coven's moldy old ass."

"Not sure calling them moldy and old will help."

"I'm talking about their castle. But the Templars pay the Watchers a fortune for wards and spells that we're continually renegotiating. I can expedite those contracts or hold them up, even explore other options if needed. Threatening their money is the one thing the Watchers react to."

"At least you have a plan C. If this doesn't work, and if the Watchers can't—or won't—help, then Isa can cross over a hellgate. As a half daemon, one trip home to Granddad, or whatever she calls him, and she'll become immortal."

Immortal? What the fuck. Why hadn't Isa said anything to him about this? Gray's chest tightened, and it took all his willpower to maintain a blank expression.

"You knew that, right?" Cyn asked.

He forced a grin—managed a grimace. "Plan C."

"Well, let's hope it doesn't come to that. Not the place any part daemon would want to go at the best of times, right?"

Isa going to Hell? His stomach roiled with something sour and acidic. And then his cell pinged with a message from Templar HQ. He thumbed the screen open.

"Fuck off!" He reread the directive.

"What?" Cyn whipped around.

"The council agrees that all focus goes to St. James. They also wanted to push Isa for more visions."

"No care for how vulnerable it leaves her after?" Cyn said.

"They want to investigate more adrenaline options to see if that can stave off the fatigue."

"That's not an option long-term, though. There are health consequences for Isa if she goes down that route."

"Yeah," Gray said. "They noted my comment on that and asked me to investigate other pharmaceutical options."

"What, drug her?"

"They're just focused on the job."

"Of course, the myrrh is important, but—"

"R-104B is all that matters, Cyn. But that's not the worst of it. The Watchers want me in Cheshire to speak about what happened in Rome. And *our* council said yes. I'm leaving today."

"No way. You're in the middle of an investigation. That's not right. Even with R-104A returned, you still need to be here for the myrrh."

"Politics."

"Well, I'm glad it's you and not me. I don't have time for that BS."

Hell. Neither did he. But this was the job, so Gray did what he always did and buried his personal thoughts. "I'll go tonight—"

"Hold on," Cyn said. "Why does it have to be in person?"

"Because the Watchers are so old-fashioned, they're stuck in the Middle Ages."

"What about Isa?"

Gray bit back a sigh. Good fucking question. What to do with Isa? Her visions of R-104B were on the right track—in fact, without her, they'd be in a whole fuck load of trouble.

"She stays with me," Gray said. And it was because of her use in tracking the relic—no other reason. "At least this gives us the opening to get their help if your spell doesn't work."

Gray spent the next hour reviewing footage of everyone entering and leaving the vault facility for the seven days prior to R-104B being taken.

Zero sign of the theft. But R-104B hadn't gotten up and walked out on its own.

Which meant someone had tampered with the footage from the start. But access to the vault and surveillance feed was heavily restricted.

No question, this was an inside job. The bigger question was, how far up the company did this go?

Gray ordered a review into all the security guards at the St. James compound to check for crossover with employee records at the lab and then added a second review into the missing lab director.

Everyone in that facility had just become a suspect, too.

He'd hit send on his second directive when the soft, rhythmic whisper of Isa's breathing picked up pace.

"She's coming out of it," Gray said to Cyn.

"I don't sense anything." Cyn held Isa's wrist again.

And then Isa's eyelids fluttered open. The tightness that had been crushing his chest released with a whoosh, and he scrubbed a fist over his sternum before he could stop himself. Then he forced himself to stand still and ignored the look Cyn sent him.

"I'm going to make a call. I'll be in the shop." And then he could feel his relief in privacy.

"Isa? Isa, can you hear me?" Cyn leaned over Isa as he left the room.

((●))

Isa woke up to find Cyn at her side, and Gray nowhere to be seen. Cotton filled her mouth, and pressure twinged in her bladder.

"Did it work?" she croaked. "And what time is it?"

"Finally. Here you go." Cyn held a glass of water up to her. "Drink this. And it's 8:00 p.m."

Isa chugged the water back. "Thanks. Now I need to pee."

"I need to test—"

"And I need to move." Isa eased up off the bed. "Wow, I'm steady on my feet. Thought I'd be wonky after that spell. Although I have to say I'm getting sick and tired of all this sleeping."

"Pfft," Cyn said. "I *never* leave a spellee wonky. And sleep all the time? Sounds heavenly."

"Wait until you're the one doing all the sleeping."

Minutes later, Isa rejoined Cyn and took a seat at the little dining table. "How do you handle the lack of sunlight? I'm feeling ..."

"Claustrophobic? Uncomfortable?"

"That too. Any chance you know where my mobile phone is?"

"Here with your purse."

"Thanks." Where was Gray? He'd been there when she'd fallen asleep under the spell's influence. And part of her had thought he'd stay to make sure she was okay. But as he'd said, he'd already spent too much time looking after Isa instead of focusing on the myrrh.

"Gray's making a call in the shop," Cyn said. "He'll be back soon."

"Is he okay?"

Cyn frowned. "Okay? Need some context there, Divine One."

"It's Isa. Just Isa. Seriously, everyone has to quit calling me that."

"Why? I like it." Cyn shrugged. "Here, have some tea before I do the blood test. Gray said you drank this shit. Personally, I'm a coffee girl. But each to their own."

Isa rolled her eyes. "As in, did Gray sleep, eat? He was ... off this morning—last night, I mean."

"Well, apart from the small break where I made him rest —the entire time you were out, he sat beside the bed either watching you or his laptop."

Warmth spread in Isa's chest. He'd watched her? Not that they'd ever spoken about any feelings between them, but that made it sound like he had some ... nice thoughts toward her. Which was better than the opposite.

Cyn took out a small medical kit and withdrew a syringe and a petri dish. Then she took out a vial of violet-colored liquid.

"This is how the test works," Cyn said as she slid the needle into Isa's vein. "If you're cured, your blood stays bright red. If it hasn't worked, your blood will turn violet— basically, the poison can still overtake your cells. So I do this." Cyn injected several drops of Isa's blood into the petri dish. "And then I do this." She took the poison vial and measured out two drops. "Then we wait."

The crimson drops mingled with violet. At first, they kind of danced around each other, like two magnets repelling one other. Then the dance slowed, the drops mingled ...

Please, please, please let this work.

The red stayed strong.

Yes! Isa's breath whooshed out, and she jumped to her feet. "You did it!" She grabbed Cyn and threw her arms around her.

"You two are getting close," Gray said from behind her.

Isa whirled around. "It worked!" She launched herself at Gray and hugged him, too. Only registered how stiff he stayed at the last moment. She leaned back and stared up at him. "Why aren't you excited? This is brilliant news."

"Uh, Isadora." A note in Cyn's voice made her stop and turn back.

In the petri dish, the drops were all violet.

Her gut sank. Damn, damn, damn. But she forced herself to smile. "Thanks for trying. So I'm heading to the Watchers."

"Looks like we're both going to Cheshire," Gray said tonelessly.

"Huh?" She stared at the petri dish until his words made sense. "Wait, I know you need to be here for the myrrh. You don't need to come with me."

"Believe me, I don't want to go either. But the council have ordered me to Cheshire for another reason."

"Oh." She cut him a look. Maybe that's what had pissed him off this time? "Is there any way I can go instead? I mean, I need to go for this spell, but—"

"No. Council orders." Gray's jaw ticked, and the glacier in his eyes made her heart thud.

"Okay, so we're going to England—where did you say?"

"Cheshire. There's some good news there."

"What?"

"Eve and Raph are heading there, too. They'll arrive before us. I've got the plane being prepped now, and I want to be in the air within forty-five minutes. Cyn, I need to keep us off the radar in case anyone's watching Marcella or the apartment. Do you have a Templar vehicle here?"

"I've got my 'stang."

"You drive a Mustang?" Gray said. "What the hell, Cyn?"

"I'm a high priestess, Grayson. It's part of my character, and it fits me perfectly. It's cherry red."

"Shit. I wanted something inconspicuous."

"It's got all the mods, so it looks like a pleasure toy, but it's got bulletproof glass and a full weapon system—both offense and defense—installed. And it's so conspicuous no one will expect you to drive that."

"All right. We'll take your car. I'll get Marcella and Tank to run decoy, just in case, and then meet us at the hangar. Marcella can drop your toy back."

Cyn said, "I'll have it around front in ten minutes."

"Do it." He leveled a look at Isa that made her blood chill. "Get your things. We're leaving."

Wow. Talk about cold. Gray had been in a foul mood off and on for as long as she'd known him, but he hadn't been this cold to *her* before. What by the stars was going on? Why was he angry now?

"I'm so sorry," Cyn said and patted Isa's arm.

"Uh, sorry for what?" Isa forced her attention back to Cyn.

"That the spell didn't work. You okay?"

"Sure. Absolutely. Just thinking."

"Well, I might not have removed the poison, but about controlling your visions, I've got something stronger than that ring for you." She gestured to the cabinet behind her. "Try an obelisk or an orb. They can help channel the part of you that's linked to the future. I have plenty of them here, and since you're working with the Templars, you're welcome to one of mine. Check them out while I get the car."

Isa glanced over at Gray. He was typing so loudly on his laptop the keys might be permanently damaged. And not looking at her at all.

"Is she serious—I can just take one of her crystals?" she asked him.

"Templars don't joke." He still didn't look at her.

She rolled her eyes. Seriously—how had she thought

having sex with this ass was a good idea? Well, the sex had been great. But his post-sex bedside manner sucked.

"Maybe try tapping the keys instead of bashing them?" she said sweetly. "You're connected to that laptop like a life-line. Would hate for it to break on you."

Before he could say anything, Isa spun and went back to Cyn's bedroom.

Five minutes later, Isa returned dressed and carrying her handbag and mobile phone. Basically, she had everything she had to her name at that point in time.

Ignoring Gray, she headed to the shelf Cyn had indicated.

Geodes, orbs, and obelisks in all sizes and hues rested on the shelves, and some on timber stands. And at the very back, a stunning hand-sized obelisk in a warm yellow color caught her attention.

She picked it up—it was heavier than it looked—and a cool tingle spread through her hands.

Wow.

"Car's ready," Cyn said from the doorway, then she nodded at the crystal Isa held. "That's apatite. Gold apatite. I haven't used that one in a while. How does it feel?"

"As soon as I picked it up, my palms tingled."

"That's the best reaction you can ask for—sounds like it's yours now. Right, do you know how to care for your crystals?"

"No clue." Isa held the obelisk to her chest. "But I'll do whatever you say."

"Cleanse it under the moon and sun. Spend time with it, hold it, and gradually you can tune the apatite into the same frequency as your body."

"Time to go." Gray snapped his laptop shut. "Grab whatever you're grabbing."

"Grab?" Isa said. "I'm being gifted a very special crystal."

"And I don't care if you're being gifted all the jewels in the world," Gray said. "Take it and let's go."

Heat rushed through her veins, and Isa lifted her chin, whirled to Cyn. "Ignore him. I'm not letting you go without saying thank you and goodbye properly."

The high priestess's eyes lit with something that looked very much like delight. "Oh, I will. I'm well used to his shitty moods. Don't let him get to you, either."

"Pfft." Isa raised her voice on purpose. "After everything I've dealt with, handling one cold prick is not a problem."

"Better a cold prick than a dead diviner." Gray jerked his chin at the door. "I'm waiting."

"Ouch. Icy, Ace. Even for you." She forced a laugh. But inside, a little part of her heart iced over. Gray was back to his curt, cold self. And she hated it.

"Ace?" Cyn choked on a laugh.

Isa whacked her on the back. "My nickname for him. At least, it was. I'm changing it to Ass." Cyn laughed but turned it into a cough when Gray glowered at her. "And I love your place, by the way." Isa refused to let the icehole Templar stop her from making the most out of whatever time she had left. "I'd love to come back one day."

"No one's said that before. But sure."

"Cut the jokes." Gray gestured to the door. "This is what we're going to do. I'm driving, you—"

"Enter fancy red car. Passenger side. Got it." She brushed past him.

A scowl shot across his face. And she was thrilled to at least get some reaction from the ice man.

22

———

Isa made a beeline for the shiny red low-slung car in the alleyway, but the hairs on the back of her neck crawled as she slid into the seat, and she couldn't stop herself from looking around.

"Is it a vision?" Gray said, climbing in beside her.

"No." She rubbed her neck again. "Just an ... odd feeling."

"Stay sharp. I'll be going fast, and I'm not stopping for anything. We need to get you to your *last chance*. Right?"

Guilt made her stomach queasy, but she just nodded and looked out the window. The other option was one she'd never dreamed of considering. But now ... she glanced at Gray. Should she tell him?

He might just find a hellgate and throw her through to be rid of the problem so they could focus on the myrrh.

But her mother had sacrificed everything and everyone she'd loved so Isa and Raph would lead normal lives. How could Isa just say, *'Hi, Mum. Also, the twenty-five years you've been trapped behind the thirteenth gate have been for nothing.'*?

And then there was the whole being a subject of her

grandfather's court and everything that went with being at his—and his lords'—beck and call. Slavery. Servitude. Baby factory for daemons because who wouldn't want to have a blood relative of the big man himself?

The memory of her death vision played through her mind. Her visions *always* came true. So even *if* she crossed over now and cured the poisoning, ending up dead in a ruby dress wouldn't change. Just because daemons didn't age didn't mean they couldn't be killed. It only took a lot more damage.

A shiver shook through Isa. No, thank you.

Getting a cure, staying *human* for whatever remained of her time in this world was the right plan.

True to his word, Gray maneuvered them through the heavy downtown LA traffic. The city passed by in a kaleidoscope of colors and lights. Then, out of nowhere, a silver sedan shot into the intersection they were passing through, headed straight at them.

"Gray!"

"Fuck. Hold on."

Gray hit the gas, did something with the gear stick, and the car launched forward.

Rubber screeched. Horns blared around them. But Gray just did more of that stick shift and pedal maneuvering, and they raced ahead on the road.

More horns blaring and the squeal of tires locking up echoed behind them, and Isa glanced over her shoulder as the silverish sedan came roaring up behind them. "They're coming again!"

"I see them." Traffic ran heavy around them, headlights shining at close and regular intervals in both directions. But instead of easing into a gap in the traffic, Gray jerked the steering wheel, and the car hurtled sideways. "I need to lose them before we get to the airport. Hold on."

Gray checked the rearview mirror, then hit the brake, did another crazy thing with the gearshift and the wheel, and the car went into a one-eighty spin, jamming her against the door with the force of the turn.

Isa yelped.

But Gray didn't even curse. His lips stayed tight, his glittering gaze locked on the road as he punched the gas and took them into the traffic, heading in the opposite direction. Then, at the next turn, he sent the tires squealing and took them off on another road.

Isa twisted to look out the back window and stared until Gray had taken half a dozen zigzags.

"Can't see them." She dropped back into the seat. "Holy crap, but my heart is pounding so hard right now."

"Almost there."

Sure enough, the high fence of the private airfield loomed ahead. "Never thought I'd be so happy to see an airport."

"We'll drive right into the hangar."

"When did you learn to drive like that?" She couldn't stop herself from looking back one last time. "And is there anyone else—?"

"No one else is following us." Gray glanced at the rearview mirror and then down at the display in the center console. "We're clear for now. And I'm a Templar. Defensive and offensive driver training is mandatory. The bigger question is, how did they find us?"

"Someone could've followed us from the lab? Or what if this is about Cyn? We're in her car after all."

"Either possibility is a problem. Cyn needs to maintain her cover."

Gray hit a button on the car console. The gate ahead slid open, and then they were through and heading toward the same hangar they'd arrived at, although the rest of the airfield was closed up.

"What's Cyn undercover for? No, wait—you can't say. Fine. I'm just glad you were driving. That was damned scary. And my scare threshold is getting higher these days."

Gray's lips tightened, but then the hangar door rolled open, revealing the same jet—or at least, it looked the same—and the two crew who'd come over with Isa and Gray from Australia.

Gray parked the Mustang. "Stay. I'll be back."

"Excuse me? I'm not a pet dog you tell to stay put."

"Never said you were. But you're a Templar employee, and I want you out of the way and protected behind bullet-proof glass in case shit hits the fan—which happens remarkably often around you. So yes. *Stay*. Do I need to make myself any clearer?"

Damn, he was angry. And serious.

"You don't have to be an ass about it." She yanked the car door shut so hard that the crew members across the hangar jumped.

Gray stopped, then turned and glared at her. She glared right back, then flipped him the bird before turning to face the opposite direction.

Grayson No-Bloody-Last-Name could take his stinking moods and go sit on a pole. Anyway, she had work to do.

Isa took the obelisk Cyn had gifted her, closed her eyes, and focused on the image of the myrrh.

The apatite warmed. But ... nothing else.

Someone rapped on the car window.

"Shit," Isa gasped. She carefully placed the crystal in her lap then opened the door. "Rohan. You scared me."

"You scared *me*. You were sitting there as still as a fucking statue. So, you coming out?"

"Apparently, I'm to stay inside the car." She rolled her eyes. "According to his High and Mighty Bossiness, anyway."

"Then I'll come in."

Why not? It would keep her mind off the fact that nothing else was working right now.

Rohan slid into the driver's seat.

"Not closing it?" She nodded at the door.

"Your Templar's already suspicious of me."

"He's not my Templar."

"Doesn't change the fact he's watching me like a hawk." Rohan's eyes shone with a fierce inner light as he regarded her.

"Why are you here?" Isa asked.

"Passing through—I've just come from the hellgate. I've got news about the bounty."

"What?"

"The job is simple. Bring you through the tenth gate— alive—and get a damned big reward. That means we can rule out most of the lesser lords. But at least Gray took out two bounty hunters. Don't know how many more are out there, though, so you need to keep cautious until we find out who this is coming from."

"We?"

"I'm enquiring on my side of the gates—also alerted your grandsire about the bounty. Man, he was ..." Rohan whistled and shook his head.

"Who lives beyond the tenth?"

"The Lords of the Gates, your mother and grandsire, and his inner circle. Isa, you should know, I'm also from beyond the tenth gate." He shot her a look. "But it's not me."

"Call me batshit, but I trust you. So we can rule out my

mother and grandfa—well, you know. But what about the others? That's nine daemons, right?"

"Eight."

"No—gates ten through thirteen, plus the five High Lords."

"The thirteenth gate doesn't have a lord. Only blood relatives of the Lord of Hell can travel through that door, so there's no need for a gatekeeper."

"So what—my mother could leave any time she wanted?"

"Well, she's not locked there."

"Ah yes, she is. Her father caged her there."

"That's not how she put it. She said staying behind that gate was for protection. Hers and yours."

"How do you know that? Wait—you've spoken with my *mother*? How? Rohan, which gate are you from?"

"I think that's clear."

Isa's palms tingled. "Holy shit. The thirteenth? We're related?"

"It's a hell of a distant tie—pun intended—but yes, we're related."

"Wow. I'm … speechless. Have you met Raph?"

"Not yet, but if the opportunity comes up, I'll take it. Listen, I need to leave soon, but first we need to talk about him." Rohan nodded to where Gray paced back and forth.

"Gray?"

Rohan lowered his voice. "You can't trust he'll always have your best interests as his priority. He's a pro, and he's ruthless. He'll say and do whatever's required to get this relic back. Which I understand—his job is fucking important—but I don't want to see you hurt."

"Gray and his motives aside, why is this so important to you?"

"You. You're important, Isadora. You're ..."

"What?"

"The granddaughter of the Lord of Hell. You're part daemon, part human. And you're a diviner. No wonder the Templars want you. And Grayson is a Templar first and always. That's their motto—once a Templar, always a Templar. He can't ever be anything else."

"Well, you don't need to worry. I know exactly who Grayson is, and his priorities."

"Good." Rohan dipped his head. "Then, I'm out of here. Got a date with an informant. See you round, cuz." He winked, then left the car as fluidly as he'd slid in.

Isa couldn't help but stare at Rohan as he strode out of the hangar. She had a relative. Holy shit. She and Raph had a relative. She had to call her brother—

"Everything okay?" Gray's voice broke her train of thought. He stood in the open door of the car.

"Yes, of course." How did he walk so sneakily?

"We're leaving now, so you can board the plane." He pivoted, only to stop and turn back to her. "Rohan had a lot to say."

"He told me about the bounty hunter. Did he tell you too?"

"Yes, so we know someone from high up in your grandaddy's world is after you." His phone rang. "Hold on." He stepped a few feet away. "What? When?" He flicked a look at Isa. His mouth pulled tight, and his eyes went dead flat. Isa's stomach knotted. Not that look again. "Prognosis? ... Okay, keep me updated. Security level one. Keep it to Templars only."

And then he just stood there, staring at the cell.

Isa's stomach tightened further.

"Fuck!" Gray whirled to Isa, and something terrible

blazed in his eyes before he reined in whatever that ... fury had been, and his gaze returned to the expressionless mask he assumed way too often.

"What is it?" Isa crossed her arms to ward off the sudden chill that flew over her. "Come on, Gray. Something's wrong. Tell me. Is it ... Raph—Dad—?"

"It's Marcella and Tank. They left the apartment at the same time as we left Cyn's to draw off any potential tails. And it worked. Too well. Twenty minutes ago, their car came under heavy fire by two men in a silver sedan."

The blood left Isa's head in a rush. "H-how are they?"

"Marcella's banged up. The car crashed into a building, but the airbags deployed, which they think kept her injuries minor. She took down the assailants—one's dead, but the other's being transported to a Templar holding cell now. He's already confessed they're bounty hunters—they followed us from the lab yesterday and were waiting for us to leave. When they lost you and me in the traffic today, they went back to the Templar apartment and picked up Marcella and Tank instead."

"How's Tank?"

"In the ER. Critical. The gunman focused on him."

Isa couldn't contain the strangled sob that escaped her. And then the next and the next.

This was all because of her.

23

Around nine hours after leaving LA, and sitting opposite Gray in the Templar's jet, Isa blinked as she came out of yet another short vision.

She rubbed her forehead as a dull ache thudded behind her eyes. Damn it.

"Anything?" Gray said.

"Just the same—the incense burner held in gloved hands. Nothing more."

"Color of the gloves? Material?"

"Black. Leather looking. And I get the sense they belong to a woman, but I can't be certain."

"Can you try again?"

"Sure." Isa took a deep breath. "Before I do, any word on Tank and Marcella?"

"Yes."

She stared at him for a beat, waiting for him to elaborate ... anything. He just tapped away at his frigging laptop.

"Damn it, Gray, why do you have to make everything so damned hard? I just want to know if they're okay. Not even okay—is Tank alive? How about that?"

"Tank's prognosis is not good. He's on life support."

Isa's chest went tight. Damn, but she wished she could go back and never come into this picture. What if this was all because she'd told Gray about her vision? If she'd done nothing, maybe this all would never have happened. Marcella wouldn't have been injured. Tank might not be ...

A lump stuck in her throat, and she had to swallow hard to force it down. Squeeze a breath into her lungs.

And Gray just sat there. Tapping into his bloody laptop. The urge to punish him for his responsibility surged through her.

"Don't you care? They were attacked—and Tank still might die—because of a job you ordered him on."

"That's their job."

"The job you ordered them to do."

"Of course I care!" he exploded. "I brought Tank into this team. I put him in harm's way. I ordered him to act as decoy, and that's why he might die any moment. And I'd do it again because what we're working on is more important than his one solitary life. We have to make sure that every single fucking human on this planet doesn't end up dead. And that's exactly what will happen if—"

"If what? What's this giant deadly secret that's so bad you can stomach having someone you say you care about getting murdered?"

"I can't tell you."

"No. No, don't you dare shut me down. You can bloody well tell me. I've signed your NDA. I've seen the people after us. I already know what the thing is we're looking for. So tell me!"

"What, like you've told me everything?" Scorn filled his gaze.

Isa's stomach tightened. "Okay, let's do this. Ever since

we had sex, you've been colder than a polar blast. So what's the deal? Come on, I'm a big girl. Be honest. Did you hate the sex? Has something even more earth-shattering come up since then that I don't know about? Or are you just a prick that sleeps with someone once and then gaslights them?"

"We had sex twice, if I recall. So clearly not number three. And the fact is, there doesn't need to be anything more earth-shattering. I'm dealing with a crisis here, and that's where I need to focus. So yes, we had sex. But that was a lapse in judgment on my part."

"A lapse in judgment? Gee, thanks. Way to make a girl feel special."

"You asked. I'm telling. I have a job to do, Isadora."

"Fine. You focus on your relics. I'll focus on my visions and researching the supposed spell the Watchers can do."

"Why?" Gray asked, his tone light and breezy. "There's always your family connection to fall back on."

"What was that?"

"You know. How if you cross through a hellgate, you'll become an immortal." He clenched his jaw so tight it ticked. "How all the work I've been going through to fucking find a cure has been unnecessary."

But Isa refused to back down from his glittering gaze. "You have no frigging idea what you're talking about."

"What—so you can't just become immortal and the *entire* poison issue disappears?"

"Wow. You say that so easily. Like no biggie"—she clicked her fingers—"I'll just to go to Hell now. You have no clue what becoming an immortal in my grandfather's court would mean."

"It's also a way to *not die*."

"So if you knew, why didn't you say anything?"

"I found out yesterday. Because Cyn told me instead of you." He jabbed a finger at her. "You lied to me."

"I didn't lie—"

"You didn't tell me the entire truth, so that's as good as a lie. That's what I hate. And you can call it anything you want. But there's telling the truth—the intent of the truth—and not."

Damn. Damn, damn, damn. Should she tell him the rest of it? But what if he kicked her off the team?

Isa's stomach roiled. She was such an idiot. How had she gotten herself into this situation? Except no. She'd gotten into this for a reason. She just had to convince one pissed off Templar Knight that everything she'd said—or not said—had been for a valid reason.

"Isa, why are you looking like that?"

She chewed at her lip before lifting her chin. Whatever the outcome, she'd face it straight on.

‹‹‹●›››

Gray's gut knotted like someone had tied it into an iron chain. Across the table, Isa's face paled. She closed her eyes and took a deep breath.

"What, by the *fucking* gods"—he pulled himself up, reined in the urge to shout—"is going on?"

"I've seen you before. In my visions. Before last week, I mean."

She'd *seen* him? Bile crept up his throat.

Isa stared down at her hands before her gaze flicked back to him. "For years. A hundred times. Maybe more."

Gray's breath locked, and all he could do was stare at her

until pain clawed at his chest and the need to breathe forced him to inhale.

"What—what have you seen?" he asked.

"So many things," she whispered.

"What do you mean *things*?"

"Usually snippets of your life. Getting a tattoo. Training in some kind of martial art in a field with mist rising off the ground. Shooting a gun. Working at your laptop. Lots of those. But with the snippets, I never had the context behind the vision. And I never knew your name, not until I met you at Raph's. But that's not everything."

What the fuck could be more than this? The bile that had risen in his throat hardened to stone.

"Back in Australia, when I convinced you to bring me with you, I ... exaggerated how I can focus on something and then have a vision. At least, I had been exaggerating when we started out. But I can do it now. Kind of, anyway." Isa's beautiful, lying, treacherous eyes went glassy with unshed tears.

Gray couldn't have moved if he'd wanted to. Betrayal sliced through his gut.

"I'm sorry—"

"What the fuck?" His blood turned hot, and he clenched his hands to avoid grabbing and shaking some sense into her. "Isa, this is not a game. What the hell do you think we're doing here? You lied to come with me? What, so you could get away from your 'good' life?"

"No! It wasn't like that. I exaggerated—not an outright lie—because I *knew* I could help you, and look, my visions did. Would you have gone to Fathom LA without me? I don't think so."

"That's not the point. You lied to me."

"Not outright. And let me ask you this—would you have let me come if I'd said I *believe* I can do this?"

"We'll never know, will we? Because you didn't trust me to tell me the truth."

"This isn't about trust."

"Isa, this is *all* about trust. Clearly, you don't trust me. You've proven that. And how can I trust you knowing you've lied—fine, *withheld* information from me all this time?"

"I'm sorry."

"Yeah, now you're found out."

"No, not because of that!" That light she got when she was about to go to battle entered her eyes. "Let me be clear—I'm sorry I had to lie. Yes, I feel like shit for the lying part. But I lied for a reason that I still believe in. I knew I could help you. And I did. So I'm not sorry for that part."

"What about the rest? You lied about your options with the poison. While I've been fighting to find the relic *and* keep you safe, you fucking lied to me. And what about hiding the fact you've seen me at least a hundred times— like what, some voyeur watching my life?"

The past washed over Gray in a tsunami of memories and feelings. Living on the street. Stealing and lying just to feed his brother and him. The cold. The hunger. Emptiness. Helplessness. The day he'd lost his brother ... And that was before he'd come to the Templars. What about the fights he'd been in? The people he'd killed? Had she seen all that? The acid roiling in his gut threatened to erupt.

Fuck. Well, who cared? That was his past. He'd gotten through that, and he was going to get through this fucking shit right now too, by focusing on what mattered. Dealing with the Watchers. Getting back to the US. Finding fucking R-104B.

He lunged to his feet and grabbed his laptop.

"Gray! You can't just walk off. We have to talk about this."

"Isa, I have zero fucking clue what more to say to you right now. And if I do say anything, it's going to be out of anger. So yes, I can stop this conversation. I have work to do."

‹‹‹●›››

An hour after Isa had dropped her truth bomb from hell, they landed in the private airfield maintained by the Watchers. The ancient coven employed decent wards, so Gray didn't object to the lack of physical security around the hangar.

Isa's face was pale, but the light of battle still shone in her eyes, and every time he looked at her, the urge to shout and let his fury fly surged through him.

So instead, he shut his mouth and led the way to the silver SUV the coven left for arrivals.

"Where to now?" Isa asked through chattering teeth as she looked around. Not that there was much to look at—the hangar had the plane, a workstation, and the car. "Hello, Gray? I might piss you off, but you can tell me where we're going."

"Ashforton castle. Through Ashford, the village at the base of the hill, then up to the castle from there. Get in."

"Want me to drive?" She lifted her chin. "You slept for like an hour on the plane, so you must be exhausted."

"And you're not meant to drive. Now get in."

"Exhaustion can be just as dangerous as me having a vision. At least I know when one's about to come on."

"Not happening. Now, for the last time, *get in.*"

Isa huffed as she sat down as if he was the one in the wrong here.

"Damn, but it's cold," she muttered. "What time is it?"

"Shit, you're shaking so much your teeth are rattling. Here, take my coat, use it like a blanket. The car will heat fast."

"Thanks."

"I need you awake so you can keep searching for R-104B, not comatose because you're freezing. And it's 4:00 p.m."

Her nose wrinkled. "So 8:00 a.m. back in LA. And I have no clue what time it is back home."

"2:00 a.m. tomorrow."

"Impressive party trick. Do you always know the time around the world? No, wait—it's a Templar thing, right?"

Gray didn't have to look at her to know she'd just rolled her eyes.

"So what's this castle like? And why is it so ... gloomy here? You said four in the afternoon, right, not morning?"

"Sun sets earlier here than in Australia. Plus, the Watchers keep this place shrouded in shitty weather—fog, sleet, snow even—as an extra layer of protection for the castle. Now, enough chitchat. I need to watch where I'm driving."

"Yes, *boss*." Isa turned away to look out into the mist-shrouded surrounds. Which suited him just fine.

Why *hadn't* she told him about the crossing-over option for the poison? Why didn't she want to make that step? Fucking immortals ... that was some family she had.

And what did this all mean for R-104B? The relic was his focus—it had to be number one above everything else right now.

-‹‹●››-

The drive through the little village and up the wooded hill couldn't have been icier if Isa had been sitting in an igloo in the middle of a blizzard.

And damn Grayson No-Bloody-Last-Name, because yes, she'd withheld information from him, but she had valid reasons. And she'd helped with the myrrh. But no, he didn't see that at all—not Mr. Black-and-White-and-No-Shades-In-Between-Grayson.

Patches of gunmetal sky, several shades deeper than the mist hovering over the ground, peeked between the overhanging trees as they drove up the hill. Eventually, they turned one more long bend and reached a stone wall extending into the forest in both directions, with a dark timber door at one section, and a gravel turnaround area. Beyond the wall, mist-hugged trees loomed into the sky.

This was it?

"This isn't it," Gray said as he parked in the graveled area but didn't turn the engine off.

She wrinkled her nose at him. How did he know what she was thinking?

"We wait here until someone comes and greets us."

"I'm going to look around while we wait," Isa said.

"It's freezing outside."

"No different from inside." She gave him her sweetest smile, then slammed the door behind her. It might've been juvenile, but it felt good.

"Stay near the car," Gray barked through the window.

"Yes, boss."

Isa shivered as the icy air bit her cheeks. Gravel crunched beneath the soles of her shoes, and she stamped her feet to keep them warm. Damn. Maybe she should've stayed in the car.

"Isa?" A laconic, familiar voice cut through the silence. "Why the hell are you standing in the freezing cold?"

Isa spun around. Her brother emerged through the door in the wall.

"Raph! You're here!" She launched herself at him and hugged him tight and then dropped to her feet. "Where's Eve?"

"She's talking to the guy in charge."

"I can't wait to see her again. How long have you been here?"

"We arrived last night." He glanced over her shoulder. "So I know why we're here. And I know why Gray is here. But I have no damned clue why *you're* here."

"Crap. There's a lot to tell you."

"Clearly. Starting with, *why are you here*?"

"Calm down. I had a vision of the myrrh—" Shit. How much could she tell Raph? She glanced over as Gray joined them. "Is he cleared to know about the thing we're working on?"

"Yes."

"Thanks, snappy." She didn't hold back with rolling her eyes before she turned to Raph.

"Snappy?" Raph quirked one eyebrow.

"That's his nickname for when he answers in single-syllable words. Anyhow, I had a vision of the—"

"Why are you even giving him nicknames?" Raph demanded.

"It'll all make sense when you let me finish." She glared at Raph. "Are you going to interrupt me again?"

Raph raised his hands. "Fine. No more interruptions."

"Okay, so—"

"Hello!" Eve appeared in the doorway. Raph's eyes lit up, and he held out a hand for the powerful witch. Wow. Raph hadn't acted like this around a woman ever.

Mind you, Eve looked stunning in black denim jeans and a long, fitted black jacket with a fur trim that hugged her tall, curvy frame to perfection.

"Told you I'd get here first," Raph said.

"Only because I had to work out arrangements with Warrick." Eve turned to Isa. "I couldn't believe it when I heard you were coming with Gray."

"Hello again to you too." Isa wrapped her arms around Eve and held on tight.

"Enough with the hugs and feely shit. Let's actually get to the castle before we freeze our asses off." Gray stomped past them.

"Ignore Grumpy Gray. Tell me how you two are." Isa linked her arm in Eve's and steered the taller woman over to Raph. With the iciness pouring off Gray, she'd be far better walking between these two.

"Forget us," Raph growled. "You need to spill everything, Isa. Now." He scowled at Gray before turning back to her.

Damn. Protective big-brother Raph was still present. This might be tricky.

"Let's walk and talk," she said in a rush. "Like Gray said, it's freezing out here. So, where's this castle?"

"You'll see it soon," Eve said. "The outer wall is warded, so you need to be taken through by someone from the castle. Me." She smiled as she led them through the wall. "We walk up from here. There's a path, though, and it's not that far. So what's the story?"

Isa took a deep breath and told her brother and Eve everything—well, almost everything. Raph didn't need to know what she and Gray had gotten up to one hundred percent of the time.

"Bloody hell," Raph breathed. "So you need this spell in the next thirty-six hours, max. Okay, that's our priority." He turned to look at Gray. "I get you need the myrrh, but this is Isa's life."

"Clearly," Gray said.

Isa sighed at Gray's cool response. Still pissed, of course. She ignored the stare drilling into her shoulders and instead spoke to Eve. "Do you know of this spell they're all talking about?"

"Not that I can think of. But that doesn't matter. Once we have the spell, I'll make sure your ritual goes right."

"Thank you." The queasiness in Isa's stomach settled for a moment. She had Eve. They had the spell. So she didn't have to face the question of death ... or life forever.

Then they rounded yet another bend, and all thought fled as a monstrous, craggy, stunning castle loomed from the forest ahead.

"Castle Ashforton," Eve said.

"Wow," Isa breathed. "It looks like something out of a fairytale—except darker. Gloomier. And it's huge."

"The original fort was built around fifteen hundred years ago," Eve said, "with battlements and turrets added over the next thousand years. There have been a few minor recent updates, but mostly it's cold, dark and dreary. Except for the library."

"You really lived here?"

"For ten years." Eve tucked her hands into her pockets. "Come on, we enter through the gatehouse. Now, did Gray tell you about the magical wards?"

"Some."

"Okay, quick recap. No mobile phones past the gatehouse—they won't work. No going inside the library without an escort—which means you need approval. Warrick, the castle bailiff, is in charge of everything inside, but you can ask any of the Seniors—they're the teachers and officials—for help. Trainees can give you guidance, but any approval you need must come from a Senior. And most, most important, if you see anyone casting a salt circle, never cross it."

"Don't worry," Raph said. "She gave me the same speech, and it's not as bad as it seems."

Inside the gatehouse, a man in his midforties with short dark hair, wearing an impeccably cut navy suit, stood checking a pocket watch. He frowned and then glanced up at them.

"Everyone, this is Warrick, the bailiff. Warrick, you know Grayson, right? And this is Isadora Smith, Raph's sister."

Isa couldn't stop herself from checking out the hot bailiff —was he a witch too? Was everyone at the castle a magic maker? She'd have to confirm with Eve later.

"Ms. Smith." Warrick inclined his head. "I understand you're here for a specific spell. Our librarian is checking the library records now. I don't expect it to take long before we have the information you require."

"Hi," Isa murmured.

"And, Grayson," the bailiff continued. "The council wish to thank you for seeing them on such short notice. They're waiting for you as we speak." He flicked one look at Raph, and something in that gaze made Isa's hackles rise.

"Isa needs this spell as a priority." Gray folded his arms. "Your council can wait, surely?"

"The librarian is searching now. We understand the urgency of the situation."

And then Warrick took an actual key from a thick chain

around his neck and opened the arched timber door at the other end of the gatehouse, pushing it wide to reveal a circular courtyard.

Isa forced herself not to gape this time—seriously, could this place get any more stunning?

Eve and the bailiff led them to a plain-looking door on the other side of the courtyard and into a cavernous room— if you could call it that. Stone walls held fabric hangings, ancient weapons, even suits of armor. At the end, where they all stood, a staircase with the same texture and color as the walls led up to a timber arched door. Tables and chairs filled the center of the room, and several overstuffed armchairs faced an enormous stone fireplace at the far end. Three young adults sat at one table, but a look from Warrick and they scrambled to their feet and practically ran out through a door.

"This is the main gathering hall. I know it looks medieval," Eve said like that was a bad thing.

Medi-*wonderful* was more like it. Isa twirled around, trying to take it all in.

"It's cold at the tables." Eve gave Warrick a pointed look. "I swear you did that to discourage us from hanging around here. But if you nab an armchair, it's not too bad."

"If I recall, Evangeline, you never liked to sit down here at the best of times," Warrick murmured.

Raph tensed and shifted, as if ready to take on the bailiff. Isa glanced over at him—what was with that?

"Well, the company was never as good as it's right now," Eve said easily.

"I'm sure." Warrick's gaze took them all in but landed on Raph for longer than anyone else, his eyes tightening for a fraction of a second.

Tension filled the little space, and Isa glanced between them all, then over to Gray.

Gray's sigh was loud enough that he must've done it on purpose, and then he clapped. "Alright, I don't know what the fuck is going on here, but we're on the clock, Warrick. Isa needs this spell, and I need to get back to the US, which means getting your council meeting over and done with. Can we do this?" He made a sweeping motion with his hand.

"Of course. Evangeline, Grayson, come with me, please. Ms. Smith, our librarian will collect you shortly—please make yourself comfortable here in the hall until that happens."

Isa smiled as Eve mouthed, "Chairs by the fire."

"Now, Mr. Smith." Warrick turned to Raph. "You'll wait here until we've conducted our business. You're not to leave this hall for any purpose, if you do—"

"No," Eve said. "Raph's coming with Grayson and me. I wouldn't be standing here right now without Raph."

The bailiff stiffened. "This is coven business. Human-world business. And Mr. Smith is ... not of this world."

Isa stiffened. If Raph wasn't of this world, then what was she? And why wasn't she getting the same icy treatment as her brother?

"Your Watcher is right," Gray cut in. "*Raphael* was integral to the retrieval of R-104A—the relic of gold. He's also contracted with my organization, so as the Templar in charge of this case, not only do I vouch for him, but my official recommendation is that he join your council for this conversation."

Isa mentally cheered. Grayson was standing up for Raph. And the pressure that had tightened in her chest over the last hour after the fight with Gray loosened. For all his icehole approach, he was loyal to her brother, and for that, she'd give him an ounce of grudging respect.

"Fine." Warrick's cheeks ticked. "This way."

Eve rolled her eyes, but then she winked at Isa before they followed Warrick to the other side of the hall and up a set of stone stairs and disappeared through a door at the end.

And ... she was alone.

For a moment, nothing but the hushed crackle of the fire and the last echo of the door shutting filled the hall.

"Isadora?" a soft voice said from behind her.

Isa spun around as a willowy woman with gorgeous dark skin and hair, and the purest amber eyes Isa had ever seen, walked through yet another doorway. A pair of denim jeans hugged her long legs and a thick, oversized coppery cable-knit jumper made her eyes gleam like gold.

"Yep, that's me. Hi," Isa said in a rush after she'd stopped gawking.

"My name is Cecelie; I'm the librarian. I've been looking for a spell to counteract amorice—is that right?"

"Yep, I'm the poisoned one." Isa couldn't stop herself from checking Cecelie out. This spectacular woman was the librarian?

"You appear remarkably well given your poisoning." Cecelie looked at her with a funny expression before she gestured to the doorway she'd come through. "Come this way. As the Vertex spell books don't leave the library, I'll take you there."

"Are you allowed? Eve said I'm not meant to go there without approval."

"I'm the librarian. I can take you anywhere I wish."

Okay, don't argue with the librarian. Isa followed Cecelie into a long, high-ceiling corridor. Arched windows let the light in, and many doorways led to who knew where.

"Did you say Vertex spells? As in, the tip of a triangle?"

"Yes." Cecelie beamed. "Do you know how we learn spell craft?"

"Ah, no. I'm an artist, and I know shapes."

"We classify spells in the triangle—those at the base are the easiest, least dangerous, and anyone in the coven may learn them. Those at the Vertex are the most powerful and the most dangerous."

"My spell is one of those?"

Cecelie nodded and then stopped before the last door. "This is the library. There are many rooms and levels, so please don't leave my side unless I give you permission— that's for your safety, as some nooks have magic of their own, and by standing within the vicinity, you're at risk of triggering their latent powers."

"I'll stick to you like glue." Because that wasn't scary at all. A library with magic of its own?

Cecelie frowned, but then her expression lightened. "Ah —because glue is sticky."

"Uh, yes. You haven't heard that before?"

"No," Cecelie replied with a smile. "But I've never left these grounds, so that's not surprising."

"Wow. As in, you were born here? And you've never left?"

"Yes, as in I was born here. And no, *you* are the amazing one. You're undertaking the *renascentia sanguinem* spell."

"The what spell?"

"Rebirth of the blood; it is a transformation spell."

Cecelie opened the door into the cavernous library. Row after row of bookshelves led to a giant arched window looking out over forest and sky. Couches and reading tables filled the middle of the room, with spiral staircases on both sides leading to a mezzanine level that wrapped around three walls.

"This way," Cecelie said. "We lock the Vertex spells in the upper level."

Isa followed the librarian up the stairs, through an imposing locked wrought-iron gate, and into a tiny area overlooking the window.

"Here we are. However, only the highest practicing Watchers could cast this incantation."

"Eve said she'll help me. But what about you—do you know the spells, too?"

"I'm the librarian, so I know of them. Why?"

"What's so amazing about me undertaking this one?"

"I thought you knew." Cecelie's face clouded over. "You're undertaking a permanent transformation hex that acts on the blood, which means every part of your body is under pressure. Because of that, it's one of the deadliest incantations we have. This spell has been cast three times that we know of, and two of these times, the recipient died."

Isa's stomach sank. Well, damn. One more spell she had to fake being scared of.

24

GRAY'S MOUTH went dry as Warrick led them higher and higher into the castle. Would Isa be okay? These Watchers had zero tolerance for anyone outside their walls—they better treat her right. And what if she had a vision? Would they know how to look after her?

"Gray, everything okay?" Raph elbowed him.

"Yeah." He rubbed the back of his neck and battled back the loco-ass urge to run back downstairs, grab Isa and keep her safe with them. But she was a big girl—and as she kept telling him, she could stand on her own two lying, duplicitous feet. "Just antsy to get back to the US," he said. Not a total lie.

"We're here," Warrick intoned in his stuffy voice. He opened yet another wood-paneled door, and his time led them into a small stone-walled room. "This is the antechamber. Evangeline, you'll go in first. Grayson, you and your associate will wait here until called."

Raph growled, "Get fuc—!"

"Shh, this is standard." Eve placed a hand on his arm.

"I'll see you soon." Then she followed Warrick into the room, and the thick door shut in their faces.

"What's that about?" Raph whirled around. Stone-cold fury replaced his usually laid-back grin. "If they do one fucking thing to hurt her, I'm going to rain fire on their asses."

"Like Eve said, this is standard Watcher protocol. They're stuffy and old-fashioned, and everything's got to be done according to their centuries-old rules. Why the hell do you think I flew here in the middle of an investigation? But this *is* just procedure. Eve did nothing wrong. You and I know it. Believe me, I've dealt with these asses long enough to know how this works."

Eventually, the door opened, and Warrick gestured for Gray and Raph to enter a circular room. Tapestries and banners covered the stone walls, but it was as cold as the Templar's icy training grounds in Boston.

Three women and a man, in a mix of ages from their fifties to their who-knew-how-many hundreds, sat at a half-circle table. Large windows showed the sky behind them, and Eve stood in front of them.

Warrick made the introductions, but Grayson already knew the council members, so he focused on their expressions as he stepped forward and explained his official findings.

"And my conclusion into the incident with the relic of gold is that Watcher Evangeline is not responsible for the theft. Furthermore, Evangeline was instrumental in the R-104A's return and the containment of the true thief."

An hour later, Raph and Eve had also given their versions of events and answered question after question posed by the councilors when finally, the oldest councilor present, a woman with long green hair, stood up.

"We will take this night to review your evidence and gather at sunrise tomorrow to confirm our findings. Evangeline, you'll be confined to this castle until that time. Grayson and your associate, we thank you for your testimony and ask that you make yourselves available to us for the night should we have further questions. Our bailiff will ensure that we met all your needs while you're here. You are all dismissed."

Fuck. Gray ground his teeth. Patience. Patience. Patience. "One night. I have a pressing matter back home."

Raph tensed. Shit. These Watchers wouldn't tolerate interference here—if Raph did or said the wrong thing, that could go badly for Eve, and at the very least, make tonight fucking uncomfortable, so he jabbed an elbow into Raph's ribs and muttered, "Don't say a thing. Wait for me outside."

"Bloody stuffed-up pricks," Eve spat as soon as the door closed behind them.

"What the fuck was that?" Raph exploded.

"Listen," Gray said, "I know we need to talk. But can we check on Isa first? We've been over an hour up here."

"Why are you so focused on my sister?"

Gray resisted the urge to rub the back of his neck—Raph was way too perceptive.

"Isadora's been instrumental in our search for R-104B, and she's currently poisoned." Why the hell did he have to keep pointing this out to people? "I'm responsible for her, that's all."

"Sure as shit, you're responsible," Raph snapped. "I can't believe you brought her here."

"Let's just say there's a fair bit you don't know." And one bit Gray had zero idea on how to tell his friend. What was the protocol here? Did he tell Raph that he'd been with Isa, or was that even crappier because then he was talking about Isa behind her back?

Freaking hell.

Gray had to talk to Isa first—and then he'd tell Raph. And hope like fuck his friend didn't hate him forever.

He held a groan. This was why you didn't bang your best friend's little sister.

25

ALONE IN THE LIBRARY, Isa stared through the giant window to the night-blanketed forest. She was back to another spell.

Everyone would want her—expect her—to fear the transformation hex. But how could she? Her death vision had clearly shown Isa's end. And she'd had more than enough time to reconcile herself to that outcome.

"Isa?" Eve called out from behind her.

Isa turned around as Eve walked over to the window too. "How did your council session go?"

"We'll find out tomorrow."

"Did you hear Cecelie found the spell?"

"I did. But are you sure you want to do this? Cecelie told me the risk."

"Absolutely sure. So, will you help me?"

Eve nodded. "If that's your wish, then yes."

"Thank you. I was worried that with the odds of things going badly, you wouldn't do it. I need to tell Raph everything's going to be okay—don't want him worrying."

"He and Gray are speaking outside. Raph doesn't know about the spell's risk yet.

"Thanks. Would you mind if I had a chat? Just him and I?"

"Of course not. I'll bring him in, then take Grayson down the main hall to arrange rooms for you both. Looks like we're all staying here for the night. Be back in a minute."

Isa took another deep breath. One problem down. Now to make sure her overprotective big brother didn't get in her way.

She took a seat at one of the reading couches as Raph came over.

"Eve said you wanted to chat?"

"Yeah, but to be clear, I'm not asking permission for this. I've already made my mind up but wanted you to know. From me."

"Isa. What's going on?"

"The spell to get rid of the poison has a frigging low chance of success, but it will work. Trust me."

"Oh hell," he breathed out. He dropped to the couch with a thud. "Have you ... considered crossing over, become part of Grandfather's court?"

"Of course I've thought of it. And the answer's no."

"Shit, Isa," Raph whispered. "There's one other option. I have to tell you something."

"What?"

"Isa, you know my gift—"

"You always called it a curse. I see why now."

"No! No, I finally found the way to use it as a genuine gift. I called the shadows. I had to. It was the only way to save Eve. But there was a tradeoff. I had to agree to serve our grandfather."

Isa searched Raph's face. The strain she'd expected to see wasn't there, though. Instead, resolution and determination lay behind his eyes. "I'm sorry, Raph. I know you never wanted that."

"That was before I listened to your advice—when you told me to embrace the dark, I did. And I saved Eve's life. *You* saved Eve's life. So yes, I finally see our power for what it is. An incredible, special gift. But here's the thing, if something goes wrong during the spell and you die, I'll send the shadows to catch you like I did Eve, and bring your soul back before you cross. But that means your life is bound to mine."

"Bound?"

"As in, Eve and I are now linked—if one of us dies, so does the other."

"And if you had to catch my soul, and then something *else* happens to me in the future—and I die—you and Eve would too?"

"Well, yes, but that won't happen."

"Sure." She smiled, even though her stomach soured. For the first time that night, fear—for Raph and Eve—made her palms sweat. Now this spell had to work.

⟨⟨●⟩⟩

An hour later, Isa followed Eve into a small circular room. Lanterns hung on the walls—no modern lighting in this section of the castle—and large windows let the moon-filled sky fill the space with pale light.

Raph came in after them.

"Can I come in, too?" Gray said in a low voice.

"No." Eve set her satchel on the floor. "Your presence may affect the spell, and I need everything to go right here. The only reason Raph is staying is as backup. In case ..."

"Fine. I'll wait in the main hall." Gray's jaw clenched, and he turned to Isa for a moment—something blazing so hot in his eyes that her breath stopped. Then he whirled and left.

Isa held in a sigh. It would've been nice to have him there—he might be an icy prick, but his calm approach had soothed her anxiety in the past, and damned if she didn't want that again right now.

But he wasn't, and there was nothing she could do about that fact, so Isa pushed the urge to ask him to stay out of her mind.

"All right, where do you want me?" Isa asked. "Let me guess, sitting down, facing you, in the center of a triangle of candles?"

"How did you know?"

"This isn't my first spelling."

"Well, let's hope it's the last. The good thing about this ritual is that it should be a permanent antidote to this poison, so you'll never have to worry about it again."

"Love an upside." Isa smiled, but the fast pound of her heart made it hard to hold the grin steady.

The memory of the vision of Gray leaning over Isa, gun in his hand, blood pooling beneath her, replayed through her mind. Isa was going to get through this night—she just didn't know in what form.

‹‹◆››

Gray leaped to his feet for the hundredth time as the doors to the hall swung open. His breath let out as Warrick entered the hall with a tray of food.

"Any word?" Gray raked his hair back. "It's been three hours."

"No. But these spells take—"

"I know, I know. You said that the last ten times. Listen, I need to contact my council. Seriously, have you ever thought about opening up just a fraction and letting—at least officials—have access to their comms?"

"The Watcher's watch, they never—"

"Engage. I know that too." That had been Eve's exact point to the council. "So, to make contact, I head back to the gatehouse, right?"

"Correct. I'll have one of our seniors meet you there to take you through the ward. They'll be at your disposal while you're here. Also, we have scheduled a snow spell for tonight as an added precaution with you all under our roof. Please take care out in the grounds."

"I'll go now."

"But the food—"

"I'll eat it cold."

"Of course. Is there anything else we can assist with? We're aware that you're taking time out of your schedule to assist us here."

"Yes, actually. One more thing. Who's your best diviner?"

"All Watchers can divine through spell craft; however, magic differs depending on the practitioner and what you seek. Might I enquire what you're looking for?"

"I can't say. So who's your best? Eve?"

"She's one of our most powerful witches, yes."

"Rough ballpark on time frame for a divination spell to work?"

"That's impossible, Grayson. You may as well ask how long is a strand of magic."

The creak of the door opening stopped Gray, and both

he and Warrick turned around as Raph walked down the stairs. Cheeks pale. Eyes wild.

Gray's gut seized, and an odd pressure in his throat stopped him from asking the question that burned on the tip of his tongue.

"It worked," Raph muttered. "But the spell was tough. Shit, tough to watch—and tougher still on Eve and Isa."

Gray's knees went weak, and he gripped the edge of the nearest table.

"They both need to rest," Raph continued. "They've gone to their rooms."

"Would you like food sent up?" Warrick asked.

"Nah, I'll come down when Eve wakes up."

"In that case, congratulations on the success of the spell. I shall see you anon." Warrick nodded and then left the room.

"*Anon*?" Gray shook his head. "Who speaks like that?"

"Stiff-assed bailiffs, apparently."

"Hey, before you go. Isa—is she alright?"

Raph tensed and turned around, his eyes narrowing. "Eve said so, but Isa's wiped out. There was a moment ... well, it was touch and go with the spell, apparently. But I didn't need the shadows, so that's the main thing."

"The shadows?"

"The daemon guards who protect the gates of hell. Because of good old grandaddy, I can control them. That means I can use them to stop souls traveling the gates—any gate—from this world to another."

"So what happened in Rome? And not the sanitized report I got through the council."

"Forneous attacked Eve in the piazza and cut her with a hellblade—one nick and your soul is severed from your body. Eve was dying, and I—I called the shadows to me. In exchange for the gift, I gave up my mortality."

"Fucking hell."

"Yeah. One way to put it."

"So if Isa had ... died during that spell, could she have crossed over and then become immortal? And then she'd be fine?" Gray leaned forward over the table.

"It doesn't work like that. Yes, as half-daemons—*alive* half-daemons—Isa and I can cross over and become fully daemon. But even then immortality isn't exactly true. We can still die, it's just harder to kill us."

"And Eve? She's not a half-daemon."

"Doesn't matter. If we die in the human world, we die. The only thing that can stop it is if our souls are caught before they enter a gate—any gate—by someone who also exists in the mortal world. When you return to this world, you can live for as long as the person who caught your soul is alive. You're linked. Forever."

Gray let out a long whistle. "So, you and Eve ..."

"Yeah. She's coming to terms with it. And I—well, this world is better off for having Eve in it, period. I'm just relieved I could use my power to save her. I would've given up anything to do that." A shiver visibly shook through Raph.

"You really feel that strongly for her?"

"Yeah." Raph took in a deep breath. "I do."

"That's awesome, man. I'm thrilled for you—and Eve. I can see you're biting at the bit to head upstairs, but I can ask one more thing? What does it mean—now you're immortal?"

"At its most basic, I'm not human anymore. You saw how Warrick reacted to me—part of that was Eve, for sure. I swear he's got a thing for her. But the rest was me—he must know somehow. I guess people react differently to daemons. But any more than that? I haven't had time to find out how being part of my grandfather's court will impact me—us."

"What do you mean?"

"Daemons from a higher gate, or with more power, have a level of control over anyone from a lower gate or with lesser power."

"But your grandfather's the Lord of Hell."

"Yeah, still have no clue what that means for me. I'll have to wait and see."

Icy fingers trailed down Gray's spine. So if Isa crossed over, she'd be at the mercy of any daemon with more power than her?

"Is that it? I really need to get back to Eve."

Alone again in the hall, Gray stared at the crackling fire.

Shit. Isa could've died tonight. Right then—during that spell—she could've left this world. And then what? How fucked up would this world be without her to light it up?

His gut knotted.

No, not even thinking like that. Gray pushed himself to his feet, hauled in a deep breath, and headed out into the freezing—fuck, *snowing*—night to contact *his* council.

A half-hour later, he'd wrapped up his talk with the Templar Council and was back in the castle shaking his hands to get warmth back into his fingers. Someone offered to find him something hot to eat, but he told them not to worry. He was so tired he just shoveled in whatever was on the tray Warrick had provided, then headed up to grab what sleep he could.

Isa was right about fatigue being dangerous, and he needed all his senses working for the next day.

Gray found the room—chamber—whatever the hell you'd call the space assigned to him. An ancient four-poster bed lurked in the darkness at the far end. The stone walls were bare but for a door on one side.

He stripped his jacket off and dumped his satchel on the bed, right beside a book.

Who the hell had left him a book?

He picked it up and turned it over. *After Today* by Jacqueline Hayley. Some kind of dystopian fiction, by the look of it. A sudden urge to lie down and read, turn the paper pages, get lost in some other world rather than this fucked-up one surged through him.

He eyed the bed. The book. No, he didn't have time for fiction. Shut-eye was the only thing he was doing.

But he had zero chance of sleep without knowing what —who—was on the other side of that door.

The next dark room was a replica of his. But a chattering sound echoed around the stone walls.

"Gray?" Isa's voice floated up from beneath the blankets. "What are you doing?"

"I'm going to sleep. What are *you* doing?"

"I'm sleeping—or trying to. It's freezing. Even with all the blankets."

Shit. "Is it because of the spell?

"Could be because it's *frigging snowing* outside, but yeah, Eve said I might be cold for a while."

"I'll check with her now—"

"No, she'll be sleeping. The spell took every ounce of energy she had. I'll be okay. But ..."

"But what?"

"I know you're pissed at me and all, but can you shelve that—for a while—and sit with me?"

Gray held in a sigh.

"Please?"

Her whisper made the hairs on the back of his neck

prick, and hell if he had a choice then, because before he'd even thought it, his legs took him to the headboard.

"Fuck," Gray said. "Is there a light here?"

"Don't think so."

"Hell. Move over."

"You don't have to sound so shitty."

"Yes, I do." He eased down onto the bed, drew the blankets back, and climbed in. Isa yelped. "I'm shitty. You should be in a warm room."

"Who cares? Right now I'm so cold, I'd share a blanket with anyone—well, practically anyone."

"Fuck, you're an icicle."

"You should know."

"What do you mean?" Gray held Isa against his side as another shiver shook through her, and then she tucked her icy hands under his shirt. He jumped.

"Shit, Isa."

"Sorry, but you're so warm. Am I too cold?"

"It's fine," he muttered. "So what's with the ice comment?"

"How your nickname's Ice."

"Ah." He'd heard his nickname spoken in whispers before, but few had the guts to say it to his face.

"Do you mind the nickname?"

"No," he said honestly. "Don't give a fuck what the teams call me as long as they do the job."

Another shiver shook through Isa, and he tightened his hold around her until it subsided. He really should have let her go, but the way her body pressed against his, and with the intimacy of the dark, the silence except for their breathing ... Fuck, he never wanted to let her go.

"So," Gray said, "do I say thank you for the book?"

"You got it?"

"Yeah." Something warm unfurled in his chest.

"I know you probably won't read it now, but the next moment where you have nothing urgent to do—no worlds to save and all that jazz—trust me, do yourself a favor and escape into a book world. And a dystopian romance—"

"You gave me a romance?"

"Absolutely. Steamy and passionate, and the action scenes are amazing. You'll love it. And are you really just going to bed?"

"Had to go to the gatehouse for a call with my council. But we got a lead, so it was worth freezing my ass off."

"What's happened?"

"We put a track and trace order on the lab director, and our satellites intercepted a call coming from an island in the Caribbean."

"Let me guess—St. Barths? Isn't that where Kai's going on his yacht?"

"Which is why Marcella is heading to the Caribbean right now to set up a base of ops."

"What about Tank?"

His gut tightened. "Still on life support. But he survived the initial operation, and they're prepping him for transportation to our hospital in Boston. We're not giving up on him. He's young, strong, and we have the best doctors, plus witches, working on healing spells."

Isa's breath hitched, and her arms tightened around him. "I'm glad he's getting the best care."

Yeah, me too. But Gray just held onto Isa. Her warmth. Her vitality.

"Gray, can I tell you something?" Isa whispered into the darkness. "I was thirteen when the visions started. So for thirteen years, I've seen the future. Never the past."

Gray inhaled with a sharp intake of air. "Then you never saw me before then?"

"No. Is that important?"

"Yes, yes, it is. I've seen some fucked-up things, been in some fucked-up situations. I can't imagine—don't want—anyone else seeing those times. Those things." He suppressed a shudder, and then her arms wrapped around him.

"Your brother?"

Gray's stomach clenched. "I don't talk about Carson much." *Ever*.

"It's okay, you don't have to tell me."

"Isa ..." He sighed. "It's a shitty story."

"I've seen so much of you, but never anything about a brother."

"That's because he was just a kid when he died. We were thirteen."

"*What*? Oh, Gray. That's awful."

"Yeah, told you it was shitty."

"No wonder you hate drugs so much. How did he get involved in that ... life?"

"Carson and I were street kids from early on. Single dad and he wasn't the best character to start with. He quit on us when we were about ten. Guess he thought he'd done his job to that point. We were already mixing with rough crowds before he bailed, and so we just stuck where we were."

"Didn't child services or someone like that look after you?"

"Our old man was into some fucked-up dealings, all illegal, so he did everything he could to stay below—or totally off—the radar, and that extended to Carson and me. We barely went to school. Moved around when we did. So after he left, I found a gang who worked stolen goods, but Carson didn't have the patience for that line of work, and he went with another gang entirely—they dealt illicit drugs."

"Shit."

"It wasn't all bad. Every now and again, we'd get a local who'd give us a little help. One baker would leave out the leftovers that hadn't sold for the day. He used to make the best cinnamon rolls. Carson and I would meet up there. It was our thing, I guess. But it wasn't long before he got into the crap he was dealing and OD'd."

"Gray ..." Isa's breath hitched. "I'm so, so sorry. For you both."

"Yeah, it sucked. But old news now."

"Maybe we can talk about something else? Like ... how you became a Templar?"

"Ah, now that's a good day to talk about. It wasn't long after Carson died. Basically, I picked the pocket of the wrong person. Well, turned out to be the right person. She was a Templar Knight in New York and only caught me because I stole a warded purse. She was, uh, impressed with how good a job I did, and took me under her wing. I stayed with her and the Templars at their compound in Boston—"

"Wait—is that why you don't have an actual home?"

"Yep. I've always lived in Templar residences, and to be frank, I have never wanted my own place. But picking that Templar's pockets was the best thing that could've happened to me. When I turned sixteen, I applied to be a trainee and never looked back."

"Thank you for telling me." She tightened her arms around his waist, and her breasts rubbed against his side.

Heat surged to his dick, and every part of him zeroed in on the way she fit against him. A sudden image of her naked, wrapped around him—

"You know, I'm warmer now. And Gray—what I said about you being an icicle before? Well, right now, you're the total opposite."

He bit back a groan. Icicle? He was on fire for her. But he shouldn't be. He should get the fuck out of that bed. Grab her a hot water bottle or something.

"I know you're angry with me. But tonight showed me something—that there's no use being shitty when life is right here. And there's something else I want. Right here." The whisper of her breath caressed his lips, and in the dark, her lips pressed to his. "Can you keep the pissed-off-ness shelved for a little longer and want me too?"

26

In the darkness, heat flowed through Isa's veins and Gray filled her world. His arms holding her, his chest against hers, the rasp of his breath in her ear.

Please, please, want me back.

"Isa, I could've lost you tonight." He pressed her hand to his chest. "This knot lodged right here while I sat downstairs fucking waiting to hear if you'd come back or not. So yeah, right now, being angry means jack shit. What matters is you're alive. And want you?" He shifted her hand lower. "What does this tell you?"

Her core flooded. She went to make a joke about men and their dicks, but laughter was a million miles away.

"I don't want to think about tonight. I just want to think about this, us." Isa drew in a shuddering breath and pressed her forehead to his chest.

"Shh," he whispered. "I know. And hey, we can sleep if that's what you need. I'll hold you—"

"No. What I need is this." Her mouth went dry. "But can I be in charge this time?"

For a moment, only their breathing filled the dark, then a groan rumbled from him. "*Issi*. Tell me what to do."

"Lie back. Wait—condoms. My handbag is beside the bed."

"Stay there. I'll get them." He rolled away from her, and instantly she missed the solid, hot presence of him pressed against her. But he was back in a flash and rolled her right back into his arms. "Now, where were we?"

"Here." Isa felt for the hem of his shirt. "Off. Now."

They yanked and tugged their clothes off, legs and arms and bodies rubbing as they got rid of everything. And then hot, hard muscles tensed beneath her touch.

She pushed him back. Damn, but she wished she could see him now. Just imagining how he'd look spread out for her pleasure sent a pulse of heat to her core.

She straddled his thighs.

"Can I do one thing?" Gray whispered. His hands settled on her hips, then one snuck down across her belly, and he swept a thumb up her seam to her clit. "Fuck. You're already wet."

Isa ground against his touch. "I'm always wet for you."

He stroked her again. "I want you so much, minx. My Divine One."

Isa rose on her knees, felt for his dick at the entrance to her body, then slid down, and his hot, hard length filled every part of her again.

Her nipples pebbled. Her body hummed at the intrusion.

Gray hissed, and his fingers dug into her flesh. "Minx, this is ..."

She rocked back, let her head drop, and savored the stretch of him seated all the way inside her.

"Perfect," she finished for him. "Frigging perfect."

His hips lifted, pushed her into the air with the force of his movement.

"Uh-uh. You said I could be in control."

"I never—fine." A low growl swept through him, but his hips lowered to the bed.

"Good boy." Isa lifted herself high. Moaned at the hot glide of his flesh through her body. Teased herself with his dick against the rim of her entry. Flowed back over him.

Maybe because of the dark, maybe because the man from her dreams was with her right now and her time with this wonderful man was limited, but every other sense went into hyperdrive.

Gray's delicious aftershave.

The swoosh of flesh on flesh. The rasp of breaths drawing in, shuddering out. The heat of him beneath and inside her.

Every scent, flavor, caress and murmur imprinted on her.

She lifted again, surged back down. Her body tightened, the pressure climbed.

"Isa ... Isa ... Isa ... So close." His fingers bit into her hips.

She rocked. The pressure mounted.

He hissed her name again. She wished she could see him—but even in the dark, she knew his eyes were on her.

She lifted again. The coils tightened.

He surged beneath her, met her thrust for thrust. But she couldn't quite—

"Touch me." She grabbed his hand and moved it to where their bodies met. He stroked her clit, strummed it over and over. Then he surged high. She slammed low. They ground against each other.

Her core clenched. Sparks flew behind her eyes.

And her orgasm exploded.

"Fuck. Can't hold back," Gray hissed. Then his arms

banded around her. He drew her down to his chest, and he hammered into her. "Fuck. Fuck. Yes, Issi, yes!"

Her orgasm reignited, and the world around them disappeared in a white-hot rush.

‹‹‹●›››

Gray woke up in heaven. The sky outside the arched window had turned from black to charcoal, lighting the room enough to make out forms and figures.

Isa's soft, warm body filling his arms. Her breasts pillowed against his side. In her sleep, Isa's lips were softly parted, her determined chin a sexy little edge to her face.

How good would life be to wake up to this every day? His chest tightened.

Last night had been ... mind-blowing. World rocking.

Damn it, why—how—did she make him feel like this? Sex was a release. Fun, sure. But always easy to walk away from without another thought. Not this ... consuming, shifting, fucking loco-ass urge to dive into someone and never leave them.

He wasn't after a relationship. Hell, he never wanted to be responsible for another person in his life. But Isa ... what would life be like if he were with her outside of this fucked-up situation?

Her joy in living. Her laugh. The way her smile was like a balm to every fucking hurt he'd ever had? He could get drunk on her.

But Isa was right.

His job was everything. It took every ounce of his focus. And the fact was, with Isa around, his focus had fractured. He couldn't allow that to happen.

Damn. He needed to stay away from her. She was too dangerous for him. To him. And fuck, look at the life he lived—he was too dangerous for her. Literally.

He blew out a hard breath. Fact one, he had to find R-104B still. Fact two, he had to cut it off with Isa. Yes, he needed her help, but he'd already been an asshole to bring her into his world. The more they had sex, the greater the risk of an emotional connection developing that he didn't want. Which would make him an even bigger asshole.

So he soaked in the sight of her. This moment had to last a lifetime because it had to be the last time.

The door creaked open, and he tensed as a figure appeared in the doorway—and then Raph stepped into the room.

Shit. Shit. Shit.

Gray raised a hand and whispered, "Don't wake her. I'll meet you downstairs in the hall."

Raph's gaze cut back to Isa. Then he backed out of the room as silently as he'd entered it.

Well hell. This had to happen at some point. Looked like that time was now. Gray eased his arm from under Isa and tucked her under the blankets before he slid from the bed and pulled his clothes on.

Then she rolled to her side as if looking for him, and he pushed a pillow to where he'd been.

The lump in his throat turned into a sour feeling he ignored as he turned his back on Isa and left the room.

Moments later, Gray entered the hall, and the tension pouring off Raph where he stood in front of the hearth made his gut churn harder. Well, this was fitting. Time for Gray to face the fire, too.

"Isa was upset last night," Gray said. "She asked me to

stay with her." *Because she found comfort when he was near her.* His gut churned even harder.

"So you were just shirtless in the bed with her? Shit, Grayson!"

"Don't yell."

"I'll fucking yell if I want to. She was tired, had just undergone a near-death ritual, and you go have sex with her?"

"It wasn't the first time—"

"What? Fuck, she's twenty-six. You're ten years older than her. And that's not even considering your life experience. She's sheltered. Shit, did you take advantage of—?"

"Hell, no. You know me, Raphael."

"Yeah, I know you wouldn't do that. Sorry. Shouldn't have said that. But Isa, she's had such a shitty time, you know? With what her visions do to her, and with pricks like Liam. She needs protecting—"

"She's not weak, Raph. Yes, her visions make her life challenging, but she's not weak."

"I know. It's just ..." Raph dropped into the nearest chair. "Gray, fuck knows we've been through some shit together. Listen, sit down, will you? And don't give me that look. Yes, you're a decent man. But you're also completely dedicated to what you do. And maybe Isa's not weak, but she's inexperienced. And you always said no relationships. No love. So has your motto changed?"

"Whatever Isa and I are to each other, I'm not out to hurt her. And no, I don't think I'm good relationship material. The opposite. I'm the last person anyone would want to be in a relationship with."

"You're allowed to fall in love, you know?"

"Just not with your sister?"

"I never said that. I only want the best for her. But right

now, I'm talking about you. Your life. I know what happened to your brother cut you deep, but—"

"Fuck that shit off. There's not enough therapy in the world to deal with my head. Now, I need to get back to the US. The Watchers better get their shit together fast."

"You do that every time I bring this up."

"What?" Gray shoved a hand through his hair. "Get antsy because some bureaucratic bullshit has me over here in England talking to a room of stuffy old shirts instead of tracking down R-104B?"

"No. Change the subject when I bring up relationships. As in every. Single. Time."

"Can't take a hint much, can you?"

"And now you go on the offense. Classic Grayson." Raph sat back and stretched his legs.

"You know, I thought you'd be pissed off if I even *thought* about your sister. Where's that Raph, instead of this get-inside-my-head-BS Raph?"

"Oh, he's there, but I'm way more interested in your head right now. Because even if it's not with Isa, you still deserve to find happiness."

"What, like you and Eve?"

"Well, you can find your own person to fall for, but yes." Raph shrugged. "Gray, you're thirty-six, not dead."

"Nope. No way."

"It all comes back to your brother, doesn't it?"

"Carson has nothing to do with this."

"I think you're lying. I think he's got everything to do with this. He was your only family. You loved him, and then when he died—"

"He fucking left me alone, and I've never wanted to love anyone again?" Gray turned away from his friend. Hardened the shell that had for a moment weakened. "Don't give me that look. I don't need your pity. And I don't need love. Don't need it. Don't want it. Not from you, not from Isa. Not from anyone. I don't need anything fucking else but to find R-104B."

"Don't need my love?" Isa's soft voice echoed from behind him.

27

ISA SHOOK HER HEAD. Gray didn't want her love? Who said she even felt that way for him? Yes, she liked him—when he wasn't being Icehole Grayson—and clearly, he found her attractive, but she'd said nothing about love.

But ... maybe she could *love him?*

Shut up, inner voice.

Anger glittered in Raph's gaze as he scowled at Gray.

"Oh no, no way." Isa cut her hand through the air. "You might be my brother, Raph, but you don't get to dictate who I bang—or don't. Ever. Is that clear?" She whirled to Gray. "And you. Why did you tell him anything? Do you report to all your lovers' families after you've had sex?"

"No." Gray scowled. "Raph checked on you this morning —found us together."

"Isa, it's not the same. Gray's been my friend long before you ever met him."

"Well, there you're wrong." Isa folded her arms. "I've been seeing Gray in my visions for years. I just didn't know who he was until recently."

"What? Him?" Raph's mouth dropped open.

"Yes, so I don't want to hear one more word about Gray and me." She lifted her chin and held his gaze. "I'm an adult. I make my own decisions. And even *if* I was in love with the icehole"—she sent Gray her most withering look—"that would still be *my choice.* So the only thing I want to hear is that you're not going to discuss my sex life ever again. Unless I bring it up, anyway. Got it?"

"Wow, Isa. You go, girl." Eve clapped her hands as she joined them. "You're a spitfire, aren't you?"

"She always has been. Just not usually this vocal." Raph snaked an arm around Eve and brought her to his side. "Hey, princess. How you feeling?"

"Better now. Thanks for letting me sleep. So, Isa, what's brought on the change of being so vocal?"

"Association with someone else I can think of," Raph muttered.

"Don't blame me," Gray muttered back. "Your sister's been outspoken for as long as I've known her."

"Whoa, hold on. You all need to stop talking like I'm not here. And you"—Isa glared at Gray—"don't get to talk about me at all."

The sound of someone loudly clearing their throat came from above. They all looked up at the landing. Warrick stood at the top of the stairs.

"Good morning, all," he said. "The council are meeting now and have asked me to advise they expect to have this matter wrapped up within the hour. Ms. Smith, they also asked me to convey to you it would be best if you stay under our roof for several days. This is to ensure you have no serious repercussions because of the transformational spell."

"Wait—what?" Gray said.

Isa looked at Eve. "Is that true about the spell?"

"It's possible. But if you stay here, it won't be a problem. Between Warrick and me, you have the two strongest Watcher spellcasters to handle anything that comes up."

"And," Warrick continued, "if you stay with us ... We understand that while you are a diviner with advanced capabilities, you are looking to strengthen your proficiency in focusing your craft?"

"Um, yes," Isa answered, "if you're saying I want to have more control?"

"Quite so. Well, we would like to offer you a room here at Ashforton, for as long as you need assistance with that skill. Cecelie has found some books that may be of use."

"So you can use her visions, you mean?" Gray said slowly.

"I'm sure we can come to an arrangement." Warrick nodded at them all and then disappeared.

Isa didn't even glance at Gray. If these Watchers could really help her gain control over her visions, they could have a permanent retainer for as long as she had left.

Isa turned to Eve. "Can your books help me learn how to control my visions?"

"Technically, yes. Your heritage means that you handle powers—like magic—differently than us, though."

"Like how a high priestess handles magic?"

"Exactly. And we have some ancient, rare texts, some not even from this world. They may be useful."

Holy shit. Isa could learn how to focus on her gift—then she could really have a purpose for her visions. She glanced at Gray. His shuttered expression gave nothing away.

Isa asked Gray, "What about the reason I'm with you?"

"Looks like you need to stay here," he said.

"I guess I could pass along any information I get."

Gray met Isa's stare, and then finally, his jaw ticked, and he nodded once.

"Then I'm staying here." In a foreign country, with a group of witches who gave her the creeps—well, except Cecelie and Eve—in an ancient castle that seriously lacked heating.

"Don't worry, I'll be here to look out for you, little sis." Raph smiled at her. "I need to chat with Gray. Try not to get into any trouble for a few minutes."

She rolled her eyes at him. "Why does everyone think I'm getting *into* trouble? Maybe trouble just comes at me?"

"Whoa. Sorry." Raph put his hands up. "Don't hit me."

She snorted as he backed away.

"Can I join you?" Eve came over carrying two steaming mugs. "Hot chocolate. Want one?"

"Sure. Not my normal breakfast, but why not?" Isa took a sip, and when the rich, chocolaty goodness hit her tongue, she couldn't help a sigh. "This is bliss."

"I know, right? One of the best things about my time here."

"Speaking of your time here." Isa leaned over the table. "What's with all the weird looks between Raph and Warrick? And also, he's hot. What's his deal? Single, taken, you know?"

"Single. And he's not bad if you like the stuck-up their ass type. He's also a powerful witch dedicated to Ashforton's safety. So as much as he's a dick, the castle is lucky to have him. And the Raph thing ..." Eve sighed and shook her head. "I swear, there was never anything between us, but Raph seems to think Warrick's got something for me, and Warrick, well, he doesn't like off-worlders. Now, maybe there's someone else we should talk about." Eve cut her eyes to the other end of the hall.

Isa followed her gaze to where Gray and Raph were talking. The flickering light of the fire nearby sent a warm glow over the Templar, giving him the complete opposite appearance of the iceman.

"Oh yeah, we need to talk." Eve laughed and then lowered her voice. "When did you two get together?"

"How'd you guess?"

"Apart from how he looks at you, you mean?" Eve snorted. "Have you seen the heat in that gaze? Yowza—*I'm* seared, and I'm just sitting beside you."

"That steam is as much from anger as anything else right now. And yeah, we've got together a couple of times, but I don't see that happening again."

"Do you want it to?" Genuine concern replaced the humor in Eve's gaze. "Gray is ... difficult. He's a Templar. And for him, that means one thing comes first, always. And that won't be the person he's with."

"I know." A shiver prickled down Isa's spine. "And do I want to be with him? He's like a prickly ice giant. And he's detailed and focused and calm and capable, and when he touches me, my mind fizzles and my body goes up in ashes."

"Oh wow." Eve sat back with a thud. "You're into him."

"Yep."

"So, what's the problem?"

"Let's see. I lied to him, exaggerated another topic, and then withheld something else."

"So you've got trust issues. Been there, done that. You can work through them."

"Not if he's not into me in the same way. Let's drop it. I just don't see a relationship, you know?"

But even to Isa's ears, her last words rang false. Not that it mattered. There couldn't be any happily ever after between Isa and Gray.

Maybe she should've guarded her heart more—but who cared? Leaving this world having been with Gray—having developed feelings for him—might be among the best things to ever have happened to her, and she wasn't going to regret that.

Isa and Eve had just finished their hot chocolates when Warrick reappeared with a message that the council was ready to see Eve.

Isa's heart filled her throat as her friend stood up and squared her shoulders. Please, please let them give Eve the all clear.

"I'll be bringing Raph with me," Eve said.

Warrick frowned but said nothing else before he led Eve and Raph back up the stairs to wherever this special council meeting took place.

"So you're staying?" Gray's voice carried across the hall.

Isa swiveled to face him. "Yes, you're okay with that?"

⸱⟨⟨●⟩⟩⸱

Okay with that. Gray's gut tightened even as Isa said the words from across the hall. He wanted to yell, hell no. Because yes, he needed her—for R-104B, and ... for himself.

And that was the fucker. Needing her for himself was the death knell on any thoughts of being close to Isadora Smith ever again. No matter what Raphael said, Gray wasn't against relationships. He just had another world to focus on. And zero desire to be responsible for another person.

So, he forced himself to nod his head. "We can do this remotely. It'll be fine." *Lie.* Having intel instantly was always best. But he was taking second best this time around. "And you need to be here." *Truth.* "Plus ..."

She walked over to him, and he stood up, too. "Plus what?"

Damn it. Was it better to rip the plaster off now or let whatever was growing between them slide gently into nothingness? After all, he was leaving, and what were the odds he'd run into Isa ever again unless he intentionally went to Australia to find her?

"Gray, stop right there."

"What?"

"Trying to handle me. I can see you figuring out what—or not—to say. Just be honest. I won't break apart. Surely I've handled enough shit by now for you to trust that, even if you don't trust me."

"Don't take it personally. I don't trust anyone. If I misplace my trust and shit goes bad with these relics, the consequences are fucking bad. And let's face it, you haven't been honest with me either."

"And you know why. So you can take your 'don't take it personally' and shove it up your ass. We've been sleeping together. Oh, I get it. The sex was convenient, right? That's all it was. Fine. I get that. Good to know where I stand."

"What? How did we get from trust to sex? And convenient? Isa, nothing about *you and I* has ever been convenient." He shoved a hand through his hair. "I can't believe you said that."

"Then fine. Don't trust me with shit to do with the relic. But at least trust I'm not going to collapse screaming at something you think I don't want to hear." She folded her arms and her chin raised. Isa battle-mode.

"Fine. This is the truth. It's time to put an end to this." He gestured between them. "No more sex. This—as in you and I—shouldn't have happened. I knew it. But I got caught up in the fantasy."

"And you just decided this now?"

"I've decided now is the time to call it. Cut the rope."

"Like I'm tying you to me or something? And why? What changed from last night to now?"

"Nothing. And that's why I'm sorry I let it go this far. We can't have a relationship, Isa. And I know—I can see it—you and I are heading for that if we let this go on any further."

"And why the hell not?"

"Because I'm a Templar. I have a job to do that's fucking dangerous. And because you've almost been killed, how many times now, Isa?"

"Hate to break your pity party and all, but only one of those times was because of you. Every single other time was because of who *I* am. And do I need to remind you who my grandfather is? Listen, Grayson, if you don't want to be with me, fine. I'm a big girl and yeah, I might not like it, but I can handle it. But don't you dare try to use the fact that your world is too damned dangerous for me. Don't you fucking dare."

Twin spots of color bloomed on her cheeks, and Isa whirled around. Hell, she was mad. No, not mad. Furious. And maybe hurt.

His own chest tightened. Freaking hell. Hurting Isa was the last thing he wanted. But he didn't—couldn't—say anything more. This was the way it had to be.

Isa's stomping across the hall and up the stairs was the only sound echoing through the hall until the door above the stairs creaked open. Eve and Raph reappeared, blocking her exit.

"I'm cleared," Eve said as they walked down the stairs, forcing Isa to backtrack. "The council even agreed to work on improving the deficiencies I outlined."

"That's wonderful!" Isa said with a brightness to her

voice that made him look carefully at her. Her smile was huge, but did anyone else see the way her cheeks clenched like she was hiding a grimace? "I am so pleased for you."

"You okay, Isa?" Raph said.

"Sure am. Just absolutely thrilled for Eve." Her smile lit up another watt, and Gray wanted to puke. She was hurting. That fake smile and tone might satisfy Raph and Eve, but Gray saw the truth. And he hated it. Hated himself.

"Good. Because Eve was magnificent." Raph picked up the witch's hand and pressed a fast kiss to her palm. "She faced down that old—the council—and told them like it is. That they were too page-and-protocol bound, and that if the Watchers wanted to see a purpose into the future, they needed to look within."

"It did the job." Eve shrugged, but the relief and satisfaction on her face spoke volumes. "And they asked me to lead a review of all our spells. It means spending more time at Ashforton, although I don't have to be based here permanently. But first up, I'm going to see my mother." Eve looked over at Raph. "*We're* going to see my mother. After the last few weeks, I've realized how important family is."

"And then," Raph said, "Eve's coming back to Australia to stay with me for a while—at least until she needs to be back here for the spells."

"Wow." Isa kept right on smiling. "That's wonderful, Eve."

"And Mum's in Glastonbury, so I won't be too far away."

"Isa," Raph said, "we'll stay here until everyone is comfortable that the blood spell has settled, and then we'll go. But we'll come back and pick you up on our way home so we can all head back to Australia together. Eve thinks seven days max."

Aaand, still smiling, Isa said, "Take all the time you need.

If Warrick's happy for me to stay here and work on my visions, then that'll work perfectly."

"Um, Isa?" Raph said, eyes narrowed. "What's wrong with your face?"

"Nothing at all. But I have to go now. Talk to you later." She took off up the stairs.

Gray swallowed the bile that rose in his throat. Fuck.

"Gray? You're good for Isa to stay here, right?" Raph asked after the door had shut behind Isa.

"Absolutely," Gray lied through his teeth.

28

FIVE DAYS after Gray had left Ashforton, two days after the Watchers declared the blood spell completely settled, and one day after Eve and Raph had left to visit Eve's mother, Isa found herself in a seminormalized routine at the castle.

She dressed as soon as she woke up because she'd learned fast that every moment she spent alone, her thoughts went in one direction.

She had breakfast in the hall, mostly on her own with Eve and Raph gone, since the castle peeps up at this early hour ate in their workrooms, and the trainees—when they did eventually come down—sat in their study groups, or even on their own like Isa.

Then she met Cecelie around 8:00 a.m., and between her other tasks, the librarian helped Isa decode the books about controlling daemon abilities. Which was just as well because some texts were in French and Latin, even Old Norse, and the librarian read them all.

So Isa made her way to the library as usual, and several hours after starting a promising book—thankfully in Old

English, so she understood most of it—Cecelie popped her head around the bookshelf.

"How are you going, Isadora?"

"Think I've found something here. Apparently, a tenth-gate daemon named Artifice—this was a long time ago—came to the human world and basically got it on with several witches. One of those witches, Giselle, wrote this book as a record for her child, who was part daemon. I've got a lot more to read, but this looks like first-hand knowledge."

"Giselle ... interesting. She lived here over five hundred years ago. She's also a direct ancestor of Evangeline. Is there anything else you need?"

"No, I'm good. A hundred pages down, only ... two hundred more to go."

As soon as Cecelie left, Isa flipped to the next page in the book.

Ink sketches covered the next two pages, depicting a hand touching the tip of a crystalline obelisk, like the one Cyn had given Isa, with something dribbling down the finger. Below the drawings, someone had written, *find the future, blood will tether. Cut the tie, blood will sever.*

Huh. That had to be blood dripping down the finger in the sketch, then. So she just had to bleed on an obelisk?

Isa remembered Cyn's comments about crystals and daemons, and excitement rushed through her. She raced up to her room, grabbed her obelisk, and resumed her place against the stone wall, and reopened the book.

The drawing still looked as simple and as explanatory as last time.

Find the future, blood will tether. Cut the tie, blood will sever. She mentally replayed the words one more time. Okay, she had this.

Isa pressed the crystal into the tip of her thumb and pulled it across her skin. She hissed, but she kept going until a bead of blood welled. "Ouch."

There were no instructions, so she concentrated on R-104B, remembering the image of the censer Gray had shown her, and whispered, "Find the future blood will tether—"

Stars flashed across Isa's vision; goosebumps raced up her arms, and the library whisked away as she hurtled darkness faster than ever before.

(((●)))

"Isadora? Isa?"

Awareness returned like a peaceful ocean wave rolling across the sand, retreating, then surging again. Gentle but implacable.

"Isadora, can you hear me?"

The bookshelves wobbled into view, along with Cecelie and Warrick's worried faces hovering above her.

"Why am I lying on the floor?" Isa asked.

"Here, let me help you sit up. I'm guessing the reason you were asleep has something to do with that." Cecelie nodded at the book, still open to the page Isa had read from on the floor beside her.

Isa pushed herself up till she was sitting again and battled back the swimming sensation in her head.

"Isadora." Warrick helped her to her feet and then stepped back and folded his arms. Disapproval dripped from his expression.

"Hey." Isa wet her lips. "How long was I sleeping?"

"I found you an hour ago," Cecelie replied. "I don't know what time you completed the ritual, though." Her beautiful eyes narrowed. "Isadora, you shouldn't have done that. Never, ever, can you try an incantation without proper instructions and protection in place."

"Sorry to have caused any ... commotion." Isa tucked the book under her arm.

"Steady." Warrick helped her to her feet. "I take it you found an incantation that worked? But did you read the next page before you started?"

"Damn, but I'm wobblier than normal. And no, just the page with the spell. Why?"

"Read it," Cecelie said, and held out the book.

"Okay, it says, 'prudence ...'" Isa wrinkled her nose. "Who says prudence?"

"Read."

"Fine." Damn, but the librarian could be bossy. "*Prudence* is required in the operation of this ritual. An imbalance is caused when the most immoderate—what does that mean?—energy is drawn upon that results in a universal inability to draw any prophecy for a period of at least one full turn of the sun."

"Immoderate means more than normal," Cecelie replied. "Most is a superlative—so using the spell gives you access to far more energy than you would usually have."

Oh shit. Isa snapped the book shut. "No wonder I slept for such a long time afterward."

"No doubt part of the sacrifice required for accessing that energy."

"So I won't have any visions for the next twenty-four hours?"

"That's how I interpret it." Cecelie nodded.

"Then at least I had a vis—" Isa froze. Oh shit. *The vision.*

"What is it?" Warrick glanced around. "Are you okay?"

"Yes. I saw—" Isa shut her mouth. Shit, shit, shit. She'd

seen Gray and the myrrh—and maybe even herself. But she couldn't tell Warrick and Cecelie that. Isa's own death vision flashed back through her mind. Holy shit.

Shit. Shit, shit, shit! Was this all connected? Had the time really come?

Her breath clogged in her throat, and her muscles tensed as her body was preparing to run off and hide from her future without Isa even making that decision. She had to wipe suddenly clammy palms over her jeans.

"Are you alright?" Cecelie asked.

"Yeah, I am." As if saying the words steadied her, she was finally able to take a breath.

No, she wasn't running anywhere.

If the vision of someone saving Gray was truly connected to Isa's death vision, then that's the way it was.

"I need to make a call. Now." She glanced between the bailiff and the librarian. "It's urgent."

"In that case, I'll help you to the gatehouse." Warrick unfolded his arms. "Come on."

As soon as they reached the wall and cleared the wards, Isa called Gray.

"Isa. Have you had a vision?" His clipped, deep voice made her heart clench, and she slumped against the wall—held a hand up when Warrick reached out to steady her. "I'm okay."

"Isadora?" Gray said. "What's going on? Who else is there?"

"Everything's okay. I found a spell that helps with control, and had a vision."

"What did you see?"

"Someone's going to shoot at you."

"Good to know nothing's changed."

"Not joking, Gray. Someone's going to shoot at you. And

... the *thing* you're after is there. And, and I think ... I think I stop them—by pushing their gun away."

"Where?"

"I couldn't tell exactly. But I think a boat. And considering where you're going ..."

"Tell me exactly what happened."

"It's nighttime. You're in a bedroom with open glass doors leading to a deck. Lights shine off the water in the background. And someone has a gun pointed at you—I didn't see who's holding it, but it's pointed at you and goes off. But someone pushes the gun high at the last second."

"What am I wearing?"

"Black suit, white shirt. No tie."

"Okay, nothing out of the ordinary. And you saw R-104B?"

"Yes. In your *hand*."

"Fuck. Well, at least you've seen me and R-104B together. I'll take that as good news."

"Uh, what about the gun and someone shooting at you?"

"Isa, I get shot at a lot. And you said someone saves me, so not that big a deal."

"Gray. You need to take this seriously. Can you send the plane for me? I need to get there."

"Isa, did you see yourself in that vision?"

"Not exactly, but I've seen a very similar scene with me ..."

"With you?"

"Nothing. But I think the arms that I saw pushing the gun away could've been me."

Gray's sigh echoed down the line. She could just imagine him pinching the bridge of his nose.

"Right now, you're safe with the Watchers. It sounds like you're onto something with the crystal and the spell, so stay there. Call me if you have any more visions. Now, I've got to go. Take care."

The line went dead.

Isa stared at her mobile and couldn't stop her mouth from dropping open. He'd hung up on her? And *take care*? Oh, damn no. She was right on this—someone, and everything in her gut yelled that someone was her—was going to save Grayson No-Bloody-Last-Name's ass on a yacht in the Caribbean.

She jammed her mobile back in her handbag and stood up straight. "Warrick," Isa said, "thank you for everything you've done for me, but I need to get to Los Angeles."

"As in, you wish to depart Ashforton?"

"Yes." But shit, how was she meant to get from Cheshire to the US? Frig. Unless ... "Warrick, there are no true diviners in your coven, right?"

"Correct."

"What about ... what if we do a deal? I'll practice divination for you if you help me get to Miami?" There was only one way Isa knew to get herself on that yacht, and Kai St. James had given her the entry ticket back in LA. "And help me find some clothes."

"You'd do business with us?"

"Yes." Isa licked her lips. "Divination is a tradeable commodity. And as my precognitions are always accurate, I can guarantee you that what I have to say will be useful."

She met Warrick's gaze, the doubt in his eyes clear.

But damn it, she would do this.

29

At 9:00 a.m. on New Year's Eve, Gray stood on the balcony of the Templar's newly purchased villa overlooking Port de Gustavia as St. James's yacht dropped anchor. The deeper waters beyond the island of St. Barthelemy's private marina made the perfect playground for superyachts.

Anticipation surged through Gray, and he headed back inside to view the incoming yacht on the surveillance equipment Marcella had set up.

"*Enchantress* has arrived. All feeds up and running?" Gray asked.

"Yes, boss."

"Okay, then the show's about to start."

"You really think R-104B is on board?"

"Certain enough to be here in person. Though Cyn is keeping watch in LA, and we've got surveillance on all other St. James facilities as a backup."

"But why invite you on the yacht if it's there?"

"St. James actually invited Isadora and me—she's who he really wanted here. And I think his plans changed after he saw us at the lab. We know they moved R-104B, probably the morning before we got there, and if you were a narcissistic, lying traitor, where would you hide your most powerful asset?"

"Somewhere close," Marcella said. "And mobile."

"Exactly. And right now, St. James is on the yacht. Plus, he has a lab there—ostensibly for the marine biology research that he sponsors, but it makes for a convenient, sterile, contained environment. What's the latest onshore chatter from the yacht?"

"Something about a VIP guest flying in today."

"We've already got the names of everyone on board, right?"

"Everyone we've seen so far, yes."

"Has this mystery guest been identified?"

"No." Marcella looked up from the comms station. "Also, the current guests are heading to one of the nudist beaches for lunch. They leave in an hour."

"Perfect. I'll go aboard once they've left. And get the passenger manifests for all incoming flights today—charter and commercial—I want to know who this mystery VIP is."

"Before you go, Atticus de Payens called—something about 'did we actually need to buy the villa, and not just rent it?' Will I have to pack all this gear up and move us?"

"Don't worry, Atticus knows the cost of doing business in our world." Which was the entire reason the Templar Knights had a financial division. "Leave him to me." Gray phoned Atticus and said, "Atticus, stop bothering my people," as soon as the other man picked up.

"Then don't go spending millions on luxury villas."

"*One* necessary villa. Luxury's just a bonus. Now, why are you calling my people?"

"Update on the SJC. It took a lot of digging, but looks like the corporation was running dangerously close to the red. St. James had even sold off assets—on the down-low—but then stopped about two weeks ago. Cash flow has returned, but I can't trace the source."

"Well fuck," Gray said. "I have an idea about that. Thanks, the pieces are coming together now."

"No worries. And really—just buy a standard, run-of-mill villa next time?"

"The place is on the books now. And who knows, after this is all done, maybe you and your fiancée could come and check it out.

"Not a bad idea. And hold up—you're suggesting using Templar property for personal pleasure? Who are you and where's the real Grayson?"

"Fuck off."

"In all seriousness, take care and get R-104B back."

"I intend to." He hung up the call and turned back to Marcella. "Any word on the passenger manifests?"

"Still coming through."

"Okay, review the list, send me any notables on priority. I'm doing one last check on my equipment."

One hour later, wearing chino pants and a white shirt with the sleeves rolled up, Gray stepped onto the private dock where St. James's tender was docked. The small boat St. James used for ship-to-shore transfers was fancier than most of the other boats moored around them.

Grayson handed over his ID and faked a calm expression as a security guard waved a handheld weapons detector over his bags. He'd purposefully left his handguns ashore so they wouldn't set off any metal detectors, and had packed his nylon composite knives and carbon fiber lock picks into a hidden compartment inside his bag that should withstand any manual search.

Because passing this security check was the next

obstacle to be cleared on his path to retrieving R-104B. So much so that Gray didn't even argue as the guard did the standard two-handed pat down.

"Hope you don't mind the start to the cruise, Grayson," said a relaxed, low Boston accented voice, announcing St. James's arrival.

"Not at all." Gray turned around and forced a smile that was the exact opposite of the rage curdling in his gut. "Good to see you again. And I completely understand." Oh, he got it, all right. But he was playing the long game now, so he stayed in the easygoing character. "Here—I'll save you the need for the rest of the pat down. Let's see, ankle-holster—left and right—empty, of course. There you go. And as you can see, nothing up my sleeves or under my shirt."

"Wow, you're unarmed?" St. James smiled, but the grin didn't reach his eyes.

"Didn't think weapons were necessary for a social-work environment."

"Social and work?"

"Well, I can't entirely leave work behind—you know how it is. As much as I'd like to just sit back and enjoy your yacht, I'm hoping to get a few minutes with you about your lab in LA. I've found out some information about a product being made there—and you're probably not even aware of this, with as many businesses as you have."

"Why am I not surprised?" St. James laughed and clapped Gray on the shoulder. "Always working. But of course we can chat. And while initially I was disappointed to hear your lovely fiancée wasn't joining you, now, well ... I can't say I'm displeased."

"Mm." What the fuck did that mean? Gray met the other man's eyes with a bland expression—he wasn't giving St.

James shit here to go on. St. James's interest in Isa had been off from the start.

Gray's cell pinged, but before he could look at it, a black limousine with tinted windows pulled up at the end of the dock.

"This won't be awkward, right?" St. James asked as he stared at the vehicle as the driver opened the rear passenger door.

Huh? Gray turned too, and in the sun's glare ahead, a tiny, curvy figure emerged and approached the security guard.

"Hey, handsome," a frighteningly familiar voice said.

Handsome? Gray fought to keep his expression calm, but inside, his gut was so freaking tense he could bounce rocks off it.

Her shining dark hair skimmed shoulders left bare by a strapless olive green jumpsuit, with the lightweight fabric setting off her gleaming skin to mouthwatering perfection.

Fuck. Fuck, fuck, *fuck*. What was Isa doing here?

Gray went to reply, but Isa flashed her beautiful smile at St. James instead, and the other man stepped forward and took her arm.

The tension in Gray's gut erupted into a boiling lava pool. What. The. Hell.

"Lovely to see you, my dear," St. James said in that smarmy tone. "I was delighted to receive your RSVP."

"Excellent," Isa said. "I was worried I might've left it too late."

"Not at all. As I said in LA, my casa, your casa—or my superyacht, your superyacht." He tilted his head back and let out a loud chuckle.

What was this about LA? Gray tried to hide a scowl, but before he could say a word, his cell pinged with an incoming message from Marcella. *Isadora Smith. Arriving eleven o'clock.*

No shit, Sherlock.

Biting back a sigh, Gray turned back as St. James put an arm around Isa's bared shoulders. She stiffened, but then she seemed to relax and even laughed at whatever smarmy fuckery St. James had said.

"Well, thank you," Isa said in a bright voice pitched a little too high. Gray stilled. "And look, you've found Grayson, too."

"Yes," St. James said, "I wasn't expecting you to arrive so close together. Do you need a moment to"—he waved a hand between them—"clear the air?"

"Not really." She shrugged one of those dainty shoulders. His gaze suddenly caught on the way the sun sparkled across the warmth of her skin. "I'm sure Gray and I can enjoy your yacht amicably." She glanced at him. "Well, Grayson, lovely to see you again. Kai—I could really do with a refresh if that would be okay?"

"Of course, of course," St. James, the ever-fucking host, said. "Your suite is ready. Now, most of the guests are at the beach. If you go, I'd be more than delighted to join you."

"Ooh, the beach? That sounds divine."

Gray stared at Isa even harder. She might be permanently positive—annoyingly so, sometimes—but she'd never been inane or ditzy, and that was how she was coming off now.

"It is stunning," St. James continued, seemingly oblivious to Gray's scrutiny of Isa. Or maybe the other man just passed it off to their broken relationship. "It's nude, although you can wear as much ... or as little ... as you like."

Gray's hackles rose. St. James and Isa together, nude, on some idyllic beach? Over. His. Fucking. Dead. Body.

Except no, he didn't have any right to tell Isa who she could or couldn't get naked with. Not unless it somehow impacted his case.

Sour acid roiled in his gut. And St. James *was* a person of interest, so Gray shoved down his glee at the thought of throttling the man.

"Well, I'll see how I feel once I've had a rest." Isa smiled up at St. James.

"If you decide to join them, let a steward know or come find me."

St. James steered Isa toward the tender, the two of them speaking in an animated BS conversation about island life, leaving Gray to stare at their backs.

Well, fuck. What was he, chopped liver?

Then his phone pinged again with another message from Marcella. *One more name of interest on the incoming passenger manifest. Parsons.*

Gray's breath whooshed out. Only one Parsons sat on the Templar watch list—the one that the daemon Forneous used for his human-world dealings.

What were the odds another Parsons was flying onto the island today? Fucking low.

Although, the fact Parsons was flying in meant there wasn't a hellgate portal nearby. Good to have one plus up their sleeve—Gray hadn't taken on a daemon army before and wasn't looking to do so any time soon unless he absolutely had to.

And if this Parsons was Forneous, it meant something very important was on this island.

Was it R-104B? Isa? Both? A shiver trickled down Gray's neck.

Damn. Back to this fucking question. He fired a quick message to Marcella to get reinforcements down from

Miami. Something was going down tonight; he fucking knew it. He just didn't know what. But a certain diviner seemed to be at the heart of it.

Isa tensed as if she was going to shrug away from St. James's arm, but then she smiled as he handed her down into the tender, only to stop and visibly steady herself.

"Damn," Isa said, "wasn't expecting it to roll like this."

"Don't worry, you'll become accustomed to it in no time." St. James kept hold of her hand.

Gray unclenched his fists—hell, he hadn't even known they were closed—and followed them.

Head in the game. Head in the game.

"I've never been on a yacht before," Isa said as the boat took off. "What should I expect?"

"Superyacht, technically."

Of course—because having a yacht was way too beneath St. fucking James. Gray held in a snort.

"Wow," Isa breathed as the full height of the ship towered above them. "When you said yacht, I was thinking something like a sailboat."

"Oh, I have one of those toys, too." Of course he did. "But this is where I like to see in my new year. And I have a feeling I'll be enjoying this new year more than any before."

Not if Gray had anything to do about it.

"It's huge. How many levels are there?" The enthusiasm in Isa's voice was clear as she stared up at the yacht. At least she was distracting St. James because if the billionaire turned around right now, there was zero fucking chance Gray could hide the urge to throw daggers into the man's back.

"We call them decks," St. James said. "Now, we'll pull up alongside the hull, and then one of the crew will meet us and help you up the stairs that lead to the entry foyer on the main deck."

Sure enough, a crew member in blindingly white pants and shirt waited on a small set of steps.

"Mr. St. James," the crew member said when they were all on the deck. "The marine biology team have requested you below deck as a priority."

"Thank you. Please let them know I'll be there shortly." St. James turned to Isa and Gray. "Apologies. Duty calls."

"You're so good," Isa all but cooed.

"Well, it's not hard to give back. Now, I'll leave you here with the crew. They'll take care of everything you need, including unpacking your bags."

"Wow. You've thought of everything."

"Of course. I wanted to make tonight perfect for you."

Gray bit back a gag and instead murmured a thanks and pretended to be interested in the yacht—oops, superyacht. Which seemed perfect because St. James took a hold of Isa's hand again.

"Isadora, please, enjoy the facilities today, and remember to let me know if you want to visit the beach; otherwise, Maurice, my chef, is serving lunch by the pool. I hope to join you there later."

"If you'd like to follow me," the crew member said to Isa and Gray. "Each deck has its own lobby and can be accessed from the central elevator or stairs."

"Lobbies as in plural? Wait, how many levels—decks, I mean, are there?" Isa asked as they walked. "And how many cabins?"

"We have seven decks, thirteen guest suites, with a crew of fifty-two on board. The main deck, where we are now, holds the primary saloon—"

"Sorry to interrupt, but did you say saloon?" Isa said as

the crew member kept walking. "I haven't heard that term before."

"Of course, it's a sailing term. It's the largest of our interior cabins where Mr. St. James relaxes with his guests. Also on this deck, we have the pool, dining hall and four guest suites." The crew member stopped in front of a door and gestured to Gray. "This is your suite, sir."

"Thanks. But actually, I'd like to take a look around. Why don't I follow you up?"

He and Isadora were going to have a word. No matter what. She'd just bounced blindly into the middle of an operation, one where the stakes were deadly for everyone.

Hell, for the entire world if they got this wrong.

(((●)))

Gray's look might've seemed bland to anyone else, but Isa could clearly see his grin had a shark's bite and the hard edge to his gaze was a sledgehammer.

"Why not?" Isa took a leaf from the bloody-minded Templar's book and forced a serene smile.

"You're on upper deck three, Ms. Smith," the crew member said. "We'll head back to the lobby and take the elevator."

Holy. Shit. Marble, stone, timber finishes filled each room in endless elegance and luxury. This was more like a floating palace than a yacht.

Any other time, she'd have been in awe, but she had a reason for being here and she was finally—well, nearly—about to get alone with that reason.

"You know, I think we can find our way," she said to the crew member. "No need to walk me up."

"If you're sure—"

"She's sure," Gray growled.

Isa sighed and shook her head at the crew member. "Ignore him. He's hungry—no breakfast. But yes, I'm sure."

On the way back to the lifts, the crew member gave them a fast rundown of the rest of *Enchantress*: the two lower decks were crew only, main deck they'd seen, deck one had a cigar lounge, cellar, movie cinema, more guest suites and a sun deck. Deck two had a lounge, the gym and yet more accommodation. Deck three had the bridge, a sundeck and two guest suites—one of which was Isa's—and deck four held the helipad and St. James's private suite and deck.

Holy shit. This really was a floating palace.

As soon as the lift doors closed, Gray whirled to her.

Yikes. Fury tightened his face, and his eyes glittered as he stared down at her, looming over her like some dark, furious giant.

"What. The. Hell, Isadora?" he ground out in a furious whisper. "Why are you here? And how the fuck did you get here? What happened at Ashforton?"

"Hello to you, too. I knew you wouldn't be happy to see me—but this is going overboard."

"Overboard? The only thing overboard is going to be you when you pack your bags and get off this yacht."

"I'm not leaving!" Her hackles rose. "I had a vision of this yacht and the fact is I'm part of this, Gray. So don't even bother going all boss-mode. I've helped you all along with the myrrh, and you're not getting rid of me now."

The lift stopped, and the doors slid soundlessly open to yet another lobby, this one furnished in cerulean blues and creams and sandy golds.

"This is me." Isa took off and didn't look back to see if Gray followed.

Which, of course, he did. And she didn't even need to hear his steps—the fury and tension pouring off him filled the air around him like an explosive charge.

But she refused to hurry. Instead, she found her door and entered the suite.

Another exquisite space filled with gleaming marble and timber, all so tactile she wanted to run her hand over everything. A giant bed sat at one end with a built-in mirrored dresser opposite. One wall had a doorway leading to an ensuite and the other a huge window looking out toward St. Barths.

But not the view from her vision—either of them.

"Don't get comfortable." Gray stalked in behind her and shut the door. "You're not staying. Grab your bags and don't say a single word."

Isa whirled around to face him. "Gray, you're not hearing me. I. Am. Not. Going. Anywhere."

"Shh," he growled. Then he crowded her back against the timber cabinets. The heat charging the air around him brushed over her with sensual fingers, and her body tightened in a heartbeat. Why did she want him so much? Especially when he was in prick mode like now?

"What are you—?"

"Wait." He leaned into her ear, and his breath sent a shiver down her spine. Her nipples pebbled. "Let me check if your room's bugged. Don't say a word until I finish.

The shiver that trickled down her spine this time was all cold, and she stood in silence while he did something with his watch, then took his mobile phone and pointed it all around the suite, before finally nodding and stepping back.

His eyes were still tight, and his jaw clenched, but at least she could breathe now. Angry Gray she could handle.

Hot-and-bothered Gray, who made her want to jump his bones, was another story.

"What's that?" She nodded at his watch.

"Modified radiofrequency scanner—Templar tech to check for listening device signals coming from the room. There are none. And I have an app on my cell to check for any surveillance cameras."

"Shit. You really think he'd have bugged my suite?"

"It was a possibility. I'd bet everything I own mine is. Another thing you need to know, I don't have direct comms to Marcella—St. James has this ship locked down tight—so if we need to get a message to her, it's strictly cell phone only. Now. What the fuck are you doing here?"

"A month before I met you—in person—I had a vision. Of me. And I can count on one hand how many times that's happened. I wore a red dress and was in a super-fancy bedroom with glass doors overlooking a deck and water."

She almost told him what she was doing in that vision, but clearly, now wasn't the time if she was going to convince him to let her stay. And no matter what, if this was where where she met her maker, so be it. Because saving Gray's life—saving the myrrh—made it even more vital now.

"So?" Gray asked.

"So that same room was in the vision where someone shoots at you. That's how I know I need to be here. I'm going to stop you from getting shot tonight."

"Fuck. I don't want you anywhere near this place. I'll arrange—"

"No."

"—for you to fly—"

"Gray." Heat surged through her, and she shoved his chest. "You're not listening! I said no. I'm going to save you."

"Then tell me everything again, and I'll be on the lookout—"

"It doesn't work what way. And you know it."

"You could be wrong."

She didn't bother countering that, and from his expression, he didn't believe it either.

"Fine." He tunneled a hand through his hair. "But hell, Isa, I'm almost certain Forneous is coming here tonight as well. You know—the daemon whose minions shot at me in LA, and who clearly said he wants you alive?"

Isa's stomach tightened, and she had to swallow the lump that lodged in her throat.

"Yeah," Gray said. "So I think that's more important than any threat against me right now."

"No way." She lifted her chin. "Hear me out. I'm going to save you tonight, Gray, I know it. But say I leave right now, and then you get shot—who's getting the myrrh off this yacht?"

The color drained from his face.

"You need me. But one thing—why is Forneous coming here? Does he know Kai?"

"He's not just after you, he's after R-104B too, remember?"

"Why? What makes a two-thousand-year-old incense burner so important?"

"Fuck." Gray's expression tightened for a moment before his gaze locked on her. "Okay. We need to make this fast. Remember the copse of myrrh trees that lets humans communicate directly with the gods? We think the drug those women took in Fathom LA is designed off R-104B—a synthetic version anyway, with some of the same properties as the real deal, but a hell of a lot of others that are bad. As in deadly with prolonged use."

"And what else? I can see there's more."

"This is a secret that goes far beyond the NDA you signed. You cannot tell anyone this. Ever. I'm serious, Isa."

"Of course." A chill shook through her. ·

"On its own, the relic of myrrh has a unique power. But whoever *holds* the three gifts together—the gold, the myrrh and the frankincense—can control the hearts, minds and bodies of humankind. That's the true power. And that's why we keep the gifts separate."

Isa's mouth dropped open. "That's ..."

"Serious."

"Uh, understatement much? Gray—you should've told me from the start. The people we're dealing with—do you know who they are? Shit."

"I know who they are, Isa."

Her face went pale. And then her eyes narrowed. "You really don't trust me, do you?"

"It's not about trust. How many times do I have to say that? It's about life and death—of this entire world. Your dad. Raph. Eve. *Everyone*. That's what matters. Which is why I'm being honest with you now. Because frankly, with Forneous, St. James and R-104B possibly right here, I need you."

"You don't sound happy about that."

"I'm not. I wanted you far away from this end of the operation."

"Well, you may not want me here, but I am. So now you're putting me to work. I'm fine with that. In fact, that's what I want."

"Shit. This is about your gift, isn't it? You want to do good in the world."

"What's so bad about that?"

"Fuck, I don't have time for this shit. Listen, you're back

on the Templar payroll as of now, got it? That means you do what I say—"

"When you say." She rolled her eyes. "Of course I've got it. It's been your mantra all along. Any other lectures before you leave so I can get ready to go to the pool?"

"I don't lecture."

"Sure." She didn't bother hiding her eye roll this time. "So, what are you planning?"

"I need to search the onboard lab. St. James has an audio blocker on the yacht because the only transmissions we've been able to pick up have been ship-to-shore comms."

"And you can't just walk down there?"

"I could. But if I'm wrong and R-104B isn't on board, St. James will know for sure he's a suspect. Right now, he's wondering—and nervous—but I don't want to scare him into doing anything stupid."

"How can I help?" Isa said.

"Keep St. James occupied. The less he's thinking of me, the better."

"He wants me to work with him—for him, I guess—although he presented it like a partnership. But he's just another Liam."

"With a lot more resources. Don't underestimate him."

"I won't. Now, let's head to the pool. I want to be visible, and I'd prefer not to go to the nudist beach—today, anyway. I just need to change into my swimwear."

"Fuck, Isa."

"You know I'm right. Now go. I'm going to say you and I spoke about keeping things civil between us over the weekend, but that you understand it's over. Then I can stay close to Kai."

"That's one more thing you need to fill me in on." His jaw clenched, and a different light filled his eyes—one that burned hotter than anything. "When did St. James proposition you?"

"Back in LA, at the lab."

"Why didn't you say anything?"

"I never considered taking him up on the offer, and things went to shit from there till ... well, mostly until now. Now go."

Gray's stare seared Isa for such a long moment she had to stifle the urge to drag him to her and kiss those firm, delicious lips. Mess up that perfectly styled hair.

"Isa." His eyes dipped to her mouth.

She stepped forward. Heat pooled in her core.

But he shook his head and stalked out of her room.

Holy shit. She stumbled back and dropped to the bed— equal parts desire, anticipation and a sense of fate rushing at her, surging through her veins. But there was no time to consider the tumult of feelings—she had a pool party to get to. Although, banging Grayson No-Last-Name one last time would've been damned fine.

And just shy of ten minutes later, Isa refused to give in to the urge to gawk at the luxe furnishings as she took the lift to the main deck, walked through the dining hall, then the huge saloon that could seat twenty people easily, and out into a covered deck with an actual pool at the back of the yacht. Oops, superyacht.

And of course, the first people she saw ... Rochelle, from Fathom LA, and Gray. Close together. The platinum blonde, with her perfect hair and makeup and flawless skin, lounged by the pool in a teeny black bikini. She wore a giant diamond pendant that, even across the deck, glinted in the midday sun.

Rochelle raised one hand in a languid wave before turning back to Gray where he sat on the edge of the pool, his legs in the gleaming blue water, and his strong, muscled chest making the perfect foil for Rochelle's pale gleaming skin.

Great. Just great. If this night—or the next few—were her last, no way was she spending one single moment blighting her eyes with that action.

Isa hit the buffet and grabbed whatever was in front of her, then took a seat far away from the two by the pool.

And that was *not* jealousy making her stomach clench.

30

THE SUN SAT low on the horizon when Isa finished showering and wrapped herself in a fluffy white towel and approached the wardrobe, only for a sharp knock at the door to make her pull up short.

"Isadora, it's St. James. May I come in?"

Shit. What now?

"One moment." She pulled the towel tight around her and opened the door a fraction. Kai stood, all blond and handsome, looking even more striking than normal in a white tux and blue shirt that matched his eyes perfectly. A crew member stood behind him holding a small ivory box and a garment bag. "Kai, what can I do for you?"

"My apologies for interrupting." His gaze flicked over her. "You make me want to tell everyone downstairs to hold the party. Ms. Smith, I do believe you and I could have the best celebration right here and now."

"Oh, really? And would I get a say in this party?"

"Of course. I'd let you say yes, and please, and then maybe even scream."

What the—?

"But sadly, I have to be downstairs." The interest lingered in Kai's expression, but he laughed it away. "However, after our lovely afternoon together, it struck me that you might not have much in the way of jewelry. So perhaps you might like to wear something from me?" He clicked his fingers, and the crew member held out the ivory box.

Kai opened it up to reveal two fine strands of diamonds and a huge ruby pendant nestled inside.

"Wow." She'd reached out and touched the stunning piece before she'd realized and quickly pulled her hand back. "It's beautiful. But I can't take this."

"Please. You've been a joy to have on board today—and I would've been bored stiff with any of my other guests."

"That's lovely, but I still can't accept—"

"Then borrow it. Think of this like a preview into how luxurious life will be when you're working with me on a permanent basis."

"I haven't said yes yet."

"Ah, but you're here now. I've got the next few days to show you how amazing this life is. Plus, you're my special guest this evening, and I would love for you to shine as brightly as these gems do."

Oh, ew. He wanted to show her off. Well, since she had to pretend to like the man, at least she'd be wearing something pretty.

"In that case, I'd be delighted to borrow it."

"Excellent. I look forward to seeing you in my jewels. And since you've said yes, I had something else flown in late this afternoon." Kai waved a hand, and the crew member stepped forward with the garment bag. "This dress will match the necklace to perfection. Hang the bag in Ms. Jones's cupboard," Kai directed the crew member.

"Wow—I mean, thank you, but I already have a dress—"

"No, no. I insist." Kai picked up her hand and held it like a prized possession. "You are my guest aboard *Enchantress*. Let me spoil you. Let me turn you out as beautifully as you deserve."

Ew, ew, *ew*. "I'm sure it's stunning, but it could hardly fit—"

"My crew confirmed your size when they unpacked for you. Trust me. I would not have you look anything less than spectacular."

Of course not. Kai wanted her to look good enough for his yacht. Oops, superyacht. "When you put it like that, how can I say no?" She gave him her best smile and patted his hand where he still held hers. "Now, since I have all this gorgeousness to wear, I'd better make sure my hair and makeup look good enough to match."

"You look beautiful as is, but I'll leave you to enjoy your preparations."

After Kai had left, Isa closed the suite door and placed the box carefully on the dressing table.

Diamonds and rubies. Not what she'd expected to wear tonight.

Then another sharp knock rapped on her door, harder than before. Crap. If Kai had changed his mind about spending 'time' with her right now, he was shit out of luck.

She tightened the towel again and opened the door.

Her breath whooshed out.

One large Templar Knight wearing a perfectly cut black tuxedo loomed in her doorway, while he stared down the corridor.

"Gray, you look …" Devastating. Mouthwatering. So frigging hot she wanted to drop her towel and get her hands on him.

"Did I just see St. James on this floor?"

"Yes, you did, and hello to you, too." She peeked either side of the short corridor, then pulled him into her room. "What are you doing here? We're not together, remember? Did he see you, too?"

"Of course."

"Then you have to go."

"I know, I know. I just need one minute to talk about tonight. We can pretend I'm trying to get you back or something. I didn't get ..." His gaze traveled to where the towel end was tucked between her breasts to hold it in place. "You're naked."

"No, I'm wearing a towel. Now, what—?"

"And St. James was in here, just now?"

"Oh, shut that growling down. Kai was at my door to give me a necklace and dress, so I don't look out of place tonight." She pointed at the box on her dresser.

"What?" He whirled around. "The fucker."

"It's because he doesn't want to be seen with someone ordinary."

"You're not wearing them."

"Of course, I'm wearing them. I'm distracting him, remember? Now stop muttering to yourself and tell me what you want to say."

"Fuck." He shoved a hand through his hair. "I got into the lab—"

"What? How? When?"

"While you were lounging and swimming with St. James this afternoon, I created a small distraction for the crew. No sign of R-104B. So now I need to check his suite. There are fireworks at midnight in the harbor. I need you to keep St. James with you, and when everyone's focused on the fireworks, I'll head to his deck."

"How do I make sure I keep him distra—oh. You want

me to kiss him?"

"No. Just distract him."

"You want me to 'just distract' him at midnight—*on New Year's Eve*? What else am I meant to do?"

He stared at her, his stormy eyes implacable.

"Fine." She shook her head. "But I'm not some super spy, you know that, right? And my distraction skills are pretty lame."

"You've got this." Gray stepped close. "Trust me, you're the most stunning thing on this ship—and that's with no makeup, no jewels, wearing a towel. I can't imagine how amazing you're going to look tonight. St. James won't stand a chance."

Warmth unfurled in her chest. Bloomed low in her belly.

"Isa." Gray shifted. His body brushed hers. His gaze dipped to her mouth. She inhaled sharply; his warm, spicy scent filled her.

"I wish ..." She licked her lips, and his eyes darkened until they were a turbulent ocean of heat and want. Damn, but she wanted to kiss him. To dominate those firm lips and see him lose control. To have one more graygasm. To wrap herself around him. Under him. Over him. To connect one last time.

Except she *should* step back, push him out the door and put on whatever pretty outfit Kai had gotten her.

"You wish?" he breathed.

Oh hell, if this really was the last time she could be with Gray, she was damn well going for it. For him. And so what if her feelings for Grayson ran deeper than his did for her? That just made this opportunity even more frigging important.

She dropped the towel. "You. Now."

"Minx," Grayson rasped. Then he lunged for her.

Their mouths met in a tangle of tongues and lips. Her blood ran thick and heavy, and tension gathered in her core.

"Pants." She fumbled with his belt and his zipper. Got her hands under his waistband, found his dick, and the hard, hot length made her body drench even further. Need clawed through her. "Condoms in the draw—"

"Let me—"

They scrambled for the box, and then he had one foil packet out and ripped it open even as she shoved his pants and trunks down.

"Gray, hurry."

"I've got you," he bit out, staring down at her, his eyes blazing. Condom on, he whirled her around and bent her over the dressing table.

She lifted onto her toes and watched his reflection in the mirror as his gaze locked onto her core.

"Fuck, Isa." Gray smacked her butt, then ran a thumb up her seam, and she closed her eyes as the friction made her body clench. "Eyes on me, minx."

He gripped her hips, and as soon as she met his gaze through the mirror, his lips pulled tight over his teeth, and he drove into her with one hard thrust.

Yes, yes, yes. He was so deep, so hard, so big. This was what she needed. Who she needed.

Then her thoughts scattered. Her body constricted, and she moaned, clutching the edge of the dresser to hold steady as he withdrew, then plunged into her again.

Hot tension roared inside her, and she ground against every thrust.

"Isa, Isa, Isa." He groaned as he hammered into her. Her body tightened. His pace quickened. "Fuck, yes, baby, yes. Take me. Take every fucking part of me."

A growl vibrated through him; he yanked her to him as he slammed hard and high and hot; stars burst across her vision.

"Issi!"

Her body convulsed, her eyes squeezed shut, and she couldn't contain a shout as the most overwhelming orgasm of her life exploded through her. Yet somehow, for all that, when Gray bent over her, whispered a kiss to her spine, she felt it all the way to her soul.

When she managed to open her eyes, Gray's reflection in the mirror filled her view.

Pure, total, perfection. Her heart brimmed with the force of their connection, and without doubt, in another life, she'd have pursued a real relationship with him.

And that's when a lump gathered in her throat. Fate be damned, why did she have to feel so much for this man now, right when her time was almost done?

She bit her lip. *Don't go there, Isa*. She'd had this with him—and that was what mattered.

After her heartbeat returned to normal, she forced her trembling lips to steady and kept her tone light. "Well, Ace, that was one way to be fashionably late for the party." She wiggled her backside and stepped forward. Refused to acknowledge how her body missed him instantly. "Time to go now, though."

"Shit. Isa—"

But the longer she was around him, the bigger the temptation was to tell him everything and just have him hold her —which would be disastrous.

She stepped back. "I've still got to get ready, so you go. Make sure Kai sees you quickly. Don't want to lose any ground I've made."

Gray's face tightened, but then he blinked and whatever

his thoughts were, they disappeared beneath his standard aloof expression.

"One more thing," he bit out. "If Parsons—Forneous—does turn up tonight, I don't want you alone, at all. Stay on the main deck. One thing we know about St. James, he's not going to risk you. And neither will I."

His jaw clenched, and then he left her suite. The pressure in the air dissipated, and her breath released. Damn. She hadn't even known she'd been holding it.

That man got to her. No other way of putting it.

But she couldn't afford to think of Gray. She needed all her concentration on the night ahead—including figuring out how to distract the resident billionaire and hold her nerve for the next few days or however long she had.

She took a fast shower, and by the time she'd applied her makeup and brushed her hair, her pulse had calmed, and her hands were steady as she clipped Kai's bling around her neck.

She stood up to look at Kai's dress when her apatite crystal caught her eye. She quickly slipped it into the clutch bag she'd gotten for the onboard party. One more jewel was going to the party tonight.

Then she unzipped the garment bag. A swathe of ruby silk gleamed in the suite lights.

The exact color of the dress from her death vision.

Her breath punched from her, and a cold shiver trembled all the way to her heart. Well, no need to wonder how many days remained.

Fate had come calling after all.

Which was as it needed to be. Because the only thing that mattered tonight was that she saved Gray. And Gray would move heaven and earth to keep the myrrh safe.

Which meant saving everyone she loved. Shit, maybe the entire world.

《《◆》》

Gray didn't have to wait long between making his way to the main deck—the pool had a dance floor covering it now—and St. James finding him. The billionaire had Rochelle draped on one arm, a glass of champagne in his hand, and daggers in his eyes.

He made a direct line for Gray. "Grayson, I hope you haven't been making Isadora ... uncomfortable."

"I doubt it. She seems to have found her feet just fine." Time to play the part of the jilted lover. "Now, since I'm here and single, Rochelle, might I spend some time in your stunning company? Perhaps you can help keep my mind occupied."

"Grayson, it would be my pleasure to occupy more than just your brain." Rochelle tipped her head back with a throaty laugh. "And here I thought this was going to be another yawn fest of a superyacht party."

"Excellent." Kai raised his glass to them, then a light entered his eyes as he stared at something behind Gray. "You two enjoy yourselves. I'm going to."

As Gray turned, Isa appeared in the doorway to the lobby.

His breath seized.

Fucking. Hell. If the gods had wanted to make a more perfect creature, he couldn't imagine how. Like in LA, that inner gleam was back, and hell if every person there didn't stand up and pay attention when Isadora Smith strolled across the deck.

The red of her dress licked her skin like a liquid gem, with a slit up one side almost hitting her hip, revealing the length of her leg with every step. She turned to speak to someone, revealing the dress dipped to the hollow of Isa's back, all held together with two ridiculous straps tied between her shoulder blades.

One flick of his fingers, and he'd have that tie undone, the dress down at her feet, and those sexy legs back around his—fuck. He shut that thought down. Getting hard in the middle of the party wasn't the plan.

But no wonder St. James had run to her. The skin at the back of Gray's neck itched, and he rubbed a hand over it before he could stop himself.

"Are you sure you're over our delectable Dora?" Rochelle asked.

Our? What in the hell did that mean? Gray kept his expression neutral as he turned back to Rochelle. "Dora who? Now, let's get a drink."

But the itching on his neck didn't stop. And over the next five hours, every fucking time he turned around, there was St. James and Isa. Dancing, talking, laughing.

And everywhere, the fucker was touching Isa—his hand like a possessive brand, on her lower back, on her neck, on her shoulder.

The urge to launch himself across the deck, yank the billionaire's fingers off Isa and pitch him overboard surged through Gray's veins in a primal tide. Clawing, roaring, demanding to be unleashed.

Gray had never been closer to losing control. Which was not an option.

So he buried that itching deep, refused to look at it, think about it, fucking acknowledge it. He just had to get to midnight. Because R-104B was all that mattered.

31

AT TWENTY MINUTES TO MIDNIGHT, Kai said he needed to use the restrooms. Thank you, gods. Isa made a beeline for the back deck and gave in to the urge to shiver for the first time all night. Her skin had crawled for so long she was surprised it hadn't skulked right off and slithered to hide somewhere in the corner.

True to his word, Kai had stayed by her side all night. His touch, a light pressure of fingers, had remained on the hollow of her lower back as he shepherded her from one group of laughing, chattering, sycophantic people to the next.

Isa felt like a new toy on display.

But he'd also been genuinely attentive. Maybe he was waiting for her to have some vision he could swoop in to help make his next business deal profitable. Because business and profits had been the talk of the night for most of the people present. That and whether they should buy another island or the next mega yacht or superyacht or whatever the frig they were called.

But no way did she want a vision happening. Every time

the slightest ... inkling of a vision trickled through her, she'd reach inside her clutch, grab her crystal, and hold on for dear life until the sensation passed.

The only good thing to come of the entire night so far had been that her control seemed to be improving.

Isa took a deep breath of crisp night air, squared her shoulders, and turned back to the party.

No sign of Kai yet. And Gray ... where was he?

She'd tried to catch his eye all night, but his attention had been locked on Rochelle, a blonde goddess in her pearlescent sheath dress and perfect tan.

Even if it was a ruse, Isa's gut had roiled with a queasy mix of acid and bile, and she'd forced herself to stop trying to make eye contact.

But now ... well, the fireworks were happening soon. Where the frig was Gray?

Probably with Rochelle. Who was nowhere to be seen either.

Isa's stomach knotted. Shit. Gray, Kai and Rochelle were all nowhere to be seen. But Gray wasn't meant to disappear until midnight.

Isa plastered a smile over her face and made her way across the deck and into the saloon. Still no sign. Maybe they were on deck one?

She'd checked out the cigar lounge, cellar and sundeck, and still nothing, and only had the movie cinema to go on this level. Isa pushed the door open into the darkened room ...

Two familiar figures were visible on the farthest recliners. Lips locked. Bodies facing each other.

Isa's breath punched from her, and she stumbled back, lost her footing and landed on her butt in the corridor.

No frigging way. Gray and Rochelle? Except Isa didn't

have any claim to him. He could kiss Rochelle—for real or whatever reasons he had—as much as he liked.

But that didn't stop Isa's stomach from roiling.

"Are you okay?" A crew member appeared at her side.

"Yeah, sure." Not really. But Isa swallowed the lump of lead wedged in her throat and pasted that damned fake smile back on. "One too many glasses of bubbles, that's all. Uh, can you tell me where Kai's gone?"

"I believe Mr. St. James was heading to his suite. I can get a message to him—"

"No, no. All good."

Except, not all good. Gray was meant to be going up to Kai's suite any minute. Damn, damn, damn. What to do? Gray and Rochelle would come out soon, no doubt, and she wasn't going to be standing there like a stunned mullet when they did.

Isa needed to get Kai out of his suite and back down to the party before Gray did his thing in the billionaire's room.

Isa glared at the door. Whatever the frig was going on in that cinema, one thing wasn't in doubt—Gray would be in Kai's suite at midnight.

Stomach still roiling, Isa ran to the lift and jabbed the button for the top deck. But of course, it went back to the main deck, and she had to fake a smile and make frigging small talk with a couple who wanted to get to their suite on deck two by midnight, and then finally, *finally*, the lift chimed on Kai's deck, and she darted out. The double doors to the owner's suite were closed.

She knocked once. Held her breath.

Nothing.

Damn. She was about to knock again when someone grabbed her fist from behind.

"What are you doing here?" Gray's rough voice whispered in her ear.

"Getting Kai out of his suite." She spun to face Gray. "He's in there now," she whispered back.

She couldn't help but check out his lips—which were the redder because of his kissing.

"No, he's not. I just passed him on the stairs." Gray checked his watch and then glanced over his shoulder. "Fuck. The elevator is coming back up—that'll be the security sweep."

"He has security here?"

"All night. I had to create a distraction downstairs to get them called away. Change of plans. You're with me." Gray took a keycard from his pocket and held it against the security plate.

"But—"

The door locked snicked. Gray pulled her through the suite doors after him. The space was massive—like, space for the sake of space, to show off wealth, and definitely luxe, but cold, hard, soulless—with a huge bed, a circular mirrored light, and doors leading off in different directions. Gray strode straight to one shadowy corner while Isa remained near the entrance.

"How did you get Kai's room key?" she asked.

"Picked his pocket on the way up. Now. What. The. Everlasting, motherfucking, gods damned hell are you doing here?" he whispered. "What happened to the plan?"

"Saving your ass!" Isa whispered back. "Kai disappeared fifteen minutes ago, and when I go to tell you, you're *kissing* Rochelle. Then I found out Kai was in his suite, so since you were *busy,* I came up here to get him out."

"Well, he's back at the party now."

"How did you get up—?"

"The stairs. Now, stand there with your back to the wall and don't move. If shit—"

"—goes down, you need to know where I am." She held in a sigh as Gray stared hard at her until she did as ordered.

"I've downloaded the deck schematics," Gray said, "so I've got a good idea of where a safe would be, but I need to check each area one by one. The guard is by the elevator, so we have to be quiet."

He disappeared into the study, the barest scrape and rustle telling Isa he was moving things around.

And then she glanced up.

Holy. Shit. The room leading to the deck, the night sky beyond, and further out, the twinkling lights of St. Barths' harbor perfectly framed ...

A shiver shook through her. But she straightened her shoulders. Whatever happened tonight, it happened. And she saved Gray. Gray saved the world. That's what mattered.

"And I wasn't kissing Rochelle. I needed to get out of the main party, and she followed me. Which made for a good cover. Then she ... launched at me."

"Not my business if you did." Isa forced a shrug that was the opposite of the churning in her belly. And what did that even mean—he had to leave the party?

His jaw clenched, then he headed for the walk-in closet. "This thing is bigger than my entire suite."

"Why did you have to leave the party?"

Silence but for the ongoing muted sounds of his search until he reappeared at her side.

"Because of you." He disappeared into the ensuite.

Her? *Her?*

"Hell. Not in here." Gray walked to the middle of the suite. Stared at the king-sized bed. "Time's running out. Need to search around the bed. You look there—feel along the paneling and under the mattress for anything out of the ordinary. I'll take this side."

Isa dropped to her knees and ran her hands along the brass inlay and the gleaming timber panels. But she had to know one thing.

"Gray, I know we're not a real couple—fine." *So* not fine. "But what's with the possessiveness? We don't have to do the act anymore."

He muttered something under his breath.

"What was that?"

"I said it wasn't an act."

Isa couldn't stop herself and rose to her knees. The churning in her belly had morphed into a knot of tension, and her heart picked up pace to pound hard and fast. What was he saying? But while he'd been whispering to her, his gaze stayed where he ran his fingers along the same brass inlay she'd been following on her side.

"Wait—fucking hell. *Yes.*" He pressed his hands into the panel hard.

A section of timber beside the bed swung open.

Isa's mouth went dry—either from Gray's comment or that this entire mission was about to end. Because, of course, he'd found a hidden compartment. Was there anything this man couldn't do?

But that meant the rest of her vision could unfold soon. She scrambled to her feet.

"Common lock. What an idiot," Gray muttered as he withdrew a pen from his jacket and twisted the end off.

"What's that?"

"Standard Templar lock pick."

Of course. Isa glanced toward the door. How long did they have? Should she tell him? But what would he do? Try to stop her, no question. She backed into the walk-in closet until she could see Gray but not the suite entry.

Gray did something with the lock pick, then a moment later reached into the wall. Relief whisked across his expression, and his shoulders dropped before he whispered, "Thank fuck."

He leaned back, cradling an ornate brass censer like it was a newborn babe.

A flash of energy punched through the air. The hairs on the back of Isa's arms pricked. Wow. Had that come from the relic of myrrh?

"Gray." She swallowed hard. Time was up. "I—"

The click of the suite doors opening and then closing echoed through the room. Isa's heart stopped.

"Well, well, look who we have here," a cool, feminine voice murmured.

Shit. Was that Rochelle? Isa stepped back farther.

Across the room, Gray's mask of cool indifference froze into place, and he shifted the censer into his left hand. His gaze never once moved to Isa.

"And here I thought we were meeting up on the deck," the feminine voice purred.

"We are." Gray's lips curled into a dead smile. "Just a different deck than planned. And that's an interesting accessory. Can't say the black matches your dress, though."

"Oh, I don't know. White dress. Black gun. It's all in the shades."

"So what's the play here, Rochelle?" Gray said.

It was her. The club owner would be the one who shot at Gray? Isa bit back a hiss. The bitch. She'd been all over Gray day and night, and now she was going to shoot him?

"Simple really, darling," Rochelle drawled. "You hand over the relic, I don't shoot you."

"Somehow, I don't think that's going to stop you, especially since you clearly know what this is."

"Oops, you've got me. And such a shame. I really did want to taste a Templar. Especially one so ... masterful."

What the frig? This chick was batshit.

"Now, take out your cell and throw it into the hot tub."

Damn. *Her* mobile. Isa turned her phone to silent, then looped her clutch around her wrist.

"That's going to make it hard to keep in touch," Gray said.

Isa's heart pounded so hard that Gray and Rochelle could probably hear it. How could Gray sound so calm? Isa bit back a hiss as he reached into this jacket and took out his mobile, then tossed it over his shoulder. Perfect aim, of course. The phone hit the water with a splash.

"Good shot. And I know, so sad we're not going to be able to continue our time together after tonight." Rochelle laughed. "Oh, I crack myself up. But seriously, we don't want you calling any of your friends, do we? And I'll be taking the relic now."

"Since you know what I am, you also know I'm not giving it up."

"See this little thing here? It gives me all the power right now."

"If you shoot now, the guard out there will come running."

"No, he won't. I sent him to get Kai. Now, stay very still—"

Gray tensed, reached back with his right hand.

Isa recalled the vision of Gray being shot at one last time. Locked the position of the gun in her mind. Then she lunged into the bedroom.

Gray's gaze cut to her. His eyes widened. His face twisted.

Then only the gun filled her view, and she ran straight into the hands holding the weapon and pushed it high.

Crack! Crack! Rochelle screamed. Gray grunted. The mirrored light shattered, and shards sprayed everywhere; then, the entire fixture crashed into Gray, and he collapsed beneath the tangle of metal and mirror.

Isa stumbled into the wall with Rochelle. Clanging overwhelmed her ears, but Isa scrambled back to her feet and spun to Gray.

Underneath the smashed light, he lay on his side, blood running over his brow from cuts on his forehead. Her heart stopped.

"No. No, no, no. Gray!" Isa shot forward, only for Rochelle to grab her arm.

"Don't fucking move," Rochelle hissed. She raised her gun. "You shouldn't have interrupted, Dora. Now you're going to go too—"

The suite doors slammed open, and Kai strode into the room. "What the hell?" Kai spun around, his mouth dropping as he looked at them all.

"Kai," Isa said, "we need an ambulance, Gray's—"

"Kai, darling," Rochelle purred. "Perfect timing."

"The myrrh!" Kai spun.

"Sh. The product's fine. It's there." Rochelle jabbed her gun toward the bathroom. "It fell when I shot him."

"You shot Grayson? Fuck, Rochelle."

"Of course I shot him. He was about to ruin our plans."

A flash of heat roared through Isa, and she launched at Rochelle, but Kai intercepted her and spun her into him.

"Now, now," Kai said. "Don't move."

"Let me go." Isa yanked her arm from his hold, but he tightened his grip, pulling her closer.

"I said don't fucking move."

"He had the product." Rochelle spat. "What did you expect me to do?"

"How about let him take it?" Kai pinched the bridge of his nose. "I swear, you're fucking dumb sometimes."

"Don't call me dumb."

"Then don't make dumb choices! We already have the formula. I was handling Grayson. I had her." He waved a hand at Isa. "I could always have got the myrrh back if we needed it again. Now I have to clean up this mess. Fucking useless bitch."

Kai had *her*? Not likely. But Isa took the opportunity to search the room. A weapon ... she needed a weapon.

"I'm your business partner, Kai," Rochelle said, her cheeks flushing red. "It was my idea to use the myrrh. *I* broke the ward spell. The product is selling through *my* clubs."

"And it's my lab, my chemist, my facility that I got you into. So fucking what?"

"So fucking this. If you had returned the myrrh as soon as you had a sample, like I said, they'd never have found it missing. But no, you had to have more. Well, I can find a new chemist—and quite frankly, your formula is shit anyway. It kills too many users. And if they're dead, they're not buying any more, are they? I don't need you anymore, *darling*." Rochelle shifted her aim and pulled the trigger two times. Two more cracks thundered through the suite.

Isa screamed.

Outside, more cracks boomed. Fireworks fractured the sky.

Kai made a wet, gurgling grunt, then stumbled and collapsed into Isa. She cried out as Kai's weight took her down with him.

"And I'll take this," Rochelle said in a singsong voice.

Isa heaved Kai off her chest and dragged in a breath as Rochelle emerged from the ensuite with the incense burner.

"No fucking way," Gray muttered. He rolled to his knees and grabbed at his upper arm. Dislodged metal bars and mirrored glass fell off him as he staggered to his feet.

Isa gasped. Thank you gods. Not dead. Not dead.

From the wounds on his head, blood ran down his cheek, over his jaw, dripping to the floor in bright red splashes. Her favorite color.

She crawled the rest of the way out from Kai. Shit. The billionaire's lifeless eyes stared straight through her. Blood and gore surrounded holes in his head and neck. Her stomach roiled. Her head went fuzzy.

"Again, Grayson?" Rochelle's chilling voice cut through the buzzing filling Isa's head. "You just don't give up, do you? What stamina. Now I'm really disappointed we never got to fuck. This time, just die, will you?"

32

GRAY'S WORLD SHARPENED. Isa on the ground, covered in blood. R-104B in Rochelle's hands. The pulse of blood through his veins, pumping past the wound in his arm. The cuts on his head. The gun barrel pointing at him again.

No. Fucking. Way.

Gray launched himself at Rochelle, forced her arm high, and with his good shoulder, rammed her into the wall. She screeched. The gun dropped.

But pain roared through him, and he dropped to his knees.

"Oh, Grayson. Still falling for me?" Rochelle's echoing laugh as she scrambled over him and ran from the suite made the hairs on the back of his neck prick.

"Gray!" Isa reached him. "Here, let me help you up."

"Are you hurt?" He ran a hand down her face. "You're covered—"

"Kai's. I'm not hurt. But you are. Come on, sit on the bed."

"No, need to go after R-104B. Call the police. Phone in study."

"What? You've been shot. You need a doctor."

The pain in Gray's arm was a fucking bitch, but his arm wasn't useless, and he was alive. Pain would have to fucking wait.

"Not shot. Grazed." Gray picked up the gun Rochelle had dropped. A Glock 19. Reliable, durable, and a model he had experience with. He quickly checked the magazine, popped it back into the pistol, then racked the slide to load a round. Ready to go.

He grabbed Isa's hand. "Call the police. Marcella's monitoring all outgoing comms, so she'll know. She *has* to know —to put a ring around the yacht, just in case ..."

"Fine. But don't you dare die, Grayson No-Bloody-Last-Name. You owe me an answer."

"Acord. Grayson Acord."

"What? Did you just tell me your last name? No, no, no, no. You tell me after you're back and safe. Not now, you asshole. I hate it when you're nice."

Gray couldn't stop a smile as he lurched into the hallway. Gods that woman got to him. But right now, he had to get another woman. The elevator display showed it had stopped on the main deck, which made sense. Rochelle could access the tender, and the crew would help her without question.

No time to wait for the elevator, so he took the internal spiral stairs down to the main deck lobby.

On his left, laughter and music and the tinkle of crystal filled the air coming from the saloon and pool deck. These people had zero fucking clue what was really going down on board right now. But he turned right through the doors to the outside deck, then followed the curve of the ship toward the tender.

Two voices echoed near the waterline, becoming clearer the closer he stalked toward them.

"... shove us off, now." Rochelle, zero question.

"Unfortunately, another group of guests have boarded *Enchantress*, and Mr. St. James has said to say here in case anyone—"

"*St. James* has said I can use this tender any time, right? Listen, you either shove us off now or I'll get you fired, and then you can shove off this boat permanently."

Fuck. Rochelle couldn't leave. No time for stealth now. Gray ran for the stairs leading down to the tender. The small boat rolled gently with the motion of the water, with two figures on board. A crew member was at the helm, and Rochelle stood over her, back to Gray as he descended the steps.

"Don't start that engine," Gray shouted. His head swam, but at the top of the steps, he braced his legs and grasped the railing with his free hand.

Rochelle spun to face him. Her face twisted, the night shadows deepening the grooves around her cheeks.

"Why won't you fucking die?" She whirled back around and shoved the crew member aside. "Get out of my way. I'll do it myself."

"Rochelle!" Gray raised the Glock 19 and checked his aim. While he'd shot this model plenty of times in the past, without knowing the ammunition in use, or the idiosyncrasies of this specific weapon, he had zero idea of the accuracy of the sights. Which meant aiming for the center of mass was his only option. "One warning only. If you turn that engine on, I'll shoot you. You're not leaving here."

"Fuck you." She tucked R-104B under one arm, yanked the keys from the crew member, and jammed them into the ignition.

"No thanks." Gray pulled the trigger twice, hitting Rochelle dead center in the chest.

Rochelle started at him—raised a hand—then dropped in a heap. The censer fell beside her. The crew member screamed.

Gray kept the gun on Rochelle as he staggered down the steps. The fire in his arm pulsed harder, but he didn't stop, he just jumped into the tender.

"Call the police," he ordered the crew member. She stared at him in horror before scrambling around him and running back up the steps.

Fine. Don't call the police. Run away shouting. Whatever, as long as it got the authorities out here fast.

He reached Rochelle, lying motionless on the deck. Dark red blood pooled beneath her and he knelt at her side, felt for a pulse. Nothing. Her eyes were still open, but looked up to the night sky above, lifeless, unaware of his presence. Well, that was one less problem to deal with.

Then he carefully picked up R-104B. He exhaled hard. Thank the gods; finally, the relic was back in his hands. He wasn't letting it go again.

Maybe it was relief—or possibly the pain flaring through his arm—but his knees went fucking weak, and he had to steady himself again.

He turned the censer over—

A chill cut through him. One panel at the bottom had broken off.

Oh hell. When had that happened? He dropped to his knees—hissed as pain ricocheted through his arm—and searched the bottom of the tender. *Fuck*. Nothing. Hell, could it have happened in the suite when *he'd* dropped the relic?

‹‹‹●›››

With her heart sprinting, Isa stumbled into the study. Telephone ... telephone ... nothing. A radio. But she had zero idea—

Shit. She wrenched the zipper on her clutch bag open and fumbled around, but her hands were shaking too hard. So she dumped everything on the chair—crystal, lipstick, *mobile*!

"Shit." She knelt and thumbed her phone open. But what number did you call in the Caribbean? Back home she'd call 000, and they used 911 in the US.

Think, Isa, Think. Gray had said Marcella was monitoring all outgoing calls, so Isa just had to make any call ... She swiped through her contact list to Raph.

"Uh-uh. Put that down, please," said an unfamiliar man's voice.

Isa yelped and spun. A stranger stood in the doorway. He wore an exquisitely tailored suit, and his dark hair had been combed back from a face that somehow seemed ... ageless.

"No. I'm calling the police."

"Never mind, they're on their way. Right now, *I* need you to come with me." The man stepped closer. "Put that down and I won't hurt you."

Oh frig, what now? Isa hit the call button, then dropped her mobile onto the chair. Even if her call went to voicemail, Raph would hear this conversation. And then surely, between Raph and Marcella, they'd figure out Gray and Isa needed help.

"Where's Gray? Did you hurt him?"

"The Templar? Not here, thankfully. Now, come." The man checked his watch. "I've been waiting a long time for the pleasure of your company, Ms. Smith. My future queen."

Her breath stalled. "I'm not going anywhere with you."

"And I say you are." He turned and said to someone outside the study, "Go. The Templar must have my relic."

"Your relic?" Isa licked her suddenly dry lips.

"Yes, mine. Just like you. Finally. Now, if you come willingly, this will be much easier; if not, my men will have to make the trip rougher."

"You're ... Forneous?" Shit. How long could she stall for?

"Nice to see you have brains as well as beauty. Our progeny will be blessed."

"Our what?" A hysterical laugh escaped her before she could stop it. "You're one batshit mofo if you think that's ever happening."

"No, I'm the Lord of Hell."

"Uh, no. My *grandfather* is the Lord of Hell. You're one of his minions."

"Pathetic little human, you know nothing. Your grandsire is too busy seeing to his precious realms to worry about what's happening in this one. Which makes it, like you, ripe for the taking."

"So this is all about power? You want some of your own?"

"Some? Oh no. I want all the power. And I'll start with this world. With you as my queen—"

"Holy shit. You're behind the bounty? That's why Triulf called me Highness—"

"Triulf failed me. She's lucky her dispatch happened this side of the gates. However, with you and your visions on my side, your grandsire will have no recourse to counter me. And once I have the three gifts, *I* shall rule all humanity."

Of course. It always came back to her visions. Sour acid roiled in her belly. Damned curse—except no. Her *gift* had saved Gray tonight when Rochelle had shot him.

Shit. Isa needed a weapon. Something—somehow—to stop this prick from ever getting what he wanted.

She reached back, her fingers grazed the chair, her lipstick. The open bag. The crystal.

The crystal. A thought shoved into her mind. Holy shit, was that even possible? But she'd need to be close.

Please, please let this work.

Isa grabbed the obelisk, then raised her chin. "I'm not going anywhere with you. You'll have to carry me out of here." Damn. Too obvious?

"With pleasure." Forneous's smile made her blood ice over. "I might even take a taste of the goods right here."

"Get fucked." Her stomach roiled, but she held her chin high.

"I intend to." Forneous dragged her into the bedroom.

Shit. Now or never. And please, please let Gray get his butt back up here soon.

Isa pretended to struggle against Forneous's hold on her arms, and as he dragged her closer, she whirled and plunged the obelisk into the back of his hand. Gouged it along his skin and cried out the divination spell.

"Bitch." His snarl filled her ears before stars hurtled across her vision.

An endless rocky plain extended in all directions beneath a twilight sky, with giant charcoal clouds billowing on the horizon.

Isa spun around and came face to face with a figure made from flames, with dark yawning eyes and steam rolling off its shoulders.

"Shit," she yelped. "Who—what—are you?" An odd taint filled her mouth. Ash. This was not a future like she'd seen before.

"What did you do, bitch?"

"Forneous?" Holy *holy* shit, what was happening here?

"How did you bring me to the thirteenth realm?"

"Is that where we are?"

Shit, Isa ... think ... think ... this was a vision. A future. Except, whose future? Her stomach clenched.

"Tell me how you did this." Forneous slapped her across the face.

"Fuck you!" Tears stung her eyes, but something more important than the pain made her gasp ... Why was she feeling anything in a vision?

Although, she *could* control this now. She looked down. The apatite obelisk still warmed her palm.

Focus, Isa. Whose future was this?

"We're in my world now, diviner." Forneous twitched, and a giant barbed tail whipped from his back and hurtled through the air toward her. "I'll take you apart piece by piece and leave only what I need. But you will be mine, foolish child."

"Run," an unfamiliar voice whispered inside her head.

Isa jumped back, but the spiked tail grazed her arm.

Fire erupted down the limb, and she stumbled to her knees.

"Run," the voice said again.

A hysterical laugh erupted from her. Run where?

"Do you like my pain, foolish child? Do you want more?" Forneous laughed, and his tail whipped toward her again.

Then the billowing clouds on the horizon expanded, darkened. Roiled like the nausea in her belly. Parted to show huge, black wrought-iron gates.

"Run!" the voice screamed.

There was only one way to do this. She lunged to her feet, gripped the crystal and screamed, "Take me to those gates!"

The vision shifted. So fast the entire landscape rushed by, and in the blink of her eye, she stood at the foot of two towering gates. From a distance, they'd appeared made from metal, but up close, they were formed of solid black crystal.

The billowing clouds still roiled around them, and through the round bars ... nothing but more mist.

Where was Forneous? Isa whirled around. Far on the horizon, a flaming speck roared. Was that him?

Relief flooded her. She'd gotten away! But where did she go now?

"He comes," the voice spoke again inside her mind. This time, the tone was almost ... feminine.

"Where am I?" Isa spoke aloud. "Have I crossed over?"

"Nay, this is the vision realm. It straddles the human world and the realms of the otherworlds."

"Who are you?"

"You know who I am. Look."

A slender feminine figure, with hair and eyes like Isa's and Raph's, appeared through the mist on the other side of the gates. The person held out their hands, only to stop and step back.

Her mother. A sob caught in Isa's throat, and she stumbled forward.

"Do not come closer."

"But ..." I love you. I miss you.

"And I you. So, so very much. Everything I've done, leaving your world, being apart from you and Raphael, is because of my love for you both."

"I know—we know. And we're using our gifts to make our world better."

"This too, I know. And I'm so very proud of you both. Now, I cannot stay long, Isadora, so listen closely. If you end this vision before Forneous can reach you, his soul will be trapped in this

realm while his body lies dormant in the mortal world. You can trap him here."

"Forever?" Adrenaline jolted through her. She could get rid of Forneous right now?

"No, his minions will find him and return him to his body. But be warned, daughter of mine, the veil between the vision realm and the otherworlds is gossamer thin, and these gates have their own power—if Forneous takes you through the gate here, it will be as if he has done so in my realm."

"Oh shit. I'll become fully daemon."

"And he shall have a power over you that I, and even my father, will be unable to sever. He nears. You must leave now. As must I."

"I would also speak," a new voice murmured into her mind.

A shiver shook through Isa.

"Yes, Granddaughter, you know who I am. Know this, the bounty upon you has been nullified. But I cannot control those who live outside Hell."

"Can't you just kill Forneous?"

"That's not possible at my hands."

"Then whose?"

"Only the blood of the blood through great sacrifice can wield that power. He nears. Leave, Granddaughter."

"Wait, I have so many questions—"

"Return to your world," her mother said. *"And to your Knight—"*

"You know him?"

"Of course. To ensure the safety of the relic of myrrh, I seeded your visions with the Knight from the moment your gift evolved. You and your Knight had to be together at the necessary point in time. You must depart this realm, Daughter mine. Now."

"You saw all this?" Holy. Shit.

But her mother stepped back from the gates and into the dewy embrace of the mist.

"No! Come back!" Isa reached out a hand, but before the echo of her words had vanished, the last glimmer of her mother's form was gone, and she disappeared into the nothing beyond as if she'd never been there at all.

No. No, no, no. She'd finally met her mother, seen her, talked to her, and now she had to let her go? Isa's chest tightened, and the urge to run to the gates surged through her—

A deafening roar punctured the air, and Isa whirled around. Forneous charged across the rocky plain. His steps grew louder. Heavier. Until the ground shook beneath her feet.

She screamed, and terror shoved every other thought except run for your fucking life out of her mind.

Forneous bellowed again, and suddenly he launched into the sky, fire streaming in his wake as he shot through the air. At her.

The yawning void of his eyes and mouth loomed in the sky. The acrid tang of char and singe burned at her nose.

With her heart thrashing in her ears, Isa jammed her thumb over the point of her crystal and screamed, "Cut the tie, blood will sever."

33

GRAY RAN BACK up the steps to the main deck and bolted through the door to the lobby. Inside the saloon, voices were beginning to rise. Looked like the crew member had done her thing. Thank the gods.

"Hey!" a strange man, early thirties, six foot three, shouted as he emerged from the elevator. "You the Templar?"

Fuck. What now?

"Who's asking?" Gray raised the Glock 19.

The male drew a knife from his jacket and threw it at Gray.

The blade whizzed past Gray's head as he pulled the trigger, but the man darted back into the elevator, and the bullet smashed into the wall.

Shit. Fast was one thing. Speed like that was nonhuman. Gray ran for the elevator, but the doors closed before he got there.

The deck display lit up all the way to four.

Isa.

He ran for the stairs.

Please, please, *please*, not Isa. The words shook through him with every step up the curved staircase, up and up and up. Please, please, *please*.

Gray hit deck four, and he lunged through the suite doors just as the knife-throwing man, who held a double-ended dagger, was pulling an unconscious man off Isa. Isa lay on the ground, her body limp like a broken and battered doll, covered in even more blood than before.

Gray's breath punched from him.

"Don't fucking move." Gray brought the handgun up again.

But the stranger yanked Isa in front of him instead and yelled, "Drop the weapon."

"No." Gray stepped nearer.

"Don't come closer. This is a hellblade." Knifeman pointed one end at Isa's back. Her eyes were open, but her head lolled to the side. "One prick and her soul will be severed from her body. Now drop the weapon."

Fuck. So she was alive? She must be in a vision. For one moment, only the thrashing of Gray's pounding heartbeat filled his ears, then he rasped in a breath.

Head in the game, Gray.

Daemon. Zero doubt.

"What did you do to her?" Gray stepped sideways and opened his line of sight.

"Me? What did she do to my lord?" The daemon countermoved, keeping Isa between them.

Lord? A fucking daemon lord? The pieces fell into place. Forneous and Knifeman must've been on the tender that arrived right before he'd shot Rochelle. Shit. Isa had done something to *Forneous*?

"Listen, why don't we both lower our weapons? Tell me what you need."

"My lord." Knifeman jerked his chin at the older man. "And the myrrh."

"I can't give you the relic. But you can take the old guy. Forneous, right?"

"Lord Forneous *and* the relic. Then you get the girl."

"You know who I am, so you know I *cannot* give you this relic." *Isa, Isa, Isa. I can't give up R-104B for you.*

"Then the girl dies."

"Wait. You do that, you lose your bargaining power. Right now, you can get out of here with the old guy. You hurt the girl, that all changes."

"The relic!"

"Not happening." Gray changed his target and shifted to Forneous. "But I'll take *him* out in three seconds. Your move. Three, two—"

Knifeman gnashed his teeth like a shark, then dragged Isa to her feet. She was small, but she was still deadweight, yet Knifeman didn't even flinch as he picked her up.

No. No, no, *no.* Gray's heart stopped. Please gods, *no.*

Knifeman threw Isa at Gray.

"Fuck." R-104B in one hand, Glock 19 in the other, Gray lunged for Isa and caught her around the middle with his forearms. She slumped against him.

Behind Isa, Knifeman lifted Forneous onto his shoulder, spun and ran for the deck.

Gray lowered Isa to the floor, then took off after Knifeman, but as Gray reached the deck, the daemon, still carrying Forneous, leaped over the side of the ship.

Gray lunged for the railing, but by the time he got there, there was nothing to see but dark water lapping against the white hull of *Enchantress.*

They were gone.

Fuck! He spun and ran back to the suite.

Isa lay on her side, her hair covering most of her face. The brilliant ruby silk of her dress was stained darker by the blood on her torso. More blood coated her arms.

"Isa." He dropped to his knees. Her hair was stuck to the blood splattered up her neck and cheek, and he brushed it back as gently as he could.

Her beautiful eyes were open. Unseeing.

His heart stopped—was she—?

((●))

"Isa. Isa, can you hear me?"

The world swam back into view. Isa opened her eyes to find Gray at her side.

"Thank the gods," Gray breathed. "It's been a fucking hour, Isa!"

"What—"

"You came out of a vision for a second, and then you went straight to sleep—didn't even say a word. And you've been that way all this time."

"Hey, not my fault. Used the spell—it really knocks me out." She sat up, but fire arced through her arm.

"No, don't move. You've been wounded."

"Shit, you can say that again." She hissed and cradled it to her side. Black-edged slices raked down her arm. "Not again."

"Yeah, they're nasty. Looks like you've been burned *and* sliced open. Cyn has a high priestess connection who she's arranged to come out with the paramedics—they're not far off now." His cheeks tightened, and his gaze bored into her. "What the hell happened?"

"Cyn's here?" Isa asked.

"No, Marcella is. She called Cyn for some options."

"Wait—what happened to you? Do you have the myrrh?"

"Both pieces."

"Both?" Isa craned her neck and tried to see—there it was. On the bed behind him. "There's someone else here. You need to get the myrrh away—"

"Shh, no need to worry. He literally jumped overboard carrying Forneous."

"You let him get away?"

"Isa, you ..." Gray swallowed visibly. "You were lying here. Not moving. Covered in blood. I thought you were dead," he whispered.

Holy shit. Had her death vision happened? And ... she wasn't dead? Her heart began to pound. "Um, can you say that again?"

"What, the part where I thought you were dead?"

"Never mind." She mentally replayed the death vision. It matched perfectly with what Gray had said, as well as the room. Her dress. The blood.

Her breath caught, and she grabbed Gray's arm. "It's over. Holy shit, Gray, it's over!"

"Are you okay? Stop trying to sit up and lie down."

"Yes, yes, I'm okay. You're here. The myrrh's here. I'm here. I'm the best I've been in forever. Let me sit up."

"Fine, I'll ease you up—you can rest against the bed. But don't move from there."

She reached up with her good hand and cupped his jaw. "Are you okay? Is your arm—"

"Shh. I'm good. You and your vision, you saved me." He pressed a kiss to her palm and then cradled it between his. "Thanks to you, only left a gouge." He winced. "Hurts like hell, though. So what happened? The guy who took Forneous said you did something to the daemon lord?"

"Well, I went to the gate of Hell, I guess you could say."

"What? You crossed over?"

"No, I went to the vision realm. Which I never knew was an actual realm until now. It sits between this world and Hell, and maybe other worlds, from what my mother said. And Gray—I saw her. Talked to her."

"Stop. You what?"

Isa took a deep breath and told him everything.

"So Forneous is trapped." Gray rocked back on his knees. "That's what you did to him?"

"Not forever, but yes."

"Well, thank fuck. With R-104B back in our custody, Forneous out of the picture—for now—Rochelle and St. James neutralized, and your bounty removed, we have some breathing room."

"What about the drug?"

"I've got a team raiding the SJC lab in LA now to collect all remaining traces of the synthetic myrrh."

Tears burned in Isa's eyes, and she opened her mouth—but couldn't get any words out. She'd survived. And had come out with control of her powers.

A wave of relief and joy flooded her, and she couldn't keep tears from forming.

"Hey, you okay?" Gray slid an arm around Isa's good side and held her to him. And she breathed him in, steadied herself before she could speak.

"I am." She wiped the dampness off her cheeks with her good hand. "It's just ... holy shit, Gray. We did it."

"Yeah, we did."

Someone knocked at the door, and they both turned as Marcella entered the bedroom.

Gray rose to his feet and picked up both pieces of the incense burner.

"Hey, boss. Hey, chica. Good to see you in the land of the awake again. Boss, we've got the scene here locked down. Here's your backup cell. The chopper is five minutes out, and the witch and paramedics are two minutes out."

"Chopper?" Isa glanced at Gray. She couldn't hold back a smile when he immediately started tapping away at the mobile.

"I'm taking the myrrh to Boston via Miami now. I want R-104B locked away, at least in a temp site, until we can work out a new permanent location."

Gray was going now? "Just you?"

Gray's jaw clenched so hard his cheeks ticked, and he glanced at Marcella. "Can you give us a minute?"

"Can do. I'll head down and meet the paramedic's tender."

As soon as the door closed behind Marcella, Gray turned back to her. "Isa, I'm so proud of you. I couldn't have done this without you."

"So a civilian in your professional world wasn't such a bad decision after all?"

"Guess not." He smiled, but it didn't reach his eyes.

"Gray—I have to tell you something, and you need to not yell at me. No—don't speak. Just listen." She took a deep breath and blurted out the part of the death vision she hadn't told him.

When she was finished, Gray just stared at her.

"Gray? Now you can say something."

"What the ... you ..." He shook his head. "Freaking hell, Isa. All this time—you thought you were going to die? And you still came here?" He pressed his hands to his eyeballs before horror spread across his face. "Why? Why would you do that?"

"Because—"

"Shit. That's why you turned down any more art commissions. You were tying up all your loose ends."

"Gray, I fully believed I was going to die. I'm still ... I'm still processing that's not the case."

"Why didn't you tell me?"

"Because I know how protective you are. Just like Raph and Dad. You'd never have let me get anywhere close to this case. And look what I did, Gray! My gift helped to save you —helped save the myrrh."

"Freaking hell."

"You know I'm right. But this is the thing, when I reconciled myself to my fate, there were three things that I knew I wanted—had—to do. The first was the easiest—wrap up my commitments, yes, like my artwork. The second was harder because it wasn't just for me. I needed to use my mother's gift for good."

"That's what's driven you all this time? To use your gift for good before you die."

"Yeah—I was upfront with you about using my gift for good. Just not why now."

"And the third?"

"Well, that's a bit different. For years, you've been in my dreams. My own personal X-rated movie. And when I realized we were going to work together, I knew one more experience I wanted in this life—to bang you in reality. And Gray, we—you—were so frigging amazing, it kicked ass all over my dreams. But the thing I didn't see coming, never expected to happen, was for my heart to get involved, too. And even as I fell more and more for you, I didn't worry because risking a broken heart didn't matter. But now ..."

She took a deep breath. Aimed for the stars. "I want us to be together—for real. And after how much we've handled in the last few weeks, a long-distance relationship should be frigging easy to work out. So what do you say? Would you like to make our fake relationship a real one?"

"Isa." Gray's eyes deepened to a turbulent blue, but then he stepped back. His mouth flattened. "I am ..."

"Going to Boston without me." Pain crushed her chest, almost as real as if she'd been hit with Forneous's tail all over again.

"Yes."

Gray's words back in Cheshire replayed through her mind: *"I don't need love. Don't need it. Don't want it. Not ... from Isa."* Holy goddess, he'd said it then and meant it.

Well shit. This was it. Gray was heading off into the night. His implacable expression said it all.

And she'd gotten her life and control but had lost the one thing she hadn't realized she'd wanted. Gray.

A huge fiery knot lodged in her throat, but she forced it away.

"Marcella's staying here. She'll arrange your flight to Cheshire. Raph and Eve are waiting there already. Marcella tells me they've been calling everyone they know to find out where you are. They'll be relieved to know you're okay. I know I was." His gaze locked on her as if he didn't quite believe his words.

Outside, the *whomp whomp* of a helicopter grew louder and louder, but Gray still stared at her. His eyes burning.

Isa blew out a shuddering breath and somehow kept the tears stinging at her eyes from falling.

"Chopper's here," Marcella said from the corridor. "The witch and paramedics are on their way up now."

"Coming." Gray still stared at her.

"It's okay, Gray. You go. And yes, I'm fine. Well, my arm hurts, but I really am okay." Except for my breaking heart. "Thank you for giving me the opportunity to discover who I really am. And prove my mother's gift. That means everything to me."

She couldn't hold the tears back anymore.

"Always thanking me when I almost get you killed. Fuck." Gray dropped his head, then dropped to his knees. He cupped her jaw, and his turbulent gaze held hers captive. "Thank *you*, Isadora. My Divine One. For saving me, and our world."

He ground his lips to hers, and she tasted the salt of her tears in the kiss. Then he let her go and strode out of the room.

34

GRAY SCRUBBED a hand over his face as he unlocked the front door to his apartment in the living quarters of the Templar compound. A flick of the light switch and his one-bed apartment lit up.

It had been three weeks, five days, and—he checked his watch—thirteen hours since he'd last seen Isa.

He dumped his satchel on the dining table, his overnight bag in the bedroom, then made a straight line for the kitchen.

Caffeine. Gods, give him caffeine.

He opened the cupboard, reached inside, and stopped short.

A box of chamomile tea sat right beside his coffee. Fuck. Since when had the Templars stocked Isa's tea?

His gut seesawed, and he shoved the door closed. Then he hung his head.

Why did Isa permanently occupy a place in his a mind? Hell, occupy wasn't even close. More like she had freaking dominion.

Because it wasn't just the tea. He'd walked into a café last week, and the person before him got a cinnamon roll. One whiff and Gray had walked right out. Someone wore red, and he saw Isa in her dress. Kissing her on her red couch. Someone laughed, and all he knew was that it wasn't Isa's laugh. He woke up every single morning with a raging erection and the phantom echo of Isa's lips whispering his name.

Every part of his world had an Isa lens. An Isa imprint. Fucking hell. He hadn't wanted this connection. Hadn't wanted any of this.

Hadn't wanted to love her. His gut sank.

Love.

Fuck, fuck, fuck.

The lobby buzzer rang, and he hit the intercom without even looking. "Yeah?"

"What a greeting," a familiar voice said.

"Raph?" Gray straightened. His heart picked up. "Why the hell are you freezing your ass off in Boston?"

"Good to hear your voice too, man. So, you going to let me up?"

Gray hit the buzzer, then flipped his laptop open and punched in the code for the Templar message board. No issues showing up with Australia. He entered Isa's name into the search engine. Nothing popped there either. Okay, so this didn't have anything to do with Isa. Probably.

"What's going on?" Gray demanded the moment Raph entered his apartment.

"What do you mean?" Raph gave him the side eye. "Just visiting a friend. And hi, good to see you."

"Yeah, yeah, you, too. So, really. Why are you here?"

"Eve's meeting with your council tonight. She's renegotiating Watcher contracts."

"Gods, glad it's her and not me."

He cut Raph a glance. Would his friend mention Isa if anything was wrong? Or was the fact that Raph hadn't said Isa's name an indication that everything was okay with her?

"Same here." Raph slowly turned around, looking at everything in the room. "Is this really where you live? It's like a display home. Where are your photos? Your personal shit?"

"I don't have time for personal shit. I'm barely here enough to need anything other than a bed, a power point and a coffeemaker. Speaking of coffee, want one?"

"Sure." Raph took his coat off and slung it over the nearest chair. "So you just got back? Where have you been?"

But what about Isa? How's she doing? Gray bit his cheek to stop himself from mentioning her name.

"Seattle, closing up the last Fathom club and making sure zero synthetic myrrh slipped through our net. Thank fuck, looks like it's all done now." Gray focused on making them each a coffee but couldn't hold back the question any longer. "So, how's your sister?"

"She's cool. That's part of the reason I'm here."

"What?" Gray whipped around. "Why? Is she okay? What's happened now? I swear, your sister gets into more trouble than any other being I know."

"She asked me to put in a formal request for her to work with the Templars."

"Why? She's already an advisor."

"As a diviner. Level one."

"Fuck. But that means everyone will know what she can do."

"That's what I said. But she's hell-bent on doing it."

"Why didn't you stop her?"

"Why? She's capable enough."

"Of course she is. After how she handled Forneous, she

can handle almost anything. That's not the point. She doesn't want everyone to know her power. If she goes on record as a D-one, I can't stop word from getting out."

"Why do you care so much?"

"It's not about caring—"

"Then why does it matter?"

"Because *Isa* matters."

"So you do feel something for her. I knew it."

"What the fuck are you on about now? Raph, I swear if you're messing with me—"

"No, no. I really am here with Isa's request. But I'm also here because my best friend, a man who I respect, who's one of the finest guys I know, has feelings for my sister. And I want to know what he's going to do about them."

"Nothing. Nothing is what I'm going to do."

"But why?"

"Work—"

"Nope. Don't give me that BS. Look at Eve and me—our jobs are half a world away, but we're making our relationship thrive."

"My world isn't safe—"

"Nope again. You can't say your world is too dangerous for her anymore, and you know it. Hell, Isa might be too dangerous for your world. What else is there?"

"I never wanted to love again," he whispered. His gut churned. "This was never meant to happen in the first place!"

"I know, believe me, I know how you feel. But looks like that ship has long sailed. So now you get to decide what to do about it."

"What if she doesn't feel the same way?"

"What if she does?"

-(((●)))-

With the late summer sun swathing the hills beyond her studio in rich amber, Isa applied another stroke with her pallet knife to the painting.

Then she stopped and eased back from the easel. Almost done. What else did it need?

But her eyes crept to the canvas leaning up against the wall. *Paint me. Paint me.*

"No, not yet," she told the painting. "I have to finish this commission, then I can spend some time with you."

Damn, now she was talking to her paintings. Not surprising, given the subject.

Her mobile phone pinged, and her heart did a triple beat. Was it—nope. Just Raph, checking in, asking how she felt. He'd messaged every single day since their return. But she got it now. When you cared about someone, their safety and well-being mattered. She sent back a quick reply saying she was okay and to say hi to Eve and turned back to her easel.

When her father knocked at the studio door and walked in, she didn't even turn around.

"One minute, Dad. I'm going to finish this commission today if it kills me."

"Then don't let me stop you," Gray's voice said.

Isa whirled around, and her heart shot into her throat.

Gray. *Inside* her studio. Leaner than when she'd seen him. Hair messy. Beard untrimmed.

"What's wrong? Are you okay?" The urge to launch herself at him and never let go surged through her, but Isa crossed her arms instead. He'd made his call about them.

Gray shoved his hands in his pockets but didn't say anything.

"Gray, what's going on? Is it Tank? Oh god. Is he dea—"

"No, he's out of the coma. Shit, I thought someone would have told you."

"Clearly not. Then wait, is it the myrrh?"

"What? No—that's locked away. It's about Liam. I wanted you to know he won't be bothering you again. The team did a deep dive into his business dealings and found some serious legal issues. He'll go to jail for a very long time."

"You came all the way here ... to tell me that?"

"Not really."

"Don't tell me you need my help with something. Another relic's missing?"

"No. Well, yes. But that's not why I'm here." He scowled. "Seriously, Isa." He looked around, his gaze touching on the caramel leather couch. "That's new."

"The ... blood and stuff wouldn't come out of the old one."

"And the painting on the easel? It's similar, but not the same."

"I couldn't save the original. And it's different because I'm a different person from when I did the first take."

Gray nodded, was silent for a while longer, shifted on his feet. "The cleaners did a um ... great job on your place. After the mess that was created by the ah ... the incident."

"Dad told me the Templars took care of all the cleaning. Thanks, by the way."

"Of course. Least we could do after how much you did for us." Gray nodded again.

What the frig was going on here?

"Right ... So you're okay. The relic's okay. Are you here to talk about my stuff, then?

"I spoke with Raph," Gray said in a rush. "He said you've formally requested to work with the Templars as a diviner— level one and all."

"That's right."

Gray headed for the painting against the wall. Her stomach tightened, and she leaped off her stool and stood in front of the unfinished canvas.

"I'm going to embrace my gift." Isa lifted her chin and held his gaze. "I'll pick the jobs I work on, but I'm not hiding what I do—who I am—anymore. Not for anyone. So, if the Templars ever need a D-one, you know where to find me. Hold on. You're not here to stop me, are you?"

"Gods no. You're an asset, Isa. We'd be lucky to have you on board."

"Thank you, that's high praise coming from you." Warmth curled in her chest. Damn it. How could he make her so emotional just by saying something nice? "So you're here to hire me? Make me sign a waiver in blood or something?"

"None of that, either. We don't need a diviner at this very moment."

"Then I give up." Isa planted her hands on her hips. "Why are you here?"

"Because while the Templars don't need a diviner, it turns out I do." He stepped closer.

Her heart picked up, and damn her traitorous body because heat bloomed where he held her, then rushed to pool lower in her belly. But no, this man had decided he didn't want to even try for a relationship with her. She wasn't going to push something on him he didn't want.

Then he stared at the ground and muttered something.

"What was that?"

"I said you're right. And that I'm sorry." Gray raised his

head, and a storm lurked in his eyes. "I thought a clean break was best. Was even possible. But I was wrong."

"Whoa—wait up, the mighty Grayson, wrong?"

"I'm serious." His gaze stayed on hers. Her mouth went dry. "Can I—can we sit? I want to talk about us." He backtracked to the couch before she had a chance to say yes or no and sat down. "Please?"

Holy shit. Gray had said please.

He shoved a hand through his hair. Then undid the top button of his shirt. Crossed and uncrossed his legs.

"Frig, calm the farm. I'll sit down." Isa sat on the end of the couch. Tension poured off him, and an answering tightness crept through her belly.

He wanted to talk about them? After everything that had happened, what the hell did that mean?

"Okay, you've got me here," she said when he showed zero sign of speaking.

"Right." He swallowed visibly, and she went on even higher alert. "Isa, we've known each other for not much more than a month, right?"

"I've known you for most of my adult life. But keep going."

"Well, I *haven't* had visions of you for years. But you wormed into my—"

"Wormed? Stop right here. No matter what you're about to say, you're not making me out to be a worm."

"Isa. Forget the worm. I'm saying that for the last four weeks, I haven't been able to get you out of my head. Hell, my life. I read the damn book you gave me. And loved it. Every time I make a coffee, whether I'm in LA, or Seattle, or wherever, even at the Templar compound, I see chamomile tea nearby—and since when the hell did we stock that? Someone laughs, and I think *that's not Isa's laugh*. Someone makes a snarky comment, and I'm like *Isa would've said it this way*. And if you have any kind of affection toward me ... that might one day become more ... like a feeling ..."

"Feeling?" She swallowed the lump that lodged in her throat. "How about we just say the word? Love. To be clear, that's the *feeling* you mean?"

"Fuck. Yes, that feeling. But stop. Please. Let me get this out."

She folded her arms again. "Fine—speak away."

"So if that type of feel—*love* ... might one day be possible, the fact is, I *would* want that."

Everything inside Isa stopped.

"But on the yacht, I told you how I felt, and you still left. Even in Cheshire, you said it—you didn't want my love."

"That's the hard part. I used to think having a relationship, of having someone I care for, who cares for me back, was a responsibility. And I never wanted to be responsible for someone again."

Her heart pounded so hard its thud filled her ears.

"What changed?" Isa whispered.

"Me. From the moment I saw you in Raph's apartment, this knot tightened inside me, right here." He scrubbed a fist over his chest. "I tried to stop it growing. Tried to shove it deep, deep down. But it just kept spreading. At the club that night when I touched you. Kissed you. Inhaled your perfume. Wanted you. That wasn't an act.

"My body had been aching for you since that day at Raph's, and instead of focusing on the job, I leaped at you. And then, when you'd been shot at and drugged, instead of monitoring the building, I made to love you. But the fact that I took my mind off the job scared the hell out of me. I thought I was a risk to the job, to you—your life. So I decided to cut this off with you before this knot grew any bigger—before you had any feelings for me, before I did something that caused you harm.

"But after the yacht, going back to my empty apartment, I realized our entire life is a risk, and that's the way it is. You're a part of our world. Danger is a part of our world. And hell knows you're more equipped than me to deal with an entire element of it.

"And then, and this is the kicker, I figured it out—the knot that grew in here. It's love. There, I said it. Love. I have zero clue if you feel the same or have any feelings that even border on that, but I had to let you know. *That's* why I'm here. And yes, love is a responsibility.

"But it's also an honor to say I feel that way for you because you're brilliant. You're funny and sharp and kind and strong and the most amazing part of this world—all the worlds—and I don't want my world not to include you."

"I thought you didn't want me," Isa whispered past the constriction in her throat.

"Want you? I can't breathe without you. Want is easy. Want is a taste and be done. But you ... Isa, you're a fucking craving that I can't live without."

"But you're always so ..."

"Aloof? Icy? That's how I get shit done. How the dangerous relics under my responsibility don't get out of control and fucking kill someone—or everyone."

"You don't seem icy now."

"That's because I can't be—not around you. There's this part of me right fucking here that I bury everything behind, but you get under it. Fuck. You shatter it. And now I have zero idea about what's coming next. But I'll tell you this. I'm not easy, Isa. I'm not a lapdog you just pat, and it trots away until the next feed time. If we do this, I'll fucking destroy anything and anyone who wants to hurt you. You call me bossy, and I am. I know it. Is that what you want? Do you really want *me*?"

"Gray." Isa gave in to her urge this time and threw herself at him and held on tight.

"Wait," he said hoarsely. "Please tell me. Do you want this too?" His jagged breathing filled the silence. "Want me?"

Oh, holy shit. The fire shining in his gaze burned a path right to her core—but behind that, behind the prowling, lethal edge, his desperation—

"You might dress in a suit and tie, but I see you, Grayson Acord. You're a warrior, and you wear your civilization in a whisper-thin veil on top of your true self. And yes, you're bossy, but I've got my share of that and will boss you right back. And the fact is, I love all that about you. I love you. Have loved you for years. How could I not? You've lived in my dreams, in my mind, and when I had the chance to have you for real—I didn't leap, I dove for you. I took that moment back in LA because even if that was all I'd ever have with you, I was going to have it. But oh, I wanted more. I want it all."

"Isa."

"Wait. I need you to see something." Isa pulled Gray to his feet and nodded to the canvas against the wall. "It's from the first night we made love. That night left a mark on me, Gray, and I never want to forget the most dangerous, sexy, heartbreakingly handsome warrior I've ever seen, who could make me orgasm with a word. It's not the only one." She turned and took the next canvas—this one facing the wall—and turned it around.

"Who's—wait. Me?"

"From predawn, the night after the club. Even though the rest of the city was sound asleep, you were working nonstop to keep them all safe. Alone."

She stepped back, tried to view the piece objectively. But it was impossible—Gray had made too much of a profound impact on her for her to retain any impartiality. Just looking at the painting of Gray sitting in the penthouse lounge, head bent over his laptop, fierce concentration on his face, his white shirt open to proudly display his tattoos, and a giant shield and sword standing on one side of the couch, a knight's helmet on the other, made her chest tighten with emotion.

"Do you really see me like this?" Gray whispered.

She reached for his hand and held it tight. "Yes. You're our warrior, with or without the armor. I see it—those of us who really know you—we all see it."

"*Isa*. But you're wrong about one thing. That night, I wasn't alone. You were right there. By my side." He drew her to him and stared into her eyes. "And that's where I want to be—by your side. Forever."

"So, any ideas on how's this going to work—you and me?"

"Long-distance relationships can't be that bad, right? And maybe, when you're ready, you could come over to the States, since I guarantee you'll be getting jobs all over the world now you're registered as a D-one. You'll need a crash pad for when you're in that part of the world. Maybe we could eventually find a crash pad together."

"And when I'm not gallivanting around the world or crashing in the States, I've got this place right here. Which is also the perfect detox from the world *for you* when you're between jobs. You need somewhere you can escape the rest of the world and just be Gray Acord. Read. Breathe. Do your fancy martial arts thing, jiu ..."

"Jitsu."

"That's it." Isa reached up on tiptoes and brushed a kiss over his lips. Heat pooled low in her belly.

"Sounds like an excellent plan, my Divine One," he whispered against her lips.

"I thought so too, Ace," she whispered back. "But I have an even better one. Want to christen my new couch?"

"Hell yeah."

EPILOGUE

Six months after officially entering the Templar books as a D-one, Isa picked up her pallet knife and scooped up a kernel of delicate yellow paint, the perfect color for the crisp early spring morning outside her studio window.

A new season, a new beginning. Just like another new beginning.

"Morning," Gray murmured from behind her. He pressed a kiss to the base of her neck. "Tea?"

"Love one." She leaned into his kiss. "So, imagine my surprise when I came downstairs this morning and found someone had read another of my romance books."

"Yeah, yeah. It was too dammed good, plus my body clock was on another time zone, and you were zonked."

"Not surprising after all those orgasms. I stopped counting after four."

"Well, I was away for three weeks. I had to make it count. But you sure you're good? You really were tired last night."

"I think there might be another reason for that. I was going to tell you this as soon as you got back—but then we made love, and I fell asleep, and—"

"Isa, what's going on?"

"I think—that is, I did a pee test, but I really should go to the doc to make sure it's right." Isa took his hand and folded it in hers. "Remember last month how we had that flight back from the US, and we gave the mile-high shower thing a go, but we'd run out of condoms?"

"Fuck." Gray's eyes widened, and then a slow, heart-melting smile curved his lips. "Isa. Really?"

"Looks like."

Gray picked her up, and she yelped when he twirled her around. "So I take it you're happy?"

"Fuck yeah, I mean, yes. Shit, I'm going to have to swear less."

"Calm the farm. You've got plenty of time before that's an issu—" Isa grabbed Gray's hands. Prickles flew over her neck; the hairs rose on her arms.

"Isa, what is it?"

"Vision," she gasped. "It's okay. I'm ... controlling how fast it comes in." She eased down to the couch, ran her thumb over the tip of the crystal pendant around her neck, and took a deep breath. Used the spell to let the stars gather one by one.

"I'll be here when it's done." Gray's steady voice eased her into the darkness.

A man sat at an enormous desk, a floor-to-ceiling window framing a city lit up at night behind him. He stared down at his clenched fist, then his fingers uncurled to reveal a tiny brown seed in the middle of his palm.

The man looked up. His lips pulled back in a tight smile.

"One seed of myrrh," someone said from behind Isa's point of view. "It was on the floor in the bathroom. I found it before I took your body away. Is it enough?"

"It will be."

Oh frig. *Cut the tie, blood will sever.* Suddenly the crystal in her hand heated, and Isa visualized herself running the pad of her thumb across the tip of the obelisk. Cut the tie.

The vision whisked away.

"Gray," she gasped.

"What? What is it?"

"Forneous has a seed. As in the myrrh."

"What? Here, sit up. Got you some water. Are you okay? Is the baby okay?"

"Shh, I'm—we're—fine." She took a sip and blew out a steadying breath.

"Then tell me everything."

"But why?" Isa said after she'd told him. "The true power of the gifts only happens when all three are together. Even if Forneous gets one seed, the gold is safe behind Eve's ward. So why would Forneous still be after the myrrh now?"

"That's what has me worried. Whatever the hell is going on here, I don't like it one fucking bit."

"Hey, come here." Isa interlinked their fingers, let him pull her close and tuck her head under his chin.

"But I know one thing," Gray whispered into her hair. "You're my light, Isadora Smith. I love you. Whatever else is coming at us—all of us—I can face it when I've got you."

The End

ALSO BY HM HODGSON

Relics and Legends

A Wreath Of Thorns

A Relic Of Magic And Gold

A Relic of Magic And Myrrh

A Relic Of Magic And Frankincense

The Immortal Keepers

Book 1 The Last Keeper

Book 2 Keeper Of My Heart

Book 3 Keeper Of My Desire

Anthologies

Mermaid Kisses

THANK YOU & REVIEWS

Dear Reader, thank you so much for reading A Relic Of Magic And Myrrh.

If you enjoyed Isa and Grayson's story, can I please ask that you leave a review (even just a rating) on your favorite reading platform? Every review helps me continue my dream career as a writer.

FREE EBOOK GIVEAWAY

Can a cursed Merprince blackmail his way out of a fairytale nightmare?

Read now to enjoy this Beauty and the Beast retelling!

Download your free ebook now by joining my reader group at

www.hmhodgson.com

ACKNOWLEDGMENTS

Writing a book can be a solitary journey, but that's not the case for the entire process. And I wouldn't have it any other way. These are some of the people I want to give my thanks for their support and input into bringing AROMAM to you today.

First, my husband Henry. He fields endless questions, brainstorms with me, listens as I talk out the entire plot on long car rides (sorry-not sorry!), and supports my need for coffee and the time and space to write.

Writing peeps—in particular Jacqueline Hayley, Louisa Duval, Melanie Pickering, , Tanya Nellestein and Jennifer Westgarth. Next is my family—our group chat is filled with book-related questions, and a special call out to my sister Julie who always has a unique perspective and suggestion when I run into a literary wall!

Then there's the people who helped with specialized knowledge. My mother and artist Val (some of my fondest memories growing up with an artist for a mother were going out with her on location and playing in the bush while she painted landscape scenes). My father Chris for his expert advice on the criminal mind (not because he is one—he was a cop for 20 years). The wonderful Doctor Julie Epstein for her medical advice. And finally, Gary List for his help with the layout of superyachts and general information about ships (not boats, as I originally called them!). Any factual mistakes made are purely my own.

I'd also like to give a shout out to a very special reader, Cecelie, who I met at Bookfest Australia 2022 and who lent me her name for my librarian.

Beta readers Renae Black, Tanya, and Val, with extra special callouts to Davida De La Harpe and Jaqueline Hayley for their in-depth manuscript reviews, and ARC readers Timothea, Sarah and Jas for looking at this novel before anyone else.

Amanda Pillar from Smoking Hot Covers, whose artistic skill brought AROMAM to life visually.

This then brings me to the editors I count myself the luckiest writer ever to work with: Sarah Proulx Calfee from Three Little Words Editing, whose expertise with copy, story and character is invaluable, and Jo Speirs from Nurturing Words whose final proofread, eye for detail, and absolute care for my manuscript gives me the confidence to hit publish on my book baby.

Thank you all. AROMAM would not be here as it is today without you.

ABOUT THE AUTHOR

Award-winning Brisbane author, HM Hodgson, writes about romance (steamy scenes a must!), intrigue and magic. Magic that moves worlds and takes her to another place.

In 2021, HM Hodgson won the Romance Writers of Australia First Kiss competition with the first kiss scene from her novel, Keeper Of My Heart, as judged by producer and director, Tosca Musk. in 2023, Hodgson also won the Australian Romance Readers Association award for Favourite Continuing Romance Series 2022 with The Immortal Keepers.

When not writing or reading or daydreaming about her next literary hero, you can find her sipping coffee and eating chocolate (or more often than not, both at the same time).

Keep in touch with HM Hodgson at: www.hmhodgson.com

THE END

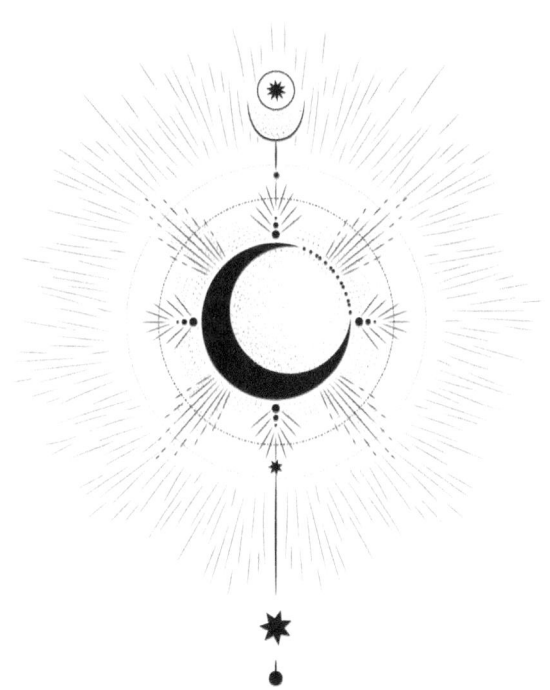